Praise for *Melaleuca*

'A page-turner with purpose. Refreshing, surpr--- d propulsive. Angie Faye Martin is a name to watch.'

—Tracey J--- --- *ft Unsaid*

'Indigenous writing ha--- --- ,iction, now it's crime fiction's tu---

—A--- ---thor of *It Takes a Town*

'Angie Faye Martin brings a fresh, authentic perspective to the much-loved genre of the Australian outback thriller. Compelling, thought-provoking and twisty, *Melaleuca* is both a gripping, tightly plotted mystery and an unflinching exploration of the dark underbelly of institutionalised racism and corruption in Australia. Fans of Jane Harper's *The Dry* and Hayley Scrivenor's *Dirt Town* will love it.'

—Kate Horan, author of *The Inheritance*

'This intense, heart-wrenching and beautifully written novel introduces a bold and important voice in Australian crime fiction. Set in a small outback Queensland town, it features the resilient, courageous and marvellously flawed Aboriginal detective Renee Taylor. When a savage murder takes place and is connected to historic mysterious disappearances, the investigation starts to expose gross injustice, racism, cowardice and corruption – not just in Australia's murky past, but in its present as well. Realities some will do anything to cover up. An atmospheric, compulsive read that I defy you to put down.'

—Karen Brooks, author of *The Good Wife of Bath*

'*Melaleuca* is rich with authenticity and heart, and each character feels tangible and familiar. Angie Faye Martin skilfully paints a picture of outback Queensland so that the scents, sounds and heat become a physical experience for the reader. Dual timelines can be hard to get right, but the author deftly weaves a satisfying – and horrifying – conclusion. Detective Renee Taylor is sure to be one of Aussie crime's new heroes – I look forward to seeing what happens next to the new Sergeant of Goorungah.'
—Laura McCluskey, author of *The Wolf Tree*

'A fresh new voice in Australian crime. I couldn't put it down.'
—Tricia Stringer, author of *Head for the Hills*

'Powerful First Nations crime noir that interrogates law enforcement and how it intersects with Indigenous victims. *Melaleuca* is a compelling exploration of a police officer caught between two worlds, small-town complicity and justice long overdue.'
—Dinuka McKenzie, author of *The Torrent*

'In *Melaleuca*, Angie Faye Martin brings an important new voice to Australia's rich rural crime tradition. With a gutsy First Nations heroine, an atmospheric setting and a shocking crime that exposes a small town's prejudices, this is a book that deserves a large and enthusiastic audience. I'm already looking forward to this author's next book.'
—Cassie Hamer, author of *The Stranger at the Table*

'Atmospheric and blistering. *Melaleuca* will leave you wanting more. What a remarkable debut.'
—Fleur McDonald, author of *The Prospect*

'A blistering outback noir that doesn't flinch away from Australia's Indigenous history at the hands of colonisation and the ongoing ramifications. Martin expertly weaves past and present, exploring the way history echoes through generations and the ongoing struggle against decisions made far from you that have real world consequences in daily life. Tense, vivid and real, *Melaleuca* will keep you turning pages as hidden truths finally come to light.'
—Alli Parker, author of *At the Foot of the Cherry Tree*

'An essential, compelling and genuine new voice in Australian crime fiction. As someone who also grew up in regional Queensland, the places and people of Angie Faye Martin's *Melaleuca* are viscerally recognisable. Given the global popularity of Australian rural noir, it feels overdue to have a First Nations author and protagonist set a murder mystery in a small town. Angie Faye Martin's *Melaleuca* hits it out of the park: a police procedural threaded with ACAB worldweariness, dark twists and black humour. Full of heart, blistering with outraged lived experience. I hope this isn't the last we'll see of Detective Renee Taylor on our shelves.'
—Clare Fletcher, author of *Love Match* and *Five Bush Weddings*

'A ripping crime story, told from a refreshing perspective. It will keep you turning the page and second-guessing yourself as Detective Renee Taylor exposes the darkness of murder and racism in a country town. A well-told story with unexpected revelations, great characters, an authentic voice and a truly satisfying resolution.'
—Jo Dixon, author of *The Shadow at the Door*

Photograph: Greg Dries

Angie Faye Martin is a writer and editor of Kooma, Kamilaroi and European heritage. With a Bachelor of Public Health from the Queensland University of Technology and a Masters of Anthropology from the Australian National University, Angie spent many years working in policy roles in state and federal government before launching Versed Writings in 2019. Her work has been published in *Meanjin, Garland, The Saltbush Review* and *The Rocks Remain*. She is a member of the First Nations Australia Writers Network (FNAWN) and accredited with the Institute of Professional Editors. *Melaleuca* is her debut novel.

Melaleuca

Angie Faye Martin

Aboriginal and Torres Strait Islander peoples should be aware that this book contains names of deceased persons.

MELALEUCA
© 2025 by Angie Faye Martin
ISBN 9781867270881

First published on Gadigal Country in Australia in 2025
by HQ Fiction
an imprint of HQBooks (ABN 47 001 180 918),
a subsidiary of HarperCollins Publishers Australia Pty Limited (ABN 36 009 913 517).

HarperCollins acknowledges the Traditional Custodians of the lands upon which we live and work, and pays respect to Elders past and present.

The right of Angie Faye Martin to be identified as the author of this work has been asserted by them in accordance with the *Copyright Amendment (Moral Rights) Act 2000*.

This work is copyright. Apart from any use as permitted under the *Copyright Act 1968*, no part may be reproduced, copied, scanned, stored in a retrieval system, recorded, or transmitted, in any form or by any means, without the prior written permission of the publisher. Without limiting the author's and publisher's exclusive rights, any unauthorised use of this publication to train generative artificial intelligence (AI) technologies is expressly prohibited.

This is a work of fiction. Names, characters, places, and incidents are either the product of the author's imagination or are used fictitiously, and any resemblance to actual persons, living or dead, business establishments, events, or locales is entirely coincidental.

A catalogue record for this book is available from the National Library of Australia
www.librariesaustralia.nla.gov.au

Printed and bound in Australia by McPherson's Printing Group

For Pedro

Goorungah is a fictional town in southern Queensland about two hundred kilometres west of Brisbane. It is based on the town where I grew up – Oakey – but my characters and their actions are not representative of any of the people from this town, past or present.

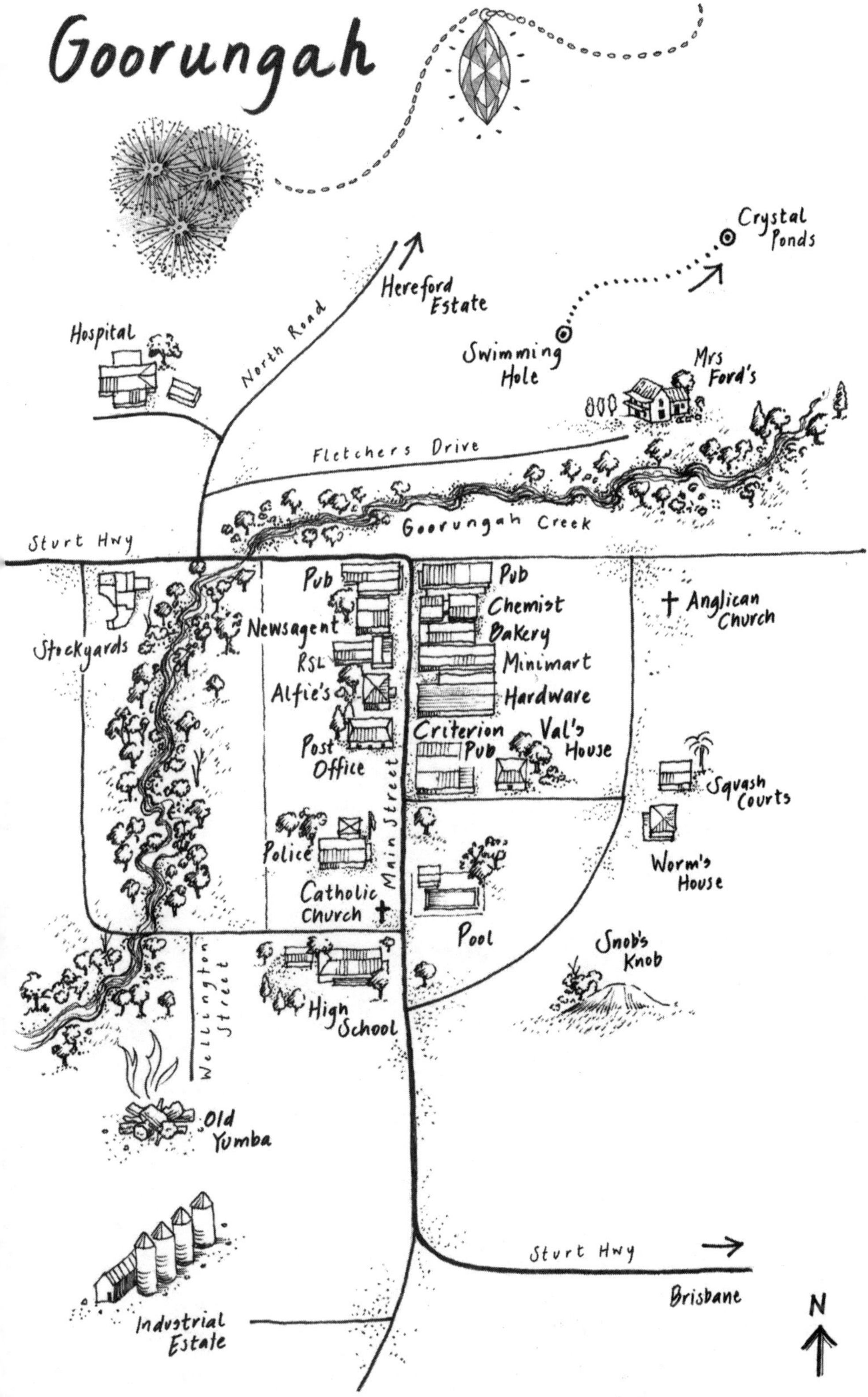
Goorungah
Crystal Ponds
Hereford Estate
North Road
Hospital
Swimming Hole
Mrs Ford's
Fletchers Drive
Goorungah Creek
Sturt Hwy
Pub
Pub
Chemist
Bakery
Minimart
Hardware
Anglican Church
Newsagent
Stockyards
RSL
Alfie's
Criterion Pub
Val's House
Post Office
Squash Courts
Police
Worm's House
Main Street
Catholic Church
Pool
Snob's Knob
Wellington Street
High School
Old Yumba
Sturt Hwy
Brisbane
Industrial Estate
N

Prologue

Light was breaking on the horizon as she ran along a dirt driveway, trying not to trip or stumble in the potholes. She reached the wire gate panting and paused to look in both directions. She could see an endless straight bitumen road with fields of wheat on either side, canopied by a vast universe of distant stars. It wouldn't take him long to notice she had escaped, to find her again in this dry, flat landscape.

Hurry up. Choose.

She chose the west and ran away from the rising sun, hoping to stay hidden in the twilight shadows. Her feet were soft and bare but adrenaline prevented her from feeling any pain from the rough stones. She heard the sound of a familiar car engine starting and pushed to run faster.

Headlights came from behind and she threw herself into the tall grass on the side of the road. As she expected, it was him. She watched the car drive by. The window was down, his elbow resting on the door, and she could see his eyes scanning the fields for movement. Cold, hard eyes. She crouched as low as possible, heart pounding, waiting and praying for the car to pass.

When the headlights had faded into nothing, she crept back out onto the road. She looked again in each direction, knowing she couldn't return to where she had run from, nor go in the direction the car had taken. Enormous paddocks of long grass lay on either side, gently swaying in the early morning breeze, but to one side she could just make out the silhouette of trees on the horizon. At least it would give her a place to rest for a moment, think of the next move. She made up her mind and bolted towards the foliage.

The grass whipped against her legs as she fled across the paddock, and eventually she tumbled down a steep dirt bank, landing hard in mud. She found her footing, wiping the sweat off her forehead, and looked around with all the fear and exhaustion of day-long hunted prey. She could just make out dirt slopes on either side dipping down sharply into water.

A log that had fallen across the mud stretched into the creek. She crawled along it, careful not to slip into the stream, and leaned down to cup some water into her parched mouth. Hesitant at first, careful not to make a sound, then gulping more hastily. Something plopped into the creek nearby breaking her focus on drinking, making her gasp and jump. A turtle or a fish perhaps. She was paralysed by fear.

Retreating back from the log, she dragged herself up to her feet and continued along the creek bed, climbing over fallen timber and squelching through deep sludge to get away. To where, she did not know. Just away. As far away as she could possibly get from the hell that lurked behind. She ran as far as she could along the muddy creek bank until she collapsed exhausted in a small clearing. Her chest rose and fell, sucking in the cool morning air which felt sharp in her lungs, as adrenaline pounded through her veins. She knew fear, and she knew dread, but this was nothing short of utter terror.

Two eagles circled high overhead as she lay outstretched on her back in a damp green clearing, too physically exhausted to move.

Melaleuca

The sweet smell of melaleuca blossoms reminded her of the warm lemon and honey drink her mum made when she had a sore throat. Her throat hurt now. Everything hurt. She rubbed her forehead, squinted against the ever-brightening sunlight and rolled to one side to break the glare. The soles of her feet throbbed and her legs were red raw from the grass lashing them.

Someone was playing a piano. At first she thought she was hallucinating, but no, there was music on the breeze. It reminded her of the church her mum always watched on television. Someone was close by. She would allow herself a few more breaths to muster the energy needed to climb the hill that lay between her and the source of the music before making a dash to safety. Such a sweet melody had to indicate a haven.

The gentle sway of melaleucas filled her vision with their soft creamy petals blossoming cloud-like from trunks of gnarled-up layers of bark. Then the sound of a twig snapping jolted her upright. Her heart gave a sudden primal thump.

'I knew I couldn't trust you.' A hoarse, deep voice came from behind. He loomed overhead. Cold eyes. 'I wanted to trust you. You know, I tried so hard to trust you.' She could see the mark on his neck from where she'd scratched him that morning. A thin red line oozed tiny bubbles of blood.

She moved her hands to shield her face. 'Please don't. I'll be better this time. I promise.'

His eyes stared back at her. 'I've already given you too many chances. You betrayed me.'

Before the scream could escape her mouth, the boulder came crashing down.

Chapter 1

Tuesday 8 February 2000

She loved the crisp morning air of the countryside. Running felt easy when the air was cool and dry. Morning jogs in the city with its dense humidity felt like running in a bulletproof vest but here in Goorungah Renee glided through the streets. The sun poked its way above the horizon and the streetlights flickered off. Her ankles felt good. Her left ankle was still healing from when she had been pushed over by some guy at a domestic. She wondered what kind of work lay ahead for her now she was back in the country.

She reached the most elevated point of her route, affording a view across the sprawling country township. It was so quiet. A few trucks had passed her, carrying supplies for further out west, but she still hadn't seen another person. The country town slept.

Houses stretched across the plains. Slightly grander ones lay to the east, Snob's Knob as the locals called it. But they weren't really mansions. No one with any real money would stay in a place like Goorungah. The more modest dwellings lay to the west; they were more likely to be public housing. And then a little bit of everything in between, including her mother's house right down there, smack in the middle, just off Main Street. Despite the differences, it was the same as in the city, any city for that matter – rich sides and poor sides.

Melaleuca

Her favourite part of the run was coming up. It was a long gentle slope back down into town. The thin layer of perspiration made the air feel cooler on her skin. She had been running for almost an hour. On her first day back, three days ago, she'd mapped out a path to do every morning during her rural secondment – a ten-kilometre route around the perimeter of town, enough to keep her fit for her return to Brisbane. She slowed to a walk, checking her watch. Fifty-five minutes.

She would need to pick up her pace to see results.

'Careful of them snakes.'

Renee jumped and looked around, searching for the owner of the deep raspy voice.

'I've seen three come past here in the last month.' An old man was sitting alone in his garage surrounded by dust and tools and random bits of steel and rusty farm machinery.

'What colour?' Renee stopped outside the fence, hands on hips, still panting, sweat dripping from her forehead. He looked hard at her and she knew the answer. 'Brown?' The most venomous. That's one of the few things she knew about her dad. His totem. His Lore deemed that the brown snake would protect anyone from that nation and never harm them. She liked to think that this protection extended to her, despite knowing so little about traditional ways.

The old man nodded. 'It's dry. They're coming up for water. There was one right here sunnin itself yesterday.' He picked up his walking stick and pointed to a bare patch of dirt in the front yard. 'Right there.'

She looked around. The place looked dishevelled. He looked dishevelled with his messy thin grey hair and leathery sunburned forearms poking out of his rolled-up, crumpled flannelette shirt sleeves. 'You take care of yourself, hey?' She wondered if he lived alone. If a man like him was bitten by a brown snake with no one to call an ambulance, he'd die in a matter of minutes.

'Don't you worry about me, love. I shot the bastard. *You* be careful running on those back roads, especially in the dark. Never know what you might come up against.'

Renee nodded, feeling a strange vacuum in her stomach. She should be thankful for the warning, but his brutal watchfulness told her otherwise.

Her mother's house was a simple worker's cottage, located just around the corner from Main Street behind the Criterion Hotel, one of the old pubs. Goorungah was no exception to any other small town in regional Queensland in that it had one pub per five hundred people. So in Goorungah there were three pubs plus the RSL, which Renee had noticed was becoming increasingly popular among the elderly residents since its recent installation of centralised heating and cooling. And five new poker machines.

She eased the gate open, wincing as it screeched on its hinges in protest. Renee had hated her mother's house when she was younger, with its large overgrown garden and loose timber panelling. The school kids would tease her that she lived in a creepy old ghost house. Her first day of primary school, after her mum had dropped her off, she'd stood in the playground looking around at the other kids waiting to see who would suggest the first game ... They all played together but no one asked her to join in, not the girl who lived in the ghost house. But now she liked it. The place had character. The tall pines gave it shade and privacy, and the wooden floors kept the interior cool in the harsh outback summer.

Any luck her mother would still be asleep and stay asleep long enough for her to tend to a few outside chores before her second day of work at the station. She sat for a moment on the front steps, removing her shoes and socks, thinking about how much she wanted a drink but she couldn't bring herself to go inside to the kitchen sink and risk waking her mother. She turned on the tap in the front yard and ran the water for a moment, letting all the dirt flush through, then cupped her hand beneath to form a pool of water. Those blissful gulps were the most enjoyable reward for running. She splashed water over her face and dampened her hair. It was going to be a scorcher.

A saucer beneath the tap filled with water. Her mother must have put it there for the birds. She thought of the old man's warning about the snakes. Such a shame that the creeks were drying and they had to leave their natural habitat for water, but even more of a shame if she stood on one and it bit her on the arse. She flipped the saucer over with her toe and let the water wash over her feet. Sorry, snakes. You'll have to go hydrate someplace else.

She raked the leaves from the front lawn, swept out the garage and driveway, and took the mats down from the clothesline. They had been so filthy. Her mother had once kept the inside of the place spick and span, but when she had arrived home three days earlier on Saturday, there was a thin layer of grime over everything. Renee had spent most of the weekend washing clothes and cleaning the house. She should have visited more often. Oh, the guilt. Had she really not noticed that things had deteriorated so much or was it wilful blindness? She reached into the kitchen to grab the bucket of leftover scraps and ventured out the back to her least enjoyable chore.

When Renee was a kid, the backyard had been filled with her mother's vegetable patches, neat rows of carrots and lettuce, but they were long gone now. Too much maintenance. However, her mother would be darned before she'd ever get rid of those bloody chooks. They clucked quietly away in their little hen house, their fat little tummies all feathery and fluffed up. Actually, the chooks were kind of cute. It was the rooster with his cocky mohawk and long sharp claws that she didn't like. Big Red. She had already had two failed attempts at collecting the eggs and had fallen asleep devising a new strategy last night.

As she approached, the rooster stuck out its chest and strutted back and forth along the wire cage, taunting Renee, as if to say 'These are *my* hens'. Renee undid the latch of the small square door in the roof and threw half the scraps into one corner, and watched as the three hens scrambled in a frantic flurry.

Peck. Peck. Peck.

Big Red stood back. That's okay, she'd expected this. She knew he was simply being a nice guy. 'I know you're a real man, Big Red, letting the ladies go first.' She stepped a little closer. He lifted himself higher, pushing his chest out. 'I'm going to put your share over here in this corner.' As calmly as possible, Renee threw the remainder of the scraps into the other end of the cage as Big Red scratched his claws in the dirt. Then he strutted over slowly to where she had dropped the scraps. Renee moved back, and he snapped at the pungent vegetable peels, looked around, and then went down for a second peck. She stepped back further, out of his vision, and delicately placed her hand on the cage door, turning the handle, pulling it open and crouching over to crawl in. Big Red, falling in nicely with her ploy, continued pecking away in a hungry frenzy; the hens had slowed down, pecking more calmly now, finding their fill. She crawled further in, as quietly as possible, and reached the back of the cage where the nests were lined up in wooden boxes.

Brruk.

Three pearly eggs, one in each box, lay cosied up in nests of straw. Good work, girls!

Brruk.

She picked up the first one, stretched out the bottom of her shirt and placed the egg in her makeshift carrying vessel. She hurried to collect the remaining two and placed them in her shirt. She turned.

BRRRRRRRUKK!!!

Big Red came at her, a storm of feathers whirling. Claws in mid-air, evil beady eyes, screeching and scratching at her. She turned her back to him, shielding her face, one hand holding the edge of her shirt carrying the eggs, the other scrambling for the latch. She burst out of the cage, slammed the door shut, then turned back to confront his hostility.

'You little punk.'

Brruk.

Laughter erupted from the back patio. She looked back to see her mother standing in a faded nightie in the morning sun holding her stomach, doubled over in amusement.

'It's not funny, Mum!'

'Sorry, darling. But it kind of is ...'

Renee frowned, as her mother tried to breathe and gain composure. 'Well, how the bloody hell do you do it?' Miss Chook Whisperer.

'Big Red knows I'm his friend. We understand each other.' She started to heave with laughter again. 'Sorry, darling. How are the eggs?'

Renee looked down into her shirt. 'Yeah, they're fine.' She'd almost twisted her sore ankle again trying to protect their delicate shells. It was a miracle they were still intact.

'Good. Come inside, I'll put the kettle on.'

'I'll just grab a shower.'

Renee had never got out of the habit of speedy showers. If you have ever lived through a drought, you know the art of a quick shower. Most people would be surprised at how thoroughly you can wash your body in sixty seconds. She could hear her mother out in the kitchen banging around pans and cutlery and cringed at the thought of her injuring herself.

The bathroom filled with a warm soapy fog and she allowed herself a moment to stretch her neck under the water flow. The shower head was better here at her mother's house. Better than the one back home in her cheap little rented apartment that poured rather than sprayed. One small saving grace to being back in Goorungah. Maybe it would be good to have a short break in the country, get fit and focussed, and then by the time a carer came along, she'd not only leave her mother behind with a clear conscience but be in better shape than when she arrived.

She towel dried her short curly hair, and took a moment to look at her face in the mirror. She was vain enough to admit she was pleased she looked no older than her twenty-eight years. She watched what she ate, worked out regularly and her skin care routine albeit simple (soap and cream) was consistent so that her skin was always clear and smooth and her muscles were lean and defined. The only thing she couldn't control was the melancholic gaze that stared back. She frowned to shake the self-pity, wrapped the towel around her body and returned to the bedroom, the one she'd grown up in. She had come to visit her mother for weekends but it felt strange being back in her childhood room knowing she would be staying for a lot longer than that. On previous visits, Renee would purposefully only bring a small backpack so she had an easy excuse for returning to the city. She opened the wardrobe, half expecting to see her high school uniforms hung neatly along the rack, and pulled out a clean blue ironed shirt and dark navy slacks. Back to uniformed policing – the compromise she had made to be close to her mother. The only job available in town had seen her drop her hard-earned detective rank back down to constable. So much for the ten years she'd spent working in the city to earn that status. Now she was back in Goorungah on secondment. She threaded her belt, placed her gun in its holster and looked in the mirror. Just a few weeks, Renee. You can do this.

'Here, Mum, let me do that.' Renee reached for the loaf of bread. Her mother was struggling to untwine the wire tag and open the bag. 'I don't know why you insist on buying this crap. And you're a nurse.'

'I *used* to be a nurse. Besides, I like white bread. I can digest it better. And I don't get all the pesky little seeds stuck in my teeth.'

Renee turned to put the bread in the toaster, rolling her eyes. 'Have a seat, Mum. I can take care of this.'

'Why don't you grow your hair a little? It's so beautiful when it's long and curly,' her mother said, ignoring her request to sit, reaching out to touch her face.

'I like it short. It's more manageable,' Renee said, shaking her mother's hands away and turning back to the toaster, which was dirty and covered in stains. The tray was filled with crumbs and Renee remembered the cockroach she'd seen scurrying down the hall the night before. She picked up a pen from the mug on the table that held everything from letter openers and hair combs to the odd receipt, and scrawled 'roach bait' on the ever-growing list of things to buy and do that was stuck to the fridge.

'Such a practical daughter I've raised.' Her mother sat down at the table, pulling her fluffy dressing gown around her wire-thin frame. She looked smaller these days. So frail. And her hair had thinned.

'Did I hear you up last night?' Renee asked. It was impossible to do anything in that house without being noticed. The wooden floorboards creaked at the slightest movement. Renee's aptitude for stealth police operations was no doubt a result of years of perfecting the ability to move through the house without making a sound to escape and enjoy midnight teenage escapades.

'Wasn't me. Slept like a baby for the first time in weeks, thanks to that morphine.' Renee looked hard at her mother. 'Oh, and the joy of having my beautiful daughter back home with me.'

Renee smiled. 'Don't get used to it, Mum.'

'What? You or the morphine?' Val snapped back.

'You know what I mean.' The toaster popped and Renee smeared the toast with butter and honey then sliced it into four pieces the way Val insisted. 'Here you go, a meal fit for a nine-year-old destined for diabetes.'

Her mother grinned, clumsily taking one piece in her twisted arthritic hands. Renee returned to the bench, then cracked two eggs in a pan.

Melaleuca

'You sure you don't want an egg?'

'No.'

'Even after all the trouble I went through this morning collecting them for you?'

Her mother looked up, seeming a bit guilty this time, no doubt reflecting on her outburst of laughter at her daughter's distress, and now Renee couldn't help laughing.

'*See, Renee!* It was funny, you agree now, don't you?'

'Yeah, Mum. But, seriously, why do you still have those chooks? They're just extra work and they stink.'

'They don't stink.'

'They ...' Renee stopped. Don't argue.

'They're my pets. I like them. They keep me company.'

'Hah! Bullshit, Mum. It's because you're a tight-arse and you don't want to spend money on eggs.'

Val went quiet and looked down at her toast. Her knuckles had gotten worse, so gnarled and knobbly. Her wrists were twisted and her hands looked squashed, as though they'd been wrapped in bandages like the Chinese once did to make the feet of women smaller. Renee thought of bird claws when she looked at them. Honey was smeared across her mother's face. 'I'm sorry, Mum.' Val looked so little and sad. Not the formidable woman who had raised her and taught her never to take shit from anyone. Renee thought of a photo she'd once seen of Val at her age. In it, she's standing on the beach with a group of similarly vibrant young women lined up in flared jeans and white thongs. Val stood tall in the middle with her lustrous blonde hair and sun-kissed skin, blue eyes sparkling with excitement. 'What's on today?' Renee plated up her eggs and joined her mother at the table with a fresh pot of tea to share. 'You gonna go have a flutter at the pokies?'

'No, because I'm a tight-arse. Tight-arses don't gamble.'

'Come on, Mum.' Renee poured the scalding tea into her mother's cup. 'You know I appreciate everything you've done for me.' As it came out, Renee wasn't sure if she really meant it. If Val had just listened to her doctor and put her name on that waiting list, Renee would be knee-deep in a new case rather than working as a constable back in Goorungah.

Her mother took a sip of tea and Renee started on her eggs, after covering them with a good dousing of Worcestershire sauce. Her life in the city seemed so far away. In the city she had her own place in the inner suburbs, an easy ten-minute bike ride to work at headquarters. Her apartment was nothing fancy, but it was hers and she loved it, frustratingly weak shower pressure and all. The pub next door meant that it was always noisy, but she'd grown used to the smashing of glass bottles as they got emptied out of the dumpster each morning. She had been raised in a house next to a pub, after all.

'Renee, do you think I like this set-up any more than you?' Val asked, picking up on her silence. 'I don't want you to have to sacrifice your career for me.'

'Look, Mum, it won't be much longer. I got a message from social services yesterday. We're third in line for the next carer.'

'That's what they always say, Renee. They don't give a rat's arse about us country folk. I saw it time and time again when I was nursing at the hospital. Folk on waiting lists for caregivers for years! That's where I'd be now if I didn't have you, you know? Over there in the old people's wing.'

Renee knew it was true. They'd been 'third in line' for months now, but no use admitting her own doubts to Val. One of them had to stay strong. 'I'm not going anywhere, Mum. Not until we can sort out a carer for you. It'll be good for me to have a break from the city. I'm going to get fit and healthy and enjoy this country air.' She wished her mother wouldn't test her like this. Val knew how much she wanted to return to the city.

She took another sip. The tea would help her adjust to the heat. She had become acclimatised to Brisbane's coastal humidity in the past ten years. This scorching dry heat now felt uncomfortably foreign. She could handle it for a few weeks, a few months if she absolutely had to. Please let it not be for so long. She imagined all the cases she would miss. Her desire to become a cop had become a sore topic over the years. Renee never knew why it was so hard for her mother to appreciate her desire to enter law enforcement. Val was a nurse after all – a similarly practical, community-oriented occupation. But she had always told Renee that she expected more adventure from her – go to university, travel overseas, see the world, blah blah blah. But Renee wanted structure, a career path, independence and the chance of owning her own home one day. She had considered going to university to study law but that would mean winding up with a massive student loan debt. So she figured she'd become a cop, get paid, get some experience, and then perhaps go into law. Because there was no way Renee was ever putting herself in a financially vulnerable position. She reached across and squeezed her mother's hand and was met with a tight smile and big sad eyes in return.

Chapter 2

The Goorungah Police Station had been built in the 1970s and had a certain blunt ugliness to it. A perimeter of concrete, no trees, just perfectly manicured lawn and a limp Australian flag dripping from the pole out the front. It was in the centre of Main Street opposite the community centre and adjacent to the post office, less than five hundred metres from Val's place.

Renee's chair was too high for the desk but she wasn't staying long enough to bother changing it. She looked around the office, shifting uncomfortably in the starchy, stiff uniform she was no longer used to wearing, wondering how she would fill the hours that lay ahead.

It was Tuesday and her second day working there. She had arrived by seven, keen to escape the house and the expression on her mother's face. Her colleagues' seats were empty. Stacey Appleton, the administration assistant, would be in first after dropping her kids off at school, three noisy ratbags Renee had had the pleasure of meeting briefly yesterday afternoon when they came in after school looking for money from their mum to buy gut rot like Nerds, Whiz Fizz and Gob Stoppers. Renee found herself fascinated by the simplicity of Stacey's life. She cooked cupcakes for her children, competed in the mixed netball competition on Tuesday nights and spoke incessantly about *Neighbours*. She was an all-round lovely person and Renee couldn't stand her. She wasn't entirely sure why she disliked Stacey so much. Perhaps it was because Stacey would never have played with the kid from the spooky house. The kid with the absent dad. The Aboriginal kid. Stacey was the type of person who could simply be herself in this world, knowing that people would console her when she was sad or scared, laugh at her when she made a joke, let her rest when she was tired, and believe her when she spoke. Life came easily to people like Stacey in a way it never had, and never would, to Renee.

Sergeant Mulligan, who ran the small station, had a medical appointment that morning and said he'd be in late, and if Monday had been anything to go by, Constable Roger Madden would be in around nine.

It was late summer and, although turn-of-the-century exhilaration had well and truly subsided (accompanied by a silent communal sigh that the Y2K millennium bug had not wiped out all the computers), the heat had not yet relented. It was already stifling in the office. The others liked the air conditioning blasting, but she preferred it off – open windows, fans whirring, fresh air. The police station was as ugly on the inside as it was on the outside – an open-plan office with three desks, cold lighting, stark white walls and linoleum flooring. Mulligan had his own office to one side, and there was a small kitchenette and holding cell down the corridor at the back, which also led to the car park. There was nothing endearing about this place. Renee shuddered to think of the brutality that would have occurred inside these walls in years gone by.

Yesterday she had spent the morning with Stacey, setting up her computer and phone. Then she'd had her introductory meeting with Mulligan. She'd met him before at community events and a few times when the country cops came into the city for training, but she'd never had an extended one-on-one conversation with him. They had spent half an hour going over the basics – what he wanted her to focus on while she was there (traffic, juvenile crime and domestic violence) and his expectations for general office conduct.

'Do you know your way around town then?' he'd asked, leaning back in his chair. His face was freshly shaven, his boots shiny and his uniform immaculate. Renee guessed her new boss, her *temporary* boss, was in his late fifties. He kept his mousy brown hair neat and short and smelled of sunscreen. He reminded Renee of her high-school maths teacher – he had a formal yet pleasant disposition, as though he were following a strict set of internal life rules. Renee wondered if he was a religious man because he had that certain confidence to him people of faith emanated. She envied those people.

'I grew up here,' Renee had reminded him. He wasn't the first person to treat her like an outsider since her return on Saturday. Gone ten years and suddenly she was no longer considered local, despite at least six trips back a year to check on Val, which you would think had to count for something.

'Right.' Mulligan had nodded and returned to scanning the pages in front of him. Renee, seated across from him, had glanced around the room. There was a framed map of Goorungah on one wall and a whiteboard on the other with a few telephone numbers and names scrawled across it in blue ink. A shiny beige filing cabinet sat in the corner adorned with a vase of artificial flowers, a family photo and a set of handcuffs. Renee had wondered if Stacey was responsible for the floral arrangement. In the black-and-white family photo, two adults stood in front of a low-set Queenslander. A boy, neatly dressed, socks pulled high, stood between them.

Mulligan had seen the direction of her gaze. 'My parents. The photo was taken when I was a boy.' The way he'd imparted the information so matter-of-factly suggested he was not open to further discussion about personal matters, which was completely fine with her.

'Handsome couple,' she'd said to be polite, even though there was nothing remarkable about them. They stared at the camera stiffly. Only the mother smiled.

Mulligan's eyes had returned to the papers in front of him and Renee sat up a little straighter. 'It says here that you were promoted to detective two years ago ...'

'Correct. I've been mainly assigned to domestic cases in that time – burglaries, home invasions, assaults, homicides ...'

Her boss in the city had sent her staff profile to Mulligan so he could get across her work history. It was a glowing file and she was proud of her achievements. Her physical strength and excellent hand-to-eye coordination, coupled with sharp intellect and low tolerance for bullshit, meant that she rarely got herself into sticky situations, but when she did, she could masterfully manoeuvre herself and those around her to safety. She'd half expected Mulligan to comment on it, but he'd moved on.

'And what were you doing beforehand?' Mulligan squinted as he read.

'I worked general duties for six years, following my initial training at the academy.'

'In Brisbane?'

'Yes, mostly Brisbane. But we went all over the southeast region. Spent a little time on the Gold Coast and up around Caboolture. But yes, mainly in the city.'

'It's changed a lot over the years ...' Mulligan would be old enough to have lived through the Fitzgerald Inquiry. He had tapped his pen on the desk while carefully reviewing the papers. 'Well, it looks like you've certainly achieved a lot in your short career. Must be a bit of an anticlimax being back here in little old Goorungah.' Was this a test of her commitment?

'I'm just grateful to be here, Sarge.'

'And you don't know how long you might be out here ...?' He'd continued leafing through the files.

'It depends on personal circumstances.' Surely her boss had given him the run-down on Val. She didn't want to have to rehash it. 'It depends on how well my mother gets on.'

'Yes, how is Val?' he'd said, placing the folder aside and looking up. 'I'm very sorry to hear about her situation.'

'She's fine. We're working on getting a carer. There's really no other option for us at this stage. So I appreciate you facilitating my secondment.' She was appreciative to a certain extent – Mulligan and human resources had been negotiating the secondment logistics for weeks but being back in uniform once more after so much work to become a detective felt awful. But it wasn't forever, just until they could sort out something more permanent for her mother.

'It may not be as exciting out here as in the city, but we'll do our best to keep you on track.'

'Thanks, Sarge. I'm willing to do whatever needs to be done.'

'We've had a lot of burglaries lately. The young ones are getting into drugs – stealing and hocking whatever they can get a hold of. Mrs Brian was in here just last week – someone had jumped through the window and stolen jewellery when she was down at the chemist filling a script. Took her grandmother's wedding ring. Wouldn't even be worth that much, but the sentimental value – immeasurable. Little bastards.'

'I can follow that up for you,' Renee had said, reaching into her back pocket for her notebook.

Mulligan had shaken his head.

'First, I want you to shadow Constable Madden. He's on traffic patrol this afternoon out near the highway.' Renee had taken a deep breath at the thought of shadowing a PC and made notes to hide her reaction from Mulligan. 'I don't know why everyone thinks it's okay to roar through this town, like we don't have little ones crossing the road. It's the truckies and the city folk on their way further west, thinking they can go at lightning speed with not a care in the world.' Mulligan got to his feet and went to the map. 'Right here. Do you know this intersection?' He'd tapped at the corner of the highway and the road out to the industrial estate. 'Set up there. I won't have any of my locals hurt in a car accident. Not on my watch.' Mulligan was unlike any of her supervisors in the city. Those cops had become hardened to the cold reality of what humans were capable of doing to each other. It never ceased to amaze her how some of them could go home and forget about the job, having glimpsed the underbelly of society, but Mulligan seemed to care. Perhaps he was the type of cop who would seek and deliver justice?

She had left his office with a renewed sense of focus and was met by Stacey and Roger Madden, who insisted she join them for lunch at Alfie's, the local cafe. There was no getting out of it, so she'd accepted and walked the short distance down Main

Street, hoping not to bump into her mother on her way to play the pokies. Alfie's hadn't changed since she was a kid. The entire interior remained coated with a thin layer of grease and dust, and the place smelled of burned fat and tomato sauce.

'Sarge said there's been some break and enters lately,' Renee had said to Roger after they'd ordered and found a table. Stacey had spotted 'one of the other mums' out the front of the cafe and appeared deep in conversation, so Renee had figured she'd take advantage of the opportunity to ask Roger a few work-related questions.

'Yeah, a few,' Roger had said, pushing a mouthful to one side, nodding. Burger juice dripped from his chin and he'd made it worse by wiping it with a serviette and spreading it further to the sides of his cheeks. 'Kids hitting the hard stuff way too young. It's sad to see. Not like when we were young, you know? Sneak out with a bottle of Mum's Passion Pop or play goon of fortune under the Hills hoist.' He'd taken another mouthful before finishing the one already in his mouth and Renee had put down her sandwich, hoping her appetite would return once Roger had finished.

'The good old days, hey? So, these kids—'

'I'm sorry to hear about your mum.' Roger had cut her off mid-question, steering the conversation back to the personal. 'You know she helped my wife, Trish, through our first pregnancy.'

'Oh yeah?'

'Couldn't've done it without her – so supportive. Trish still talks about her.' He'd put his burger down. 'We should come around sometime.' Renee had found herself shaking her head. 'Not to stay, just to bring you some food. Trish is a fantastic cook. Does your mum like Vietnamese food?'

Melaleuca

Renee loved Vietnamese food and was tempted to accept the offer but really wanted to keep things professional. 'It's okay, really. But thanks. Sarge said he wants us to go on traffic this arvo …' she'd said, steering the conversation again back to her realm of comfort.

'Oh yeah, he did mention that. How'd your meeting go with him this morning?'

'Fine. He wants me to shadow you.' Renee had imparted the news through gritted teeth, almost hoping Roger wouldn't hear, thinking there may still be a way to wiggle out of the arrangement. 'Just for a few days, I think.'

Roger had paused, tilted his head to one side and studied her a moment. His blue eyes were kind.

He knows, Renee had thought suddenly. He knows that I am finding this hard.

Perhaps she had misjudged him – he was better at reading people than she thought.

'Coolio.'

Renee had cringed. Maybe not.

'I thought you were a detective in the city. I should be shadowing you!' No shit. 'Gee whiz, now I'm a bit nervous.'

After lunch, Stacey had gone back to the office and Roger had taken her ten minutes' west of town to set up the speed camera on the Sturt Highway, as per Mulligan's instructions. They'd parked alongside the road in long dry grass, next to a towering dead gum, its skeletal remains shiny grey against a perfect blue backdrop.

'So, tell me more about this drug problem. Who's running the show?' Renee had asked, lowering her binoculars to look across at Roger.

'There's a bloke here you're probably going to wish you never heard of.'

Renee had smiled gently, as though Roger were a child, and nodded for him to proceed. She'd been a cop in uniform in the city for eight years! Did they think she was a snowflake?

'His name's William Gawlor. Worm. And as the name suggests, he's a real low-life. He's behind most of it, although there's probably a few randoms that swing through as well.'

'Tell me more about Worm.' Renee vaguely recalled hearing about him growing up, but it was always whispers and stories cut short with that wide-eyed 'you know' look between the adults. She'd heard her mum and a few other adults talking about him when she was a teenager but never thought too much of it back then. Looking back now as an adult, she wondered if that was why her mum had always been so worried about her going out late at night. She had spotted a family of kangaroos resting under the skeleton tree, flicking the flies away with their ears.

'Spent a bit of time behind bars years ago, but he's back on it now. We just can't get enough on him. Nothin sticks.'

'He lives in town?'

'Yeah, over behind the squash courts. Trish tells me that she sees him there from time to time chatting with the young ones.' Roger's face had reddened. 'I'll smash him if he ever goes near my daughter.'

Renee had turned to look at him. She couldn't imagine him smashing anyone.

Roger had met her gaze briefly, lifted his chin and turned to looked out of the window.

Huh. Like she thought, he could read people.

A semi-trailer had approached, rattling in the distance, and Renee picked up her binoculars again. 'Look at this bastard coming along.'

Roger had raised the speed camera and held it as the long snake of the truck approached, its roar startling the roos, one of them bounding out onto the road. The monstrosity rushed past, thumping into the roo, sending its body skidding along the roadside, tail and legs bumping and rolling. Renee had closed her eyes.

'140 kilometres,' Roger had said, checking the display. 'Fuckin lunatic.'

That was yesterday. Now Renee sat in the empty office, wondering how the hell she was going to remain sane in the company of Stacey, Roger and Mulligan by day and her mother by night, when the phone on the desk opposite her started to ring.

'Goorungah Police Station, how may I help you?' she asked, standing at Stacey's desk to take the call.

'Yes, hello?' A woman's frantic voice came through the receiver. 'You need to come quickly. I …' The caller sucked in her breath, as though she was struggling to speak.

Renee picked up a notepad and pen. 'Calm down. Take a deep breath and let it out slowly.'

'I found a woman,' the caller wailed. 'A body. Hm. I don't know. Very badly hurt. Maybe she's dead. I don't know. Ah – down by the creek. Please come quickly.'

Renee pressed the phone closer to her ear. 'I'm sorry, ma'am. Can you please repeat that?'

'A woman's body. It's all bloody. She wasn't moving. I don't know if she's alive. Down by the creek.' Renee thought she recognised the caller's voice. There was something familiar about the tone – slightly pompous despite the breathlessness.

'You found a woman? Just now?'

'Yes, what are you doing? Hurry up and come!' The woman was starting to cry. 'Whoever did it might still be out there.'

'I'm on my way, ma'am. Where are you now?'

'17 Fletchers Drive. Hurry.' Renee pictured the house in her mind. It was the one at the end of the road along the creek. She had run past it a few times on previous visits, but it wasn't part of her more recent route.

'Ma'am, I'm on my way. Are you by yourself?'

'Yes.'

'I need you to lock all the doors and stay inside. I'll be there right away.'

Renee ran down the corridor and out the back to the parking lot. Still no one else had arrived. The navy-blue sedan blinked twice as she pressed the open button on her key. Given she had been the last person to drive it after patrolling with Roger the day before, the air conditioning was off and the rear-view mirror was in place. She turned the key in the ignition, wound down the windows and sped through town, grabbing the radio to call an ambulance – the operator assured her they would be out immediately – then to call Mulligan. No response. She remembered he had a medical appointment that morning.

'Sarge, I've got a call-out to Fletchers Drive. A woman's called in. Says she's found a woman by the creek, a body. Maybe deceased. I'm going now. Meet me there. Number seventeen – house at the end.'

Chapter 3

Two tall steel gates greeted her upon arrival at the property at the end of Fletchers Drive. They were encased on either side by the thick stone wall that ran along the front of the property. It was unusual to see security being taken so seriously in the country. Val still left both front and back doors open every night, a habit that Renee was trying to get her out of, and that was before she'd become aware of the spate of break and enters in town. She drove closer and the gates opened before she had a chance to reach for the button. Glancing up, she noticed a camera to one side and imagined the fear-stricken caller examining her on a screen inside the house. A gravel driveway lined with pine trees led her up to an impressive double-storey slate and brick house.

She rang the doorbell and peered through the glass panel in the front door to see a grand entrance with polished wooden floors, a high ceiling adorned with a crystal chandelier and a long staircase leading to the upper level. She was about to bang her fist on the door when a woman's face appeared at the glass. She remembered where she knew the voice from. It was one of the ladies who had taught religious education classes at primary school. She strained her memory to recall the name, but all that came back to her were recollections of the unanswered questions she and her classmates had posed.

If God exists, why are kids starving in Africa?
If God exists, why haven't we had any rain?
If God exists, why did so many people die in World War I and II?
She felt a sudden pang of guilt for being such a smart-arsed little brat – as if the poor religious education teachers would have known the answers. Mrs Ford. The woman's name came back to her. The door opened and a thin woman with grey hair tied high in a bun, immaculately dressed in a silk blouse and long floral skirt, stood before her.

'Thank goodness you're here.'

'Mrs Ford, I'm Detect ... Constable Renee Taylor.' She flashed her badge. 'We need to move quickly.' The woman wore a dazed look. Renee was familiar with this expression on the faces of first responders and witnesses to serious trauma. Witnesses would often lose all sense of agency and become childlike upon the arrival of someone they deemed authority, safe. 'Mrs Ford. Show me to the woman.'

'By the creek.' She pointed. 'Down that way.'

'You need to take me down there.'

Mrs Ford stepped back. She was shaking and clearly did not want to return. Renee scanned the front lawn for movement. 'We will be safe – you're with me. You need to show me. Do you think you can do that?' Renee's patience was running thin. If the woman was still alive, they needed to get her medical assistance asap.

Hand on gun, Renee followed Mrs Ford down a long gravel pathway that led from the side of the house towards the creek. They went through a large iron gate embedded in the thick stone wall and covered in ivy, then continued downhill along a track, leaving the manicured lawn to enter lush native bushland. It

Melaleuca

was quiet apart from the corellas nibbling and squabbling in the branches high above and the occasional distant rumble of a freight truck. Mrs Ford glanced around like a mouse watching for a hawk then stopped dead as they entered a small grassy space. 'I would prefer to stay here.'

Renee followed Mrs Ford's terrified gaze to the far edge of the clearing, then began running towards the mound of leaves there. She had seen many severely injured people come back from the brink of death so there was always hope until the heart stops beating. She jerked to a stop, punched by the sight of the bloodied mess. A woman's lifeless body lay in the grass, her face partially caved in and her hair matted with blood and dirt.

It was difficult to guess her age, maybe late teens or early twenties. Renee leaned down to place her finger on the woman's neck. The sound of the ambulance siren flooded her senses when all she wanted to feel was a pulse along the carotid artery. She closed her eyes hard, summoning strength to proceed. A sudden flashback to those religious education classes: *If God exists, why?*

The body was carelessly covered in leaves and branches that were insufficient to hide it from the view of a passer-by. The woman was wearing denim shorts and a faded purple singlet. A thin gold necklace trickled down into the creases of her neck, and at the end of the chain dangled a yellow stone pendant, softly sparkling with the morning sun. A boulder lay nearby, and the earth around the body was covered in blood. Her feet were covered in mud and her legs were scratched with signs of bleeding, which could have been the result of running through dry vegetation. Her skin was the same shade of light brown as Renee's. *Who did this to you?*

She put gloves on and reached down again to feel the girl's skin. Still warm. The killer might not be far away. Renee walked back over to Mrs Ford. 'Did you see anyone down here this morning?'

'Not a soul.'

'What time did you find her?'

'I'm not sure. I came down here for a walk, as I do every morning. Perhaps about quarter to seven? There's never anyone around, usually. It's serene.'

Renee could relate. The world is more peaceful when people are sleeping.

'Do you recognise the woman?'

Mrs Ford shook her head. 'I only know a few of the coloured girls in town, the ones who come to church on Sundays.'

Renee managed to stop herself from rolling her eyes. This was the kind of racism she had grown up with. In the city, people made an effort to hide their prejudice, but out here in good ol' Goorungah they let it all hang out. Racist? Oh no, not me. There was no use calling it out – it would only make things worse. Best to pretend not to hear it, not to feel it.

Renee turned from Mrs Ford and searched the surrounding paddock, taking in the scene. There were no tyre tracks, and besides it would have been difficult for a car to access the clearing with the creek on one side and steeply sloping scrubland on the other.

Renee wondered where the girl could have come from – maybe a house in town. The spot was only about three kilometres from Main Street. She would have had to cross at the bridge or swim to get to this side of the creek. Renee looked down towards the water – it was about ten metres across to the other side, and even though the water had evaporated throughout the summer, she knew from swimming there as a kid it was still deep in this part. The woman's clothing was muddy but dry, so she couldn't have swum across recently or her clothes would be wet. She may have crossed further upstream where rocky boulders and fallen logs provided stepping stones but this was further from Goorungah. How would she have got out there? Maybe she did run away from the town but crossed the bridge, which was further downstream, just around the corner from Main Street.

Renee peered over into the edge of the creek where the water had receded and the dried mud along its banks looked like cracked chocolate. She noticed a single set of footprints coming up the bank. She walked carefully across to the other side of the clearing, where the track sloped up the hill. Here she found another set of prints going back up the hill. Shoes. Probably boots, worn by someone with a large body judging by the depth of the markings.

Her phone buzzed. It was Mulligan.

'I'm here, I'm out the front of the gates. The ambulance is here too. They've been ringing the gate bell. Where the hell are you?'

She'd given them her mobile number – why hadn't they called her?

'I'm down by the creek. She's dead. Tell the medics there's no need to rush.' She could hear Mulligan relay the news followed by muffled voices.

'Is he at the front gates?' Mrs Ford asked. 'Tell him to turn to his right and follow the path down. That will bring him directly here.'

'Did you hear that?' Renee asked Mulligan.

'On the way.'

Heavy steps came crunching through the bushes and she looked up to see Mulligan moving down the track, followed by two paramedics who Renee instructed to keep back for the time being, so as not to contaminate the site.

'Sarge.' Renee beckoned Mulligan to follow her down to where the body lay, instructing Mrs Ford to stay where she was. 'She's down this way.'

She watched as Mulligan took in the scene, a pained expression forming.

'Did you know her?' Renee asked.

His face showed no signs of recognition. Renee had been away from Goorungah for ten years, so she had lost track of many of the locals, especially the younger ones.

'There are footprints over in the mud,' Renee advised, pointing down to the creek bed. 'And boot prints over there, up the path. Whoever did this must've gone back up there.'

'Did you see anyone?' Mulligan asked.

'No.'

'Did Mrs Ford?'

'She was down here by herself, didn't see anyone.'

'Righto, I've already called in backup. We need to put up roadblocks around town and start searching the area. They can't be far away, whoever did this.' He glanced back across the clearing to where the old lady stood. 'And Mrs Ford called it in?'

Renee nodded. 'Yeah, about forty minutes ago. You know her?'

'Yes, I know her. Bit of a gossip. You'd think someone who lived out here on the outskirts of town would keep to themselves but she's always stickybeaking.'

'She used to teach religious education at the primary school, right?' Renee asked.

'I vaguely remember something along those lines. Were you a student?'

'Briefly.'

Melaleuca

'Lucky you. Mrs Ford,' Mulligan called out in greeting as he headed over. Renee followed.

'Sergeant Mulligan, good morning.' Mrs Ford, shoulders hunched and shivering despite the heat, squeezed her hands together tightly. Suddenly so pitiful, in the face of the sergeant.

'You've had a terrible fright this morning, Mrs Ford. We're going to need your full cooperation for the next few hours to find out what's happened here. Do you understand?'

Mrs Ford nodded as Renee stood still listening for signs of life – noises, footsteps, car engines. 'Something very evil has happened here.'

'We know, Mrs Ford, and we're going to find out exactly what. I need you to tell me what you were doing out here this morning?'

'I was going for my morning stroll, as I do every day, as I told your officer.'

'Did you see anyone?'

Mrs Ford shifted uncomfortably from side to side, face looking dangerously pale. Renee wondered if she was going to pass out. It was not unusual after witnessing such a horrific scene.

'Not a soul.'

'What time were you down here?' Mulligan continued with his questioning, seeming unperturbed.

'About six thirty, quarter to seven. I don't know. Can I please go back home now? I don't feel well.'

Renee heard footsteps coming down the path and all three of them turned towards the sound, startled by the arrival of another person. 'Who's that?'

'Must be Roger,' Mulligan said. 'I called him on my way out here. We'll need to cordon off this area.' Renee hadn't even thought of calling Roger and felt a brief stab of guilt as her colleague emerged wide-eyed from the bush path.

'Madden, there's tape in my car,' Mulligan said in greeting. 'Go fetch it. And Taylor, you accompany Mrs Ford back home.' Renee heard him but didn't respond. Her focus had shifted back over to the body where it lay alone – cold, dirty and bloodied. 'Taylor? Are you okay?' Mulligan reached out and held her shoulder. 'I can get Madden to take Mrs Ford back up. I know it's a lot.'

Renee stepped back, looking away so he wouldn't see her face and shook herself steady.

'I'm fine.' She turned towards Mrs Ford. 'How about we go and have a cup of tea?'

Mrs Ford opened the front door and removed her sandals, then asked Renee to do likewise before coming inside. Renee bent down and unlaced her boots, taking the opportunity to scan the front yard for movement or anything out of the ordinary. When she stepped inside, it smelt old and musky, and the air was cool even though it was heating up outside. 'Would you like that cup of tea?'

'Thank you.' Renee never accepted such offers in the city, but she knew in Goorungah refusal of such hospitality would be met with suspicion and she thought it would help Mrs Ford to have something to do. She followed Mrs Ford along marbled black-and-white tiles into a wide-open kitchen, passing a spacious, starkly furnished room – a small table with a thick book on top, a wooden cross on one wall and a grand piano, shiny and black, with sheet music neatly arranged on top.

'I don't know what the world is coming to. Do you have any idea who may have done such a terrible thing?' Mrs Ford asked, switching on the kettle, peering out the window as though checking if anyone was hiding behind the bushes.

'Not at this stage, Mrs Ford. Are you sure you didn't see anything unusual this morning? Anything at all that may have seemed out of the ordinary?' The kitchen was stark. There were no family photos, only crosses and the occasional pieces of golden-framed scripture.

'No, I woke up just after dawn. I rehearsed some songs on the piano.' Mrs Ford thought for a moment. 'I usually leave the house about six thirty.'

Renee got out her notepad and scrawled down: *Left house at around 6.30?*

The kettle switch clicked. 'Milk or sugar?'

'Just black, no sugar.'

Mrs Ford poured scalding water in two cups and handed one to Renee.

'And last night? Were you at home? Any visitors?'

'I ate dinner around six, watched some television and went to bed around nine,' she said, looking to the ceiling as though to recall events.

'Did you hear anything unusual?'

Mrs Ford frowned and squinted her eyes – it looked like she was straining to remember the finer details. 'I don't think so. The possums were carrying on till the early hours. Nothing out of the ordinary.'

'And when you woke? Did you hear anything?'

'No. But the piano drowns out the background noise. I get lost in my own little world when I'm playing.' Mrs Ford sipped her tea. Renee blew on hers and pretended to take a sip, not able to stomach anything after the scene she'd just encountered down by the creek. 'I remember you now.' Her eyes narrowed, no tenderness apparent in her recollection. 'Quiet little thing you were. Always so keen to learn. The other kids gave you a hard time. How's your mum? Valerie? She looked after me when I had my hip surgery. Always knew the right thing to say and when to keep quiet. There's an art to that, you know? Lord knows, I certainly don't possess it, blabbermouth that I am.'

A frail man appeared in the doorway, tall but slightly hunched, with hollow eyes, red around the lids, his lips cracked as if from biting or licking too much. He appeared ghostlike in faded white pyjamas that hung loosely on his body, and his black hair was stuck to his forehead with sweat. Renee guessed he was in his thirties. 'Mum?'

'Archie! What did I tell you about moving about without your frame?! My goodness, you will tire yourself out. Get back to bed.'

Mrs Ford grabbed a mobility walker from the corner of the room and guided him back down the hallway. Renee watched as mother helped son back towards his bedroom, which lay off the long hallway. It was obvious he could move unaided, albeit slowly. She followed them into the bedroom uninvited and watched as Mrs Ford fixed the pillows around his head, wondering why she had not mentioned her son.

She considered asking Mrs Ford why she had said she was alone and decided it was best not to be confrontational at this stage. 'Archibald, is it?' He nodded. 'I'm Renee Taylor. I'm from the Goorungah Police Station.' The younger man looked at his mother, searching for what appeared to be reassurance. 'The body of a young woman was found down by the creek this morning. Do you know anything about that?'

He shook his head, and looked again at his mother then back to Renee. 'What are you talking about?'

Mrs Ford stepped closer to her son and took his hand. 'It's okay, Archie. We're safe here.'

'Your mother found the body on her morning walk. You didn't hear her on the phone to the police station?'

'I already told you this, Constable Taylor. Archie was asleep.' She hadn't mentioned this previously. Why was she lying?

'If you wouldn't mind, Mrs Ford, I'd like to hear from Archibald directly.'

'It's okay, Mum. I can answer the constable's questions.' He patted his mother's hand and smiled at her weakly, indicating to her to take a seat next to his bed. 'Please, Mum.' Mrs Ford frowned back and Renee thought for a moment that she was going to refuse, but he tensed his grip around her hand and gave her a hard stare. 'Really, Mum. I'm okay.' Mrs Ford took a seat next to the bed and turned her gaze to Renee like a lioness ready to pounce. 'What would you like to know, Constable Taylor?'

'Where were you this morning?'

'Right here.' His gaze was strong, as was his voice. Both defied his frail appearance.

'And did you hear anything?'

'I heard possums early in the morning. They often wake me up when they carry on in the branches at night, especially if my pain medicine has worn thin.'

Renee glanced around the room, thinking of her mother and all the paraphernalia that goes with managing chronic pain. There was a blood pressure monitor on the bedside table, along with cups, tablets, little bottles, a hardcover entitled *Mysteries* *of the Ancient Egyptian*s bookmarked with a $5 note, and a pair of spectacles.

'Do you mind if I ask – what is your condition, Archibald?'

'I was diagnosed with muscular dystrophy when I was five. I take corticosteroids and a few other drugs to help with the pain.'

'Constable Taylor, is this really necessary?' Mrs Ford interjected once more, leaning towards her son and placing her hand on his again.

'Mrs Ford, a woman's been murdered,' Renee said, with an ironic air of moral superiority. Her old religious education teacher responded by stepping back and Renee turned her attention back to Archibald. 'When you heard the possums, did you get up? Look out the window?'

'Not until dawn. I heard Mum on the piano, and that's when I went to the bathroom. But I didn't leave the house, if that's what you're wondering. I came back in here and went to sleep.' He paused and glanced down at his hands. 'Who was she?'

'We don't know yet.'

'What did she look like?' Another candid query – morbid curiosity or fear for the wellbeing of a friend?

'Is there something you want to tell me, Archie? Do you know a young woman who may have disappeared? In …' She paused to consider how best to phrase the question, '… in distressing circumstances?'

'No.'

Renee met his calm gaze. There was something serene about this young man despite the circumstances. Could it be that having to endure so much physical pain daily made everything else small in comparison? She thought of her mother and her moods – delirious with pain one moment and dazed with medication-induced numbness the next. Did this man also experience drug-induced mood swings? Her phone started to ring in her pocket. It was Mulligan.

She turned away to answer the call. 'Sarge?'

'Taylor, come to the front gates. I need you here now.' He sounded stressed.

She moved towards the bedroom door. 'I'll be in contact, Mrs Ford. If either of you thinks of anything do call me straight away.'

Archie inclined his head and silently watched her exit.

Renee walked past the tall pines and manicured rose gardens of the Ford property and met Mulligan at the front gates where dried gum leaves swept across the rust-coloured dirt, guarding the path that wound down to the clearing where they had found the woman. The crime scene investigations van had arrived and was parked next to the ambulance. Renee was surprised to see it there so quickly – it was a two-hour drive from headquarters. Unfortunately, the van was not the only vehicle. An endless stream of cars crawled down the country road. Some held one lone snoopy passenger, while others had two or more people, all rubbernecking to see the action. She spotted the old man from that morning who had warned her about snakes. They locked eyes and he slowed down his knocked-about, rusty old Holden ute.

'What's going on?'

Before Renee could respond, Mulligan interjected. 'Nothing we can comment on at this stage, Norm, so just keep moving.'

'Come on, Rod,' Norm said, leaning out his window. 'You can tell me.'

'Norman, move along.'

Norm snorted, clearly unimpressed, but he drove off. It was a dead-end street, so all the cars needed to turn around at the entrance to the Ford property. Renee wondered if Mrs Ford was watching the procession from her security camera.

'Where are all these people coming from? Don't they have jobs?' Renee asked Mulligan. 'How do they even know? Reckon they followed the ambulance down?'

'Mrs Ford,' Mulligan grumbled under his breath, motioning back towards the house.

'Really? You think she was up there on the phone?'

'It must've been her. She probably called one of her church friends before you even got here.'

Renee thought that unlikely – Mrs Ford had been too shaken to call anyone. 'Maybe they picked it up on the radio,' she said. There were bored hobbyists out there who liked to listen in to police radio. And news travelled like wildfire on the bush telegraph. 'Or it might have been the crime scene van? That got here fast.'

'They were in the next town finishing up on an aggravated burglary. Druggies looking for stuff to hock, no doubt,' Mulligan said grimly. 'It's a plague out here.'

'So where are we up to?' Renee asked and Mulligan advised her that forensics and the ambulance were down on the scene and extra cops from central had been sent out to help set up roadblocks around town.

'I want you to stay up here and guard the entrance to the path. Don't let any of these stickybeaks come down to the scene. You understand, Taylor?'

'Sure.' She would have preferred to return to the scene. 'Madden's still down there?'

Melaleuca

'Yes, he's keeping watch ...' Mulligan seemed distracted. He was looking into the distance.

'What is it?' Renee followed his gaze to the last car in the long winding procession. It was a white van with a brightly coloured television news channel logo across the side.

'Channel Five's here,' Mulligan said. 'Won't take long for the others to come now.'

'What are we going to tell them?'

There was no identifying material, and no one had been reported missing yet.

'Nothing.' Mulligan turned to walk away. 'Just keep them calm. Tell them we're handling things. You've worked in the city. You know how this goes.'

'I've never dealt with the press. We have a special unit for that.' Renee did not like nor trust the media.

'Well, Taylor. Welcome to Goorungah where we're flooded with resources.' The sarcasm wasn't lost on Renee and she glared at him. 'I need to get back down to the scene. You can handle it.' He patted her back and turned away.

A sense of profound loneliness enveloped her as she walked towards the gathering press, trying to process the horrific details of that morning into a form appropriate for a news audience of millions.

'Hi there. My name's Jillian Crawley.' A woman came from out of Renee's line of vision, interrupting her thoughts, and reached out her hand with an exaggerated sense of self-assuredness. 'I'm from Channel Five.' Her puffy bright yellow dress and skinny legs ending in pointy stilettos made Renee think of a canary.

'Constable Taylor.' Renee shook Jillian's hand, noticing her thick geometric eyebrows and pouty swollen lips. Such unnecessary pain.

'We heard that a young woman's body was found here this morning.'

'There is a suspicious death under investigation.'

'Any ID?'

'No comment.'

'Any suspects?'

'No comment.' And so the game begins.

'Any chance we could get a filmed statement from Mulligan at the Goorungah Police Station?' Renee had seen this coming. They'd want something to put up as soon as possible to beat the other stations to the story. 'It's in the community's best interest if you provide me with a statement.'

If they arrested the perpetrator or they had concrete information *then* they would let the community know. It would allay their fears that a murderer was loose in their midst at best, or at least show that they were pursuing the investigation competently, if they had yet to make an arrest. But it was advisable to release minimal detail till they had something to say in these early stages. Both Jillian and Renee knew this.

'We're investigating, Ms Crawley. When we have anything to tell the community, we will call a media conference. Now please step back. You are encroaching on a crime scene.'

Renee turned away from the media and the rest of the crowd. She had handled it as best she could but the feeling of dread from this morning persisted. The same feeling as when she'd encountered Norm in his rusty old shed, the same feeling as when she had found the body. It had moved from the pit of her stomach up into her chest, like the heaviness of a humid day. Everyone was watching the show but did anyone care about that woman down by the creek? Where were the people who loved her?

As the afternoon wore on, Renee stood guarding the entrance to the path as the forensic team went back and forth from the van to the site. She had accepted a demotion to work here, but that didn't mean it didn't sting that she was relegated to crowd management while Roger was down at the crime scene, no doubt contaminating evidence.

The film crews and reporters hovered at the side of the road, ready to jump on any new information, as the locals continued their parade past the entrance to the track.

Renee knew that an outdoor crime scene was the most difficult place to get evidence and she desperately wanted to return to the scene to check they were being thorough in their collection of samples, but Mulligan had instructed *Constable* Taylor to stay here and watch. At least it hadn't rained. That was often a problem in Brisbane. Thunderstorms frequently washed away any trace of evidence or DNA if a body had been discovered out in the open.

When the onlookers hushed and froze, all staring towards the entrance to the path, Renee knew before turning around that it was the body coming up. There's something about coming face to face with the inevitability of what lies ahead for all of us. The dread it incites.

The first time Renee saw a dead body was not actually on the job, but during her first year of training as a cadet. She was running early one morning in the park along the river and as she crossed under the traffic bridge, cars and trucks roaring overhead, she came across the body of a man who had thrown himself over the edge. It was the most disturbing scene she'd ever witnessed in her life, and the details remained photographically etched in her memory. The man was morbidly obese and his remains had burst over the bitumen upon impact. When she'd called emergency services, they'd asked her to stay nearby and it was during those ten minutes of waiting that she seriously considered whether she could make it as a police officer. Was she strong enough? Before his death, the man had been sleeping on a mattress in the dark, damp concrete cave under the steel pillars of the bridge, and for the rest of the day all Renee could think about was how alone he must have felt.

Now as she stood in the heat of a late Goorungah summer watching the forensics team stroll past with the body of the young woman on a stretcher, Renee understood that those doubts made her human. They meant she would never become like some of the cold-blooded psychopaths she'd crossed paths with over the years as a detective, nor the apathetic professionals who no longer cared about seeking justice and only wanted to climb the ranks to better pay and conditions.

It was her vulnerability that made her strong.

The news crews sprang to attention and turned on their cameras like vultures all wanting to get a good shot just as Renee noticed the thin plastic white sheet covering the body was coming loose and starting to slide. She lurched over as it slipped away from the body, revealing a fleeting glimpse of the woman's crushed face, and pulled it back up over her, re-securing it to the edge.

'What the hell was that?' She ran up to the chief medical examiner who was walking a few steps behind. 'Did you even see that?'

'See what?' He kept walking towards the van and Renee chased after him.

'The sheet slipped. It nearly fell off.' She looked at him incredulously, waiting for a reaction but he calmly walked on.

'Calm down. We had it under control.'

Like hell you did, she thought. She vaguely recognised him from the city. 'It's Petrovic, right?' He had slicked-back black hair and *The Blues Brothers* Wayfarer sunglasses.

'Do I know you?'

'I've seen you at a few scenes. In the city. I'm here on secondment.' Renee hated saying that out loud.

'Right.' Petrovic opened the door to the van, eager to move on. 'Mulligan wants you back down there. He's sending that goofball cop up in a minute.' She figured he was referring to Roger Madden.

'So you're done?'

'The rest of the boys will keep sweeping. We have plenty of blood samples.' Her death was a result of blunt force trauma to the skull and there are ample capillaries in the head so Renee was not surprised.

'Anything else?' Renee watched as the forensics team wheeled the covered body into the back of the van.

'The fingerprint expert will be here in half an hour but I don't hold much hope on her finding anything. There are some loose hairs we can run for DNA. Any idea who she was?'

Renee shook her head. 'Not yet.'

'Not one of your mob?'

Renee raised her eyebrows. What was it with some people? 'No. She is not one of my *mob*. We don't all know each other, you know.' And who the fuck do you think you are? she wanted to say, but settled for an icily contemptuous smile. Renee didn't like this man, but she would need to get on with him.

He responded by shrugging, a 'don't be so sensitive' lift of the shoulders, and got in the van.

'When can we have the lab report?'

'Soon,' he said before slamming the door.

Roger came up the hill and told her they could swap watch. Renee returned to the clearing as the remaining few forensic officers scouted the area for samples. Mulligan was pacing the perimeter, searching for items forensics may have overlooked. Renee joined him.

'Did Petrovic tell you anything before leaving? Was there any identifying material on her?' Renee asked.

'Nothing,' Mulligan said. 'No ID. No wallet. No bank cards. Obviously, we'll know more when they do the full autopsy, but for now we really don't know much at all.'

'Any calls to the station?' Renee asked. Stacey was monitoring the phones in the office.

'Just the media. And headquarters has been checking in all morning. They won't give me any extra resources but then when something like this happens, they're all over it because they're afraid of the news reporters. It's all politics.'

'What about family and friends of the victim?'

Mulligan shook his head. 'No one.'

A forensics officer called Mulligan over and Renee was left standing by herself.

A lone magpie landed on a low branch a few feet away, puffed up its feathers and warbled into the void.

Chapter 4

On the way back from the crime scene, Roger and Renee grabbed a sandwich and some water. By the time they walked into the office, Mulligan was in full flow.

'I don't want you to miss a single call, Stacey. We're going to have all sorts dialling in today: community tip offs – I don't care how absurd their claims are, I want to hear all of them; family and friends of missing loved ones thinking that the girl is theirs. I've already had HQ up my arse with instructions three times today. And the media – the media is already all over this like a rash. They are calling all the time. Any questions, the answer is "We are doing everything we can, and the community should rest assured that they are in safe hands. There is nothing more at this time." You got it?'

Stacey sat up straight in her chair, fiercely nodding and scribbling notes. 'Yes, Sarge. I got it.'

'Good. And this goes for you too, Taylor and Madden. Any calls from the media, that's the answer. Do not leave space for doubt. We are handling this. Understood?'

They nodded in unison. He slammed back into his office. Then threw the office door open again and glared at them. 'Come on then!'

They nearly tripped over each other on the way in. Renee pulled out her lined notebook and placed it on her lap with pen in hand, pulling a loose curl back behind her ear, ready for the sergeant's briefing.

Mulligan shut the door, walked across the room and closed the curtains to block the view of prying eyes. The media frenzy had followed them back to the station and set up on the footpath out the front, cameras and microphones at the ready. He turned to Roger and Renee and took a deep breath. 'Right. Let's go over what we know. A young woman, probably Aboriginal, in her late teens or early twenties, was fatally injured, probably with the boulder we found beside her body, sometime in the early hours of this morning.' Renee watched Mulligan turn away to wipe old notes off the whiteboard. 'What else do we know?'

'Mrs Ford found her at around 6.45 am when taking her usual walk,' Roger offered. He had spent a suspiciously long time in the men's bathroom after returning from the crime scene and Renee suspected he was more affected by the grisly sight this morning than he was willing to let on. It wasn't every day you came across a dead body, especially not in Goorungah. It may have been the first one Roger had ever seen. She reminded herself to go a bit easy on him. 'She saw and heard nothing. There were two sets of prints – footprints and boot prints,' he continued, seeming to have it together again now, even quite spritely as he offered his thoughts. 'But only the boot prints left the scene, leading away up the path, towards the road.'

He fell silent. Renee studied him and wondered his age. Stacey had said on Monday that he had a wife and two kids. She guessed around thirty-five. Certainly older than her, but he had such an innocence about him. For someone in their mid-thirties his face was remarkably lacking in character – there weren't any lines on his face, forehead or around the eyes to indicate any patterns of joy, melancholy, frustration or fear. This event might give him a few wrinkles.

Mulligan added Roger's contributions to the whiteboard and turned back to face them. 'Right. What else?'

'She'd been running. Her feet were covered in mud and her legs were lashed, probably from bush foliage or long grass,' Renee added, remembering the red scratches across her calves. 'Maybe she had escaped from something – she didn't have time to put shoes on.' Had this woman been running about the same time she had gone for her jog that morning, or possibly earlier? She would have also experienced the heat and dry air, maybe yearned for water in the way she had.

Roger sat up, holding a pen he'd been toying with. 'Yes, what if the woman was in dire circumstances and didn't even have any shoes – maybe she'd been abducted from someplace else, like over on the coast, and held in a vehicle against her will, until her captor got distracted and then she made a break for it?' It was imaginative, but it was a plausible theory. They couldn't rule out anything at this point.

'Let's not speculate just yet, Madden,' Mulligan said. 'What do we know for sure?'

'We know what she was wearing – denim shorts, singlet and a necklace,' Renee recounted. 'And we know that she wasn't carrying anything that would help us identify her, like a purse or driver's licence.'

'Okay, good. What else?'

Renee strained her mind, thinking of the details of the morning ... A young woman, alone, early hours of a summer morning ... in Goorungah ...

'There were prints along the bank, and her feet were covered in mud ...' Renee thought out loud.

'But her clothes were dry ...' Roger added. 'Which means she hadn't crossed the creek. Maybe she was trying to find somewhere narrow to swim cross the creek, to get into town to find safety.'

'Not necessarily. She could have crossed further upstream where it's shallow. You can get across the creek by jumping across the logs further up.'

'Or she could have crossed at the bridge,' Roger suggested.

'I don't think so. The prints were pointed westerly, towards the bridge. I think she crossed further upstream and she was running west. If she was looking for safety in town, she was shooting too far north.' Either town was not safe, or the young woman wasn't familiar with the region.

'Okay, park that for now. What *don't* we know?' Mulligan asked, eyeing them both closely.

'Her identity,' Roger said and Mulligan scrawled *Who was she?* across the top of the whiteboard.

'Do you want to elaborate, Madden?'

'Well, no one has come forward to identify her. She had no identifying information on her. We don't know where she came from nor where she was going. We don't know if she was local or from out of town.'

'And ...?' Mulligan pressed further.

Renee stepped in. 'We don't know the cause of death, although it looks to me like a homicide.' Mulligan added *How did she die?* to the board.

He stepped back to take in the contents of the board, and then slowly nodded approval. 'Good.' Renee watched as he moved towards the window, peeked through the blinds at the media, then took a seat at his desk, leaned back and sighed. 'So *now*, let's speculate.'

'The way in which she was killed ...' Renee stumbled as an image of the woman's battered and broken face flashed before her, 'the violence of it would suggest it was someone she knew. It was personal. It looks as if the killer smashed the boulder into her face repeatedly, as if as they wanted to make her stop talking or to inflict—'

'Yeah ... but ...' Roger interrupted, then paused for so long that Renee fought an urge to speak over him. 'It was also very practical. I mean, if we return to my earlier theory ...' He checked around the room to make sure he held their attention. 'If she was abducted by a stranger and made a run for it and the killer chased after her, he may not have had any other means of killing her, so he just reaches for the closest object. There's nothing *passionate* about that, it's just *practical*.'

'Okay.' Renee wasn't thrilled about being interrupted but Roger had a point. The face had looked bludgeoned to her – and she had seen a few blunt instrument assaults in her time. But they hadn't had the results of the post-mortem yet. It may have been one catastrophic blow. She tried to control her breathing. 'And the motive?'

'To silence her, to stop her,' Roger said. 'If this person abducted her against her will, he's not exactly going to want her running off telling everyone.'

'Maybe,' Renee conceded, staring at the table, conjuring the scene. Mulligan had gone quiet.

'Okay, so what if it *was* someone she knew?' Renee said, gathering her thoughts. 'Let's assume for a second that she's *not* local. But she did know her killer.' Renee glanced across at Mulligan again. He could say *something* but he seemed to have decided to sit back and listen to their analysis.

'Maybe she was part of a group of kids,' Roger said, jumping in, 'a group of kids who came for a swim out at Crystal Ponds and they got carried away drinking, doing drugs – you know how they carry on out there. There was a huge party out there on New Year's. Didn't hear about it till the next day, when reports of one of the young girls having to get their stomach pumped came through from the hospital.'

Renee knew from her own youth that Crystal Ponds was a popular place for locals and out-of-towners alike. Families went to the main rock pools for Sunday picnics, but further up the valley were deeper, harder-to-reach pools. These rocky crevices were filled with clear icy water, not like the muddy brown Goorungah Creek that evaporated into putrid pits of rotting carp every drought. These more remote, higher-altitude pools had always been a place for thrill-seeking teenagers wanting to impress their friends by hurling themselves off the steepest ledge. 'What if something bad had happened up at those rock pools? They were drinking and carrying on, showing off to each other, and then things got out of hand? This girl saw it, then they decided she had to go ...'

'Bloody hell, Roger.' The detail was unnerving. Maybe he hadn't been so sheltered. 'If you weren't on our side, I'd start to get suspicious.'

Roger smiled hesitantly as though unsure if it was a compliment. 'I watch *Law and Order*. A lot.'

Okay. Perhaps he *had* been that sheltered.

Renee continued. 'What if she was visiting someone in town — a friend or a cousin?'

'So, yes, let's say she was from out of town but the perpetrator is local?' Roger agreed, looking at the ceiling, and Renee wondered what fully fledged dramatic scenario was formulating in his head. 'It is summer, so it's the time of year for visiting family and friends.'

'Or she might've come from one of the hobby farms,' Renee suggested, thinking back to the kids she went to school with who lived in trailers and helped their parents by selling eggs and vegetables at the weekend farmers' market. It wasn't as though she'd had a remarkably easy childhood, but those kids had it rough. Their families would move around in search of work and Renee always felt sorry for them having to start over and make new friends. 'Maybe the girl was from one of these smaller farms, visiting relatives.'

'Maybe. There's a lot of maybes going on here.' Mulligan had been peeking out the slit in the blinds again, now he returned to his seat and rubbed his eyes. 'I think it's best if we—'

'Maybe it was her boyfriend,' Roger continued. 'What if she came out here to visit her boyfriend and he found out she was cheating on him? Or she was with her boyfriend on a trip out west, and they had a fight and she escaped. That would explain why she had no identifying information on her.'

Renee was about to roll her eyes but then ... 'Archibald Ford.'

Roger was encouraged. 'Yes! Archie and this young woman met on a website for lonely romantics, and he lured her out here with profound philosophical insights about the meaning of life ...'

'Archie's sick and no doubt weak but we can't rule him out,' Mulligan said, writing *AF* on the whiteboard. It was true. Renee had seen him walking down to the kitchen so he could move, but how far and how quickly was anyone's guess – something to investigate further.

'It could've been drug related. Maybe it was Worm?' He was still fresh in her mind from their conversation in the car yesterday as someone to keep an eye on while she was there.

'Wouldn't rule out that dirtbag, no way,' Roger said, and they both turned to Mulligan, who wrote *WG* on the board.

'Well, I think we can agree that we've got some loose ends until someone calls in with further information and until we get the lab report. Roger, I want you to head up this case.'

'But Sarge?' Renee felt the heat rise in her neck. She looked across at Roger, whose flushed face instantly paled as the blood rushed to his central organs in a sudden fight-or-flight response. He didn't want this either.

'Yes.' Mulligan's eyes narrowed at her. Was he seriously going to give this case to Roger?

'Sergeant, I've been a detective in the city for two years now. I have all the expertise and experience. It would be a waste for me not to take the lead. I think it's only appropriate for me to lead this case. You don't have a problem with that, do you, Roger?' Renee tried to slow her breathing and meet Mulligan's eye.

Roger shrugged, then nodded. 'All yours, Taylor.'

Mulligan looked down at his desk, back to the whiteboard and then to Renee. He sighed heavily. 'I'm just worried that with your mother being so sick, you may not be able to give this your full attention.'

'I appreciate the concern, Sarge. It's true, Mum is unwell and somewhat reliant on me, but she's stable. And she knows everyone at the hospital, if there was an emergency.'

'Fine. But you report everything back to me.'

'I will.'

'And I mean *everything*, Taylor. Do you understand?' The vein in his neck pulsed and he clenched his fists. Renee found herself taking a half step back at the look on his face. Why was he so upset?

'I'll keep you abreast of absolutely everything, Sarge. You have my word.' Only then did he loosen his grip, take a breath and sit back down. She and Roger glanced at each other. Mulligan caught the look.

'I just want you to be careful. Breaks my heart this young woman was murdered in our town. You be careful out there, Renee. Women can't be too careful. Okay. You can deal with the press as well. Roger, go and call the cops on the roadblocks. Ask them if they've seen anything on the outskirts of town or interviewed anyone suspicious. We'll only have those extra resources for the rest of the day, so we want to make the most of them.' Roger nodded and left the room.

Mulligan narrowed his eyes at Renee. 'I suppose that means we have to put you back up to the rank of detective, Taylor.'

'Yes, Sergeant,' replied Renee carefully, resisting the urge to punch the air.

'More paperwork,' he muttered.

A pause. Renee plucked up her courage.

'And forensics?' Renee asked.

'Yes, Petrovic called and said he's working on samples and the coroner will be in tomorrow to conduct the autopsy.' Mulligan stood and shifted papers around on his desk. She was dismissed.

Renee hesitated. She felt like there was more to cover.

'We may need a facial reconstruction of the woman, Sarge. She suffered severe facial injuries, so if no one comes forward soon and a missing persons search doesn't reveal anything, we'll have to enquire around, broadcast the likeness to the media … And we should really interview any neighbours as soon as possible. As well as the townsfolk.'

'Sure.'

'Shall we also set up a formal enquiry line so we can give the number to the media at the first press conference? I thought we should schedule that as soon as we can, but I would prefer to have something to say first.' She felt her shoulders tighten at the thought of standing in front of a crowd of journalists with nothing to go on.

Mulligan waved his hand wearily at her, already absorbed in a file. 'Your show, Taylor. You're the detective.'

Renee looked at him for a moment but he didn't raise his head from the file. She returned to her desk to start the grunt work in earnest.

Chapter 5

Renee spent a few hours at her desk writing up notes before anything slipped her mind and left the station after everyone else had already gone home. She had been surprised when Stacey and Roger left at the normal time, but realised she couldn't get any further that day anyway without interviews, forensics, autopsy or missing persons information. She was beginning to realise that without a full team it would be slow work. The country town was under-resourced and much of the legwork would fall to her and Roger. But this was murder. She would speak to the sergeant tomorrow about pushing for more resources.

The media had finally left, giving up on any last-minute breaking news, and for the first time that day, Renee felt like she wasn't being watched by anyone – not the news, the locals, her colleagues nor her boss. With twilight came freedom and she sucked in the warm air as she started her walk home.

But she wasn't the only one moving at ease in the dark. Just as she turned the corner from Main Street onto the road her mother's house was on, the tail end of a snake slithered into the nearby bushes, causing her to jump back. His totem. Again. There was the warning this morning from old Norm and now an actual sighting. Renee hardly ever thought of her father any more, but today the image of his face kept coming to her mind. She had one photo of him in his early twenties. Her mother said she had his gaze – that she looked straight through people the way he did, which Val said was both charming and unnerving. It had certainly come in useful as a cop.

This is what Renee knew about her father, the few details her mother had imparted in response to her incessant requests for more information: Valerie Taylor met Floyd Chapman when she was eighteen and on her first student nursing placement in a remote Aboriginal community in far north-west Queensland. He came in one day bleeding from a deep gash in his thigh after falling off a bull at the local rodeo. Her mother said it was the first time she'd ever given anyone stitches and her hands shook with nerves. Not just from inexperience, but because of his presence. Handsome and calm, with eyes that looked deep into her soul. Renee begged her mother for more details growing up. *What'd he say? Who talked first? Did you like him straight away or did he grow on you?* But her questions were always shrugged off with promises more would be revealed later.

Renee suspected the reason her mother didn't like to talk about Floyd was that she regretted leaving him. Val was a pragmatic woman with a strong sense of moral obligation. They were similar in that sense, as much as she hated to admit it. Val always said she returned to Goorungah as soon as she found out about her pregnancy to give her child the best chance at life. Val's parents had already retired toced the north coast, so Val moved back into their house, the one she'd grown up in, and stayed there. Grandma Evelyn and Pop shuffled their plans and came back from their one-bedroom apartment by the beach. They stayed in Goorungah for two more years to help Valerie with the birth and the adjustment to motherhood. As the years went by and Renee grew up, she only visited them on the odd summer holiday when her mother could afford to take time off or to buy her a bus ticket and send her on her own. As a result, she wasn't particularly close to them. Her mainstay was her mum.

Valerie was sociable and extrovert and she would occasionally have friends over – usually other nurses from the hospital – or she'd have dinner at the pub with some of the girls she grew up with. She remembered one night her mum came home from the pub tipsy. She wasn't a drinker so it was unusual for her to stumble and slur her words. Renee was only about twelve at the time: old enough to stay home by yourself when you live in a small town close to the Main Street where the police station is within yelling distance and your mum's at the pub next door. Renee was watching TV when her mum came home and went straight into her bedroom. Then the phone rang. It was Sheree, her mum's friend. She asked to speak to Val so Renee took the phone into her mum, who was smoking out the window. Her mother didn't normally smoke.

'Mum, Sheree's on the phone.'

She stumbled across the room, beckoning Renee to give her the phone. 'What? Sheree?' Renee went back out into the hallway and listened against the wall. 'I'm not going to sit around while they talk like that. They know my daughter's Aboriginal. How can they call themselves my friend and say all those nasty racist things. It's downright fucking offensive, Sheree. I'm not going to put up with it.' Renee remembered sneaking back into her room, covering herself up with the doona and blinking the tears away. Val must've heard the floorboards squeak because she heard her bedroom door open.

'Darling?' There was no use trying to pretend. She had the covers up over her head so her mother would know something was wrong. 'Did you hear me on the phone just now?'

Renee pulled down the covers and her mother sat on the bed next to her. When her mother reached across and wiped the tears off her cheeks, she couldn't hold it in any more and sobbed uncontrollably. 'Renee, what's the matter?'

Her body eventually stopped heaving long enough for her to get the words out.

'I want you to have fun with your friends, Mum.'

Her mum held her until she stopped crying and then slept with her in the little single bed for the first time since Renee was a toddler and scared of the dark. Renee hadn't forgotten that night.

She continued walking along the dimly lit street, watching where she stepped, and as she approached the front gate to her mother's house, Renee could hear people at the pub next door and whistles coming from the indoor sports centre down the road. Sound travelled far in the stillness of the evening. She wondered if they had heard about the woman and if they were talking about it.

Renee was physically exhausted from spending most of the day standing by the gate in the heat and her stomach grumbled. She hadn't eaten anything since that hasty sandwich and she considered walking around to the cafe to buy some takeaway fish and chips, but caught a waft of sausages from the kitchen window. She peered in. Her mother was hunched over the stove, trying to turn the sausages, which were sizzling in the frypan, by holding a fork between her wrists. Renee ran up the front steps and hurried through the front door, entering a kitchen filled with cooking fumes, and reached across her mother for the fork to turn the sausages. 'Mum, let me help you with that. You'll burn yourself. I'm sorry I'm so late home.'

'It's fine, Renee. I can do it.' Her mother gently slapped her hand out of the way. 'Sorry, darling, I just wanted to surprise you with a hot meal after today.'

Renee sighed in resignation and plonked herself in a chair at the table. She was desperate to free her feet from her boots but too tired to move in that moment. 'So, you heard?'

Her mother looked at her. 'This is Goorungah, Renee. Of course I heard. It was all anyone was talking about downtown.'

'Did you go down to play the pokies?'

'I was headed in that direction, but then I ran into Meredith – you remember Meredith? Meredith-with-the-horses?' Her mother knew everyone in town because she'd worked as a nurse for most of her adult years. Valerie knew more intimate details about the residents of Goorungah than could ever be found on a police or social services file.

'No.'

'Yes, you do. Lives over near the industrial estate. Keeps to herself a bit these days, but a hell of a chick. Wish I had been friends with her instead of the nursing crowd ... Well anyway, she told me the news.'

'Oh yeah, what are people saying?'

'Body of a young Aboriginal woman was found down by the creek and that the police,' she turned to give Renee *the* look, 'are being awfully cagey about the details. Do you know who she is yet?' Renee watched as her mother turned back to the stove. Renee knew she was trying to act nonchalant, but nonchalant Val was not. She would be bursting to get more information.

'Mum, you know I can't share any details from the case. It's police business.' She heaved her tired body up and went to the front patio where she sat on the couch, unlaced her boots and pulled them off along with her socks that stunk of dirt and sweat. As she leaned back in the cushions and wiggled her toes free, she yearned for a beer but wanted to stay clear-headed in case a call came through. She checked her mobile and groaned. Multiple messages already, no doubt the vast majority media demanding details.

'Renee! It's ready.' She returned to the kitchen feeling better without the heavy boots and sat back down at the table. 'So you're on the case?'

'Yes.' She didn't want to share anything with her mother, but she couldn't deny that part. 'Sergeant Mulligan's assigned me to the lead. I'm back to being a detective.'

'Ha! That's my girl. Didn't take you long. So plain clothes?'

'Yep, from tomorrow.'

'Good. You can take off that god-awful uniform. Uglier than scrubs. So, have you been over to Wellington Street yet?'

Renee felt a sudden pain in her temple and tried to rub it away. 'Not yet.' She was planning to go there tomorrow. Renee had hated going to Wellington Street when she was growing up. She felt like the Aboriginal families judged her for being different even though she looked the same as them. There had been seasons when she was growing up that she'd hang out with some of the Wellington Street kids and have a great time, like when it was flooding and they'd all charge down to the overflowing creek and play for hours on old tyre tubes. Or a netball season when all the kids were mixed up on different teams. But she'd always return home to her mother's house and, as she got older, she always felt a little bit stuck in between, not quite belonging here nor there.

'Well, I'm sure if anyone from Wellington Street had gone missing you would know about it by now. There would've been a crowd down at the creek today demanding information.' Her mother struggled to turn off the stove and Renee leaped up to help.

'Thanks, Mum, let me plate up.' She put two sausages on her plate, cut up her mother's sausage into mouth-sized pieces, and scooped on the steamed vegetables.

'No broccoli for me, darling.' Renee rolled her eyes, too tired to argue, removed the little green trees and added an extra spoonful of steamed cabbage instead. She probably wouldn't eat it but it was worth the try.

'Here you go.' Renee laid the two plates on the table. 'Thanks for cooking, Mum.'

'I'm not completely useless, darling.'

Despite the little black tarry bits, the sausages tasted delicious, and Renee ate heartily, her mind drifting away from creeks and ambulances and body bags and on to the mundane routine of household chores. 'What'd you do today, Mum?'

'I went to the pharmacy and filled my script.' Her mother pushed the cabbage to the side of the plate then put the tiniest morsel of sausage up to her mouth and blew on it. 'I'm so sick of taking these painkillers, Renee. Next time you're in the city, I want you to get me a bag of weed. I'm telling you, I've had enough of this pain.'

'Mum, I'm a cop. I'm not going to get you marijuana.'

'Exactly. You're a cop! Should be easier for you than anyone to get your hands on some pot. Besides, when did you get so straight?'

'I'll think about it,' she lied to avoid an argument. If only it had been decriminalised. They continued to eat in silence while the tap dripped at the sink. She hadn't noticed it over the weekend.

Another job to add to her list of never-ending maintenance chores to do around the house, right after she got the cockroach baits.

'So, who do you think did it?' her mother asked, looking down at her plate, continuing to push anything remotely healthy to the sides. She picked at the sausages, trying to hide her interest. 'It was a local, wasn't it?'

'Mum. I told you. I can't share case details with you.' The familiar hyperbolic synthetic drumroll from the lounge announced the evening's news, relieving Renee from any further maternal interrogation.

'Leave the dishes for me. I like the warm water on my hands – helps with the pain.' Her mother hobbled into the lounge room and Renee cleared the table and quickly scrubbed the frying pan, leaving the easy things – the plates and cutlery – for her mother to do in the morning. Doing the dishes made her feel 'useful'.

She sat down and worked through the twenty-three messages. Mainly media, plus one from the coroner asking if she would be attending the autopsy or just wanted the report (the report was fine with her – she had a weak stomach), a few unrelated calls, a few reports of suspicious characters – one clearly complaining about his neighbour throwing rubbish over his fence – and a call regarding the area missing persons check. They seemed to have drawn a blank. Plenty of missing young women, she couldn't help but note. None meeting this description. No one calling to claim this woman. No mothers frantically discovering their daughter was not at the coffee shop as planned, no boyfriends worried that their girlfriend didn't come home after spending time with friends, no one calling in to say they'd witnessed an abduction, or worse.

Surely someone had cared for her enough to notice she had gone missing. Who was this woman?

'Renee, quick!' her mother sang out from the couch. The canary reporter from Channel Five appeared with her immaculate hair and make-up and bright yellow dress.

'Local police have set up a crime scene here in the country town of Goorungah.' Jillian Crawley stared intently at the camera, faux concern etched across her face. Renee searched the background for details she may have missed. An unusual character lurking about in the midst. A car with interstate number plates. 'We know that the body of a young Aboriginal woman was found near the creek early this morning by a local resident. It appears to be suspicious, but police are not releasing any further details at this point in time.' The camera panned the scene – dry scrub, dirt road and the forensic van. She saw the tall stone walls of the Ford property, the pines above and the endless stream of cars driving past. Jillian Crawley gave the number to call if anyone had seen or heard anything unusual.

Renee called Mulligan.

'Sarge, sorry to bother you, just thought I'd check in and see if you'd heard anything more from headquarters on the missing persons check?'

'Nothing on my end, Taylor. Chief Superintendent Dupont's been hammering me with questions all evening – mainly about how we're handling media – but no new information. Typical of headquarters – they'll pound us with requests but when it comes to providing resources …' She could hear dishes in the background and imagined Mulligan cleaning up after dinner.

'I can update Dupont from now on if you like …' Renee suggested, thinking of her old boss in the city. She wanted to be the one reporting in to headquarters. That way she could stay across any emerging information sooner, rather than having to wait for Mulligan to pass it on.

'No, I'll deal with Dupont. You focus on things on the ground here.' His response was no surprise, but worth a try.

'Are you watching the news?' Renee asked. 'Jillian Crawley just gave an update from the scene.'

'The reporter from Channel Five? Yeah, I saw it. Good that they got the hotline right this time. I've known them to screw it up.'

Mulligan would notice that kind of detail. She was learning that he didn't miss much, liked to be in control. Renee thought about the way he'd clenched his fists at her request that he give Renee the lead rather than Roger. She would have to be careful how she managed him.

'Have you heard anything more from forensics?' Renee asked.

'Petrovic reported in directly about twenty minutes ago. Don't worry, I told him you were taking the lead from here on. He said they'll provide a more detailed report tomorrow but mentioned she'd only been dead a very short time before we found her.' Renee knew that. She'd felt her body and it was warm.

'So whoever did this can't have been too far away this morning,' Renee said.

There was a long pause, and she could sense her mother listening in. She moved to the kitchen, out of earshot. 'Mulligan, do you think we're doing enough?'

'What more can we do?' The background went quiet and she knew she had his full attention.

'We should have gone over to Wellington Street today.' It frustrated her that he was being so calm even though she knew a methodical approach was best.

'Well, yes. We could have. But we didn't really have time, and besides, if anyone up there knew her or was missing anyone, we would've found out about it by now. They would've been down by the creek or at the station this afternoon.' The same thing her mother had said.

'Yes, I agree.'

'But you're not convinced?' Before she could reply he went on. 'Look, Taylor, you're leading the case now, so it's your call. But I think it's best if you get some rest and we'll start afresh in the morning. Try to get a good night's sleep.'

Renee ended the phone call and returned to Val, who was still on the couch, pretending not to eavesdrop. She looked like a kid who'd just raided the cookie jar.

'What'd you hear?' Renee asked, letting herself plop on the couch next to her mother.

'Nothing.'

'Bullshit.' Fatigue-induced silence prevailed and a repeat of some old British police drama that Renee was completely uninterested in allowed her to enjoy scenes of a bucolic countryside without taking in any of the storyline. That was until the image of kids swapping money for drugs came on the screen, which prompted her to think once again about Worm and his local dealings.

'Mum, can I ask you a question?'

'You had all evening and now my favourite show is on you want to ask me a question?' Val shifted her body among the cushions in exaggerated frustration. There was no way she would admit it wasn't her favourite show, never mind that she'd never watched it before in her life. 'The ads are on soon.'

'Fine. It's nothing important. I just wanted to know more about William Gawlor?'

That was enough to get her attention. 'Worm? That drug-dealing scumbag should've been put behind bars years ago. Is this about the case?'

'Mum!' Renee gave her a look that said *don't test me*.

'He's a rotten bastard, Renee. If he is capable of murder, you'd bloody better hurry up and do something about it because he lives just around the corner.'

'Where?'

'Next to the squash courts. Didn't your mates tell you that today?'

Renee remembered Roger saying he hung out around the squash courts. She ignored the question and asked her own. 'Has he always lived there?' Renee couldn't remember her mother, or any adult for that matter, talking about him in any specific detail.

'Yes!' Her mother was losing her patience, as though she'd covered this topic before, which irritated Renee because it was starting to seem like a whole bloody lot had been kept from her.

'Why didn't you tell me?'

'I don't know. I didn't want you to worry. I didn't want you to feel scared.' Renee tried to calm herself, seeing her mother getting rattled. So, information had been withheld with good intention.

'Well, tell me now then. How do you know him?'

'When I worked at the hospital, I noticed more people coming in on drugs. And they were getting younger too. Kids showing up buzzed on meth. Strung out and crazy.'

'Why were they coming in?'

'They were coming in with injuries, accidental or not – assault or self-inflicted. That meth, it really messes with peoples' heads.'

'And you linked it back to Worm?'

'I guess it just gradually became common knowledge. You'd hear people hint about where they got stuff from. Nurses and doctors would find out and try to report it to police but nothing ever happened. Maybe he did spend some time in jail …'

'Roger said he went in once, but it was ages ago.'

'Yeah, sounds right. But I think over the years people have given up trying to get him arrested. He spooked a few people – blackmail, threats, but this is all hearsay. I know people fear him but I haven't experienced it personally.' Her voice trailed off and they both fell silent.

Renee helped her mother to bed after she'd nodded off towards the end of her program. Her once vital body felt small and weightless, merely a leaf floating on the breeze. Renee wondered if soon she'd be able to pick her up and carry her from the couch to her bed. She pulled the sheet up – it was too hot for doonas – and tucked her in, holding out one hand with tablets and the other with a glass of water. 'Take this, Mum.'

Val swallowed the pills, handed back the glass and looked up with a tenderness Renee rarely saw. 'Promise me you'll be careful, Renee.'

Val was tough, never scared. Why this now?

'Of course I'll be careful, Mum.'

'Renee …' Her mother caressed the side of her face. 'Why do you think I never took you back to your father's community?'

'I don't know.' Renee made a point of tucking the sheets again. This was not a conversation she needed to have right now. 'It's okay, Mum.'

'Because society cares much less about Aboriginal girls. As much as no one wants to admit it.' Val said this with such gentle sincerity it sent shivers through Renee's core. She knew it was true. She'd experienced it time and time again, whether it be at work or a cafe, in a gym or at the shops – the hard stare, the unnecessary questions, the extra surveillance or the complete disregard in favour of others. But this was not something she talked about with her mother. She was wary of sharing the pain it caused her, in case somehow her mother felt responsible.

'Go to sleep, Mum.' She switched off the light and started to close the bedroom door. Her mother rolled away, over to her side, and Renee noticed an empty foil sheet on the carpet next to the bed. Had she already taken her night-time dose? That could explain why she'd been so reckless in voicing the cruel truths of Australian society that were always left unsaid between them.

'Goodnight, Mum.' Renee leaned over, kissed her mother's sweaty head, and went to turn the light off.

'Honey?'

'Yeah, Mum?'

'Did you hear – Sally Cunningham passed away this morning.'

Renee hadn't heard anything.

'Josh's mother?' Renee remembered her high-school boyfriend's mum – a sweet lady, a little shy perhaps but very generous and friendly. 'What happened? She can't have been that old.' She'd only met Mrs Cunningham on a few brief occasions, in town or at school sporting events. Josh never took her out to Hereford Downs. God forbid that he would take a poor town girl like her out to the grand pastoralist's family home.

'Heart failure. Poor thing … Fifty-four years old. Such a lovely lady. You know, darling, you never did tell me what happened between you and Josh.' They'd already covered the local drug dealer and racism tonight; her failed high-school romance was definitely not a subject they were going to talk about. 'The funeral's on Thursday. You'll take me, won't you?'

'Of course,' she whispered through the darkness. It would be an opportunity to see the locals relaxed in their own environment. Always a good chance to spot suspicious activity.

Renee grabbed a can of beer from the fridge, thankful her mother was now softly snoring from her bedroom. She went to sit on the front porch, giving up on the idea of any further active investigation for the day. The wooden floorboards creaked beneath her as she took a seat on the front steps and watched a swarm of insects buzzing in the glow of the streetlights. The heat had only slightly relented and the icy cold brew felt good. A few kids walked by holding long sticks, poking at the ground and swinging at each other for no reason other than they were country kids out late with no adults watching them.

She thought of Mrs Cunningham. She may have been a shy woman but she was well liked and part of one of the most wealthy and established farming families in the area, so the funeral would be huge. No doubt the town would be looking for an excuse to come together and talk about the woman found down by the creek. Self-interest working alongside the deepest sympathy. Everyone wanted to seem like the good guy.

Josh would be at the funeral. She took another mouthful of beer at the thought of seeing him again after so many years. So much time had passed since their fleeting high-school romance had come to an end. She felt old thinking about it. Old and jaded. She'd had relationships with men since then but nothing she'd describe as a 'romance'. A few dinner dates followed by casual sex. One guy, Mitch, she'd seen on and off for three years, but if she was real with herself, they'd never really got past the friends-with-benefits stage. He already had a kid and she didn't want the responsibilities of being a stepmother so her guard had been up from the very beginning. Come to think of it, maybe she chose him because she knew it wouldn't go further. She wouldn't take the next step. Whatever it was with Mitch, it had been very different with Josh.

If there is such a thing as a broken heart, then she grudgingly had to accept that is what she'd experienced when he left. Their romance had been intense yet short-lived.

They'd met in the high-school library. She was sitting up the back in the corner on one of the beanbags reading an Agatha Christie novel. It was the middle of winter, and she was in the habit of going to the library after school where it was warmer than home, and less lonely – her mother was working at the hospital and although the reading room was usually empty at least the librarian was around. But one afternoon she spied Josh through the bookshelves searching for something in the history section.

'You're back late,' he had said, catching sight of her. 'Renee, right?'

'Yep.' She hid her excitement that he knew her name. He was a year above her, handsome and popular, and very much on the conventionally attractive side. 'And you're Josh …?' She didn't want to stroke his ego by letting him know she knew his name. 'What are you looking for?'

He told her about his World War II assignment and, knowing the position of most books in the library, she helped him assemble an impressive pile of sources. They sat on the beanbag and browsed together, chatting and reading and chatting some more, Renee making every effort to not reveal the extent of her delight. His trips to the library became more frequent and over time Renee realised that his reasons for searching the shelves were indeed excuses to see her. Her first kiss was at the back of the library on that beanbag and Josh told her it was his too. How silly she had been back then, so easily carried away by romantic fantasies and the naivety of youth. How wonderful it had been.

They started spending time together outside school: swimming at Crystal Ponds, ice creams under the cafe umbrellas on Main Street. She invited him back to her house and they had fish and chips on the front porch. Josh had seemed at ease with the 'ghost house' and charmed her mother easily. As the school year came to an end, Josh's application to study at university in the city was approved, and the arrival of that letter marked the beginning of the end of their teenage romance. He broke up with her just after Christmas with little explanation other than he was going away. Renee thought it was because he was embarrassed by her and her single mother, the ugly second-hand clothes they wore, and the shabby wooden cottage. He insisted it was because he was moving to the city and it wouldn't be practical to keep seeing each other, even though she was planning on moving down there herself in a year.

Whatever. It didn't matter any more. She'd moved on from him. When she finished high school, she'd moved to the city to start at the academy and successfully fought the urge to contact him. Over time she made new friends, had new boyfriends and built her own life in Brisbane.

The street was empty now, silent and still except for the swarming bugs under the streetlight. She drank the remainder of her beer, went inside and lay on top of the covers staring at the ceiling, counting the glow-in-the-dark stars that she'd meticulously arranged in constellations as a kid, wondering what tomorrow would bring. She brought up images from the day, carefully reviewing all the details in her mind, analysing each moment from multiple viewpoints, not trying to sleep. That was rookie mistake number one of an insomniac. Sleep will come when it's meant to.

Chapter 6

Renee woke at the break of dawn to the sound of birds competing for lyrical supremacy; the cockatoos winning – of course – with their brash screeching, the blanket undertone of the playful lorikeets, a crow's call here and there. It was almost twenty-four hours since they'd found the body.

Something was missing but she couldn't put her finger on it. She lay in bed. It was a single bed with tall timber posts that she'd painted numerous colours, depending on her age: dusty pink when she was five, a light blue when she turned eight, bright yellow at twelve, a sudden change to black at thirteen when her 'goth' years kicked in, then back to a eucalypt green in her later teens, the colour it had stayed. Her mother had entertained Renee's decorative instincts and granted her full creative freedom of her bedroom. She stuck her leg out of the white cotton sheets and pulled the curtain across with her feet to save getting out of bed. No clouds. Another hot dry day. But why the feeling that something was missing?

Big Red.

Why was he so quiet this morning? Yesterday he had been the alarm clock for her early morning run. Big Red's morning crow was more reliable than a battery-operated watch.

She threw off the sheets and moved quickly out the back door. She smelled the blood before she reached the hen house – wafts of thick metallic sweetness. All three chickens were headless. Feathers covered the dirt. Big Red was over in his corner. His head was still attached but his stomach had been torn out, guts and intestines strewn across the pen.

'What's the matter, Renee?' her mother called out from the back porch.

'Foxes.'

'Foxes?!' Her mother started towards the chook pen.

'No, Mum. Go back inside.' But Val kept walking towards her chickens. 'Mum, I'm serious. You don't want to see this. Go and put the kettle on. Let me clean this up and I'll be in soon.'

Her mother stood staring at the chicken carcasses, eyes wide, mouth open in shock.

'Mum. Go!' Renee gently pushed her away and finally her mother turned from the ghastly scene and went back inside without saying a word.

Renee got a shovel from the shed, cleared away some overgrown weeds, and dug a hole in the back corner of the yard. She heaped the first carcass onto the shovel and laid its body to rest in the grave, then repeated the same procedure for the other two hens and finally laid Big Red on top. She filled in the hole and sat down on her knees to offer a silent farewell.

'Cruel bastards, those foxes.' She hadn't notice her mother come back out.

'Sorry, Mum.' Renee had never really liked the chooks but knew how much Val cherished them. An intense sadness washed over her, somehow magnified by the brilliant sunny day. It should have been cold and overcast.

'That's okay, love. Come inside now, you have a big day ahead of you.'

Renee showered, towel dried her hair and applied lip balm, the extent of her morning make-up regime, then glanced at herself in the mirror where she recognised a familiar look in her eyes: drive. She was going to find out what happened to that woman. Wrapping a towel around herself, she returned to her bedroom, pulled on jeans and a button-up shirt – she was a plain-clothes detective again after all – and entered the kitchen where her mother was sitting at the table with a pot of steaming tea. Three eggs lay in a bowl on the table. Her mother must have gone back out and fetched them while she was in the shower.

'It doesn't feel right to eat the eggs, Mum.' She picked one up, careful not to shatter its brittle calcium shell. 'It still feels warm.'

'Don't be a fool, Renee.' Val bumped her hip and Renee quickly moved to balance the egg. 'Crack them open and get some protein into you.'

'Hah! Like you can talk about vitamins and minerals Miss-butter-and-honey-on-toast-every-day-of-her-life. Seriously, Mum. I can't eat them now.'

'I thought I raised a sensible daughter …' Her mother continued to mutter something as Renee stood. She had an idea and went to search in the hallway closet.

'Where'd you put that lamp?'

'What lamp?'

'The one I used to study under. The white one on the bendy stand.' Renee poked around in the closet until she found it stuffed in the top back corner, its little tin shade all bent out of shape.

'Found it.' She pulled the lamp out, reached for a towel, the fluffiest she could find, and went into the lounge room.

'What are you up to?' her mother called out from the kitchen. Renee set the towel down on top of a cushion in the corner of the lounge room, then plugged the lamp into the socket, switched it on and adjusted it so its light beamed down on the towel. Then she went back into the kitchen and got the eggs, still warm to the touch. 'Renee, what on earth are you doing?' She made a hollow and lay the three eggs on the towel nest under the light. Her mother leaned around the corner from the kitchen. 'Don't you have something more important you should be doing, Renee? Like umm ... let me think ...' she said, index finger tapping cheek with dramatic exaggeration, 'finding a *murderer*.'

Renee ignored her. She stood back and looked over her eggs, pleased with her effort, hoping that the warmth of the light would be sufficient for incubation. 'I guess it's honey on toast for both of us this morning.'

The station was an entirely different place compared to the same time the previous morning. Stacey and Roger were already at their desks when she arrived.

'Where's the boss?' Renee asked, throwing her backpack down and heading to the kitchenette to fill her water bottle.

'Been on the phone since we arrived,' Roger said, tapping away at his keyboard, which was uncharacteristically industrious of him. Stacey was on another call, rigorously asking questions and taking notes.

'Anything new?' Renee asked, encouraged by the level of activity, as Stacey waved and pointed at a cake tin on her desk, mouthing the words *Take some.*

'You tell me,' Roger answered. 'Last time Sarge came out, it was to complain about headquarters again. You're late. What's kept you?'

She took a swig from her water bottle and prised a biscuit out of Stacey's cake tin. 'Little incident at home. Fox got the chickens.' On closer inspection, the biscuit had pink icing and sprinkles. She didn't want to offend Stacey by returning it to the tin so placed it carefully on her desk.

'Oh shit, I should've told you!' Roger exclaimed, raising his hands to his forehead. 'There's been a heap of fox attacks lately. They're getting a bit out of hand. Not sure why. You need a hand with anything?'

'I'm fine, Roger. Buried them already.' She left out the part about creating a makeshift incubator in the lounge room and sat at her desk to think for a moment. First, she checked her mobile to see if anything had come through since leaving home. Nothing. Then she wanted to go out and talk to locals, especially the residents of Wellington Street, but before then she needed an update from Mulligan regarding resources ... A manila folder was in her in-tray. 'What's this?'

'Photos from the scene,' Roger explained without taking his eyes off his screen. 'A guy from the forensics team dropped them off this morning.'

Renee took a deep breath, adjusted her seat to a more comfortable position, then let the contents slide out of the folder onto her desk. The photo on top was of a boot print in dry dirt. She wondered whether to get the prints team in forensics to do a search for matching brands or if it was easier to assign this task to Roger. She jotted it down as something to follow up and went on to the next photograph, which was of the boulder. She hadn't realised yesterday the extent to which its surface was covered in blood. Was it a confirmation of her sense that the woman had been hit multiple times? The autopsy was coming this morning and the report would tell her more when it arrived. Hopefully it would give her an indication of the strength of the perpetrator and that could eventually narrow down suspects.

Next photograph was a close-up of the woman's face. It was difficult for Renee to view even though she had been at the scene. If anything, it was worse in the sterile safety of the police station because of the stark contrast. The left side of her skull was caved in where the boulder had made impact but it was still possible to identify some of her facial features: dark brown eyes, high cheekbones and a broad nose. The woman's hair was cut plainly at the shoulders, smooth, straight and well cared for. The fourth crime scene photo was taken further back, maybe a metre, and showed the full length of the woman's body. Other than the gold necklace, there were no significant features like piercings or tattoos, and she wasn't wearing make-up. She was thin, malnourished even, indicating poverty and hardship but her fingernails were neatly trimmed, which to Renee suggested that she hadn't been undertaking hard manual labour like cleaning or farming.

'Taylor, you're late.' Mulligan emerged from his office, sweat already dripping from his forehead and once again smelling of sunscreen.

She put the cover of the manila folder over the image of the woman. 'Sorry, Sarge, got a bit held up with ...'

He waved her off, clearly not wanting to hear excuses, and turned to Stacey. 'Stacey, call all the trucking companies and get their rosters ...' Stacey scrawled across her notepad, vibrating with excitement. 'I want to know who was scheduled to drive through Goorungah Monday night and early yesterday morning.'

Renee shifted uncomfortably in her seat. Why was Mulligan giving these instructions? Had he forgotten he'd assigned her as lead investigator the day before?

Mulligan addressed Roger and Renee. 'I want a full report on all findings at ...' he checked his watch, '... midday. By that time we should have all the autopsy and forensics results. That'll tell us if any foreign DNA was found, and if it was, whether it matches anything in our database – ex-crims, those currently serving time, anyone who's already committed a crime and has had their DNA lodged in our systems.'

Renee felt her temperature start to rise. This was bringing back memories of working in the city and all the years she'd had to fight to be heard and respected.

'It'll also tell us about our Jane Doe: age, time of death and, most importantly, whether *her* DNA is on any databases which, unless anyone comes forward to claim her, is the fastest way of finding out the identity of the young lady. Any questions?' Mulligan scanned the room.

Renee got to her feet. She'd had enough of men undermining her in the city. It wasn't going to happen in her hometown. 'Sarge, can I've a word?' Mulligan shrugged and turned towards his office with the nonchalance of someone who's never been second-guessed in his life, indicating for Renee to follow.

He sat at his desk and she closed the door without him instructing her, which made him eye her more seriously. 'What is it, Taylor?'

'I thought you said I was leading this case?' She stood straight, hands on hips, respectful but not about to be pushed around.

A tiny vein pulsed in his neck. He looked confused and irritated at the same time. 'You *are* leading the case.'

She bit back a smart-arse remark – something along the lines of 'You've got a funny fuckin way of showing it' – and calmly began to put her argument.

'Look, I know it must be hard for you to hand over the reins, but you need to trust me.'

Mulligan squinted hard, revealing an expression Renee had never seen before. Being challenged was uncharted territory for Mulligan and his face was a strange combination of confusion, anger, surprise, maybe a dash of self-pity and victimhood. Renee knew men like this and she'd experienced many moments like these before, the pivotal moment when everything could go belly-up. It was the moment you had to hold their gaze, not look threatening, nod reassuringly, speak slowly and calmly, but above all else not pose a threat to their ego.

'I was a detective, Sarge. I can do this.'

'You *are* leading the case, Taylor. What makes you think otherwise?' This was not going to be easy. His hands remained clenched and the little vein pulsed on.

'You asked Stacey to call around the truck—'

'That's something that needs to be done, doesn't it?'

'Yes, but—'

'We're a team here, Taylor.'

'I appreciate that, Sarge, but you see—' she used her calm voice, the one she used when talking people down at armed hold-ups or off building ledges; not patronising, just calm, '—if you give orders, than it makes it difficult for me to manage all the lines of enquiry. To be the central point of contact, so I can give you full and timely reports at all stages throughout this investigation.'

'Hmm ...' His fists loosened. The veins disappeared.

'I just want to do a great job for you, Sarge.'

Eventually he nodded.

'I promise to give you regular updates. I trust you. Can you trust me?'

'Okay.'

'I'm going to head out for a bit now. I'm going to talk to the locals and I'll be back by midday to report on everything I've found.'

Renee returned to the open-plan office, where the atmosphere was busy but definitely not as tense as inside Mulligan's office. Stacey was on another phone call and Roger was tapping away at his keyboard. 'Hey, Roger?'

'Yes?'

'You're coming with me.'

Roger drove, which Renee appreciated – it would give her a chance to focus more on their surroundings. They parked in front of the post office where three old farmers sat. Norm, the man who had warned her about the snakes on her morning jog, was among them. She didn't know the names of the others but guessed they would know hers by now. They would know her mother and they would know of her absent father – a scandalous absence for their generation. They would know her address and her escape to the big city to become a cop. They would know by now that she had returned on Saturday to look after her ailing mother with the gnarled arthritic hands.

'It's a bastard, that arthritis,' they would say to each other, but not really caring. It never ceased to amaze Renee how the residents of Goorungah could know the most intimate details about their neighbours but then remain completely oblivious to other things.

'Here they come. You caught him yet?' Norm called out, lowering his newspaper to his lap, natural leader of the pack. The day was getting stiflingly hot and Renee figured the old men must really enjoy the street not to retreat some place with aircon.

'Not yet, Norm,' Roger said and greeted the other two men, Otto and Reginald. Roger was familiar with them so she didn't bother asking for their details, but jotted down their names.

'Have you seen anything unusual? Anything out of the ordinary?' Renee asked, going straight to the point.

'There were a few truckies with Victorian number plates going through yesterday. Don't often see them,' Otto offered and the others agreed.

'Okay, that's helpful.' Renee made a note. 'What about you, Norm? We spoke yesterday when I passed you on my morning jog. Did you see anything when you were sitting out the front?' The newspaper on his lap was open to a story about a serial killer – she recognised the name Shipman from the evening news. Some GP in the UK had been found guilty of murdering 250 of his patients by injecting them with opioids.

'Nothing.'

She narrowed her eyes. His speedy reply made her wonder if he was hiding something. She looked at his wiry frame and tried to estimate his strength – could he lift that heavy boulder?

'Maybe a car or truck driving past? Or someone running …?'

'I didn't see anything. Who was she?'

Renee ignored his question and turned her attention to Otto and Reginald. 'What about strangers in the street? Yesterday, or the day before? People who may have been passing through?'

'There were a few lads at the cafe yesterday I didn't recognise,' Otto said, scratching his chin. 'Roo shooters from further west – came in a big hotted-up ute with massive headlights and mongrel dogs.'

'What time was that?' Roger asked as Renee made a note.

'Mid-morning. Bunch of Aussies. Maybe one coloured bloke among them.' Norm stopped and leaned forward. 'What'd you see down there yesterday?'

'Norm. You know we can't give out any information. But maybe you saw—'

'It was a murder, hey? I saw the cover slip off the body when it was getting wheeled up on the stretcher. Gee, she was a mess …'

'Norm,' Renee warned, but he glared back, clearly not happy about being kept on the outer.

'Her head was all caved in. And bloody. Like someone threw a rock and smashed her skull.' The other two grimaced and Renee felt like picking up Norm by the collar and giving him a good shake.

'Gentlemen,' Roger said, sensing Renee's revulsion, 'we're investigating all possibilities at this stage, but the community should rest assured you're in safe hands.' He rehashed Mulligan's advice about doing all they can as if he meant it. Renee was quite impressed.

They left Norm and his mates and continued walking down Main Street, trying to stay in the shade of the awning as the temperature continued to soar. They stopped a young man with a whistle around his neck, a local sports coach maybe, but he had no news. They walked further down the street and went into the hardware store, then Alfie's, the bakery, hairdresser, mini mart and the newsagent. No one knew who the woman was, but everyone had questions. *What happened to her? Do you know who did it? Are we safe? Do you have any leads? How could this happen in Goorungah?*

They proceeded until coming across a familiar face. 'Carissa?' *Carissa Bremmer, why you st- st- stammer.* She could still hear the taunting of grade three students. Carissa had been in Renee's school year and they were only just beginning to spend time together and become friends (and bond over their mutual feelings of ostracism) when Carissa's parents sent her to boarding school in the city. She was easily recognisable though with the same thick round glasses and long slender figure. A baby hung on one hip and a toddler held her hand.

'Renee? Renee Taylor?' She smiled wide.

Roger leaned in. 'I'll go ask around the grocery store. Meet you back here in five.' Renee nodded.

'Oh my goodness, is that you?' Carissa went on. 'What are you doing back in town?'

'I came back to look after Mum, but now I'm—'

'Oh my goodness, I heard what happened yesterday. Have you caught him yet?'

Renee didn't want to confirm that it was a 'he' and fuel suspicions of a murderer on the loose. 'Carissa, have you seen anything unusual around town lately? Or heard anyone talking about things that seem out of place?'

Carissa looked up, as though sifting through her memories, and shook her head. 'I don't think so, Renee. I'm sorry. It's really terrifying.' Her toddler pulled on her worn-out T-shirt and Renee wondered how much the locals had exaggerated and built on the few facts that had no doubt been leaked by people like Mrs Ford and Norm for Carissa to appear so scared. 'Not now, Jack. Mummy's talking. Who was she?'

'We're not sure yet. Have you heard any of the locals speak of a missing woman?'

She shook her head. 'No, I haven't heard anything.' Jack tickled the foot of the baby, causing it to stir and start screaming. 'Jack! I better get going, Renee,' Carissa said, tired and apologetic. 'It was good to see you.' Renee gave Carissa her card and they parted ways as Roger re-emerged from the shop.

'What now?'

'Any luck in the shop?'

'Just news of a few more truckies passing through.' He skimmed through his notes, 'Some NSW number plates, a group of teenagers were hanging by the bus stop on Sunday morning …'

Renee could feel the eyes of the locals on her and the weight of their expectation, or perhaps the fear of discovery. After all, it was possible that the murderer was lurking in their midst, watching her right now. 'I think it's time to go door to door. Let's start with the locals on Wellington Street.'

'Isn't that racial profiling?' Roger asked anxiously.

Renee had already started walking back to the car and he was racing to catch up. She stopped and turned abruptly, so that he nearly walked into her. She looked at him levelly.

'The woman was Aboriginal, Roger. Wellington Street is where most of the Aboriginal people live. If she was white, I would start at Snob's Knob.'

Roger smiled uneasily. Renee rolled her eyes. Honestly, if anyone was entitled to have a problem with racial profiling, it was her.

She reached the passenger door and looked at him expectantly until he remembered he had the key and clicked it open. They drove past the mechanics – still the most unattractive building on the street with its tyre-strewn concrete landscape, grease and dust. Past the block of public toilets, freshly painted with a peculiar combination of native fauna and farm animals – kangaroos, horses, sheep, koalas, echidnas and dairy cows, all with interestingly proportioned body parts. One cow had legs the size of a hippopotamus while another resembled a stick insect, suggesting the mural was painted by the local primary school children. The overall effect was disturbing and charming in equal measure.

A long single pole stood out the front of the toilets with a sign that read *Bus Stop*. 'How often does the bus come through?' Roger had said someone had seen a bunch of teenagers waiting there on Sunday.

'Same as always. Once, at nine in the morning.' There was no need for a timetable – everyone in town knew the bus came from further west, stopped in Goorungah at nine, give or take thirty minutes depending on the mood of the bus driver, and continued another two hours east to the city. A return bus came back through at around three pm. Renee estimated maybe two or three people would catch that bus each week. Insufficient numbers to warrant the building of an awning over the bench. If the perpetrator had wanted to flee town yesterday without raising suspicion, one thing was almost certain – they would *not* have caught the bus.

They passed over the bridge and she couldn't help glance down at the water level of the creek. Old habits die hard. It was a shallow stretch where the water was a dark muddy brown, green algae floating around the edges. The water level had dropped even in the four days since she'd been home from the city. Renee had experienced drought and the subsequent water restrictions throughout childhood and developed an instinct for water levels. She could almost always guess within a few centimetres of accuracy where the water line would be in the local creek before glancing down.

They wound down the narrow road until they reached the level of the creek, where the road transitioned from bitumen to dirt. She spotted three kids jumping in the water from a rope tied around the branch of a giant old gum tree. 'Stop here, Roger. Let's see what those kids have to say. They may have seen something.'

Roger's phone started to buzz. 'It's Stacey. You go ahead. I'll take this just in case someone has called in.'

'Good – sing out if it's important.' Renee got out and walked down the grassy slope to where the boys were hurling themselves into the water.

'What are you boys doing here?' Renee called out. Two faces looked up from the edge of the bank, but the surprised expression was quickly replaced with resentment. They didn't want an adult coming to crash their fun. Another boy emerged from the muddy brown water and she recognised them as the kids with sticks who had walked past her house late the night before.

'None o ya business,' the smallest one said, short and staunchly built with bronzed brown skin, sun-bleached hair and striking light grey eyes.

Renee walked closer. 'Why aren't you in school?'

The boy in the water pulled himself up the bank with ease using the rope and carefully placed his feet in the roots of a towering old gum. The three boys glanced at each other, a wordless language playing out which Renee could interpret as:

Just ignore her.
But what if she dobs on us!?
Don't worry, just shut up.
She's a cop, you idiot.

Renee moved closer. 'What're your names?' The short one glared at her and Renee paused. He went to grab the rope. 'I said, what're your names?'

He gripped the rope, turned and said, 'Why don't you just fuck off and mind your own business?' The other two looked at him open-mouthed then watched as he swung wide out across the creek, let go and splashed into the water.

Charming. Renee walked closer to the other two, one dripping wet, the other completely dry. She showed her badge and introduced herself. 'A girl's body was found upstream. Yesterday. You know about that?' They looked at each other. They knew. 'You see anything?' Their eyes fell immediately to the ground and the chubbier of the two shook his head. 'What did you see?'

The chubby one looked up. 'We didn't see—' he started to explain.

'Shut ya fat face, Robert,' shouted the short cheeky one from the water. He launched himself up the muddy creek bank. 'What'd I tell you bout talkin to gunjis? Just coz she's Murri, doesn't mean you can trust her. You wanna learn how to keep your mouth shut, boi, you gonna get your fat bointhi in trouble, and mine with it.

If he hears you been talkin to the cops, he's gonna get real fuckin wild with you, boi.'

'Sorry, Calvin.'

'If who hears?' Renee asked.

'No one.' Calvin glared at her.

'If you boys saw something, then you need to tell me now.' Renee eyed the three of them. She remembered what Roger had said about Worm recruiting some of the youth in town to do his dealings. 'If you tell me now, then nothing's gonna happen. But if you keep secrets, then …'

'We're not tellin you shit. We know our rights.'

Renee eyed Calvin, a natural ringleader, then looked at Robert and the silent one. Nothing.

'Well, if you have seen something and you change your mind, here's my card.' She handed Robert her business card, knowing the chance of him keeping it was next to nil, and turned to walk away.

'And go to school,' she yelled back over her shoulder. 'You want to stay in this fuckin shithole for your entire lives?' They broke into stifled giggles – tough guys still amused by the swearing of an authority figure.

'What'd Stacey want?' Renee asked as she got back in the car.

'Forensic report is in. Mulligan wants us back there now.'

They'd have to go and see the residents on Wellington Street later.

Chapter 7

As they stepped out of the air-conditioned police car into the back car park, the sweltering heat hit them like an oven opening. Renee pulled at her cotton shirt to let air flow on her chest.

They moved quickly towards the office and shade.

Stacey looked up as they entered. 'Have you two had lunch yet?'

Before they could reply, Mulligan came out of his office. 'Stacey, get us all a round of toasted sandwiches, would you, love?' He reached into his pocket and handed her a fifty, which Stacey pocketed. She pulled out a pencil and notepad to take orders, but Mulligan barked out, 'Four ham sandwiches,' and then turned for Renee and Roger to follow him back into the office. 'Let's go, you two.'

Renee and Roger told him the little they had learned during their questioning of locals along Main Street. 'We ran into some boys down at the creek,' Renee added as they convened around Mulligan's desk.

'Oh yeah, those little ratbags from Wellington Street? Young Calvin and his crew. What'd they have to say for themselves?'

'Not a lot. But I think they're afraid of someone.' Renee and Roger had debriefed on the drive back to the station about what she'd overheard.

'I think it might be William Gawlor,' Roger said.

'Why do you say that?'

'They've been seen talking to him, hanging around near the squash courts.'

'Calvin bullied the others into staying quiet by saying "he" would be upset,' Renee added.

'Hmm ... Worm's all lawyered up these days and he'll have them breathing down our necks if we have no evidence,' Mulligan said, tapping his pen on the desk.

'No harm in asking a few questions of a citizen,' Renee said. 'I'm new to him. I'll go see him straight after this meeting.' Mulligan looked worried. She hesitated. 'Is that okay, Sarge?'

'Yeah, just don't go too hard on him. And make a record of everything that's said. He's got top-notch lawyers backing him in Brisbane.'

Renee figured Worm had taken the blame for someone in the past, probably did some time for someone higher up the chain and now he had their legal team to support him. She would have to proceed very carefully.

'Now listen.' Mulligan pulled a bunch of papers from an envelope. 'The lab report has been faxed through from headquarters.' Renee sat forward. 'I've leafed through it myself already, but I haven't had time to study it in detail. Our Jane Doe died in the early hours of Tuesday morning. Probably just before dawn.'

'And the cause of death?' Renee asked.

'Blunt force trauma to the skull.'

That much she expected. 'Was she hit once or multiple times?'

Mulligan checked the notes. Renee bit back her incredulity

that he hadn't picked this up the first time, but then he had said he'd only leafed through it.

'It says here that there were at least three, possibly four, points of impact.' The perpetrator had made sure she wasn't going to survive.

'Does it say which point of impact delivered the fatal blow?'

Mulligan squinted at her, seeming surprised by her question, and flicked through the papers. She couldn't wait to get her hands on the report later and study it herself but this was typical Mulligan style, she was learning, keeping control of things. 'It says, "The way in which the cranial skeleton has been fractured indicates that the first impact was most likely to deliver the fatal blow." So what does that tell us?'

'It tells us he wanted to be sure with the follow-up blows. But there is some research that suggests obliterating her face could be both personal and a sign of guilt.'

'Why exactly?' Roger said.

'So she can't look at him any longer.' They fell silent.

'Okay, moving on,' Mulligan said briskly, seeming unconvinced by Renee's premise.

'Signs of sexual assault?' Roger jumped in.

'No, there were definitely no signs of sexual assault.'

'Really?' Renee raised an eyebrow, a little surprised by this. The woman's clothes were indeed intact but there was something about the brutality of the scene that made Renee think sexual violence had occurred.

'What about drugs and alcohol?' she asked, thinking about Roger's earlier theory of a party at Crystal Ponds getting out of hand. 'Had she been drinking? Or using anything?'

'Nope.'

'No alcohol *or* drugs?' Although the woman was thin, her complexion was smooth and her skin seemed healthy so Renee shouldn't have been surprised. But did this also lessen the chance of her being linked to Worm? Perhaps she was a very professional drug runner and didn't dip into her own supply.

'Completely healthy. The toxicology report says that she wasn't taking anything – no prescription medication, no illicit substances or alcohol,' Mulligan explained, referring to his notes to check.

'How old was she?' Roger asked.

'Estimating mid-twenties.'

'Seriously?' Renee had guessed late teens and she was usually pretty good at estimating age. The woman's face had appeared much younger. Her skin was youthful and fresh, and there were no fine lines. How could she be in her mid-twenties? 'I'm assuming they ran her fingerprints to see if it matched anyone in the system?' If the woman had committed a crime, they'd have her prints.

Mulligan shook his head. 'No matches.'

'And the boot prints?'

'Standard work boots, similar to Blundstones. Every man and his dog has them. They're still running searches to try to pinpoint the brand.'

One less thing to ask Roger to do. She crossed that off her list.

Mulligan pulled a paper from the pile and placed it on his desk. 'This is the artist's impression.'

Like in the crime-screen photos, the woman in the black-and-white sketch had broad cheekbones and straight black hair. The phone on the desk started to ring.

'Where's Stacey? She's meant to be fielding these calls.'

'Sorry, Sarge.' Stacey peeked through the slit in the door, holding out a brown paper bag. 'But I have food.'

'Leave it there,' Mulligan said, pointing at his desk. 'I need to take this.' He picked up the phone and motioned to the door for them to leave. 'Goorungah Police Station, this is Sergeant Mulligan.' Renee tapped her finger on the forensic report, mouthing *Can I take this?* He hesitated before pushing it across his desk towards her.

Renee could hear Mulligan start to argue with someone on the other line as she returned to her desk with the forensic report. Stacey had placed a sandwich and Coke on her desk but she pushed them aside, grabbed her water bottle and opened the pages to see if there were any details Mulligan didn't have time to share.

She pored over the contents. Mulligan had covered all the main points and there was nothing in the report that brought her any closer to the identity of the woman. She sat back examining the room – Roger was on his computer, checking the reports from the traffic cops from Brisbane who had set up a perimeter around the town the day of the murder. Stacey was on a call.

Still no one had come forward. Who was this woman? Where had she come from? Headquarters had already uploaded the artist's impression of the murdered woman into the National Registry of Missing Persons. Thirty thousand people went missing every year. Most of them were found quickly, but there remained thousands of cases on the national registry. Smiling teenagers in school uniforms, confident women full of life. Many had been missing for more than five years. They were mostly women, but some men and boys appeared. People of all ages, backgrounds and ethnicities. She tried to narrow the search by area, and to women in their twenties who had gone missing in the last year.

Three women appeared. She read each profile but they were all non-Indigenous.

'How are you, Renee? How's your mum?' It was Stacey. She'd ended her phone call and was looking for some new distraction.

'She's fine, thanks, Stacey.' Renee smiled thinly and refocussed her attention on to the screen.

'Roger told me you had a nasty incident with some foxes this morning ...' Renee glanced across to find Stacey leaning over, pen in mouth, a sympathetic expression on her face. 'You don't want to talk about it? That's okay. I understand.'

Renee wished Stacey came with a volume dial. She returned to her screen but Stacey continued talking anyway.

'My sister called last night. She wanted to see if I knew anything that they aren't reporting on the evening news. She thinks just because I work at the station, I know everything! Anyway, she recognised you from the coverage. Said you haven't changed a bit since high school.'

Renee blinked hard, took a deep breath and turned to give Stacey her attention. May as well get it over with. 'Really?'

'Do you remember my little sister? Lisa Moore. She was the same year as you at school. Oh goodness,' Stacey put her hands to her cheeks, 'I just realised you're only twenty-eight. I thought you were much older. But you're my sister's age. You're so much more mature than her!' Stacey chuckled at this discovery. Lisa's face emerged in Renee's mind as much as she didn't want it to. Lisa was one of the popular girls – dux of her grade, netball captain. Very similar to her older sister, but Lisa was more driven and focussed than Stacey ... and nastier. Lisa used to tease Renee for wearing second-hand clothes and spending time in the library. It was one of the reasons Renee had been so exhilarated when Josh showed interest in her. Josh was Lisa's type of guy.

'You must remember her!'

'Vaguely.' Renee didn't bother smiling this time.

'She ...' Stacey started to say something but stopped herself. 'Yeah, anyway ... Lisa says to say "Hi".'

'That's nice.' Renee considered asking Stacey what she was going to say, but the missing persons search was awaiting. Renee tried to concentrate on her screen but out of the corner of her eye she could see Stacey sigh heavily and put her sandwich down.

'I think she might be scared.'

Bloody hell. Here we go. 'Scared of *what*?'

'Renee! A woman was murdered. *Here.* In Goorungah.'

'Yes, but we have no reason to believe it's a repeat offender.' Renee stared hard back at Stacey, head slightly tilted on the same angle. It was also true that they had no reason *not* to believe it was a repeat offender, but that was better left unsaid.

'She doesn't know that, Renee.'

'You heard what Mulligan said yesterday: "We're doing everything we can, and rest assured, and blah blah blah." Did you repeat those words to her like he told us to?'

'Yes, but still. It's natural for local residents to be scared, Renee. Besides, how do we know it's not a serial killer?'

'We don't,' Renee said. If Stacey wanted to work herself up into a froth of terror, that was up to her. She returned to her screen and widened the search by removing the date last seen and adding Indigenous to the field, but kept the location as Goorungah.

Stacey huffed and stalked into the kitchen, clearly exasperated by Renee's lack of concern for the emotional safety of the town's residents. Renee's hands froze on the keyboard. A young Aboriginal woman by the name of Caroline Forrest had gone missing in 1966. She was last seen with her friend Bessie Shields on 20 August 1966. She clicked on the tab that read *Case Notes*. There was a scanned copy of a newspaper clipping from page three of *The Goorungah Post*, which had long since ceased circulation, dated 27 August 1966, one week after the girls were last seen.

> *Two young coloured girls have been reported missing from Goorungah. Caroline Forrest and Bessie Shields, both 18 years of age, were last seen by their families on 20 August. If you have any information on their whereabouts, contact Goorungah Police Station.*

Renee wondered why she hadn't heard about this before. She remembered her mother's weary comment from the previous night: *Society cares much less about Aboriginal girls.* Why was this not considered front-page news at the time? How often did people go missing in Goorungah? Back then, the town would have been much smaller.

'Did you find something?' Roger asked. She realised she was tapping on her desk and murmuring out loud.

'No. I don't think so. It's probably not relevant but did you know that two teenagers went missing here back in the sixties?' She read the newspaper report out loud to him.

'Never heard of it.'

Renee worked out the years. 'Disappeared in 1966. That's only six years before I was born.'

'True. Not exactly ancient history,' Roger offered. 'They're still listed as missing?'

'Still on the missing persons register,' Renee confirmed. 'It's strange that you don't hear locals talking about it.'

'I've heard about it,' Stacey said. She had returned to her desk and was sipping a cup of instant coffee, looking pouty. She didn't offer any further information.

'Why didn't you say anything?'

'Why would I? They went missing more than thirty years ago. People said they'd run away. And anyway, apparently it's not a repeat offender we are looking for.'

Renee sighed and went back to the case notes on her screen. No witnesses. No interviews. No sightings. Nothing. Just the addresses of the women and the names of their next of kin. Bessie's mother, Nettie Shields. And Caroline's sister, Millicent Forrest. That was it. There was hardly anything in there. Surely there was more to record.

The notes were signed off by Stewart Mulligan and Henry Bonhoeffer. 'Was the Sarge's old man a cop here too?'

'Sure was,' Roger replied. 'Policing runs in the Mulligan blood.'

'What runs in Mulligan blood?' Renee hadn't heard his office door open. Mulligan was standing right behind them. She explained what she'd just found in the missing person's file.

'Yes, gee, that's a long time ago now. I was in my teens. They were a bit older than me. They sent out some search parties that my father coordinated as sergeant at the time, but, if I recall correctly, there was very little to go on. They lived over on the old yumba.'

Renee knew a little about the yumba. When she was a kid some of her rogue mates had pointed it out as the place their relatives used to live. But by that stage, all the dwellings had been knocked down and there were only a few bits of old sheet metal laying around, a timber stump here and there, and cleared areas in among shrubs where Renee imagined families once lived. There was still a sandy patch in the centre where her friends said the campfire had been. Only concrete slabs were left of the amenities block; the council being so keen to remove any suggestion it had once deliberately segregated the Aboriginal community.

'They vanished, those two girls. So sad for their families.'

'Do we have a file on this?' Renee asked.

'Hold on.' Mulligan moved back into his office and went to his filing cabinet. 'What were you saying about my old man?'

'Oh, just that I didn't know you had followed in his footsteps. Is that him there?' Renee asked, indicating the family photo on top of the filing cabinet, the one of Mulligan as a boy standing between his two parents. It looked like it was taken out the front of their house.

'Yes, that's him. Stewart Mulligan. He was a good cop.' He started rolling the combination lock. 'He wouldn't have missed any details, but I'll let you have a look over the file. Can't do any harm, I s'pose. He was born on the same day as Queen Elizabeth, you know? Shared a birthday with the queen herself! Best darn cop in Queensland. Here you go. Put it back on my desk when you're done.'

Renee returned to her desk and sifted through the contents of the hard-copy file. A photo of Caroline caught her attention, eyes glimmering with hope as though she held a special secret. Renee felt profound sorrow wondering what had become of this young woman. There was hardly anything else in it either. Strange. But there was nothing linking these two women to her current case. She needed to refocus. Before the forensic report had arrived, they were going to visit the residents of Wellington Street, but after hearing the boys down the creek allude to Worm she figured it was time to go and pay him a visit first.

'Stacey, have you got an update on that trucker's report?'

'What trucker's report?'

'The one that Sarge asked you to produce yesterday.'

Stacey heaved a sigh and swivelled her chair so her back was facing Renee to leaf through papers. 'It's here.' She pulled out a paper and handed it up to Renee, making Renee get to her feet and come over. There was nothing but a list of names.

'Good. Now I want you to run all these names through our databases and see if anyone has a record.' Stacey frowned and looked away. 'I'm going over to William Gawlor's place. Let Sarge know if he's looking for me.'

'Want me to come?' asked Roger with puppy-dog excitement.

'No, I want you to go and check with all the hotels around town. Get their guest registers and see if they've seen or heard anything suspicious. We'll go do the door to door later.'

She parked out the front of a low-set brick house next to the indoor sports centre, and checked her gun was locked and loaded before getting out of the car and walking across the front yard. There was no garden or lawn – just dirt and tyre tracks. Cigarette butts, slimy dog toys and chewed bones were strewn across the yard. She knocked on the door, but there was no answer apart from the deep growls of a few dogs that could be heard scratching and jumping at the fence in the backyard. She knocked again, harder this time, just in case Worm was inside sleeping or had headphones on, and she was about to leave when out of the corner of her eye she saw a curtain sway ever so slightly.

'I know you're in there. This is the police! Open up!' She banged harder on the light-framed wooden door until it opened a fraction and a waft of cigarette smoke escaped.

'What do you want?' The voice was low and raspy and when the door opened further Renee was surprised to see it belonged to a young woman.

'I need to speak to Mr Gawlor,' Renee said, flashing her badge. The woman was wearing pink satin boxer shorts decorated with the faces of little pug dogs in bow ties.

'Worm's not home.'

Renee peered behind the woman, trying to see inside. There was a four-seater red faux leather couch and giant television. The coffee table was covered in empty beer glasses, ashtrays, a few baggies and a five-dollar note. It was a much brighter pink than others she had seen. It seemed familiar.

'Do you know where he is?'

'I think he went ...' She stopped herself. Someone had coached her not to reveal too much. Young but not naive. 'Umm ... I don't know.'

'Did he say when he'll be home?'

'Nope. Didn't say.'

'I'm here about the woman who was murdered yesterday.' Ironically, this made the woman relax. She must have assumed Renee was there for other reasons, a drug bust perhaps. 'Do you mind if I come inside and ask you a few questions?'

'I don't think that's a good idea. Don't you need a warrant or something ...'

Fine. Renee didn't have time to argue, and she was right. She did need a warrant to enter. 'Do you recognise this face?' Renee put the image of the woman who had been murdered in front of the girl. If the dead woman had been a drug-runner for Worm, then maybe this teenager would know her. She shook her head and Renee searched her expression for signs of recognition. 'What's your name?'

'Tiffany.'

'How old are you, Tiffany?'

Tiffany stared back with defiance and Renee knew that whatever number was about to come out of her mouth was going to be a lie. 'I'm nineteen.' Renee was about to ask for identification but thought better of it. If she was with Worm due to drug dependence, then she needed to feel like the police were a safe alternative. If she had information with regards to the killer, then it was also beneficial to have Tiffany's trust and cooperation.

'Are you safe here, Tiffany?' Renee asked with sincerity – after all, it wasn't all about the case.

The walls came up quickly. 'Yes,' Tiffany snapped back. 'And now, if you don't have any more questions, I need to …' She paused, searching for something palatable to say to a police officer. 'Get work done.' The door slammed in Renee's face and once again she heard the dogs barking out the back.

She returned to the car, remembering where she'd seen a five-dollar note recently. She'd noticed one at the Ford property the morning before – it was Archie's bookmark.

Renee left William Gawlor's house and headed back through town and along the creek to Mrs Ford's place. Along the way, she called Roger. 'Roger, I need you to do me a favour.'

'Sure. What is it?'

'I was just at Worm's and I noticed an unusual five-dollar note on the coffee table. It was a brighter pink than others. I'm sure I saw a similar one in Archie Ford's room yesterday.'

'So what?'

'I don't know. Bit of a coincidence, is all.'

'Do you think they're counterfeit?'

'Seems unlikely. Could you do a bit of a search on them?'

'I'm looking now.'

She put him on speaker and continued through town, trying to make out what Stacey was saying in the background, but it was too muffled.

Roger came back. 'Interesting. It says there was a limited batch put out in 1995. They all start with the serial HC95. And yep, they were made in a brighter pink to differentiate them from the regular batch.'

'Oh. Okay. Probably just coincidence then. Anything happening there?' Renee asked. She could hear chatter in the background

'You're not missing anything,' Roger said. 'No new leads.'

Renee was disappointed but not surprised.

She arrived at the Ford residence and pressed the buzzer on the outside fence. 'Mrs Ford. I need to talk to your son.' There was silence. She imagined Mrs Ford peering at her on the screen in her kitchen, ready to protect her son.

'He's resting.'

'It's important.' There was a long pause before the gate opened.

The front door opened before she had a chance to knock. 'Why do you need to talk to Archie, Ms Taylor?'

'It's Detective Taylor. And it won't take long. I just need to ask him a few questions.'

Mrs Ford's hair was pulled up in the same immaculate bun as the day before and she wore a long dress again, but today she'd chosen a bright sunflower pattern that seemed inappropriately cheerful given the circumstances.

'Let her through, Mum.' Archie was standing in the hall behind his mother. Renee remembered Roger's theory from the day before. Lonely lovers meeting on a dating site. A young woman being drawn into this man's mystique – he was indeed confident and well spoken albeit physically feeble. 'I have nothing to hide.'

Mrs Ford heaved an exasperated sigh to show her distaste and moved aside to let Renee through, her cold, hard eyes examining her.

'Come through, Detective Taylor. We're okay, Mum,' Archie said.

'Fine.' She was not fine. 'I'm here if you need me.'

Archie moved slowly down the hall to his bedroom and Renee followed. She watched as he got back into bed, seeming to struggle onto the mattress, and wondered if he was exaggerating his weakness.

'How can I help you, Detective? Have you got any leads?'

She glanced across to where the book about Egypt had sat the morning before. It was still there, but the bookmark was missing. 'Not leads as such, but maybe something you can help me with. Maybe you've remembered something since yesterday that you'd like to share with me?' Maybe he'd be more willing to talk without his mother breathing down his neck. 'If you do know something about what happened yesterday, it's best to come forward now.'

'You seem to be hinting at something, Detective. Why are you back here? Do you think I was involved in the murder of that woman?'

'That's not what I'm saying, Archibald.'

'Oh right, so this is what? A welfare check?' Despite his sarcasm, he remained pleasant and non-defensive. 'Please, have a seat.'

Renee sat. 'I just came from William Gawlor's house.'

'Oh, yes, how's our local drug dispenser going?' He said it without a hint of guilt.

'He wasn't home.'

'I bet Tiffany was though. You need to get her out of there, Detective. She's too young.'

'You know Tiffany?' So this man was getting around town. Or Tiffany had come here.

'Not really. I think Worm is the cousin of the people she was in foster care with. Or something like that. She used to live down in the city with them but then came back to Goorungah with Worm for god knows why.'

'What do you know about Worm?'

'Just as much as every other local. He deals drugs and he's a real standover. I've only met him once or twice and have never had a lengthy conversation with him. Despicable man, if you ask me.'

'Archie, I know you had dealings with Worm.'

'Well, that's very astute of you, Detective. What is it? Three days into your new role, knee-deep in a murder investigation and already mapping out the local drug network? I'm impressed.'

Renee's jaw dropped in disbelief. He wasn't even going to deny it.

'Open that drawer over there.' He pointed to the side dresser. In among the asthma puffers, tissues and various medications was a plastic bag filled with weed. She opened it and took a smell to check. 'Detective, I'm not a bad person. I understand what's at stake here. A young woman was murdered and that is a tragedy. I want you to catch whoever did this, and the sooner I reveal my wrongdoings – if you want to call them such – then the sooner you will find out what actually happened down there by the creek.'

'Okay.' Renee sat back down. Was a confession coming?

'I don't know how you did it, but you've obviously found a link between William Gawlor and me. Maybe Tiffany told you, I don't know. It doesn't matter. It's true. Tiffany comes by here once a month, usually on a Sunday, and delivers me one of those bags so I can better manage the pain. I understand that is illegal, and I am willing to pay the price.'

Of course. Her mother's request for pain relief in the form of marijuana flashed into Renee's mind.

'I see. Do you know anything about the woman murdered yesterday?' Renee asked wearily, placing the artist's impression in front of him. She would deal with the illicit substance use later.

He calmly took in the details and shook his head. 'Absolutely nothing.' It was difficult to imagine him lying after he'd just been open about how he got his marijuana, but she needed to persist.

'Tiffany didn't mention a friend? An accomplice?'

'Nope. But we don't really have lengthy conversations.'

'You knew about her relationship to Worm. You must have talked at some point.'

'Obviously one has some initial get-to-know-you banter when first engaging in a transaction.'

'Is everything okay in here?' Mrs Ford asked.

'Yes, Mum. We're fine,' Archie called out, and then turned back to Renee. 'Would you like some tea, Detective?' She declined.

Archie put up no resistance to giving her a DNA sample – he was eager to clear his name.

Then she left. She ignored the bag of weed – he was a little condescending but he had been cooperative, and she didn't want to take away something he was dependent on for pain relief. Could be worse, after all.

She returned to her car and drove through town. Sometimes driving helped her think through things. Right now she knew that Worm was dealing drugs in town. Archie was getting weed from Worm, and those kids by the creek were most likely dealing for him. Perhaps the Jane Doe was too.

She passed the high school, pausing by the fence to watch teenagers playing soccer on the sports oval, and thought back to when she was a student at Goorungah High. Studying was a treat and she'd enjoyed learning but lunchtimes were lonely.

The only friend she'd made left in primary school and she hadn't clicked with anyone else, until Josh came along, briefly made her happy, and then broke her heart. Her plan had always been to finish high school and study law at university. She got top grades and was accepted into one of the best courses in the country but after reviewing the course fees and adding up the costs associated with renting, food, utilities, books and transport home to see her mother, she'd decided to become a police cadet instead. That way, she could get first-hand exposure to law and justice, and receive a salary at the same time. She thought for a moment of Archie. A life changed by illness, opportunities severely curtailed.

The school bell rang indicating the end of the lunch break and the teenagers sauntered back towards the classrooms, showcasing their low levels of enthusiasm for schoolwork, not realising how much worse things could become.

She took the turn up Wellington Street, where kids stopped kicking balls around in the middle of the street to stare as she passed, then stopped at the very end and got out of the car at the site of the old camp, thinking back to the missing persons report she'd read earlier that day. The girls had been living on the old Aboriginal camp on the outskirts of town, the yumba.

A few stumps emerged from the ground and there was a scattering of rusty iron across the red dirt indicating the remains of dwellings. The clearing was bordered by giant eucalypts and she spotted a flock of galahs sitting quietly preening themselves in the branches. She imagined what the yumba would have been like in the old days, back when the government wouldn't let Blackfullas live in town, and wondered if her father had experienced the same discrimination wherever he had lived.

She got back in the car and drove up to the first house on the left, walked up the steps and rang the bell.

An elderly lady hobbled to the front door, closely followed by her Maltese terrier. 'Who's there?'

Renee showed her the artist's drawing, and asked the same questions she'd asked earlier in the day when she'd walked along Main Street with Roger. The lady didn't recognise her but commented on her beauty, as did everyone, when Renee continued with the same results along the next four houses. The kids in the street were similarly unfamiliar with the woman, as were a young couple on their way home from playing squash.

The sun was setting and Renee needed to return to the office to write up her notes and check on any developments before the others left, although surely they'd call her if there was anything important.

At the station she found that the others had already left so spent the next hour reviewing the notes from the day before, then added what new information she'd come across that day. The discovery of a link between Archie and Worm. Locals not wanting to talk about Worm – the boys at the creek and Tiffany. She leafed through the lab report once more.

Stacey had printed out the missing persons files on Caroline Forrest and Bessie Shields and placed them in a folder for her. A peace offering perhaps after their unpleasant exchange. Renee felt a stab of guilt. Maybe she'd been a bit too callous about her sister being scared.

She leafed through Bessie's report and then turned her attention once more to Caroline's. There was something about her photo. The image looked different now that it was printed out. She leaned back in her seat and held it up. Caroline Forrest was wearing a necklace. Renee opened the folder of the previous day's crime scene photos and went to one taken of the necklace alone, set against the backdrop of a white bench. The notes read: yellow sapphire, marquise cut. She held it against the photo of Caroline Forrest – it was the exact same necklace.

Chapter 8

August 1965

Caroline sat at the back of the church nestled between her best friend, Bessie, and her older sister, Milli. The stark simplicity of the interior of Goorungah's Anglican church felt as hollow as the words coming out of Pastor Ford's mouth. Her thick heavy Bible lay open on her lap and she flicked its thin pages between her fingers. She enjoyed feeling its perfect delicacy. Milli nudged her with her elbow, hissing, 'Ephesians, Chapter 4, Verse 32,' and the congregation recited the verse in unison: 'Be kind to one another, tender-hearted, forgiving one another, as God in Christ forgave you.' Milli sat straight, chin tipped up, thick curly hair pulled back into a low bun, feet together, long black skirt and high-necked blouse neat and clean. The very picture of upright, church-going propriety. Caroline squinted her eyes hard at the page, trying to make a soul connection with the words but felt nothing. They were empty.

Caroline had left school three years ago when she was fourteen but remembered leafing through some of the old history books in the school library and admiring the lavish cathedrals of faraway lands. Maybe if this 'house of worship' was as stunning with statues and stained-glass windows, velvet fabrics, grand organs and elaborate painted ceilings, she would be more inclined to pay attention. But the stark windowless church in all its shades of brown and grey, with its ugly bare walls, scuffed wooden floors and cold hard pews did nothing to stir her soul. Besides, the church meant something different here. She continued to flick at the pages of her Bible.

Another verse was recited, and she looked around the congregation to see if she could spy anyone else that may be feeling as equally disconnected from the words. There were some nice aspects to attending church – Mrs Ford's singing, the beauty of Corinthians, the sound of the piano, but never Mr Ford's sermons. Today he talked about generosity and the spirit of giving, and all Caroline could think about was how his people had come and herded her family off the land and made them live between the swamp and the rubbish dump, and thought he had a very interesting interpretation of generosity. He spoke of sharing food and clothing, but there was no mention of land. How could they forget so easily? She wouldn't tell Pa Quincey about the sermon later when he would inevitably ask about it. 'What nonsense did the priest-man go on about today?' he would ask, and Milli would correct him. 'Mr Ford is a pastor, Pa. Not a priest. That's the Roman Catholic Church. We're going to the Anglican.'

'Whatever.'

She pushed these thoughts out of her mind and let Mrs Ford's ethereal voice carry her.

She was never entirely sure why Milli insisted on coming to the Anglican church as opposed to the Catholic Mass – it wasn't as though they had a long family history of allegiance to either religion but she went along with it, knowing she didn't have much say in their place of worship anyway. Caroline preferred to be sitting around with Pa back on the camp, as he spoke about the old times and how their people lived in connection with the land, when they knew of all the rocks and gullies and when to stay and when to move, and the meaning of an early blossom in spring or the late departure of migratory birds. Pa always said life was simple when you live in rhythm with Country, but it would be a long time before life returned to those ways. He used his hands as he told his stories and gently drew in the sand, signs and symbols that Caroline was yet to fully understand, but one day she hoped to grow in that faith, and not this one.

Her stomach growled and she squirmed in her seat, adjusting her posture to stop the rumbling, wondering how much longer the service would go on. The thick canvas dress, the one that Milli insisted she wear because it was the only one she owned that covered her arms and legs, itched her neck. Pastor Ford stood ramrod straight and tall at the front of the service behind the pulpit in his perfectly fitted brown suit, rambling on and on in his dull drawn-out voice that would have put Caroline to sleep if it wasn't for her stomach screaming out for attention. She glanced at the rows of people in front of her. All white people. Milli was the only Blackfulla crazy enough to buy in to this religious business. There were around sixty people present, a few less than normal perhaps – the cold was keeping people at home, and some locals would be at the Catholic Mass. Caroline recognised a few of the farmers and townsfolk. Goorungah was a small town after all – nearly everyone knew each other in some capacity even if they tried to pretend otherwise, building fences to keep themselves in their boxes. She spotted the local police sergeant a few rows in front. His son usually accompanied him but today Sergeant Mulligan sat alone and Caroline thought he looked more solemn than usual.

Caroline glanced at Bessie, who still had her Bible open on the first verse they'd read that morning, staring blankly into space. What on earth was going through that girl's mind was anyone's guess. Caroline stifled her giggle, knowing that if she started, there would be no hope of control and Milli's wrath would be endless. If one started laughing (or crying) the other one would undoubtedly follow.

Caroline and Bessie, although unrelated by blood, were the same age and had been pretty much raised together. If Milli wasn't taking care of them, then Bessie's mum – Aunty Nettie to Caroline – would have them over at her shack. Although the camp was scant in resources, there was hardly a dull moment with Bessie by her side because her friend always found some mischief to get into. They played together as toddlers and later as little girls around the camp. They went to school together (and avoided school together), and similarly did household chores together (and avoided household chores together). Caroline forced herself to look down, willing herself not to laugh at Bessie's absentmindedness until finally Pastor Ford said, 'Amen.'

People rose out of the long timber pews and began scuffling towards the exit as Mrs Ford began playing the organ again, as was her Sunday morning ritual. She would always play one last song so the congregation would leave the church with the music still carrying them. This, she said, was to 'keep the Lord's words as fresh in their minds as possible, until they could return to the sacred house of worship on the following Sabbath'. Or something along those lines. As Caroline looked towards the stage where Mrs Ford played the piano, she wondered how such perfect force could come from such a diminutive frame.

She bumped into Bessie, who was slowly shuffling towards the centre aisle.

'Watch it, Callie. I'm keen to get out of here too!'

Once she made it to the centre aisle, Bessie turned and grinned at Caroline, then scurried towards the exit, avoiding Pastor Ford, who always greeted people on their way out. She was halfway down the front steps when Caroline caught up to her. 'Hey! Where you think you're going?' Caroline knew very well where Bessie was going, and it was not towards the kitchen. 'We gotta help with the food today. Come on, don't be naughty. You'll get me into trouble ... again.' Bessie squinted her eyes at Caroline in a rebellious frown, and Caroline glared back, hands on hips, challenging her friend to disagree. '*You* know what day it is, Bessie.'

It was the last Sunday of the month, which meant staying to help with the charity luncheon that the church put on for everyone in the local community, even those who didn't attend the actual service. It was their way of enticing newcomers to join the fold, or as Caroline once put it to Milli, their way of bribing the hungry, but she would never say that again given the stern reprimand she'd received from her sister.

'Fine.' Bessie hunched over in defeat, kicked a stone and dragged herself back to follow her friend. Caroline walked past the churchgoers gathering out the front and continued down the side path towards the kitchen out the back. She heard her friend scurry up behind her to tickle her sides. 'I'll help you in the kitchen if you admit that you were checking out Sergeant Mulligan during the sermon.'

'Shh ...! Not so loud.' Caroline wriggled away from her friend's clutches and looked around, making sure no one heard. 'Eww! That's not even true, Bessie, and you know it.' She slapped her friend away and opened the door to the kitchen where there were two large pots sitting on top of the stove awaiting someone to switch on the gas and heat them. Caroline remembered the one other thing that drew her to Sunday sermons. Food.

'I don't like that cop, Bessie. Don't be ridiculous. Stop talkin rot!' Caroline said, safe in the privacy of the kitchen, out of earshot of their fellow parishioners, and keen to put her friend straight. 'And don't you go shooting your mouth off with silly gossip like that, you hear?' Bessie smirked back but Caroline could see that she was taking her scolding seriously. 'Besides, he's a gunji. *And* he's old!'

'How old do you think he is?' Bessie asked, lifting the lid on the first pot, peering in and then waving her hand in front of her nose feigning revulsion. 'Yuck. Pumpkin.' She stuck her tongue out and Caroline thought how cute her friend looked. Bessie had short curly hair, big round eyes, and a face so expressive the slightest crease told Caroline everything.

'I dunno, maybe thirty-five or something. Probably older.' What she was saying was true – Caroline wasn't interested in some crusty old man – but now that Bessie had mentioned him her mind conjured an image of his face. Pale skin, reddish hair, serious demeanour, so proper, everything neat – neatly shaven, neat clothes, neat shoes, neat, neat, neat. Bessie would be better matchmaking him with do-gooder Milli. Hah!

'You know he's got a kid?' Bessie went on to the potato and leek soup, took a whiff and her expression warmed. She grabbed a spoon and scooped up a mouthful. Caroline slapped her hand down and warned her not to let Mrs Ford or Milli catch her sneaking any. 'Yeah, little Rodney Mulligan junior. About our age, maybe a year younger than us.'

'Is the sergeant married then?' Caroline regretted it as soon as she'd asked, not wanting to encourage her friend.

'Nope. Lost his wife a few years ago to cancer.' She took another spoonful and this time Caroline almost wanted Milli to come in and bust her so she wouldn't have to endure Bessie's nonsense any longer.

'How do you know all this? Actually, forget it, I really don't care. I'm not interested in men …' She went to add 'right now' but her friend had already caught on and she was in a real shit-stirring mood.

'You a lesbian then? You like girls?' Bessie exaggerated all her words, slowly wiggling her body, working up to some kind of theatrics.

'Stop it, Bessie. Put that spoon down and get away from the soup before Milli gets in here.' Caroline brushed her away but it only hyped up Bessie more.

'You're gonna make this holy temple here burn down with that sinfulness!' Bessie waved her hands in the air now, her voice taking on the tones of a preacher. Caroline rolled her eyes and let her go on with her drama. One day Bessie would be an actor. If she didn't end up behind bars or seriously injured for stealing some woman's man.

She returned to the soups. They weren't even close to boiling. 'Pastor Ford is *not* gonna be happy if he hears you …'

'What's Pastor Ford not gonna be happy about?' The door flung open and Milli charged in, going straight over to check on the soup. Both girls stepped back, putting their hands behind their backs guiltily. Milli took a sip and wrinkled up her face. 'This soup is lukewarm! I told you girls it had to be hot. We gotta horde of hungry people out there and they don't want no lukewarm soup. What were you two doing in here? I could hear you carrying on from a mile away.' Milli looked from Caroline to Bessie and back to Caroline. 'I should leave you back at the camp on Sunday mornings. Actually, no. That would only make yas worse. Get over here, Caroline. You stir this, and Bessie! You go and start wiping down those chairs out there – a few of them got wet in the rain – and tell everyone the pumpkin soup will be ready in five minutes.' Bessie started towards the door. 'And the potato will be ready then, too,' Milli shouted out but Bessie was already gone.

'Callie, you stay here and help me butter these bread rolls.' Caroline wanted to go back out into the crisp fresh air with Bessie. 'That girl, Caroline! She's trouble. I keep tellin you.'

Caroline stepped back and watched her big sister busy herself wiping down the benches, putting pots and plates here and there. It was all so pointless. So much unnecessary energy being used making things neat and 'presentable' (Milli's favourite word) for people Caroline didn't care about. It would all turn into a mess within the hour anyway.

'You wanna pay more attention during service, Callie, I'm gettin sick of telling you to keep up in there. You and Bessie; womba as each other. When are yas gonna grow up and act your ages? Hey?' There was sweat dripping from her forehead, despite the chill in the air. 'You need to set an example for the young ones.' The young ones? She was only seventeen herself. She tried not to roll her eyes but couldn't help looking to the ceiling.

'Go'orn den, roll your eyes at me, girl. You'll see one day why all this is important, just you wait and see.'

Caroline had heard it all before. 'Why what's important, Milli? You don't seriously believe in all those stories, do you? That's not what Pa Quincey teaches us.' She rubbed her forehead, wondering why she even bothered arguing.

'I'm not talkin about religion, Callie. I'm talkin about *fitting in*.' Milli leaned in close, sounding it out as though Caroline had half a brain.

'Why would we even wanna fit in here? It's dull and empty. I'd rather spend Sunday mornings at the camp. If I'm old enough to be setting an example, I should be old enough to make my own decisions about how I spend my time.' She thought of Pa with his dog, leaning over the billy can with smoke floating around him. That was comfort and warmth, not this cold old wooden building filled with stories of mobs getting lost in deserts and men being nailed to crosses. And even though Mrs Ford's songs were nice, it was Pa's soft melodies that really soothed her soul. Caroline fell silent thinking about the camp and went to get the butter out of the fridge so she wouldn't have to meet her sister's sad eyes. Maybe she had taken it too far. She knew her sister was partly right in being so calculated. After all, they had nothing. They relied on the mercy of the townsfolk for nearly everything – work, albeit for pathetically low wages, a water supply to the camp, and of course, most of all, their silence. The people on the camp lived in ever-present fear that the government authorities would be notified and their children taken away.

'You think I don't wanna have fun and muck around, get myself a man, have my own family?' Her sister had given up everything to care for her after their parents died in a vehicle accident when Caroline was four years old. Milli had only been ten herself. Caroline knew this had changed her. Made her protective, bossy, cautious. 'Of course I do, Callie. Of course, I wanna life of my own. But someone has to look after you and Pa.' Milli cut into the crusty bread rolls and handed one to Caroline to butter. 'So, if that means going to church, singing some hymns, and *fitting in* then I will. That way we're more likely to get some work around here and be able to afford a decent feed occasionally, rather than sifting through the dump for leftovers. And the least you could be, Caroline Forrest, is a little bit fuckin grateful.'

'Ladies, how is everything going in here?' The pastor's wife came in holding her four-month-old baby in her arms. Milli looked mortified that Mrs Ford may have heard her say 'fuckin' and Caroline squeezed her arm in reassurance. Mrs Ford was a tall slender lady with long straight blonde hair. She was elegant upon first impression with her neat smile and thin frame, until she moved and then Caroline thought of a robot with its stiff posturing and jarring movements. She peered over their shoulders, patting them on their backs. 'Nice work, ladies. Did you enjoy the service today?' Caroline braced herself for the nauseatingly sweet person her sister was about to become.

'Wonderful, Mrs Ford. We're very blessed here in Goorungah to have the wisdom and guidance of your husband,' Milli replied with a forced smile and Caroline stifled an urge to throw up. Her sister was a completely different person around townsfolk – so proper and upright, changing the way she spoke and walked.

'I'm so pleased.' Mrs Ford took a sip of the pumpkin soup, concentrated hard and then nodded a slow approval.

Caroline could hear the crowd start to gather out under the tarpaulin and wanted to escape and join them. Milli must have noticed her grimace because she looked across with her familiar warning gaze that said, *Hurry up and say something nice to Mrs Ford.* 'The service was lovely,' Caroline muttered and Milli hardened her glare so much at Caroline that her eyeballs bulged slightly. '… Mrs Ford,' she added. Milli smiled, satisfied.

'Well, that is good to hear.'

Caroline never understood why Milli went to such great lengths to appease this woman. Mrs Ford was obviously completely unaware of the subtle interactions that went on between her and her sister. They could carry out an entire conversation without saying a word, with only the direction of their gaze and facial expressions and Mrs Ford would be none the wiser.

'Look at this chubby little fulla,' Milli complimented, squeezing the cheeks of baby Archie.

'Gentle now,' Mrs Ford warned, as if Milli had never cared for a baby, and it was all too much for Caroline. She picked up the plate of bread rolls and left Milli to coo and gah-gah over the chunky baby.

Milli, Caroline and Bessie had arrived early and spent the morning before the service putting up a tarpaulin covering just in case it rained. They knew from experience Mrs Ford would expect it done. Chairs and tables were neatly organised under the covering. It was all ugly mouldy plastic, and none of it compared to the gentle ambience of the camp early on a wet Sunday morning, with its campfire smoke hanging low in the cold air.

They laid out the food banquet-style across the tables lined up at the back of the tent – pumpkin and potato soups, bread rolls, napkins and spoons. Mrs Ford called out to everyone that lunch was ready and a long line formed. Milli gave Caroline the look that meant *wait until last*, so she and Bessie found a long bench to the side and let everyone else go on ahead.

'Look who's here,' Bessie said, elbowing Caroline in the side, motioning to the footpath. A man of about thirty years old leaned down and tied his dog to a fence post a few feet away from where

Caroline and Bessie sat, then strode towards the tent. He was tall and muscular, wearing ripped jeans and a loose flannelette T-shirt with the top few buttons undone revealing his chest. Caroline recognised the man as William Gawlor, otherwise known as Worm. Milli had warned her against ever going near the man – she worked at the local pub three nights a week and said she had watched her workmates at the pub deal with him on a number of occasions when he got drunk and out of hand. A younger bloke followed Worm. Caroline looked around – she and Bessie weren't the only ones watching the newcomers arrive. The entire church congregation had stopped their chattering and eating to look up silently.

'What're they doing here?' Caroline whispered, leaning in closer to Bessie.

'I don't know. But he's got balls coming to church lunch looking like that.' Bessie giggled just as Worm looked over and caught her smirking. He winked and kept walking, straight to the front of the line. Caroline watched closely, puzzled by his appearance at the Sunday luncheon. He had a pack of smokes in one back pocket and his wallet in the other.

'What the hell is he doing?' she whispered again to Bessie, dumbstruck as she watched Worm skip the queue. When one of the elderly ladies tapped him on the shoulder to let him know he'd pushed in, he turned around and made a show of not realising and, hand to chest, feigned an exaggerated apology. Bessie wriggled in her seat, excited by his presence and the commotion that this was causing, while Caroline continued quietly studying his movements. Her sister was overly cautious about most things, but on the matter of William Gawlor she was probably right. Worm and his mate reached the pots of soup, ladled extra-large helpings into their cups and then turned to gaze across the group of hungry parishioners, looking for a place to sit.

'Oh no ... They're coming over,' Caroline said, careful not to make eye contact with Worm. She moved down the bench so there was less room for him and his friend to sit. Please don't come over here, she silently prayed, guessing that Bessie would be praying for the opposite.

'How's it goin, girls?' she heard him ask in a deep, smooth voice that could almost have sounded attractive if it didn't belong to him. Caroline reluctantly lifted her gaze and hoped the full extent of her dread didn't show on her face. A man like this would only be encouraged by the look of intimidation on a woman's face.

'We're goin alright, boys. How you two fine fullas going?' Bessie said, pushing out her chest and making Caroline want to slap some sense into her. In the short time that Caroline had been looking away, Bessie had taken the opportunity to unbutton the top of her cardigan and reveal the little cleavage she had. 'Wanna seat?' Bessie moved further away from Caroline, allowing a space to emerge on the bench. Worm smiled down at her, took a slurp from his cup of soup and glanced back at the man he'd come with. He was younger than Worm, with long blond greasy hair tied back in a ponytail. He wore a black T-shirt with the name of some band on it and brown corduroy pants, ripped at the knees.

'Go on, Gappy.' Worm motioned for his accomplice to take a seat. 'I wanna face these two lovely sheilas and get a nice look at em.' Worm turned to find a plastic chair, brought it back and placed it down to face Caroline and Bessie, then sat back, legs apart, and grinned. 'Why haven't I had the pleasure of meeting you two ladies before?'

Bessie giggled and squirmed. Caroline was about to tell him that the reason they hadn't met was because they didn't hang out at the pub with troublemakers, but Bessie jumped in before she could get a word out. 'We've met. You just don't remember me. I was at the pub a few weekends ago. Not inside, just waiting on the street out the front. You gave me a smoke. Don't you remember?'

'Are you sure it was me? I think I'd remember such a beautiful face.' Worm smiled but looked at Caroline when he spoke.

'I think you'd had a bit to drink,' Bessie explained coyly. Caroline shouldn't be surprised by her friend's antics, but she was. Bessie was getting increasingly daring during her night-time escapades. When she got bored spending time with her family around the camp, she'd walk down to Main Street on the premise of looking around for work. Sometimes she'd go alone, sometimes with cousins who came from out of town and stayed for a bit. Caroline had accompanied her on one late-night adventure, but they hadn't run into Worm. 'Anyway, I'm Bessie, and this here is Caroline.'

Bessie stretched out her hand and Worm took it slowly and kissed it, making her writhe with delight. Then he sat back and looked at Caroline, who remained motionless. No way in hell was she extending her hand. His lips pouted as he cast his eyes from head to toe and back up again, making her shiver.

'Hi, Caroline.' She froze. There was nothing she wanted to say to this man. He laughed, making light of her rejection, and turned back to Bessie. 'Is she mute or something?'

'Nah, she's just a bit shy.' Bessie leaned forward and looked down the bench to Caroline, past the man Worm had called Gappy, now between them. 'Caroline. Don't be bloody rude.'

'Fuck off, Bessie.' This made both men laugh, and Caroline took the break in conversation to get up and get some soup.

She walked through the church congregation, now huddled warmly under the tarpaulin, towards the two pots of steaming soup. The shock of Worm's appearance had worn off and the hungry mob had returned to dipping their bread in soup and chatting away. Milli was still in the kitchen and for that Caroline was relieved because she didn't want her to see Worm and his mate. Who knew what she might do? And Caroline could already tell that Worm was dangerous. She ladled herself some pumpkin soup and then put some potato and leek in a cup for Bessie. She didn't want to go back over but she couldn't leave Bessie alone with them. Maybe if Bessie had some food in her stomach, she wouldn't act like such an idiot.

'Is everything okay over there?' A man's voice came from behind. She turned to see Pastor Ford had walked up to where she was standing. 'I don't believe I saw those two lads in my sermon this morning. Perhaps they left early and came back for the soup?'

For a moment Caroline thought that Pastor Ford was concerned about her safety but now she could see he only cared whether they were interested in his teachings. She had an idea. 'They were interested in your thoughts even though they weren't in church this morning, Pastor. Maybe you'd like to come and have a chat with them now?' If the pastor could come and talk to the men long enough, she could get Bessie away.

'Good idea. I'll be right over.'

Caroline walked back over and handed Bessie the cup.

Bessie took it with an air of distraction. 'Caroline, this is Gappy. He's Worm's cousin from the city. Tell her what you just told me, Gappy.'

Gappy looked at Caroline hesitantly, as though he were checking to see if she was indeed receptive. She shrugged to indicate she didn't care either way.

'Well, I was just telling your friend that my old man owns a yacht down in the city and if you two ever wanted to get away, I could borrow it for the weekend.' She hadn't noticed his black eye earlier, nor the large space between his two front teeth, which she figured was the reason for his nickname. Bessie continued peppering Gappy with questions about the boat, while Worm leaned back, licking the remainder of the soup from the rim of the cup, eyeing both women. His dog was starting to whine from over to the side where it was tied up, drawing some attention from the crowd.

'Have either of you ever been to the city?' Worm asked over the top of Bessie and Gappy's conversation, placing the cup down next to him. Caroline looked back over to the tent, wondering why Pastor Ford was taking so long. Didn't he want two new men to join his flock?

'No, but we want to,' Bessie said. 'What's it like?'

Worm's dog howled loudly this time, jumping up and pulling on its leash towards an elderly couple who recoiled in fright. 'Sit down, Munch!' Worm growled and it whimpered and wriggled its body back down into the dirt. 'Hmm ... what's the city like, hey? Good question. Do you like having fun or are you a bit *boring?*' He leaned in towards Bessie in mock threat and she mirrored his movements, flashing her cleavage.

'What do *you* think, Worm?' she teased.

'I think you like having fun and maybe one day I could take you there. They have discos, and big shops with handbags and perfumes, and high-heeled shoes ... Do you like that kind of thing, Bessie?'

Munch howled, while Pastor Ford and Milli remained nowhere to be seen.

Bessie nodded. 'I think I might like that, Worm.'

Caroline was starting to feel scared now. What was Bessie getting herself into? 'Bessie, have you finished your soup yet? We should go and help Milli clean up in the kitchen.'

'You can go. I'll just be here with Gappy and—'

'What's happening here? Mr Gawlor.' Caroline turned to see her sister standing there. 'I didn't see you in church this morning.' Her voice didn't falter although Caroline knew her sister well enough to note something flick across her face. This man scared her too.

'Sorry, Milli.' Caroline was surprised to see Worm address Milli with such familiarity albeit sarcasm. 'But my alarm didn't go off.' He clicked his fingers. 'What a shame, I missed the service. Maybe you could fill me in on Pastor Ford's sermon. We were just getting to that part, weren't we, girls?'

'It was about gratitude and—' Bessie started to explain, oblivious both to Milli's disdain towards Worm and Worm's sarcasm.

'Bessie. Kitchen. Now,' Milli demanded, cutting her sermon summary short. 'You too, young miss.'

Caroline stood to follow her sister – it was possibly the first time she'd ever been relieved to be called into the church kitchen – and waited for Bessie to do likewise. 'Are you coming?'

'I'll be in in a minute.' Bessie glared back.

Caroline looked from her friend to Worm and Gappy, and back to Bessie, then shook her head and left.

Chapter 9

It was late afternoon and the sun was setting over the yumba. The clouds had lifted, although a chill still hung in the air. Caroline scratched around in the vegetable patch behind their shack for herbs and leaves to put in their evening meal, listening to the soft hum of chatter across the camp and voices from neighbouring households calling in their children for dinner.

The yumba was home to about fifty people, but that number rose and fell as folk came and went depending on where their relatives lived and where they could find work. It was a shanty town of sorts set up on the outskirts of town, past the rubbish dump and next to the cemetery, bordered on the western side by the Goorungah Creek. The yumba was a scattering of shacks made from bits of sheet metal and other leftover parts collected at the dump or around town, with a fireplace at the centre and one long dirt road that led in from the town bitumen road. Some people found places to live on the large pastoral estates, but for those who couldn't, there was the camp. The council knew that the farmers relied on their cheap labour and let them stay, even going so far as setting up communal taps, toilets and showers. How generous. Caroline had heard that in other parts of the country the 'authorities' had moved entire nations onto missions or reserves, but here in Goorungah they turned a blind eye so long as the residents of the yumba made themselves useful to the white folk.

Most of their traditional language and ways of life had been lost – moved from their land, forced to speak English, it was hard for many to remember the old ways – but some traditions remained, mixed in with the new. Food, for example. Meals consisted of anything from roo tail cooked over red hot coals, porcupine, yellow belly, johnny cakes with butter and honey, native berries, to tinned ham and any kind of cheap offal from the nearby kill sheds. Some of the stories were still there too. As a kid, Caroline had been told stories of hairy men that dwelt down by the creek – the Elders had told that story to warn little kids against going too close to flooding rivers. Other stories were mixed with biblical parables to form twisted ghost stories of evil people with goat hooves, brooms standing in hallways, headless horsemen and the dreaded 666 – the number of the beast. The yumba was a wild place to live, and for the most part Caroline loved it. It was home.

There were four large extended families living in the fringe settlement, mainly descended from two nations. The Shields were the biggest family, headed up by Nettie who everyone called Aunty, even some of the white folk in town, owing to her commanding demeanour. Aunty Nettie was married to Uncle Kevin, a quiet man who kept to himself. There were whispers that something terrible had happened to him when he was a boy on one of the stations further west, but no one really knew the exact details. Aunty Nettie was protective of him and together they formed a strong union. They had five children including Caroline's best friend, Bessie, who was second in line after big brother Clarence.

'Callie, come on in here now and give me a hand with this meal,' Milli called from inside their shack. Milli was still angry with her for talking to Worm at the church. She'd tried to explain that it wasn't her fault he and Gappy had started talking to her, but Milli wouldn't listen.

'I'm coming, Milli, just give me a second.' She broke off a piece of mint and placed it in the bowl with the parsley, glanced over her shoulder to check Milli wasn't watching her 'waste time' and picked a blossom of melaleuca. She rolled it in her fingers, releasing the oils, and placed it under her nostrils, closed her eyes, inhaled. The scent was both sweet and tangy, warmed by the earthy campfire smoke. Looking up, she opened her eyes to the deep purple of oncoming night above a sunset-orange-washed horizon.

'*Caroline!*'

'Always in a rush,' Caroline mumbled as she threw the blossom into the scrub and went into their shack. Milli was sitting on the floor with a crocheted blanket tossed over her back, peeling carrots on their table made of bits and pieces of debris from the rubbish dump.

'Here.' She passed Caroline a knife and plate. 'Make yourself useful.'

'Where's Pa?' Caroline asked, taking the knife and beginning to peel.

'In bed.' He had been getting so tired lately, and the cold weather was not good on his old bones. 'Don't you worry about him, young miss. You focus on yourself.'

'How? By working myself to death like you?'

'You wanna eat, don't you?' Milli shot back, chopping bits of curly gut and sweetbread. Pa Quincey worked at the local slaughterhouse and brought back bits of offal when he could. The butcher was a generous old bloke and shared the offcuts with his workers. When Caroline was a kid, she and Bessie would hang around out the back until Pa found a quiet moment when no one was looking and hand them a good bit of meat – rump steak, lamb shanks or pork ribs – and they'd scurry back to the camp to throw it on the fire before the meat went bad in the heat. But then Pa came to know the butcher and started to like him. When the butcher started giving Pa offcuts of the meat, he felt guilty for his earlier thefts so he worked extra hours to make up for it and stopped stealing.

'And on that note, I have news,' Milli continued. 'Mrs Cunningham came and spoke to me at church this morning, while you was busy muckin around with Bessie and those other ratbags.' She spat out the word ratbags.

Caroline slowly cut the carrots, feeling tension emit from her sister. She had spent all afternoon assuring her that she wouldn't go anywhere near Worm and Gappy, but Milli was still suspicious. 'Who's Mrs Cunningham?' Goorungah was a small place with only two churches, so most people knew each other but Caroline didn't recognise this name.

'Mrs Cunningham and her husband own the big farm on the north side of town, Hereford Downs, across the creek and past the railway line. They got a herd of cattle and a few paddocks of wheat. If you mingled more with folk at church, you'd know that.' She brushed aside the curly gut and started chopping the mint and parsley into fine slices. Milli never stopped moving. Constantly doing things, like it was a race to get through life.

'So, what does she want?' Caroline had been along the north road a few times but she didn't know the farm.

'She – *Mrs Cunningham* – is looking for help around the house. She's got four sons and they all big eaters.'

Caroline knew where this was heading. She wasn't in school and she'd left her position at the Armstrongs' property a few months ago. It was only a matter of time before she was sent somewhere else to make money.

'And Mrs Cunningham heard from Mrs Armstrong that you left their place because smartypants Lola was thrown out of boarding school in the city and had to come home. Mrs Armstrong told Mrs Cunningham that you're a good worker.' Her sister smiled at her and nodded her head. 'See, what'd I tell you? These white women talk more than us. Get on the good side of one of em and you're in! I already washed your dress and apron for tomorrow so you should be all ready to go.'

'Tomorrow!' Caroline put down her knife. 'Far out, Millie! Don't I get a say in any of this? Weren't you just telling me I had to start acting my age? How am I supposed to—'

'You wanna be a bit more grateful, girl,' Milli fired back. 'You know that after losing the job with the Armstrongs, this is a godsend!' She shook her head and mumbled something under her breath. 'We can't go on survivin on my pub wage and the bit I make sellin oils alone.' Milli made the oils by gathering melaleuca leaves and steaming them until the oil separated out. The tiny jars of oil were lined up neatly along the wall near the entrance, ready to sell to whoever happened to need it. The oil was good for infections of any kind and its ethereal fragrance instantly cleared the mind of any worries.

'So you know you're going to need to be ready early tomorrow morning for your ride?' Milli asked. 'I'll have already left for my shift at the Criterion, so you're going to need to make sure you get yourself up. Callie, you listenin? Can you get yourself up?'

'Yeah, course I can. Quit naggin me.'

'It was very generous of Mrs Cunningham to arrange a ride for you to work. Not like those Armstrongs – they would've made you use them skinny legs o'yours.'

Caroline reluctantly agreed, although secretly would have preferred to walk to the new job. She liked the long stretches of country road. She started trying to add up all the stretches of road to estimate the total distance from her home to the Cunningham farm.

'You hear me, Callie?' Her sister's voice interrupted her thoughts.

'Yeah, Milli. I'm going to be fine. Don't worry about me.' She looked earnestly at her older sister, wishing Milli didn't fuss over details as much as she did. 'Sis, it's all going to be fine.' Caroline sighed, coming to terms with her fate. It had only been a matter of time before she would have had to find a new job, anyway. She grinned at Milli and gently shoved her shoulder, trying to lighten the mood. 'What would I do without you, hey?'

'Prob'ly sit out there sniffin them leaves all day,' Milli teased her back, smiling. Caroline laid out three plates, three forks and three tin cups on the little makeshift table and turned down the kerosene lamp so it lit their shack with a warm glow.

'Very good. Now go get Pa,' Milli said.

Pa Quincey was resting in his room. There were three small 'rooms' in their tin shack separated by bits of tin and cloth, enough to provide the family of three with privacy. Caroline and Milli shared the space that was previously their parents' and Quincey had a small space of his own, and then there was the common area where they ate.

'Pa, are you awake?' Caroline whispered softly. These days their grandfather was often dozing with his faithful dingo dog Star by his side. He would never admit to sleeping, saying he was just having a 'lay down with his eyes closed'. Quincey only had one daughter and that was Caroline and Milli's mother, who had died in an accident. The accident was never spoken about in their household – it was simply referred to as 'the accident' and nothing more. It had occurred on one of the big properties further west of Goorungah. Caroline's parents had finished up work for the day and were driving back towards the homestead in the farmer's ute when a bull lurched out in front of them. Her father was driving and didn't have time to brake before they collided head-on at high speed. They died at the scene. The farmer found them later that evening when they sent out a search party, and the news made its way to the Goorungah camp the following day. Caroline was four. She remembered two police officers standing at the door asking to speak to Pa Quincey. She thought they had come to take her, because she'd heard stories of the government men taking fairer-skinned kids away to live with other families, and she ran and hid under the blankets in her bed. From there she heard Pa Quincey go to the door and start talking to the officers in a muffled voice and then the silence that followed. That was all she could remember. Now she was grown, she figured Pa Quincey must have come in at some stage and found her under the blanket and told her that her parents had died in an accident, but she had no recollection of that part. There must've also been a point when Milli found out. She was ten at the time. Were they together? Did they cry? Did they console one another? It was a blank space in her mind. She only remembered the cops at the door.

She stood for a few moments at the opening to his room, not wanting to disturb Pa's sleep, imagining how tired he must feel after working in the slaughterhouse. He'd mourned the death of his only child and raised her two daughters, no doubt keeping the gunjis at bay with promises that he was looking after them. His skinny body shifted slightly beneath the blanket. Making sure he ate his evening meal was just as important as rest.

'Supper's ready, Pa.' She went in and placed her hand on his forehead and wiped the hair away from his eyes. 'You hungry? Milli's made a nice warm meal for us.'

He grinned at her, lifted himself up out of bed and hobbled to the table. She could see by his jagged movements and grimaces that his body was stiff and sore. Star followed alongside as always and plopped down next to where Pa sat.

'Evenin, Queenie,' he greeted Milli using his nickname for her. 'How was church?'

'Good, Pa.' Milli rolled her neck and lowered her shoulders, finally relaxing. 'They really love the soups on a cold day – you should see em smilin up when we arrive, hey Callie?' Caroline nodded.

'That's good,' Pa said, taking a mouthful of his meal and murmuring compliments. Caroline shared a knowing look with Pa. This was the evening ritual. They both knew Milli would relax once she was sitting at the table, all her chores done for the day, meals laid out before them. 'And tell me, how're the Armstrongs? Mm ... That's good. And the Fords?'

Milli rattled on, telling Pa all the details. He nodded and smiled and asked the occasional question to keep her going.

'And tell Pa your news, Callie.' Milli beamed as Caroline fought the urge to yawn.

'I start work at Hereford Downs, the Cunningham farm, tomorrow.' She moved the curly gut around on her plate, feeling a childishness come over her.

'Well, that's great news, Princess. Why the sad face?' Pa always brought out the self-pity in her. 'Has your big sister been bossin you again?' He said it with exaggerated seriousness. 'Do I need to have a word with Queenie?'

'Pa,' Milli warned, and Caroline's self-pity gradually shifted to delight as Pa continued to sook her up.

'She didn't even ask me about it. Just went and talked with Mrs Cunningham and organised everything. How am I ever supposed to be a responsible adult with her doin everything for me?'

Pa reached out and brushed Caroline's cheek softly with his hand. 'My poor little princess. You shouldn't even have to work. Don't these people know you're royalty?'

Caroline laughed and shook her head. 'They're crazy.'

'Pa, stop sookin her. She starts tomorrow. Her ride will be here at eight o'clock,' Milli said, half amused at the scene unfolding in front of her.

'Tomorrow?' Pa asked in dramatic disbelief, and Caroline nodded as though to say *see what I mean?* 'And eight o'clock. These people are barbarians. My princess will still be getting her beauty sleep.' Caroline laughed.

'Womba, the two of yas,' Milli said, getting up to collect the plates and shaking her head. When her back was turned Pa slipped a bit of fat from the curly gut down to Star, who took his time sniffing and licking, and then just as she turned back the dog started chewing into it.

'Pa!' Milli cried out. 'Don't be wasting that meat.' Milli and Pa locked eyes until finally Milli broke into laughter; her whole body shook. 'I dunno what I'm gonna do with you two? Bloody dreamers, the both of yas.'

The girls finished the dishes and retired to their bedroom, which held nothing much more than two small mattresses and a radio. As was their evening ritual, they turned on the radio and tuned in to *Dad and Dave*. Usually they would chuckle along together, but tonight Caroline's mind was on the new job.

She hadn't felt nervous before starting work at the Armstrong property, but now she knew what it was like, working for wealthy white people, she felt a lot more on edge. There would be more retreating into herself to ignore all the nasty things said about her people. Could she handle it, or would she snap? Milli fell asleep quickly next to her, but she stayed awake, thinking about tomorrow.

Chapter 10

Caroline woke to the sound of men chatting outside. One voice belonged to Pa and the other she didn't recognise – he spoke slowly, deeply and confidently. The camp was always chaos in the morning, people yelling and kids playing and screaming, but this morning was different. Everyone else was quiet except for Pa and this man. She rubbed her eyes and peeked through the cracks in the tin shack to see her grandfather by the fire, swirling his billy tea and looking up at a white man in riding boots, jeans and an Akubra hat. A farmer.

Oh, no.

She'd slept in, clearly. It was Mrs Cunningham's son. She leaped out of bed and found the dress Milli had prepared for her to wear neatly pressed and folded over the back of a chair. It was a plain calico dress but was missing a button. Then she'd remembered Milli waking her earlier that morning, before dawn, with reminders to sew it back on. Caroline had promised she would, then she'd rolled over and gone back to sleep. The button was missing right at the bra line. She panicked, thinking of Milli's wrath that evening if she disappointed Mrs Cunningham on her first day at work on Hereford Downs and started digging through a pile of clothes and rags in the corner of the shack, eventually finding a piece of material that would work as a makeshift apron. She wrapped it around herself and patted it down. It looked ridiculous, but better than a gaping hole at her bra line where the button was missing. It would just have to do.

She wiped her face with some water from the bucket, pulled back her hair and took another peek out. The Cunningham man was still talking to Pa and patting Star around the ears. Her stomach filled with dread. She pulled on her shoes, then she left the shack and went straight to the passenger side of the Cunningham man's truck, eyeing Pa as she passed him. He gave her the look that said be careful, be smart.

'Caroline?' The Cunningham man came over and put his hand out in greeting. She didn't want to take it but could hear Milli nagging in her ear so she reached out. His hand was big and callused. He didn't smile, just nodded and opened the door for her. 'I'm Chester.'

Chester was tall with broad shoulders and a strong jawline. His shirt was tucked into his trousers but dirty along the sleeves and she could smell diesel or some other mechanical substance on him. When he looked at her his blue eyes softened for a moment, kindly, and her uneasiness abated.

As she got in, she looked around the vehicle. He got in the other side. The smell of diesel mingled with scents of dirt, sweat and cattle. It all felt very awkward. He smiled at her. 'Ready to go?'

She looked back at Pa and Star, and wanted to tell him the truth: 'Hell no, I'm not ready'. She wanted to get out and go and sit by Pa or see if Bessie was awake yet. Take Star for a swim down at the creek, catch yabbies or play with the little kids and pretend that adulthood and responsibility were not looming. She did not want to go to Hereford Downs. She did not want to be in this truck with this smelly man with his giant callused hands. And she did not want to work for Mrs Cunningham. Instead she nodded silently.

'Alright then,' Chester said, turning the motor on and pushing the truck into gear.

Mrs Cunningham was waiting out the front of the house when they arrived, hands on hips with a scowl across her face. It was not the welcome Caroline wanted, but it was the welcome she expected.

'You're late,' Mrs Cunningham announced as Caroline got out of the truck and walked towards her new boss, a formidable woman with short blonde curly hair and a long white linen dress. No colour, no make-up and no jewellery except simple pearl earrings that spoke of wealth and solemnity. 'Caroline Forrest?'

'Yes, ma'am,' Caroline replied, looking down at her feet and feeling the world around her. She could hear Chester's footsteps moving away towards the shed she'd noticed on the way in, and another man calling out to him. She could make out the sound of horses neighing and dogs barking, chooks and a rooster. There was a slight breeze, cold air, the sun still creating long shadows in the morning light, and the smell of musk coming from this woman standing in front of her.

'I'm Mrs Cunningham. I met your sister at church yesterday. She said that you worked on the Armstrong property.'

Now that Caroline had her bearings, she raised her chin and met the woman's gaze. Her nose was pointed and her eyes were full of expectation. 'I worked for Mrs Armstrong, but Lola came home from school so they don't need me any more.'

'Good.' Mrs Cunningham nodded. 'So you have experience running a household?' She could feel the woman sizing her up, just as Worm had done at church the day before.

'I have, ma'am. And I'm a real hard worker,' Caroline added, remembering Milli's instructions to impress. 'I can sew, iron, clean, polish, cook …' She tried to remember all the other domestic duties she'd carried out at the Armstrong property. '… garden and tend to animals.'

'Well, we'll see about that.' Mrs Cunningham started walking towards the house. 'Let's go inside so I can show you around.'

Caroline looked up the sweeping entry stairs to the largest homestead she'd ever seen. Neatly carved timber panels bordered the house and fenced in a verandah, from which palms and orchids overflowed. She felt small. This was to be her new workplace. She ignored the anger inside her that coiled up like a snake in her stomach. So much space for one family.

Mrs Cunningham took a brick-paved path around the side of the house and Caroline followed. 'Guests enter from the front steps but the boys and I use this back door on a daily basis,' she explained as they made their way down the narrow path. 'You will also enter this way.' To the side of the house was a sheltered herb garden with a manicured patch of lawn and white steel outdoor setting. Caroline studied the herbs, already planning to ask if she could take some cuttings one day, recognising a few varieties that she didn't yet have back home on the camp. They reached the back door and Mrs Cunningham scuffed her feet on the door mat. Caroline did likewise.

'You can place your belongings in here.' Her new boss gestured to a small room immediately inside the back entrance. Men's boots lined the edges of the floor and dark leather coats and Akubra hats hung on a row of hooks. The room smelt of concrete, steel and damp leather. Mrs Cunningham turned to the other side of the hallway and opened a door onto another room. 'This is the laundry.' Three large piles of sheets and clothing occupied the floor space. 'I feel like I spend my entire life in here.' The air was warm and foggy with steam.

'I washed plenty at the Armstrongs' property, ma'am,' Caroline offered but her new boss didn't seem to hear her and kept moving through the house.

'Come along.'

Caroline slipped on the wet tiled floor but caught herself on the sink ledge, thankful that Mrs Cunningham didn't see. She followed her into a quiet courtyard overgrown with ivy, caladium, African violets and other exotic plants Caroline had never seen before. At the centre of the courtyard was a fishpond, its surface partly covered in lilies. Bright orange goldfish wriggled their way up to the surface and puckered their lips. It felt like something out of a movie. Caroline couldn't believe people lived in places like this so close to her, Milli and Pa on the camp.

'I'd like you to help me with watering the plants in here. It gets terribly dry around the yard, especially in the summer, and so I like to keep this space green with the laundry water. It's cold now, but come summer this place is like an oasis.'

Mrs Cunningham turned, went down a corridor and into the first main room of the house. 'This is the kitchen where we have breakfast and lunch.' Mrs Cunningham motioned for Caroline to enter. It was a cosy room with a stove to one side and a range of brightly coloured kitchen appliances. Although Caroline had none

143

of these on the yumba she recognised the toaster and kettle from when she worked at the Armstrongs' place. Caroline imagined how comfortable life would be if she didn't have to cart the water up from the communal tap to the shack every day. And if they had electricity to power things, rather than just the old kerosene lamp – they could have a proper light and maybe even a hairdryer so she could style her hair like she'd seen on the ladies in the magazines Milli brought back from the pub. Bessie would go crazy in a place like this. She could imagine her friend getting into everything and causing absolute chaos.

Caroline followed Mrs Cunningham into a grand room with high ceilings and a long table covered in a smooth white cloth. 'This is the formal dining. We have dinner in here of an evening.' The table was adorned with fine china, sparkling silver and crystal glassware. Caroline immediately felt nervous she would break something and pushed aside an image of Milli's disapproving face.

'If we have guests, this is also where we would serve them.' Caroline counted ten settings. 'When we have guests, I invite them to have a seat in the parlour before and after our meals.' She followed Mrs Cunningham further to the front of the house. The parlour faced south and it was the first room guests would enter upon ascending the front steps. She could see the horse stables through the plantation shutters. The room had a fireplace, couches with cushions and a bookcase.

'I would like you to, on occasion, serve when we have guests. Did you serve at Mrs Armstrong's?' The Armstrongs were always having rowdy parties. It was the part of the job that Caroline hated most. The men would become intolerable after a few glasses of rum or whiskey. And there was always a never-ending pile of dishes to clean late into the night after the party ended.

'Yes, Mrs Cunningham, I served at the Armstrongs'.'

'Good, then I won't need to teach you the basics of serving and dining.'

She continued to follow her new boss to the western side of the house and down a long hallway. Caroline had never seen a house as spacious and comfortable as that of the Cunninghams. It was much larger than the Armstrongs' homestead, packed with ornaments, and there were paintings, old photographs and tapestries on the walls.

'I have four boys, which I'm sure you learned from speaking with your older sister?' She didn't wait for a response. 'The youngest two share this room.' She stopped at the entrance. Caroline looked inside. There was a single bed on each side. Each bed had a shelf at the foot upon which lay an assortment of small figurines. On the opposite side of the room, a timber-panelled glass door provided a view across the paddock. Under the window lay a desk with two chairs on either side. The desk was covered with note pads and pens. 'The twins are at boarding school in the city now. Tom and David. They'll be home in a few months. And trust me, you'll know it! Messy little critters and such big eaters.'

Mrs Cunningham walked on and opened the door to the adjacent room. 'This is where Chester and Simon sleep.' Similarly, there were two single beds, but without the ornaments. On one side of the room, a desk was piled with books and paper. The desk on the other side was empty bar a single piece of paper and pencil. It was some kind of sketch but she couldn't see clearly from the entrance.

'Come along,' Mrs Cunningham called, continuing down the hallway. 'This is where Mr Cunningham and I sleep.' It was the only room she had seen so far with the hint of a woman's presence. Above the dresser hung a painting of the long driveway up to the homestead, bordered on either side by white and pink roses. There was also a bottle of perfume and a crystal platter with a scattering of gold earrings, diamonds and strings of pearls.

Caroline followed her new boss further down the hallway until they reached a door at the end and stepped outside on to a wide verandah. It stretched along the western side of the house and she could see now that all the bedroom doors she had just peeped through led to this verandah. How lucky the boys were, she thought, to be able to step outside from their bedrooms and take in this view. It stretched for miles around, across the grain sheds and paddocks of wheat. A herd of cattle was scattered to the south where the grass was greener and a line of trees could just be made out in the distance. That would be the upper stretches of the Goorungah Creek.

'This property has been in Mr Cunningham's family for four generations now,' Mrs Cunningham said, looking across the fields. 'My eldest son, Chester, will be the fourth to inherit this land.' Caroline thought of Pa Quincey and his skinny body curled up by the fireplace back on the camp. 'I need you to honour this family and our traditions, Caroline, by doing honest work here. Do you hear?'

'Yes, Mrs Cunningham.'

'If I suspect you're slacking off, or worse, if I find you sneaking off with my belongings, there will be consequences, do you hear?'

Caroline simply nodded to hide the sick feeling rising in her stomach. This woman was intolerable. How dare she suggest Caroline was a thief? Once again, Caroline felt a rage burning inside, towards Mrs Cunningham and towards Milli for not consulting her about this job.

'Yes?'

'Yes, Mrs Cunningham.' It was so cold moments earlier but now Caroline could feel the sweat beneath her arms.

Caroline breathed a sigh of relief when she was finally left alone in the laundry to fold the washing. For the next few hours she cleaned and scrubbed and followed Mrs Cunningham's directions until she was so exhausted she needed to sit. She found a place out the back near the water tank where it was cool, took a gulp of water from the hose nearby and sat to rest for a moment. It was past noon and the boys would be back soon from rounding up the cattle. Mrs Cunningham said it was her responsibility to serve lunch.

She could hear trucks coming up the driveway so she went inside. The men were sweaty and covered in mud and she watched in dismay as they threw their dirty clothes and boots around the areas she'd just cleaned. They sat in the kitchen, the informal dining area, and waited to be served. She was completely invisible to them. They ate and slurped and talked as though she didn't exist. Even though she'd worked for three years at the Armstrongs' place, she still never got used to this part of the job. They eat, we work. It was only Chester who made eye contact once and said thank you – the others went about their chewing and slurping without a single murmur of thanks.

When they were gone, she returned to folding the washing. At least here she could look out across the fields and be free of their presence and expectation. Here she could watch the sun slowly lower to the horizon and wait for her ride back to the camp.

'That's enough, Caroline.' She jumped back to reality. Mrs Cunningham had crept up behind her, startling her. 'You can go now. Chester is waiting out the front.'

Caroline was exhausted. She'd felt the time would never come. She went to fetch her things but Mrs Cunningham held out a bag.

'Here.' Caroline took it. 'Some sausages. They won't last, so you take them.'

Caroline thanked Mrs Cunningham, delighted that she'd be able to present them to Milli later, but then immediately felt suspicious. Women like Mrs Cunningham don't give away things without strings attached.

'Are you sure?' Caroline asked.

'Don't you remember the pastor's sermon yesterday? He said we must be generous to those with less.'

As Chester drove her home, she felt a different kind of exhaustion. It was more than physical exhaustion. She wanted the arms of someone who cared for her deeply wrapped tightly around her. Milli, Pa, her mum, her dad. They drove in silence along the back roads, past the wheat fields, until they got close to the camp and he looked across at her. 'It's here, right?' he asked.

'Yep.' Nearly home, she thought to herself. They passed Uncle Kevin walking along the side of the road towards town. Chester waved and Uncle Kevin squinted his eyes, seemingly to try to identify the driver. He didn't wave back.

'We don't get whitefullas along here very often,' Caroline said, not knowing why she cared for this man's feelings when he was clearly oblivious to hers. It was only partly true though. They did get whitefullas along that road, but it was mainly drunk ones on a Saturday night, driving like hooligans, coming over to scream and shout at the residents. Or the cops or government people coming to do 'welfare' checks. They continued driving and passed a bunch of kids pulling tin cans along with string, cheering and laughing among themselves. They stopped when the car passed, just as Uncle Kevin had done, and peered into the driver's seat.

'Was that your pa this morning?' Chester asked. She looked across at him. Why did he care?

'By the fire?'

'Yeah, the old man with the dog. Was that your father?'

'No, he's my grandfather. Pa Quincey. My parents died in an accident a long time ago.' She said it matter-of-factly and looked out the window as they came onto the opening to the yumba. The fire was going but Pa Quincey wasn't there. He must still be at work. She could see Aunty Nettie hanging washing by the front of her shack and searched for Bessie but she was nowhere to be seen.

'I'm sorry to hear that.' Chester stopped the truck. 'Mum said to come back tomorrow and get you. Is that okay with you?' Mrs Cunningham hadn't said anything to Caroline and she was pleased that Chester had passed on this information otherwise she wouldn't have known what to expect, and Milli would be up in arms.

'That's okay.' Caroline nodded as she got out and closed the door. 'I'll be here,' she said through the open window and turned to walk towards the shack, as she heard him start the truck again and drive away. Strange man. She wasn't sure what to make of that interaction.

'Go'orn, git!' Aunty Nettie screamed at the kids. 'Youse wanna floggin? I said git! Go get me some water.'

Caroline was pleased Chester was already out of earshot.

She found Milli out the back of their shack boiling up big pots on the fire. 'How'd it go?' she called out before Caroline could duck inside. She was desperate to lay down in her own company and enjoy some silence for a few moments before dinner.

'Good,' she yelled back, pausing to see how badly her sister wanted her company.

'Come over here, I need your help.'

Caroline turned from the shack, giving up on the idea of rest, and went to help her sister. They had collected branches of leaves from the melaleuca trees along the creek a few days ago and now they were ready to steam. Over time Milli had perfected the art of distillation and her products were in demand. Her oil was better than any treatment you could find at the chemist; its antiseptic healing properties were perfect for disinfecting cuts and scratches, and if you put a small dab on a cloth and wiped down the kitchen benches, it was great at keeping away nasty germs, better than any detergent you could find at the store *and* cheaper. She sold it to the camp residents for a quarter of the price she sold it to the chemist and other locals, and since they'd started using it around the camp, the number of people with colds and the flu had noticeably declined.

'Here, you keep stirring while I drop more leaves in.' She handed Caroline the large stirring rod. 'Do it slowly.' The oil formed on the surface. She loved the smell of the leaves but always feared the boiling water would splash on her and so she took the rod cautiously.

'Tell me more. How'd it go?' Milli asked, ripping the leaves into smaller pieces and placing them in the pot.

'It's okay.' Caroline's gaze remained fixed on the bubbling mixture. Her mind was tired. 'Can you hurry up?'

'It won't harm you, Callie. Just keep a good hold of that stirrin rod. So, what are they like? What's the house like?'

'Big.' She envied the Cunninghams with their long verandahs but would never want to live there. She felt happy to be in her little shack with Pa and Milli. Even if she did have to put up with Aunty Nettie screaming at her kids every five minutes and Milli's constant nagging. 'They have an indoor courtyard with a fishpond.'

'Holy dooly!'

Caroline immediately regretted adding this detail. Milli was getting excited; she was picking the leaves off another branch.

'And the Cunninghams? How are they? Hold it steady, would you?'

'They seem alright.' Caroline felt uncomfortable at Hereford Downs but she didn't want Milli to worry. Her sister had enough on her shoulders without having to worry about her at work. She felt the same working at the Cunninghams as she did at the Armstrongs, like she wanted to let a crystal champagne glass slip and smash on the floor, but the energy required to deal with the anticipated consequences made the act insurmountable.

Milli reached for a glass jar and held it carefully over the surface, gently tilting it so the oils flowed in. 'Mm … very fine yield today. And what about Mrs Cunningham? She seemed lovely the other day.'

'She's nice,' Caroline lied. Mrs Cunningham gave her the creeps. 'She liked that I arrived with my apron on.'

Milli's eyes squinted with suspicion. 'You didn't sew that button back on, did you?'

Caroline couldn't help laughing and eventually Milli gave in and chuckled along with her sister, shaking her head. 'You're hopeless, Caroline. You do realise part of the job involves sewing and mending clothes?'

'Yes, Milli, relax! It was fine. I just put an apron on.'

'Tell me you remembered to say "thank you" to the son ... What's his name?'

'Chester.' She watched as Milli filled the jar, held it high to assess the quality of the liquid, smiled and screwed a lid on top.

'Did you thank Chester for giving you a lift?'

Good Lord, she wasn't going to let up. 'Yes. I thanked him,' Caroline said, turning her attention to her veggie garden. 'He'll be here same time tomorrow to pick me up.'

'Good.' Milli reached over to take the stirring rod from Caroline. 'Get me some more water and then go and get some rest. You'll need it for tomorrow.'

Caroline took a bucket, too tired to argue, and went towards the tap. On the way she passed Aunty Nettie, who was changing a nappy on one of the babies out the front of her shack. The other younger ones had left after being scolded for carrying on and Caroline figured they were down at the creek. When the kids were told to go and get water from the tap, they usually used it as an opportunity to spend some time swinging from the trees into the water before returning.

'Callie, who's that gubbie come get you this morning?' Aunty Nettie called out, as the baby cried from the brief shock of exposure to the cold. Caroline put down her bucket and went to help Aunty Nettie pin the cloth at the side.

'Chester Cunningham. I got a job over on Hereford Downs,' Caroline started to explain, knowing where these questions were leading.

'Where's Hereford Downs?' Aunty Nettie asked. The baby gurgled happily, content now that he had a dry nappy. She pulled a jumper over his head and some pants up around his waist.

Melaleuca

'Over on the north side. Long way. That's why Mrs Cunningham gets her son to come give me a lift.'

'They need more people to work over there?' Here it comes. Aunty Nettie was forever trying to get Caroline to pull Bessie out of her wayward ways.

'Maybe. I can ask.' She got to her feet and reached for the bucket, as Clarence came along. Caroline had heard he'd got a job on one of the stations nearby as a jackaroo.

'My Bessie could do with a job, you know, Callie. We all gotta help each other out here. My folks helped your parents, you know? When they had nothing, my folks stepped in and got your parents that job.' Aunty Nettie stopped, realising that it was the job that had killed her parents, and looked away. 'Just try, will you, Callie? I'm worried about her.'

'I'll try, Aunty.' Caroline was worried about Bessie too.

It was late into the evening and they were finished their supper and washing up the plates in buckets warmed with water from the fire. Pa Quincey was too tired to join them that evening and had already retired to his room with Star. Caroline brought the bucket of water she'd fetched earlier into the shack.

'Be careful when you're on the properties, okay? I've heard some awful stories bout our mob workin in those big old homesteads,' Milli warned as she reached across for Caroline's empty plate. She would never say such things in front of Pa.

Caroline hadn't mentioned any of her apprehensions about Mrs Cunningham to her sister, but there must've been something in the way she gave her report that afternoon that had made her sister worry. 'Yeah, like what?'

'You really want me to tell you, Callie?' Sometimes her sister got like this. Usually when she'd had a big day at the pub and her nerves were spent. It was like she needed an outlet for some of her own rage and fear.

'I'm not a little girl any more. You don't have to protect me.' Milli was always trying to make her scared, like she wasn't already scared enough about life and what she was up against.

'We both know that's a lie. If it wasn't for me, Callie, you would've been picked up by the welfare and placed in a home or raised by whitefullas after Mum and Dad passed.'

Caroline had had enough. 'I think you would've liked that,' she challenged.

'What?' Her sister let the plates fall to the bottom of the bucket and sat up to look at Caroline. 'What would I have liked?'

'Me being raised by whitefullas. You're always telling me I have to talk proper around them, and behave myself, like they're better than us. You're a different person around them, Milli. Usin all those up-town words.'

'You really think that, Callie?' She stood up. 'You take that back.'

Caroline looked down, tired and ashamed. Her sister meant well even if the delivery was poorly delivered and timed.

'I just want you to get by, Callie. I want you to stay close to me. Family should stick together. The only reason I keep naggin bout being nice to Mrs Cunningham and Mrs Ford is because they the ones we need to have by our side to get by. They the ones with the bungoo, girl. If we don't do these little odd jobs for them around the place, and be nice, and smile sweetly, and tell them their babies are cute, you really think they gonna pay us and look after us?'

'I know.' Caroline studied her sister's face in the dim light of the kerosene lamp. Milli was darker skinned than her and the bags underneath her eyes were deep and dark. Too many years of worrying about her and Pa Quincey, and, unlike Callie, Milli missed their parents. Callie was too young to remember them, and instead of grief she just felt guilty for not having any memories.

'Don't worry, Milli. I'm gonna be fine. And I will be careful.' She patted her sister's back and Milli turned to hug her. They held each other for longer than normal and all the tension Caroline had been holding released. 'So, you don't think baby Archie is cute?'

'What are you talking about?' Milli held Caroline at arm's length where she could see her face in the twilight.

'You just said that you tell them their babies are cute to keep them onside.'

Milli stifled a giggle. 'Stop talking rot, Callie. I take that part back – lil fulla is gorgeous.'

After finishing washing up, the sisters fed Star, checked on Pa, then went to bed, turning on the radio to listen quietly to another episode of *Dad and Dave*. Once more Milli fell asleep quickly, but Caroline stayed awake listening to the sounds of the camp. A baby crying, an owl hooting, Aunty Nettie hissing at some kid rebelling against sleep. A tap at the side of the shack …?

Chapter 11

Caroline tried to ignore it but there it was again. Another tap. She sat up on her mattress and peeked out the slit in the tin. She could just make out the shape of her skinny friend a few feet back. 'Bessie! That you?' Caroline hissed through the opening. 'Go away. I'm trying to sleep.'

Bessie came closer and whispered, 'I'm going to meet Worm and Gappy. Come with me.'

'What?! No way, Bessie. Don't be silly. Go to bed.' Caroline glanced back as she felt Milli stir on the mattress next to her. 'You're gonna wake Milli and then all hell'll break loose, Bessie, now git.'

'Okay. Fine! I'll go by myself then.' She could hear the steps soften into the distance and laid back down to try to sleep. But she couldn't rest. How could she leave her best friend to go spend time with those no-goods all by herself? Moving as slowly as possible, careful not to wake Milli, Caroline took off her nightie, put on her day dress and draped a coat around her shoulders. Then she slid on some shoes and left the shack to chase after her friend, who was already well down the road back to town.

'Bessie, what the bloody hell do you think you're doing? It's freezin out here.' She caught up to her friend and pulled at her hand. The path was dimly lit by moonlight.

Bessie ripped her hand back and kept walking. 'You don't need to come, Callie. If you don't want to have fun, just go back to bed then.'

'I can't let you hang out with those blokes by yourself, Bessie. They're no good and you know it.' Bessie walked quickly ahead in the dark and Caroline hurried after her. 'Why do you want to go anyway?'

'They're fun, Caroline. And they have money. They said they'd find work for me. Isn't that what you and Mum are always going on about?' They reached the turn from the dirt camp driveway onto the bitumen road and Bessie stopped abruptly. The night was so quiet that all Caroline could hear was Bessie's breath and her own.

'Come on, Bessie. Come back to the camp. This is silly,' Caroline pleaded, but she could see that her words were having no impact on her friend as she stopped and looked down the road towards town. 'You remember what they were like yesterday. They're gross. And they're so much older than us!' She stomped her foot, trying to get her friend to take her concerns seriously.

'No, they're not,' Bessie said, turning to face her, and for a minute Caroline thought she might be getting through. At least she was looking at her and responding. 'Gappy's not old. He's only twenty.'

'Yeah, but how old is Worm?' A flicker of doubt crossed Bessie's face. 'Come on. At least thirty. What would Clarence say if he knew you were hangin out with some bloke so much older than us?' Caroline continued to beg as a pair of car headlights emerged in the distance. 'And your dad – what would Uncle Kevin say if he knew you were creepin out to see William Gawlor?'

'Stop it, Caroline,' Bessie growled, as the car slowed down and stopped on the road next to them. It didn't need to pull to the side. There would be no other cars passing this time of night. Bessie's entire demeanour changed as the car slowed down. She put one hand on her hip and tossed back her hair.

'Oh, look here, who do we have? Little Miss Soup Kitchen?' Gappy teased, winding down his window and leering out at Caroline. 'You didn't tell me you were bringing a friend, Bessie Boo.' Bessie went around to the other side and got straight in the car, and Caroline was left standing there. 'Well, you comin or not?' Gappy asked, reaching behind him to open the back door for her. Caroline could see Worm in the driver's seat. He hadn't said a word, just kept looking straight ahead, tapping the steering wheel impatiently.

'Just go, she's bloody boring!' Bessie sang out and Caroline was torn between running back to the camp or reaching in and slapping her friend for being so reckless and mean.

'Don't worry, Caroline. We'll take good care of your friend,' Worm said, leaning across Gappy, grinning widely, and then turning around to hand Bessie a bottle of something. That was all Caroline needed to decide. She reached for the car door and slid into the back seat alongside Bessie, who was already drinking fast, and Worm swung the car around and turned the Rolling Stones's '(I Can't Get No) Satisfaction' up on the radio.

'Where are you taking us?' Caroline called out over the music as Worm drove south along Main Street. Caroline thought maybe he was taking them to the city, but then he took a right turn into the industrial estate about a mile out of town. Caroline had never been to this area before and as he drove on she tried to estimate how long it would take them to walk back to the camp if they couldn't get a lift home later on. Bessie didn't care – she was too busy laughing and drinking.

Melaleuca

'You'll see,' Worm said, looking back across to where they sat in the back. He stopped the car near some bushes in front of the silos, got out and told them to follow him. He walked along a narrow path that closely passed one of the enormous grain sheds. It was dark and Caroline tried not to trip, immensely regretting her decision to accompany her friend. If she asked to go back, they'd taunt her and tell her to walk. It was best to go for the ride, let them party and tire, and then she'd get her friend back home to safety.

They walked along about two hundred yards until they reached a timber hut in a clearing behind the grain shed. Worm shone a torch onto it. 'Come on, ladies. Welcome to the Worm Hole.'

Caroline looked around for something to use as a weapon if either of the men got out of hand and spotted a thick branch to one side. That could work.

'Come inside,' Worm called out. 'We can have some privacy here.' Bessie was already inside, and Gappy stood by the entrance holding a beer out for Caroline. She took it, not wanting to cause any offence and risk pissing off Worm, then went inside.

The floors and walls were made of rough, dry timber, and the ceiling was tin, held up by huge old wooden beams. It was probably some old farmer's place, long deserted. There were cobwebs up in one corner and posters of near-naked women and bands on the walls. A coffee table in the middle of the room was covered in empty beer bottles and overflowing ash trays, and a dirty green shag rug covered the middle of the room. Worm stood in one corner next to a record player, and Bessie took up on the sofa and started leafing through a magazine. Caroline went to sit next to her, but Worm stepped in front. 'That's my spot. Gappy, get her a seat.'

She took the stool that Gappy put out and he sat down on the one next to her. 'How'd you get the bruise?' Caroline asked Gappy, trying to make conversation. She'd noticed it at church yesterday. 'Get into a fight down at the pub?'

He shook his head, warning her it wasn't a good topic to touch on, glancing up at Worm, who was busy flicking through the records, and she knew immediately where the black eye had come from.

'Right. Best mates, hey?' She didn't wait for his answer. 'So, you're from the city. How long you in Goorungah for?'

'Depends how long Worm needs me?' Gappy said and took a sip of his beer.

'What exactly is it you do for him?' Caroline asked, instinctively lowering her voice.

'What would you like to listen to, Miss Soup Kitchen?' Worm called out from the corner.

'The Beatles?' Caroline suggested, figuring if she was going to spend time in this smelly den, she may as well spend it listening to music she enjoyed. 'A Hard Day's Night' came on, much to Caroline's surprise; she hadn't thought Worm would oblige.

She took a swig of her beer hoping that maybe the evening wouldn't be so bad but she felt the same wary suspicion that came over her when Mrs Cunningham gave her the bag of sausages that afternoon. This man wanted something. She just wasn't sure yet what it was.

'I saw you with that Cunningham bloke today,' Worm said, taking a gulp of his own beer and dealing some cards. 'What are you doing with him?'

She wanted to tell him it was none of his business, but again, she was wary of causing offence. The sooner Bessie got this recklessness out of her system, they'd go back to the camp, and tomorrow Caroline would have the moral high ground to scold her about putting them in such a compromising situation. For now, though, Caroline needed to keep things calm.

'I'm working on the Cunningham property. I started today and Chester gave me a lift,' she explained. 'He'll be back early in the morning, so we can't stay late.'

'Cunninghams, hey? Snobby pastoralists,' Worm said, taking the bottle from Bessie. 'I seen them around town. Chester comes into the pub from time to time. Reckons he's a big shot because his old man owns Hereford Downs. Why would you wanna work for them? I can give you some work.'

Bessie laughed as though she knew what he was talking about.

'Thanks, but I'm good.'

'I'm keen,' Bessie said. 'What kind of work?'

Worm picked up his hand of cards and ran his eyes from left to right. 'We'll see,' he said, patting her thigh.

Caroline picked up her hand and placed a card down. She couldn't think about card-game strategy now, all she could think about was safely getting home. If she played a few rounds of cards, let Worm win a round or two, then maybe he'd drive them home before the sun came up and everything would be okay. She'd slide into bed next to Milli and be up in time for Chester to get her for work. How the hell had she gotten herself into this situation? She threw a ten of hearts down, took a gulp of beer and tried not to look at Worm's hand on Bessie's thigh.

'It might involve physical effort,' she heard Worm say to Bessie as she studied the cards. Her gaze was already drunken, which made Caroline want to take the bottle off her, but she was hesitant to create a stir. Gappy played his hand, and then Bessie followed suit.

'She looks pretty fit to me,' Gappy said. Caroline's head felt heavy. 'I reckon Bessie Boo could be a real game-changer for us, Wormie.'

'What kind of woorr—k?' Caroline said, struggling to get the words out, as Worm and Gappy glanced across at her and then gave each other a knowing look and burst into laughter.

'Uh oh, Bessie,' Worm teased. 'Looks like your friend might be interested after all. You alright over there, Miss Soup Kitchen?'

'What'd you do, Worm?' Bessie looked across, concerned.

'Don't worry, honey. We just gave her something to help her relax. She was a bit uptight, you gotta admit? We're just having fun here and she was totally killing the buzz. You want some too?'

'What'd you give m—' Caroline couldn't hold up her head any more. Her neck had gone all rubbery and her body felt heavy and floppy as it slid down to the floor. Too exhausted to resist, all energy having left her, she laid down on the shaggy rug, trying to keep her eyes open and watching Worm as he leaned over and kissed Bessie.

'Caroline.' Someone was shaking her. It was Bessie. 'Caroline, wake up.' She sat up and looked around, head throbbing. The hut was only dimly lit but still she squinted and held her hands against the light.

'What happened?' Caroline asked, as Bessie pulled her up.

'Nothing. You're fine.'

Caroline stumbled to her feet, Bessie on one side and Gappy on the other. 'What time is it?' Worm was passed out on the sofa. She felt her clothing. Everything was still intact.

'Come on. It's time to go home.' Bessie was pulling her up. 'We gotta get home before Mum and Milli wake up. Gap's going to drive us. Come on. Hurry up.' Caroline let Bessie pull her out of the shed and guide her back down the path past the grain silos. 'Don't worry, Callie. You're okay. We'll have you home soon.'

When they got back to the car and Gappy switched on the lights, Caroline noticed that Bessie's dress was unbuttoned.

'What happened, Bessie? Did he hurt you?'

'No.' She giggled and looked across at Gappy, who stared ahead blankly. 'He definitely didn't hurt me.' Caroline leaned up against the car for support and felt her body heave as it retched out her stomach contents onto the ground.

They reached the turn-off to the camp and made Gappy stop halfway down the road. 'Thanks, Gap,' Bessie said, and leaned over and gave him a kiss on the cheek. Caroline, who was too shocked and disoriented to make anything of it, got out of the car and stumbled back towards the camp.

'Get some sleep, Callie,' Bessie said, stroking the side of Caroline's cheek as she guided her back towards her shack. Dawn was breaking and the camp still slept as the fire smouldered softly. 'And don't tell anyone.' She turned and ran back towards her place. Caroline was too tired and confused to be angry and so she crept in to where Milli was still snoring softy, crawled onto her mattress and fell into a troubled, dark sleep where she drowned in her own vomit, over and over again.

Chester was waiting for her when she emerged from the shack later that morning, dazed and severely hungover, keen to escape Milli's watchful gaze. She didn't think her sister had heard anything but Milli knew Caroline so well that she wouldn't be surprised if she somehow knew how she felt. If she did, she was keeping uncharacteristically quiet about it.

'Now, make sure you be polite today. And thank Chester for the lift. You're lucky that fulla comes out here and picks you up.

No way those Armstrongs would've been that kind,' Milli said as she left for work.

For a moment, Caroline considered confiding in her and telling her everything that had happened at the disgusting 'Worm Hole' the evening before. But what would she say? It was Caroline who chose to go with strange men, Worm and Gappy no less, drink beer and play cards. She did this all of her own volition because she didn't want silly little Bessie to wind up in trouble. It was her decision, and she needed to own it. After all, more responsibility was what she'd been asking Milli for constantly over the last few months. So what if Worm slipped something in to her drink. So what if Bessie may have had sex with Worm. No big deal. She'd give Bessie the dressing down of her life later that day and that would be it. Done. Dealt with. But in spite of her resolve, pushing away of the fear, she knew she had seen true darkness last night and that she and Bessie had been lucky to escape it.

She walked over towards the ute, squinting against the bright morning light, warmed by the sight of her grandfather as he sat by the fireplace. 'You're spoilin that dog, Pa!' she said, motioning towards the enormous bone the muscular little hound was chewing with unabated enthusiasm. She figured Pa had brought Star home a treat from the abattoir.

'Not me,' Pa mumbled, as he stoked the coals. 'Chester brought it around for her.'

Caroline looked suspiciously from the dog to the ute. 'Chester?'

The old man patted his dingo dog behind the ears as he grizzled and tore at the bone.

Caroline shook her head in wonder and went to the passenger side of the ute. When she opened the door to get in she realised someone else was in the passenger seat. It was Chester's brother, who she'd briefly seen at the kitchen table the day before – Simon.

'Good morning,' he said, sliding across, making way for her. She said hello and got in next to him, pulling the door shut.

Chester leaned over to explain. 'We just need to go past the post office. You don't mind do you, Caroline?' Caroline shrugged. Why would she mind? If they were paying her, she didn't care, and the extra bit of time might help her shake off the groggy fatigue that hung over her. He drove down the driveway, and once again she felt the entire camp watching them.

'So, who's the eldest?' Caroline asked to break the awkward silence.

'Are you serious?' The intensity of Chester's reaction surprised her. He really cared what she thought? 'I'm the eldest.'

'Yeah, yeah, and the strongest. And the best looking,' Simon added sarcastically, nudging his brother. 'But not the smartest.'

'Okay, okay.' She chuckled. She still felt nauseous but her mood was lightening somewhat. Chester turned the corner and they drove down Main Street. It was busy as usual on a weekday morning with people coming in and out of shops. She saw Mrs Ford from church with baby Archie, and slightly ducked when she saw Mrs Armstrong with Lola. Not that she was on bad terms with them, but Lola was just so sickeningly up herself. They parked in front of the post office and Simon got out, saying he wouldn't be long.

'He's nervous,' Chester explained unnecessarily, as he watched his brother glide up the stairs to the post office.

'Oh yeah. Why's that?' Caroline asked, rubbing her forehead, wondering if Mrs Cunningham had any paracetamol. She didn't care about Simon, but she also didn't want to appear rude.

'He's been waiting for a letter from the university down in Brisbane for weeks now. He wants to study law. Crazy, if you ask me. But hey, like I said, he's the smart one.' He looked across and smiled. It was the first time he'd smiled at her and she noticed his eyes sparkle with warmth. 'Do you like music?' It was a question out of the blue, and he laughed at himself, making Caroline wonder if *he* was the nervous one.

'Sure, I like music.' It might soothe her pounding headache and lessen the obligation to make conversation.

'Let's see.' He twisted the knob to find a signal, tuning past the static and settling for a moment on some mournful country song. 'Oh, that's terrible.' He rolled the dial further and Caroline noticed his hands again. Tough and callused, yes. But also strong and capable, the hands of a farmer. A more joyful song came on and Chester started moving to the rhythm. His big grin made her smile.

'What's this?'

'I don't know, but I like it.' He turned it down slightly. 'So how'd you go with Mum yesterday? She can be a bit bossy sometimes.'

'She's nice.' Caroline wasn't about to tell him that she agreed with his assessment. 'Your house is so big – I can see why she needs the help. I appreciate having a job.'

Simon returned, empty-handed. 'Nothing,' he said, sliding into the bench seat.

'Don't worry, it'll come,' Chester reassured him.

'Yeah, I know,' Simon said and then reached for the dial to turn the music up. This was a side of the brothers that Caroline hadn't seen the day before. They were different men when in front of their father. With the windows wound down and the music blaring, they headed towards Hereford Downs, and Caroline felt the darkness from the night before slowly lift.

Caroline spent the morning washing dishes, scrubbing floors, folding clothes, ironing clothes and chopping vegetables and meat for lunch. Mrs Cunningham had followed her every move on the first day, but today Caroline moved around the house relatively unobserved, much to her relief because she certainly didn't have the same level of stamina as the day before.

At lunch the three men piled into the small kitchen as they had the previous day, and Mrs Cunningham served them the stew Caroline had prepared earlier. Caroline continued working as they ate and she could hear their chatter from the laundry room where she folded clothes. They discussed the maintenance of various farm machines and fought about whose responsibility it would be to attend to a birthing cow. They went into detail about the weather forecast and carefully considered the optimal date for seed planting. It was all foreign to Caroline and her mind drifted off to other places. She imagined what it would be like for her, Milli and Pa to live in the Cunningham house. She could see Pa sitting up on the verandah overlooking the fields with Star dog by his side, and Milli pottering around in the kitchen preparing her oils on the stove. Caroline imagined herself lounging by the fish pond, maybe doodling, reading a book or chatting with Bessie, until she heard her name being mentioned by the voices from the kitchen. They were planning a dinner.

Mrs Cunningham was explaining to the men that her birthday was coming up and she planned to invite Mr and Mrs Armstrong over for a meal to celebrate. That would mean Caroline would have to serve them. Her body filled with dread at the thought of tending to that family again. She remembered how she'd overheard them talking about the residents of the camp, contempt in their voices, and all the times she'd had to clean around Lola as she simply sat and smirked at her. Once Lola had deliberately spilled a bowl of porridge and pretended it was an accident, but Caroline knew better. She'd watched Caroline down on her knees, cleaning up her mess. Then there was Mr Armstrong and the way his eyes followed her around the room. He had once made a grab for her but she was too quick for him and Mrs Armstrong had walked in. After that, she was careful not to be in a room alone with him.

Why couldn't Mrs Cunningham make friends with some other entitled rich pastoralists? Caroline had thought she'd left them behind and would only ever have to occasionally mingle with them at church or pass them on Main Street. When the men left again for their afternoon duties, she re-entered the kitchen where Mrs Cunningham sat at the table, eating a small bowl of stew, relaxed now that the hurricane of men had been and gone.

'They eat so much, those boys. I sometimes wonder if they'll ever stop growing.' Caroline moved towards the sink to start running warm water to wash the dishes. 'You think it's busy now. Wait until the twins come home!' Caroline noticed the almost empty saucepan of stew with satisfaction. They had enjoyed the meal she had prepared. 'How were the sausages I gave you last night?'

'Very nice, Mrs Cunningham.' She remembered her sister's instructions and added, 'And Milli said to pass on her thanks.'

'Good. This afternoon I'd like you to tend to the vegetable patch and prepare the evening meal.'

'Yes, Mrs Cunningham.'

'This will be your daily routine from here on – cleaning floors, washing and ironing clothes and preparing lunch in the morning, then tending to the garden and dinner of an afternoon.' She returned to her stew and then seemed to remember the conversation she'd just had with the men about her birthday dinner. 'You said yesterday that you served for the Armstrongs when you worked there?'

'That's right. I did on a few occasions.'

'Good. It's my birthday soon, and it's been a long time since I've celebrated anything for myself. Too much focus on these boys lately.' Mrs Cunningham continued talking to Caroline about all the sacrifices she had made raising the boys, and Caroline murmured and nodded at the right moments as she ducked around the kitchen, cleaning and washing.

'So I need you to do a very good job, do you understand?'

'Yes, ma'am.'

'Very well. You can feel free to have the rest of that stew for your lunch.'

'Thank you, ma'am.' It was almost two o'clock and Caroline was starving. She waited for Mrs Cunningham to finish her meal and scratched the remaining stew out into a bowl, wishing she had a nice piece of muntha to wipe up the last bit of gravy.

Chapter 12

Wednesday 9 February 2000

It was dark outside. Renee knew she couldn't wait to tell Mulligan what she'd discovered on the photo in Caroline Forrest's missing persons file.

'You've found what?' he said, clearing his throat. He sounded tired.

'A link from our victim to the girls who went missing. Remember? You gave me the file this afternoon.'

'Are you still at the office?'

Renee wondered whether he hadn't heard her properly.

'Sarge, the woman who we found yesterday by the creek was wearing the exact same necklace as the one Caroline Forrest is wearing in the photo in the missing persons file.' Surely that would get his attention. 'Yellow sapphire, marquise cut.'

'Mark what?'

'Marquise cut. That's the shape of the stone, like a pointed oval. It's not a common cut, and even more rare given it was a yellow sapphire.'

'Okay.' She could hear rustling in the background and imagined him getting out of his chair and sliding on his slippers. Renee took this as encouragement to proceed.

'What more can you tell me about those girls, Sarge?'

'Slow down, Taylor. You're giving me a head spin.' She heard a tap turn on, water pouring. 'I was in my senior years of high school. It must've been summer break when that happened. They were a year or two older than me. I do remember seeing them around town though. They didn't go to school. Most of the Aboriginal people dropped out when they finished primary school, especially the girls. Harsh times, back then. They lived on the Aboriginal camp.'

'And you don't know what happened to them?'

'No. I think they would've headed to the city or the Gold Coast. Bessie was a bit of a ...' he became self-conscious, struggling to find the right words, 'a bit of a run-around.'

'A run-around?'

'You know. She was known to play up a bit around town with the local fellas. My father had to throw her out of the pub a few times.'

'What about Caroline?'

'She was working up at the Cunninghams'. Good family. By all accounts Caroline was more for the quiet life than Bessie.'

Renee started. 'The Cunninghams? You mean Josh Cunningham's parents?'

'Well, grandparents at that point, but Chester runs it now.'

Renee regrouped. Chester was Josh's dad.

'You think Bessie and Caroline ran away together?'

'That's my best guess.'

'And what about the necklace? Perhaps if Caroline ran away, had a daughter then gave the daughter this necklace ... could this be her daughter? Perhaps she came back to see where her mother was born? That would make sense, right?'

'It's just a necklace, Renee. There's probably thousands of them floating around.'

Renee stiffened. Did Mulligan really believe that?

'But a yellow sapphire marquise? It's a very rare cut, and an even rarer stone …'

'Go home and get some rest, Taylor,' Mulligan snapped. 'We'll talk about it in the morning.'

Before she could protest he cut her off, leaving her with nothing but the dial tone.

There wasn't much more she could do so she switched off the lights and locked up. The sun had long since set and the streetlights had come on along Main Street. Young men in Wranglers, boots and cowboy hats made their way through the drive-through bottle-o, stocking up on six-packs of XXXX Gold. Mothers stopped out the front of the cafe, sending their kids in to buy burgers and chips as they sat in their cars and waited with the radio on. Renee wondered if the media had put out any further updates. If they had, they hadn't got them from her, although a press conference would have to be held soon. Not that she had much to tell them. Renee thought of Stacey's comments about Lisa being scared. Goorungah did not feel like a quiet, safe place.

'Hey, Mum,' Renee called as she entered, immediately beginning to search the cupboards for something to eat. Her mother was in the lounge room watching the news in her armchair. 'Have you eaten?'

'Yes, I had leftovers from last night. Sorry, I didn't get around to cooking anything, love. My hands have been playing up something awful today. I thought we could heat up one of those tins of soup. There's a minestrone in there somewhere, and there's a loaf of bread in the freezer. Heat it up.'

Renee located the soup. 'Where's the can opener?' Renee asked, looking in the second drawer.

'In the second drawer. Where it's always been.'

She remembered she'd used it last night on the porch to open her beer, found it, opened the tin, poured the contents into a bowl and placed it in the microwave.

'How are the eggs?' Renee called.

'The what?' Her mother had already forgotten.

'The soon-to-be progeny of your beloved, recently deceased feathered friends.'

Her mother muttered something under her breath and Renee quickly ducked her head around the doorway, checking in the corner under the lamp. She breathed a sigh of relief at the three little eggs tucked up with the light warming their shells.

'Far out.' She held her chest. 'I thought you ate them for a second.'

'Darling, I might be thrifty, but I'm not completely heartless.' The microwave beeped again. 'News is starting.'

Renee carried the soup and bread in as Jillian Crawley, the reporter from the creek who looked like a canary, appeared on screen, but today she was standing out the front of Alfie's cafe. 'It's been more than twenty-four hours since the body of a young woman was found here in Goorungah, and still the police are reporting no leads. I have Mrs Moore here, a mother who is understandably very concerned about the situation.'

'Huh! It's Lisa. Mum, you remember Lisa, don't you? Stacey from the station's sister. Must've married one of the Moore boys. She was in my grade at school.'

'That little bitch who teased you for having hand-me-down clothes?' Val said, not taking her eyes off the screen.

'Yeah – her sister, Stacey, is the admin assistant at work. I wonder what she makes of Lisa dissing the police.'

Lisa appeared in front of Alfie's with a toddler on one hip. 'Everyone in Goorungah is very concerned right now. Especially parents. We have no idea who did this, and the police are telling us nothing! We just want to know that our kids are safe.'

'Reporting from Goorungah, where the residents here will undoubtedly have another sleepless night fearing for the safety of their loved ones as the person responsible for this crime remains at large and the police stay silent.' The reporter closed, handing back to the newsroom.

'What?! How can she say that?' Her mother looked at her with raised eyebrows. 'Why are you giving me that look, Mum?'

'Well, do you have anything?'

'I'm trying, Mum!' Renee got up and started running warm water in the sink to clean the dishes. She grabbed a beer from the fridge, cracked it open and took a swig. Lisa Moore! With her exaggerated fear for the cameras and her immense sense of entitlement. She had always liked the spotlight at school too.

She threw in the cutlery, squirted detergent into the running water and plonked in the plates with a crash.

'Renee! Can you keep it down out there? I'm trying to hear the television!' Val called.

And her *mother* didn't even support her. As if she wasn't doing enough and already exhausted from cleaning the house, feeding her and chasing up the useless bloody social services people.

'Fuck!' Blood leaked from her palm.

'What happened? Are you okay?' She could hear her mother trying to get out of her chair.

'I'm fine.' She didn't need a lecture.

'You cut yourself, didn't you?'

Renee went to search the medicine cabinet for a Band-Aid. Her mother may have been a nurse but there was seldom anything in their first aid cabinet. She found an old Band-Aid at the bottom of the third drawer.

Her mother followed her in. 'Is it okay? Show me.' Renee held out her palm to her mother. 'Did you find a Band-Aid?' Renee waved it in the air. 'Well, put that on, leave the dishes. I'll do them in the morning. Grab your beer and come and sit down with me.'

Too tired to argue, Renee followed her mother's instructions and fell on the couch in the lounge room. There was a talent show playing. The next contestant was a girl of about nine who stood awkwardly in the centre of the stage facing the judges. 'Mum?' Renee asked after she'd downed a few mouthfuls of beer and relaxed.

'Yes, darling?'

'Did you know the two Aboriginal girls who went missing here in the mid-sixties?'

'Huh?' Her mother glanced over. 'Say again, darling.'

'In Goorungah, almost thirty-five years ago,' Renee prompted.

'Hmm ... yes ... What were their names now? Let me think ...'

'Caroline Forrest and Bessie Shields.'

'Renee, I said let me think. I'm going to get dementia too if you think for me as well as do everything else.'

Renee gulped her beer. *Give me patience.*

'Yes, I remember them. Well, some people said they were abducted. Some said they ran off.'

'Did you know them?'

'They were a little bit younger than me. I don't know how old they were; they dropped out of school fairly early, if I recall correctly. Their families had it pretty rough back then. Bessie had an older brother called Clarence. And Caroline had a sister called Milli. Both families are still over there on Wellington Street, I think. Millicent went away but came back a while ago.'

'Did you ever go to the yumba?'

'No, but I remember when they brought in the bulldozers to get rid of the shacks and debris. That was shortly after the Referendum, 1967. Probably didn't want outsiders to see the conditions those poor people lived in. We didn't mix that much. Why are you asking me about this? How does this help? Shouldn't you be trying to find the person who killed the woman yesterday?'

Renee couldn't tell her mother about Caroline Forrest wearing the same necklace as the dead girl. Not yet anyway. If that was leaked, the media would be all over it. Renee watched the little girl. She'd finished her painful rendition of Whitney Houston's 'I Will Always Love You', and the judges clapped.

'She's going to win, this little one. What a voice!' Her mother's attention had easily switched back to the screen. 'You haven't forgotten you said you'd take me to Sally Cunningham's funeral tomorrow?'

'No, Mum. I haven't forgotten.' After another few segments, Renee helped her mother to bed and then lay on hers, once again studying the glow-in-the-dark stickers and thinking of the dead woman and how she might be linked to Caroline Forrest.

Melaleuca

Mulligan was already in his office with the door closed when she got to the station on Thursday morning. She'd woken early (having remembered to set the alarm), gone for a jog (didn't see Norm or any snakes), made Val honey on toast, checked on the eggs and made it to the station before Roger and Stacey.

She looked out the window. Townsfolk were passing by, running errands, doing the grocery shopping. Kids were in sports uniforms or had towels thrown around their shoulders on the way to the swimming pool, enjoying the last days of summer. She spotted the three boys from the creek walking side by side, the cheeky one kicking along a soccer ball.

'Good morning, Sarge,' Renee said, walking straight into Mulligan's office holding both the missing persons file and the photo of the necklace then putting them both down on his desk. 'Look at this.'

'Bloody hell, can't you knock, Taylor?' He swivelled his chair around to face her, wiping his face and putting down his toast. She could smell the Vegemite he'd layered on top of it.

'Tell me they're not the same.' The more Renee looked at the photos, the more convinced she was it was the same necklace. She pointed at the necklace forensics had taken from the woman they'd found by the creek and photographed against a white background, and then to the photo of Caroline Forrest.

'They do look very similar,' Mulligan said reluctantly.

'I want to go and see her sister before Sally Cunningham's funeral. Mum told me that she still lives over on Wellington Street. Her name's Millicent.'

'Okay. But don't go near Worm again. He called his lawyers

and they've already lodged a warning against harassment. It's been dealt with at headquarters. We can't risk litigation.'

Renee narrowed her eyes. 'He's a suspect. And I haven't even *spoken* to him yet. He wasn't home yesterday. I talked to a young woman living there. Tiffany.'

'Whatever. Just don't go around there until you clear it with me first. Leave it for today. I'll take it up the line.'

Renee kept her temper. Changed the subject. 'How are things with HQ?'

Mulligan rolled his eyes. 'They're not happy at all. I asked them for more resources, but they say they're just as short-staffed as us, which is bullshit.' It was actually true, but Renee wasn't about to contradict him in his current mood. 'I spent half an hour talking to some nitwit who oversees the hotline – reckoned his staff needed more location details in case anyone called in with information.' He raised his hands in disbelief at the absurdity of someone needing clarification on Goorungah's geography – the centre of the universe, according to Mulligan. 'And to top it all off, the bloody media is requesting updates every five minutes.' Renee pressed her lips together, feeling guilty she hadn't briefed the media yet and resentful that she had to in the middle of an under-resourced murder investigation. 'And on that note, Taylor,' he said, narrowing in on her. 'We need to hold a press conference asap. Make it a priority.'

Renee nodded and left the office, promising an update on her meeting with Milli as soon as she had finished talking to her.

Millicent Forrest's house on Wellington Street was simple brick with a garden bed of geraniums and marigolds bordering the front yard. Renee walked up to the door and pressed the buzzer. A voice shouted down the hall, 'Alright, alright … I'm coming. Just hang on there.'

The door opened and a neatly dressed woman in her fifties, with a well-rounded figure and dark thick hair pulled back in a tight bun stood just inside, holding a mop inside a bucket.

'Millicent Forrest?'

'What do you want?'

'I'm Detective Renee Taylor. I'd like to ask you a few questions.'

'Is this about that young woman?'

'Sort of,' Renee said carefully. 'Do you mind if I come inside?'

'Hold on.' The flyscreen snapped shut as Millicent went back inside and returned with a towel that she placed on the tiles to make a pathway to the adjacent lounge room. 'Quick, come in,' she said, opening the door back up. 'Flies everywhere today.'

Renee entered the lounge room, which was small but cosy, and Millicent took a seat and encouraged Renee to take the one opposite her.

'Do you know who she was yet?' Millicent asked before Renee could speak.

Renee shook her head. 'I'm afraid not. But you may be able to help me.' She put the artist's drawing in front of Milli. 'Do you recognise this face?'

Milli leaned in to study the features. 'I don't, I'm sorry. This is the woman you found by the creek?'

'Yes.' Now that she was here, despite thinking about it all night, she didn't want to raise the possibility of a link. How does someone cope with losing a loved one for over thirty years and never knowing what happened to them? Renee couldn't fathom it. The lines around Millicent's face showed years of worry and grief. But if she didn't tell her about the necklace, she may never find out the identity of the woman nor who killed her. 'Mrs Forrest, do you mind if I ask you a few questions about your sister?'

'Caroline? Why do you want to talk about Caroline for?' Her eyes narrowed.

'A necklace was found on the body of the woman who was murdered on Monday morning. It looks like the same necklace as the one your sister is wearing in this photo.' Renee showed her the photo from the missing persons register.

Millicent studied the photo and then looked at Renee, a tired gaze heavy with grief-filled years. 'Why are you showing me this, Detective?'

'I think there may be a connection, Mrs Forrest.' Her eyes brightened with a faint glimmer of hope. 'Do you know where your sister got the necklace? It looks expensive.'

Millicent went quiet and looked thoughtfully at the photo of her younger sister. Her manner seemed to change. She looked up and Renee saw the hope die out of her eyes.

'You know, I wanna believe she ran away, but I don't think she would've done that. I don't know about the necklace. She just showed up with it one day.'

'I heard she worked up at the Cunninghams' house. Did Chester have a relationship with Caroline?'

'No. He used to drive her to work. That was it.' Milli raised her head and held Renee's eyes. 'You reckon his mum would've approved of anything like that? Nice white boy. Eldest son, about to inherit the farm. Far too good for the likes of us.'

'Can you tell me more about Caroline? Have you heard anything from her since she went missing all those years ago?'

'No.' Milli turned her head away, as though she might cry, but then her face twisted from grief to something else. Anger. 'Nothin. And you people didn't help at all. Still don't.'

Renee thought about the case notes. Such little detail. Barely surfacing in the official records. She wasn't going to defend her institution. She felt ashamed of the lack of information. Mulligan had said the girls had vanished, as though that were sufficient reason for them closing the case without a thorough investigation, but surely they could have recorded notes of interviews with family members and the locations the search parties had trawled.

'What happened that day, when Caroline and Bessie disappeared?'

'I don't know. She went out for a ride on her bike and she didn't come home. You want to know more, you better do some investigating.'

'What about her friend, Bessie? Has anyone ever heard from her again? I understand her family still live here on Wellington Street too.'

'Nothin from Bessie either. They both went that same day.'

Renee asked Millicent to call if she thought of anything new and started to walk towards the door, feeling a frisson of curiosity at the thought that the Cunninghams knew Caroline. Lucky she was just about to see all of them, although Sally Cunningham's funeral probably wasn't the place to ask questions.

'Detective Taylor?'

'Yes?'

'Do you want to know what I think happened to my sister?'
Renee nodded.

'I think she's dead. Because she had a lot to live for. And if she was alive, she wouldn't have left me wonderin all these years. She wouldn't be that cruel.'

And with that, Milli closed the door on her.

Chapter 13

The Goorungah Anglican church was a lone simple timber building in the middle of a dusty paddock on the eastern side of town. When the region wasn't in drought, the church made for a picture-perfect scene, with its inviting green lawn and colourful flower beds, the kind of place fashionable young people might want to tie the knot, absorbing its vintage bucolic innocence. But it wouldn't suit them today. The grass had all dried up so the front lawn was red dirt and the gardens held only a few straggly petunias. It looked more like the scene of a western horror movie, where the scorned lover rides up on horseback, rifle over shoulder, ready to take vengeance on the newlyweds. After leaving Millicent's place, Renee had managed to make it home in time to help her mother get ready – locate black dress, apply make-up, do hair – and get to the church within five minutes of the service commencing.

After she helped her mother through the crowd, she found a pew at the back to slide into and took a moment to look around the room. The wooden floors, which had once been polished, were now dry and scuffed. The walls were painted plain white and adorned with a single cross at either end of the hall. The pews were full and people had started to stand at the back. Sally Cunningham had been well loved. She had always volunteered her time with people in need, whether at the school helping kids with homework or the other mums in the tuckshop, or at the hospital reading with the old folk or keeping new mums company. She always had something nice to say to people that would inevitably make their day a little brighter. Being closer to Sally was one of the things Renee had looked forward to when she was seeing Josh. So it was not surprising that the church was at full capacity. She spotted Carissa Bremmer and Lisa Moore. Mulligan and Stacey were at the back but no Roger. He was probably managing the station. Norm was there with Otto from the post office bench. Mrs Ford was sitting in the aisle across from them, but Archie was a no-show.

She recognised the back of Mr Cunningham's head. Straight white hair, neatly combed, expensive-looking black suit. Social etiquette required that she wait a few days to ask a grieving widower questions, but she would have to do that sooner rather than later.

Then she saw Josh. He was sitting next to a beautiful woman with long brunette hair. Two little heads popped up between them. His children, perhaps.

'There he is.' Her mother had followed her gaze.

'Shush, Mum.' The crowd fell quiet as the casket was wheeled in, laden with white lilies. Mrs Ford walked up to the organ and began playing a sombre composition that made Renee think of *The Addams Family*. Something about funerals made her feel disconnected to herself. There was no way she wanted to be farewelled like this.

'We are here today to commemorate the life of Sally Gertrude Cunningham,' began the pastor. For a man relatively small in stature, his voice carried. As she listened to the pastor go on to recount the many ways in which Mrs Cunningham had contributed to the local community, Josh turned around and she caught a glimpse of his face. The structured jawline, piecing dark brown eyes.

'Amen,' the pastor said, and the crowd echoed in unison. 'Sally's son, Joshua, would now like to say a few words.'

Josh moved onto the platform. He was thinner than she expected and seemed both grief-stricken and self-conscious.

'My mother would be heartened to have you all here,' he began, then continued with a few further shallow formalities. Renee wondered if he was altogether there. Josh loved his mother – surely he could think of something more touching to say. Mrs Ford began again on the organ and Renee noticed Josh was sweating as he descended from the stage. Not in a good place, Joshua Cunningham. His mother's passing was sudden. Perhaps he was still in shock.

The ceremony concluded and everyone was invited for tea and scones under the tent set up next to the church. The Cunninghams were invited to exit first and Renee watched as the family made their way down the aisle, smiling sadly at everyone. First came Chester, tall and still handsome like his son, but he had aged considerably since Renee had seen him. His hairline had receded and there was the kind of weak stiffness to his movements that comes with age.

Roxy, Josh's sister, linked arms with Chester as she helped him down the aisle. She still had masses of curly red hair and her look was still caught between hippy and goth, in a long black velvet dress and silver necklace. She noticed Renee standing there and mouthed *thank you for coming*.

'They're a very handsome family, aren't they?' Val whispered. Renee knew she was trying to get a reaction. 'A bit stuck-up though.' Renee squeezed her mother's hand and Val let out a little squeal just as Renee met Josh's gaze.

'Shit, sorry, Mum.' She had squeezed with more force than intended.

'Far out, Renee. I've got arth–right–tis.' Val shook her hand in pain, but Renee couldn't unlock her eyes from Josh's. He didn't smile, and neither did she. They were frozen in time – there was something new behind those eyes, something that hadn't been there before. Pain. Loss. Disappointment. Self-loathing? His wife pulled him towards the door, causing him to snap out of his freeze, and he nodded at Renee. Slowly. Warmly. It was not what she had expected.

'Did you know Chester wasn't even there when she passed?' Val whispered again, clearly not deterred by the previous pinch.

'What are you talking about, Mum?'

'My friends at the hospital. They tried to call him in the early hours of the morning and he didn't answer. You'd think you'd sleep with the phone by your bedside if your wife was in the hospital with a heart condition. But no … prick didn't answer.'

'So when did he make it to the hospital?'

'I don't know. After she'd already passed. Too late.'

That would have been the morning of the murder. Chester Cunningham had not been by his wife's bedside. What could have been more important than being next to a loved one as they pass? She would have to find out.

It was mid-afternoon and outside the air was hot and dry. Renee got her mother a seat in the shaded tent then went to find her some scones with extra jam and cream per her instructions. She'd returned to where her mother sat and was about to take a seat when she felt a presence.

'Thanks for coming, Renee.' She turned around and Josh was standing there. She wasn't sure how to greet him, whether to give him a hug, a kiss on the cheek or shake his hand – nothing seemed right – and before she could decide he leaned over and gave her a small hug. 'We really appreciate you and your mum coming.'

'I'm so sorry, Josh. I heard it was sudden. Are you holding up okay?'

He looked away, back towards the beautiful woman and two kids, and she knew the answer was no. 'I'm fine. I thought you moved down to the city. What are you doing back here?'

'I did. I had to come home for a bit. Mum's not well. Her arthritis has gotten worse. She needs a carer now and social services are taking forever to line someone up.'

'I know, we experienced the same with Mum. Hey, I saw you on the news the other night. You were down by the creek. Are you covering the murder investigation?'

'I am.' Renee nodded. 'About that, are you okay if I come and see you and your dad tomorrow? I don't want to intrude but there is something I need to talk to him about.'

Josh's eyebrows shot up. 'Really? Okay. Tomorrow is fine.' He paused. 'I can't believe that happened in Goorungah. I hope you find who did it soon.' Josh's wife called out to him. 'I must go. Thanks for coming.'

'What's this I hear about a link?' Roger said when Renee returned to the station after dropping her mother home. Stacey had ignored her when she'd walked in and even Roger looked a bit put out. Perhaps she should have told him earlier – he was pretty much the only team she had. God knows the media – still camped outside, baying for information but with less enthusiasm because of the heat – weren't on her side.

She really did need to do a media conference and release the artist's impression, but with such a small team and so much still to be done and relatively little to share – what could she say? 'We don't know who she is, she has appeared from nowhere, no one has come forward, I have one lead I can't tell you about.' She would be eaten alive. A mixture of dread and irritation washed over her. She couldn't bring herself to prioritise it. Maybe tomorrow.

'Did Sarge give you an update?'

'Briefly. He said you'd gone to speak to the sister of Caroline Forrest.'

Renee explained to Roger what she'd discovered the night before when looking at the photos. 'But Sarge doesn't think it's a big deal.'

'What do you think? What did Millicent Forrest say?' Roger asked.

'She said she didn't know where the necklace came from, but that Caroline used to work for the Cunninghams. Chester used to drive her to and from work.'

'Were they involved? Dating?'

'Milli says not and accused the police of not doing enough to find the girls. Mum just told me that Chester wasn't by his wife's side when she passed on Tuesday morning.'

'At the same time our Jane Doe was murdered,' Roger said. 'Do you think he has anything to do with it?'

Renee shrugged uncomfortably, remembering Josh's face. 'It's a lead. We follow it up. Can you go by the hospital later? See if you can talk to some of the nurses and get their version of events. I want to go and speak to the family of the other girl who went missing. Bessie Shields.'

Chapter 14

Bessie's family lived in a small timber Queenslander with a faded couch and a cluster of chairs scattered around the front porch. Renee lifted the latch to the front gate at the address listed on the online missing person's file as belonging to Nettie Shields. It was on Wellington Street, but at the very end, and was one of the houses she hadn't managed to get to the day before. A neat line of freshly planted daises lay inside the wire fence and it made Renee think that maybe this family had been able to move on from the devastation of having a missing loved one. Or maybe they fought back the grief every day in little ways like by planting flowers to beautify their front yard. She tapped a few times on the front door, stood still and waited, then knocked some more. She was about to turn away when heavy footsteps came through the house.

'Who are you?' A tall, thin man holding a cigarette peered through the flyscreen.

'My name's Renee Taylor. I'm from the local police station.' She showed her badge through the mesh as he leaned in to check it.

'You here about that Murri girl?' He didn't wait for an answer, opened the door and took a long drag on his cigarette. 'Come in then, I s'pose. Take your shoes off. What do you think this is?'

She yanked off her boots and followed him down the hallway. 'Come through.'

The walls were covered in photos and each bench or stand held ornaments and decorations – imitation flowers, small bowls of potpourri. Renee walked past one of the bedrooms, which emanated an overly sweet scent. Its walls were covered in magazine posters, a mix of African-American hip hop artists and local football players, and the dresser was piled with beaded necklaces and bracelets, hoop earrings and headscarfs. The windowsill was lined with collectable figurines from McDonald's.

She hurried after the man. 'What's your name?' she called out.

'I'm Clarence. Clarence Shields,' he answered, reaching to open the back door.

'Is Mrs Nettie Shields home?'

'Mum? Nah, she's out now. Downtown playin the pokies.' Renee imagined Nettie alongside her mother dropping coins into noisy, flashing machines.

'Do you mind if I ask you a few questions then?'

'Go ahead.' He shrugged. 'I got nothing to hide. But can we do it out the back? I'm busy cutting wood. Watch your step. Housing Commission said they'd have someone come out to fix it.' He pointed to a wide gap between the first and third wooden steps. 'That was fuckin three weeks ago now.' She followed him into a courtyard in the back yard. 'I live out there in the shed. Mum and Audrey live inside.' Clarence turned down the country music blaring from the radio and took a final drag on his cigarette before stubbing it out in an ashtray.

'Who's Audrey?' Renee looked around. It was a neatly maintained courtyard, surrounded by well-cared-for pot plants. The concrete made it feel cool. She wondered why he was cutting wood when the weather had been so warm lately, but then noticed an open fireplace to one side with a wire rack for cooking. He pulled a milk crate out for her to sit down and picked up his axe to continue cutting wood.

'Audrey's Charlene's kid. Charlene's my youngest sister, fuckin womba one she is. Can't stay off ...' He stopped himself, glancing at her feet, becoming self-conscious. He was about to say drugs. 'Mum's taking care of Audrey. My niece.'

'Do you work in Goorungah?'

'Nah, I'm on carer's allowance for Mum.' He slammed the axe down again, splitting a piece of wood. 'Are you Murri, sis? I think I recognise you from around town. Not lately. Years ago, when you was a kid.'

'My father is. But I've never met him.' Clarence looked at her with eyes mixed with pity and suspicion. She had seen that look before from other Aboriginal people. 'I was actually wondering if we could talk about your sister? Bessie?'

The gentleness left his eyes. He walked to the pile of wood, picked up a large chunk and brought it back to place on the round wooden slab. 'Why you wanna talk about Bessie for? That was a long time ago, you know?'

'I'm sorry, I know it must be difficult for you.'

He lifted the axe above his head and slammed it down, again hitting perfectly in the centre. 'Why you gotta go dredging shit up like this? Leave a poor family be, why don't you? You fullas didn't investigate it properly years ago when the girls actually went missing, so don't come round here now asking questions. They ran away, those two. Headed south where there's more action. They were too bored here in the country, wanted the excitement of the big smoke.'

'Who's there?' A wavering voice came from inside. 'Clarence, I thought they was going to come today to fix that step?'

'They were, Mum – they keep mucking us around.'

'And who might you be?' A small woman who looked as if she were in her late seventies appeared. She squinted into Renee's face from the back door.

'She's a gunji,' Clarence snarled. 'Sniffing around, asking questions she shouldn't be.'

'Now, was I talking to you?' The old lady looked fiercely back at her son, eyes bright.

'Mrs Shields, my name's Renee. Renee Taylor. I don't want to be intrusive.'

Clarence scoffed and took another whack at the wood block.

'Don't mind him. He's too sensitive. Always has been. Clarence, call the Housing mob now and bring the groceries in! And how many times do I have to tell you? *Don't. Smoke. Inside!* Renee, did you say your name was? Come inside, love.'

Nettie turned back to Renee, metamorphosing from furious matriarch to sweet old lady, her fierce alter ego momentarily at bay. 'Would you like some tea, dear?'

Renee accepted the offer and followed her into the kitchen where she took the seat Nettie pulled out for her.

'Mrs Shields, I don't want to bring up past pains, but I wanted to know if you ever heard from your daughter again after she disappeared back in 1966? Did you ever find out what happened?' Clarence came in with bags of groceries and left them on the kitchen table, side-eyeing Renee as he departed.

'Love, shouldn't you be trying to find the murderer of the girl they found out at Fletchers Drive?' Nettie turned on the kettle and started putting the cold groceries away in the freezer.

'Yesterday when I was reviewing the missing persons register I came across the details of Bessie and Caroline's disappearance.'

'Yes, and …?' She had her back turned to Renee now, rearranging cans in a top cupboard.

'In one of the photos, Caroline was wearing a necklace.' Renee waited to see if this information had any effect on Nettie but she continued moving things around. 'A yellow sapphire on a gold chain …' Nettie stopped and turned, eyes suddenly flooded with both curiosity and fear. 'You know the one I'm talking about?'

The kettle switch clicked and Nettie spooned black tea leaves into a pot, poured in the boiling water and then placed it on a mat on the table alongside two cups, before taking a seat and heaving a deep sigh.

'Was it shaped like an oval but with sharp points?'

Renee confirmed it was.

'I saw Caroline Forrest wearing that necklace one day. What's that necklace got to do with anything?'

Renee was mindful of the way Millicent had reacted when she revealed the link and didn't want to cruelly raise hope when there probably was none. 'We found a very similar-looking necklace on the body of the woman who was murdered down by the creek on Tuesday.'

Nettie picked up the pot and swirled the tea, taking time to think. She did not react in the same hopeful way as Millicent had initially, and Renee felt bad for feeling relieved. Maybe she'd had her hopes dashed too many times. 'The same necklace?' Her expression was that of cynical scepticism as she poured the tea into two white cups.

'We can't say for sure if it was the exact same necklace. But they appear very alike. And it's quite an unusual variety of stone and cut.'

'The woman you found was in her mid-twenties?'

'Yes, that's right.'

'So we know it wasn't my Bessie or Caroline Forrest.' The woman was thinking out loud now. 'If it was the same necklace, then maybe Caroline lost it and this young lady found it. You don't know who she is yet?'

'Unfortunately not.'

'No one's called in?' Nettie asked incredulously. 'Even if she did run away from her community or get in some kind of trouble with a man, we still check in with each other from time to time. News has reported a young Aboriginal woman's body found. Very strange no one's checking on her or missing her.'

'I agree.'

'Let's say, if it was the same necklace—' Renee was impressed with this woman's restraint and analysis, not allowing herself to jump to any conclusions '—then maybe Bessie and Caroline did run away. Maybe they fell on hard times and Caroline pawned the necklace for some cash. It's strange though that it's ended up in the hands of another Aboriginal woman. That's why I'm thinking the girls might have gone to another community.'

Renee couldn't hear Clarence cutting the wood outside any more and thought she heard a rustle in the garden beneath the kitchen window. 'Mrs Shields, do you think you could tell me more about what you remember of Bessie?'

'What do you want to know?'

'Anything you think might be important. What was she like?' Renee remembered Mulligan had said his dad threw Bessie out of the pub a few times. Surely a mother could offer a broader perspective.

'Oh good Lord. That girl caused me some worry.' She smiled as she said it, staring deeply into space, lost in memories of her teenage daughter's mischief. Renee saw the heartbreak when she pulled herself back to the present, shaking her head to discard the momentary lapse. 'She liked to live life to the fullest, let's say.' Nettie went on to describe how she tried to find her daughter work on some of the farms around town, but had no luck, and how she'd occasionally go to church with Millicent and Caroline, who also tried to help Bessie find her feet, but there was always a reckless rebellion about Bessie that people sensed the minute they met her. 'But then she started running off on me. She wouldn't come home until early in the morning and she stopped helping me with the younger ones. I think she had a boyfriend somewhere. She came home with things she'd never be able to afford herself. A handbag, some perfume, these giant blue sunglasses that were in fashion back then. It hurt me. And, boy oh boy, did I worry.' She paused and frowned as though sifting through the memories of her daughter, fighting through the bad ones to find the good ones. 'Do you have any children, Detective?'

'No, ma'am.'

'Think very carefully before you do. They drive you bloody crazy.' She shook her head and smiled sadly. 'She was a bit of a rebel some might say, but she had a good heart. Always up to mischief. Have you spoken to Milli yet? She might be able to tell you more. Milli was twenty-three when they went missing. Closer in age, and

I think Caroline shared a lot more with her than my Bessie shared with me.'

'I saw Milli this morning.'

'And you told her about the necklace?'

'I did.'

'Oh goodness. Poor thing. Oh well, in that case she'll be over here knockin any time soon to find out what we talked about.'

'Mrs Shields, what do you think happened? Do you think the girls ran away?' Renee asked.

'I know my Bessie. She didn't run away. She was happy here with life. It's true, she liked living in the fast lane and she wanted adventure and nice things but she loved her family. She wouldn't have run away and not got in touch again.'

'So you don't think that Bessie skipped town?'

The old lady shook her head. 'I know my daughter. If she had left, she would have got in touch to let me know she was okay.'

'Clarence thinks Bessie and Caroline ran away.' It felt cruel to challenge her on this, but she needed to know. She had a murder to solve.

'He's just sayin that. He can't handle the truth. He knows in his heart something worse happened.'

'What do you think happened?'

'I think my girl was taken. And I think there's been a cover-up. You're an Aboriginal woman. You know what that means.' This was a statement, not a question. 'Why didn't they investigate properly? That sergeant came and asked me a few questions, all of five minutes, and was gone again. They didn't care about findin the girls. Just assumed they ran away. Those girls might have been playin up a bit, they were teenagers after all, but they had families they loved, they had a whole community here. If you really want to investigate ...' and here Nettie turned the full force of her intense gaze onto Renee, 'I mean investigate properly, you could start with Worm.'

'Why Worm?'

'I'm pretty sure that's who my Bessie was seeing. The boyfriend who was buying her things.'

Renee felt a chill creep down her back. Worm again. The town's resident bad guy. The one who was, strangely, protected by distant lawyers and unnamed powerbrokers in Brisbane.

'You think Worm had something to do with Bessie's disappearance?'

'Bloody oath, I do. And I told the cops that. Is that on your file? People are scared of him but I'm too old to give a shit any more. He's the deviant gettin the young ones involved sellin his meth. Someone needs to put a stop to his rot.'

She drove back to the station, deep in thought. Could Chester and Caroline have been dating secretly? Worm may have been dating Bessie. And the woman by the creek was wearing a necklace that looked the same as the one Caroline was wearing in the photo. How did this woman end up with Caroline's necklace?

Stacey was on the phone when she walked into the office and Roger wasn't at his desk. She figured he may still be at the hospital. Mulligan's door was closed, but he would want to hear what she'd just found out. This couldn't wait. She knocked and entered when she heard him yell to come in.

'Sarge,' she said, opening the door. He was sitting quietly at his desk writing in his notepad. 'I just got back from Nettie Shields' house.'

'Right.' He nodded deliberately and Renee couldn't read his emotions. 'And?'

'Nettie corroborated what Millicent Forrest told me earlier. Nettie had spotted Caroline wearing a necklace that looks the same as the one we found on the woman by the creek on Tuesday. She also told me that she suspected Bessie was dating Worm.'

'What are you talking about, Taylor?' This time she caught a hint of frustration.

'Apparently she'd been sneaking off and spending time with Worm and coming back with gifts like handbags and sunglasses, things that she couldn't afford. And Nettie Shields told the police this, but no one ever followed up on it.'

She realised she was moving into sensitive territory, as it was Mulligan's father who was leading the case at the time, but she needed to call it out. 'Come on, Sarge, who cares if Worm's got his lawyers out? Tiffany's over there. We can do a welfare check on her if you want to play it safe and just suss out the place.'

Mulligan seemed to be thinking it over. He glanced across at his phone a few times.

'Hello?' A man's voice came from the front reception. Renee put her head out the door to see who it was. Stacey was still on a call and ignoring his arrival.

'I'll be back in a second,' Renee said. She couldn't help noticing that Mulligan looked relieved as she left. Stacey was talking about a cooking recipe when Renee walked past so she threw her hands in the air and gave her the what-the-fuck stare, which incited an eye roll and chair swivel.

A tall man in his mid-thirties wearing an unstructured linen suit stood in the reception area behind the counter. He had long curly blond hair pulled back in a ponytail and wore wooden beads around his neck. The edges of a tattoo poked out of his T-shirt neckline. 'My name's Lennon,' he said, stepping forward. He was about to extend his hand but must've noticed Renee's frown. She realised her frustration at Mulligan's caution and Stacey's lack of professionalism were evident on her face. He put his hand in his pocket, shrugged and smiled. 'Lennon McGorrie. I'm from *National Indigenous Post*.'

'A newspaper?' More media. Wonderful. 'I'm Detective Renee Taylor.'

'You haven't heard of us?' Renee shook her head. 'We're the leading newspaper for Indigenous Australia. I'm surprised.' He tilted his head slightly. She knew what he was thinking. He wanted to ask if she was Aboriginal. She had a feeling he wasn't. He was far too unaffected.

'No. I haven't.' She felt her mouth form the shape of a polite smile that gave nothing away. He was about to tell her all about it, and the quicker the better. She needed to follow up the leads around Chester and Worm.

'We report on a range of current affairs affecting the Aboriginal community – land rights, constitutional recognition, deaths in custody, the *new* stolen generation … and institutional incompetence when it comes to crimes against black women.' He smiled with satisfaction, as though he'd moved his chess piece closer to her king.

'Black women, hey?'

'Yes, Aboriginal and Torres Strait Islander women are disproportionately assaulted, falsely incarcerated, abducted and murdered compared to the non-Indigenous population.'

She felt her blood starting to rush. She was being lectured on the rights and abuse of Aboriginal women by a white man. Now would be a good time to lose her hearing.

She smiled politely. 'Why are you here, Mr McGorrie?'

'The body you found on Tuesday was that of an Aboriginal woman, correct?' He took his notepad out.

'Mr McGorrie, you seem to be under the impression I am going to give you an interview, which is not the case. There will be a press conference in due course.'

'Has the family been informed yet?' It was as if she hadn't spoken. She wondered what the tattoo on his chest was of. Probably some Chinese lettering that he didn't understand. If the tattooist had a sense of humour, it probably said *Jerk* in Mandarin.

'That's a matter we're looking into.'

'You still don't know who she is yet?'

'Unfortunately, no.' This much was public knowledge. She fought the urge to bite her lip. The family must be going through hell.

'And do you have any leads?'

'Look, Mr McGorrie, I'm simply not in a position to share anything with you at this stage that isn't already in the public arena, which is that the body of an Aboriginal woman was found by the creek under suspicious circumstances on Tuesday morning and we're looking into it.'

'So, it was a homicide then?'

'I cannot confirm that at this stage.'

He fell silent, carefully studying her face.

'Were there signs of sexual assault?' He was persistent, she could give him that. He'd chosen the right profession.

'I cannot confirm nor deny.' He nodded thoughtfully and checked his notepad. She peered over and there was a long list of bullet points. He had obviously prepared well for this meeting and he had driven all the way out from the city. 'Do you know something? Is there something you're not telling me, Mr McGorrie?'

'We're thinking of covering this case in the next issue of the *National Indigenous Post* and I was wondering if you'd like to provide a comment. It has a very broad readership from the community. If there's something you need assistance with then we could put it in the paper?'

She considered telling him about the discovery of the necklace and how it might link the current case with the two girls who went missing in 1966 – but she decided it was too early. She needed to speak to more people herself first. Such an announcement could spark fear and fuel paranoia in the town. The term 'serial killer' would be thrown around. Best avoided for now.

'You can include the hotline number. And encourage people to come forward if they know anything.' She gave Lennon the same information as Jillian Crawley. 'Just let people know to call if they know who the girl might be or if they saw or heard anything suspicious.'

'Alright.' He still looked at her as though he knew something he wasn't sharing.

'Here's my card.' She gave him her business card and watched him walk down the concrete path back towards his car.

'Who was that?' Mulligan called out from his office. Stacey had left for the day and the rest of the office was empty. Rence realised it was past six o'clock and felt a bit bad for giving Stacey a mean look before – she was probably just trying to manage after school care for her kids. It was late after all.

'Just some reporter from an Indigenous newspaper. *National Indigenous Post*,' she sang out and plonked herself down at her desk, ready to write up notes from her meeting with Nettie that afternoon. The full results of the boot print analysis were also on her desk.

If she had to admit it, she was angry with Mulligan. She needed to interview Worm and Mulligan was being cowardly for going along with headquarters. So when he walked up to her desk she busied herself, hoping he would disappear.

'Taylor. It's late. Worm is not a flight risk. Trust me.' He stood in front of her and waited until she put the print analysis to the side.

'It's fine, Sarge.' She didn't mean it. Passive aggression was her weakness and she felt too tired to fight it. 'I can wait.'

He didn't pick up on it. Oh, how peaceful it must be to have the oblivion of a confident white man. 'Good. We need to build the case more. There's still plenty of things we haven't checked off. How are you going with that boot print analysis? Does it tell us anything?'

'No.' She hadn't read it yet, but wanted him to go away.

'And someone will call through on the hotline soon. Someone will know this girl, and once that happens we'll be able to connect the dots.' He put on a jacket and started walking towards the door. 'Get some rest, Taylor. You've had a big day.' The door closed behind him.

The street was quiet when she left. Renee imagined normal happy little families at home eating popcorn, settling in to watch a movie or a comedy together. Or maybe they were sitting around talking about the unsolved murder and the possibility of a killer lurking in their midst.

'Hey, Mum.'

Her mother was lying in bed watching the same reality singing show from the night before.

'Renee, thank god! Can you pass me the remote control? I need to turn this part up. Come over here. Sit down.' Valerie motioned towards the seat next to her bed and pressed the buttons to raise the volume. 'You remember this little girl? It's the semi-finals, you know? Just look at her.'

Renee watched as the little girl ascended the stage in a feathered pink dress and gold headband.

'Oh, come on, Trisha! You got it, girl. Watch, Renee. You watch how this little one sings.' Renee poured a glass of water from her mum's jug while the girl belted out a rendition of Mariah Carey's 'Fantasy'. She sat back, took a mouthful and watched her mother sitting up in bed, clapping wildly. 'She's good, isn't she?'

Renee nodded as her mother lowered the volume. 'How are you feeling, Mum?'

'Alright, love. Took an extra pill for the pain this arvo, so I'm a bit wobbly.'

'That could explain why you're going nuts over a kid singing Mariah songs?'

'Haha ... very funny. I'd be fine if you got me some weed like I asked.' Renee didn't have the energy to argue with her. 'Ahh ... what's wrong, darling? I'm just teasing. Tell me. You look tired.' Val switched the television off. 'Talk to me, honey. What's going on?'

'Tell me more about William Gawlor. Were you in the same grade as him?'

'No. He was older than me.'

'Why does everyone do that?'

'Do what?'

'Shut down. Clam up. As soon as they hear the name William Gawlor or Worm being mentioned.'

'Darling, that man is no good. And he's *connected*.'

'What do you mean?'

'He can pull strings. No charges ever stick to him. He beat the shit out of Jill Huxley to within an inch of her life. All because she threatened to dob him into the cops.'

'How do you know?'

'I treated her.' Renee was trying to make sense of it all when her mother interrupted. 'She's dead now. Died of complications of pneumonia a few years back. Meredith Walker was also one of his victims.'

'Meredith-with-the-horses?' Renee asked.

'Yes, that's her. Go and talk to her. She might tell you a thing or two. She's braver than most.'

Renee stayed quiet. She wanted her mother to continue. This was the most she'd got out of anyone.

'To be honest, I'm surprised they even charged him for it. He's been like Teflon ever since. Can't pin anything on that bastard. And folk are too scared to say anything because they know what he's capable of.'

'What is he capable of?'

'Well, physical violence for one. He beat up Jill. I nursed her back then and she told me a few things.'

'Like what?' Renee braced herself.

'She wanted to go to the cops because Worm raped her.' Val

paused and Renee readied herself for more details. 'It wasn't the first time but this time he left bruises and bite marks. Jill knew it was enough evidence to press charges, but then after the beating she lost her nerve. He threatened her he'd kill her if she went to the cops. I tried to assure her that she was safe, but to be honest, I didn't know. Who was I to tell that she was safe?'

'Why didn't you tell me this earlier, Mum?'

'It's not up to you to do anything about Worm, my girl. That's Mulligan's job. And if he can't do it, then I don't want you getting messed up in that stuff.'

'I'm a cop, Mum. You have to tell me these things.'

'And you're also my daughter.'

A stubborn expression settled onto her mother's face. There was no moving her now, Renee knew, so she changed the subject. They stayed up late talking, Renee peppering her mother with questions about everything from what life was like for people on the yumba, to who she played with at school, and what she knew about Bessie and Caroline. They were a bit older than Val but she vaguely knew of them. She went on to ask more about Worm and how drug-use patterns changed throughout the years, from the sixties to the seventies and eighties and how it showed up in different presentations at the local hospital where she worked.

She tucked her mother into bed, reviewed the case notes and documented her latest developments, and finally checked on the eggs, smiling at the absurdity of incubating chickens under a lamp. They were still warmly nesting in the corner. It'd be a miracle if they actually hatched, but there was something important about trying.

Chapter 15

By the time Renee arrived at the station on Friday, Roger was already there so she took the opportunity to fill him in on the events from the day before.

'So Mrs Shields – Nettie – said Bessie was spending time with Worm?' Roger asked.

'Yes.'

'But Mulligan won't let you see Worm yet because Worm's gone and spooked headquarters with his team of lawyers.' It sounded ridiculous when Roger said it out loud.

'Yep. What did you find out from the hospital staff? Was Mum right about Chester not being around when Sally passed?'

'I talked to Dr Mac. He reckons that Chester came in late, at nine am, a few hours after Sally Cunningham had passed away, and that Chester was a bit on the nose …'

'On the nose? What are you talking about?'

'He smelled of alcohol.'

'What else?'

'Nothing much. He seemed genuinely upset at her passing.'

It wasn't much to go on, but the drinking was interesting. He had been drinking on the morning his wife died. Had he known he was about to lose his wife and it was a way to deal with the grief? Or was it a guilty conscience?

'Morning!' Stacey came bounding in, carrying an assortment of bags as usual, and plonked them down near her desk. 'So, I take it you made an arrest?' She looked at them, quivering with excitement.

'No. Why would you say that?' Renee asked.

'What are all the people doing out the front?' Stacey said, pointing back in the direction of Main Street with her thumb.

'What people …?' Renee got up from her desk, went to the window and peered through the blinds to see a crowd of people milling around, more joining them as she watched – people of all ages, holding signs that read *Shame on Police*, *Justice for Bessie and Caroline* and *ACAB*.

She felt Stacey and Roger peer over her shoulder. 'What does "ACAB" mean?' Renee asked.

'All Cops are Bastards,' Stacey said.

She spotted Millicent and Nettie and Clarence with a teenage girl who must've been Audrey. The three boys from the creek were there. And old Norm and his two mates stood a few feet back, snooping more than participating. And then she saw Lennon McGorrie. So that's how this started. 'Damn.'

'What?' Roger asked.

'Lennon McGorrie. He must've gone and talked to the residents along Wellington Street yesterday after he came here. I knew he was up to something.'

Renee went to her desk to check her emails. There was one from McGorrie, subject empty. The message simply read, 'Thought you might find this interesting,' and a link to a news segment from the *National Indigenous Post*.

Melaleuca

Local Goorungah police are still at a loss to identify the body of a young woman found by the Goorungah Creek in the early hours of Tuesday morning. Nor do they have any information regarding the person responsible for this unlawful killing, despite a credible link being found between the murdered woman and two girls who went missing in 1966.

Caroline Forrest and Bessie Shields were last seen in Goorungah on 20 August 1966. At the time, numerous reports were made to the police by concerned relatives regarding potential suspects, but little effort was put into locating these girls and they have never been found. Relatives of the missing girls say that the police spent less than thirty minutes interviewing them after their loved ones disappeared, and reluctantly organised a search party one week after the girls went missing when the families insisted on more being done.

A necklace was found on the body of the unknown woman that resembles a necklace worn by Caroline Forrest, a marquise-cut yellow sapphire pendant on a gold chain.

Reports estimate that Australian Aboriginal women are thirty-one times more likely than non-Indigenous women to be hospitalised due to domestic violence, and seventeen times more likely to die from homicide. Will the authorities ever devote sufficient time and resources to solving crimes when it comes to First Nations women in this county? Enough is enough. We need to rally as a community and let them know that Aboriginal lives matter. It is a gross injustice and shame to this country that we still have not moved on from where we were almost thirty-five years ago.

If you have seen or heard anything that may assist with the investigation you are encouraged to call the police hotline on 1800 999 999.

'Who are you talking about? Who is Lennon McGorrie?' Roger asked.

'A journalist. Here.' She pointed at the screen. It wasn't only Lennon she felt betrayed by. Millicent and Nettie could have given her a heads-up that they had spoken to a journalist. Did she come across as that unapproachable?

'He came here yesterday?' Roger was struggling to keep up. 'It must've been late. What time?'

'I don't know. About six maybe. I think he went and spoke to Millicent Forrest before he came here, or maybe Nettie Shields – that's how he established the link. He would've known he was going to write this story yesterday when he came here and he wanted my comment.'

'Why didn't you tell him?'

'I need to tell everyone at the same time to manage community reactions, and if we weren't so stretched for resources I would've held a press conference by now.' Roger nodded his understanding and she sighed. 'I just don't want to set off any wildfires – you know how rumours spread in this town. And like Sarge says, we need to keep the community calm.'

'They're not calm. I can tell you that right now,' Stacey chipped in unhelpfully and Renee decided she needed some fresh air.

Under the guise of buying more coffee to top up the kitchen supply, Renee snuck out the back door and took the alleyway behind Main Street to avoid the crowd. She welcomed a moment of calm as she made her way to the shops.

The temperature was still rising and the blazing heat from the past few days showed no signs of relenting. As she cut back onto Main Street, she welcomed the gush of cold air that burst out of each store as she passed by. People were running errands, popping into the newsagent to buy the paper and a ticket in the lotto, buying meat from the butcher shop for their weekend barbeques, stopping to gossip. It all seemed so normal, and Renee felt lonely. Why didn't Milli and Nettie trust her to do the right thing? Why didn't Mulligan trust her enough to let her question Worm? A feeling of being caught between two worlds rose up around her like floodwaters, threatening to drown her. She didn't feel like she belonged – neither in the community nor the force.

As she walked back to the station with the coffee, she stopped under the awning of the post office where she had a clear view of the group of about forty people huddled around out the front of the police station. They held flags and placards and were mostly dressed in red, black and yellow.

Lennon McGorrie's article detailing accusations of police incompetence stung, but it also rang true. She hated how much she agreed with him. In the city, she had experienced so many incidents that were racist, but she kept trying not to take other people's prejudice personally. But as she stood there in the shade of the awning watching the people protest, she couldn't help but wonder why her colleagues frequently overlooked her recommendations.

And there were times she was asked about all the stuff she got 'for free'. 'Did the department pay for your apartment when you moved to Brisbane?' 'Did you actually have to do the aptitude tests to gain entry?' That was a common one. And then there were the times when they had to do mandatory Aboriginal cultural awareness training and her colleagues would snigger and giggle at the presenter when he talked about the Dreaming or light-skinned Aboriginal and Torres Strait Islander people. She would sit uncomfortably wondering whether or not to address the matter by telling them they were privileged arseholes who'd benefit from shutting their mouths and listening to the presenter. Sometimes she would. Other times, she'd let it slide. You learn to pick your battles. It was exhausting. If you get someone offside, then sometimes there's more work to be done drying their tears and convincing them that she wasn't trying to be 'mean'. And then the inevitable corridor whispering. The number of times she'd walked into the tea room to have colleagues abruptly stop talking or awkwardly change the subject. Breathe, focus, carry on. But, oh, the fantasies she had of blasting them all.

The last case she had worked on involved an Aboriginal woman who had been murdered by her boyfriend. She'd called in to the station a few times and asked for help, and Renee had taken one of those calls just as she was about to go off shift. Her colleague Ian had promised her he would follow it up but he didn't and the woman was murdered by her boyfriend the following day.

That woman had trusted her and she had let her down. She should have known Ian wouldn't take it seriously, but worse still was the possibility that maybe she had known that he wouldn't take it seriously and she still left. What kind of person does that? She had even respected Ian up until that point. She couldn't bring herself to report him for failing to act on a duty of care because she felt she had also failed. She had let it slide like a coward, just like Mulligan not going after Worm. Always managing risks and toeing the line and being a team player. Renee hated herself so much she couldn't articulate it.

Lennon McGorrie caught her attention, standing to the side of the crowd.

Melaleuca

'Mr McGorrie?' she sang out and he turned to see where the voice had come from. 'Over here.'

'Detective Taylor,' he replied, leaving the crowd to come over to where she stood. 'How lovely to see you again.' His voice was hoarse and she wondered whether it was from the pack of smokes bulging out of his top pocket or shouting out calls for justice.

'Wish I could say the same. Why are you doing this? You don't even know what happened to those girls. For all we know, they were runaways and there's no connection whatsoever to this case. The necklace we found could be a replica. It's going to muddy evidence and stir up tension and fear.' He had been so reckless and he needed to take some accountability for stirring up the community.

'Caroline Forrest and Bessie Shields were not runaways. Go and ask around town. Get to know *your* community, Detective Taylor.'

'I'm from this community, Lennon, which is more than can be said of you.'

'Nevertheless, it's my job to raise awareness of racism.'

But not experience it, Renee thought. She took a deep breath and let it out slowly. She could feel the sweat dripping down her back. 'We're doing everything we can. You're creating unnecessary emotion in a group of people who are already scared and struggling with recent events. Do you really think bringing a bunch of people out here in this heat is helpful to the case?'

Lennon smiled fixedly, even as his face reddened. 'Yeah, I do. I think anything that puts the spotlight on the incompetence of your organisation is helpful. Look at these.' Lennon dumped his backpack on the ground, ripped open the zipper and grabbed a bunch of papers. He held up sheet after sheet in front of her – news clippings detailing past injustices. 'All these incidents involve the police either actively involved in the death of an Aboriginal person, covering it up or not devoting any resources to seeking justice. Young men dying in hot vans, women not receiving medical treatment, police assuming intoxication when the poor man is having an epileptic fit!'

She grudgingly took hold of the last one he held out. She met his eyes but found herself unable to hold his gaze. He turned his back on her and went to join his fellow protesters. That same guilt she'd felt when she'd handed over her duty of care to that prick Ian overwhelmed her. She hated herself.

Renee avoided the crowd again by taking the back door, and went straight to the kitchen. She turned on the kettle and ripped open the instant coffee. Renee knew the protesters and Lennon McGorrie were right. As frustrating as Lennon's arrogance was, this might be just the wake-up call that Goorungah needed.

'Are you okay, Renee?' It was Stacey. She was standing behind her, holding her cake tin. 'Do you want a bickie?'

'No. I don't want a fucking bickie.' Stacey looked like she was going to cry and Renee instantly regretted it. 'I'm sorry.' Stacey shrugged and went back to her desk.

Renee followed her. 'Really, I'm sorry. I shouldn't have spoken to you like that. I'm just really stressed about the protesters out the front.'

Stacey looked at her levelly, tears still glistening in her eyes. 'You know, Renee, I used to think you didn't have any friends because you didn't fit in, but maybe it's just because you are a bitch.'

Renee figured she kind of deserved that, even if it stung, so she mumbled 'sorry' again and went to see Mulligan, who had arrived while she was out buying the coffee. She told him of her exchange with the journalist.

'What do you reckon?' she asked, standing in the doorway to his office.

'People have a right to protest. It shows a healthy democracy. But make sure you keep an eye on them, Taylor. I don't want this getting out of hand.'

'I'm going to hold the press conference at five pm. I think we can at least release the likeness of the woman, share the connection with the necklace and update everyone. And I'm going to go and question Worm soon.' She said it as a statement, not as a question, and waited for his reaction.

'Actually, legal just got back to me. They agreed we need to interview William Gawlor. Just keep it polite.'

She said she would and then added that she planned to stop by Hereford Downs after that to see Chester Cunningham.

'Fine. But wait until these protesters leave. Take Roger with you.'

It was better than an outright refusal, and she returned to the office feeling like she had a plan forward. Roger was keeping unusually quiet. She wondered if he had heard her swearing at Stacey and was annoyed or upset with her.

After a while, she remembered Mulligan's instruction to keep an eye on the protesters and, wanting to stay in his good books now she had his permission to question Worm, she went back out the front to get a closer look. They were still yelling and holding up their placards. There was no breeze and the sun beat down as it neared mid-morning. She could feel the heat coming up from the bitumen and moved to lean against the brick fence over to one side to study their placards. There were names of people she recognised from the news. People who had died in police custody. Other media had also started to gather again, and she imagined the evening news. The pressure was about to increase.

She saw Lennon walking towards her and considered going back inside, but decided it would be more politic to stay put.

'I'm sorry if I was a bit harsh before,' Lennon said, opening his cigarette packet and offering her one.

'No, thank you.'

He took one for himself, lit it and turned to follow her gaze out over the crowd. 'Must be hard for you?' He blew the smoke to one side but the breeze carried it back over her face.

'What are you talking about?'

'Working for the cops. You're Aboriginal, aren't you?'

'I am.'

He took a long drag of his cigarette and nodded deeply.

'Mm, I thought so. You know that you're living in a society that doesn't recognise you, right? It doesn't recognise your people's right to sovereignty. That's why you feel so mixed up.'

'Why would you assume I feel mixed up?' Renee almost laughed. Who did this guy think he was?

'I can see it in your face. You haven't even come to realise yet how much society has screwed you and your people over. Once you do, you'll feel as angry as these people here today. The government has denied you everything in an attempt to assimilate your people into white culture. They've taken your land and your culture and your language. They've tried to give you a new way of thinking, Christianity and English. I'm on your side, Renee. Even though it seems like I'm not right now. I know you want to get to the bottom of this too.' He nodded again.

She stared at him incredulously then she really did laugh. 'I'm sorry, I know you mean well, it's just …'

She felt the laughter turn to anger and she shook from the energy pulsating through her. She tried to contain it, push it back down. She shuddered, wanting it to go away. If she said something offensive to him, asked him what a privileged white guy like him would know about her life, what anybody knew about how it felt to have a foot in each camp and be discriminated against by both, it would only take her backwards. She would inevitably end up managing his emotions, soothing him, trying to make him feel better while she felt worse.

Lennon looked startled by her laughter. She turned away to hide her rage and was saved by a woman with the Aboriginal flag across her chest who began chanting, 'What do we want?'

Only one person responded. 'Justice.'

'Fuckin gimme that, McGorrie.' The woman snatched the microphone away from Lennon's hands and, undeterred by the quiet response, bellowed, 'WHAT DO WE WANT?'

The crowd bellowed back in unison, 'JUSTICE!'

Renee turned back to face him. 'Lennon?'

'Yes, Renee?'

The woman's cry for justice had calmed her, grounded her. She felt her own rage vibrate in the woman's vocal chords. 'You don't know me. What makes you think you have the right to lecture me? In my own town, in front of the police station, where I work as a police officer. You've got some nerve.'

'I don't know what you mean …'

'Who are you, McGorrie?' He stood mutely, mouth slightly ajar. 'It's not a rhetorical question, Lennon. Who are you? Are you white? German? Scottish? Irish? Who the fuck are you? You dig into my identity, casually waltz around my life, my profession, my community. Tell me who I am. How about you back the fuck up, and take a look at yourself?'

'I'm ...'

'Actually, fuck off. I don't even care.'

She turned and walked away but he called after her, 'You're directing your anger at the wrong person, Renee. I'm on your side. Where are you going?'

Renee turned and looked at him, his cigarette still smoking in his right hand. 'To do my job.'

Chapter 16

A shiny new red Holden Commodore was parked in William Gawlor's driveway, and as she stopped the car out the front and turned off the engine she could hear music coming from inside the house.

'I know that song. What is that song?' Roger asked as he opened the front gate.

'"Achy Breaky Heart",' Renee said. She hated that song, but felt relieved to hear it because that meant someone was probably home.

'Yes! That's it. Billy Ray Cyrus. I used to love that guy.'

Renee supressed an eye roll. She knocked on the front door and half expected Tiffany to appear again but there was no answer, so she knocked again.

'I don't think anyone's home.' Roger's enthusiasm was on par with the teenagers Renee had watched returning to class the other day – so easily deterred. She went to the side and peered through the glass window.

'You can't do that. It's a violation of people's privacy.'

Renee waved him over. He looked around to make sure no one was watching, then joined her to peer through the curtain opening.

'I think someone's ignoring us.' The television was broadcasting some trivia show and Renee could see the back of a man's head poking up from the lounge and two big hairy feet resting on the coffee table.

'What do we do?' Roger looked at Renee for guidance, as the face of a giant mongrel, all teeth and slobber, lurched at them from the other side of the glass window, biting the air and barking.

'Holy shit,' Roger said, falling back on his bum. 'I told you we shouldn't be poking in people's windows.' Renee helped him back up to his feet as she heard the front door open from behind.

'Sit down, Chika – good dog.' A man who looked to be in his sixties opened the door and eyed the two officers. He was wearing an expensive polo shirt with white and orange stripes. Lacoste or Ralph Lauren. Something exorbitantly overpriced, denoted by the tiny animal neatly embroidered into the top left chest. His hair was combed back and his stomach bulged egg-like. His face was lined and oily, and his eyes heavy-lidded and half closed. Renee felt a shiver of distaste run through her. 'You know, it's commonly accepted protocol to knock on the door when you arrive at someone else's house?'

'Sorry, we did try …' Roger apologised, brushing the dirt off his pants and tucking his shirt in.

'William Gawlor?' Renee asked, peering inside. She could see a woman's leg hanging off the side of the couch and when she tiptoed slightly she saw the pink pug boxer shorts that Tiffany had been wearing.

'Indeed. The one and only,' he announced, placing his hands on hips and proudly letting his belly protrude even further. He smiled, but there was no joy in his eyes, just cold, calculated intensity, like a predatory reptile about to snatch its prey.

'I'm Detective Renee Taylor and this is Constable Roger Madden. We're investigating the death of a young woman. I'm sure you've heard about the body found by the creek.' She studied his face for reactions, resisting the temptation to step back, away from him.

'Mm ... I did hear about that. Terrible.' He exaggerated the word *terrible* and Renee picked up on his sarcasm.

'We need to ask you a few questions. Can we come inside?' As much as she didn't desire the prospect of being in a confined space with this man, she wanted to look around.

'Hm ... I dunno.' He looked back inside. 'Oi. Tiffany.' Tiffany dragged herself up and leaned over the top of the couch – limp limbed, with dazed eyes and a face filled with fatigue and void of expression. Renee wondered what she'd taken: heroin, ketamine, prescription pills, who knows. 'Clean up a bit, hey. We have some guests here.' Tiffany's gaze shifted from Renee to Roger and back to Renee, until recognition broke through. 'Yes, exactly. *Police*,' Worm continued, walking over to Tiffany and leaning in menacingly close to her face. 'So, how about you get off your skinny arse and clean up?'

Tiffany flinched then, dragged herself up and started cleaning the coffee table of dirty coffee cups, magazines, two mobile phones and something Renee didn't recognise until she leaned in a little closer. Toenail clippings.

'Please, officers. Do us the honour of gracing us with your presence.' Worm gestured for them to sit on the lounge, as Tiffany snuck away into the kitchen.

'Do either of you know this woman?' Renee held up the artist's impression. 'Tiffany? We would like to hear from you too.'

Tiffany came back out and looked at the picture. Renee watched her reaction closely. 'Nup, never seen her before. She's real pretty though.'

'Are you sure, Tiffany?' Tiffany was beautiful too, in her own way. Renee remembered what her mother had told her about Jill Huxley the night before. Tiffany seemed to be there by choice, but Renee wondered why. What evil games was Worm playing with this young woman? She suspected a toxic cocktail of addiction, threats of violence, low self-esteem and past trauma.

'I don't know her,' Tiffany repeated.

Worm leaned over far to his right. The sound of his neck cracking made Tiffany visibly tense. He studied the artist's drawing and exhaled acetone breath that made Renee want to gag.

'She's beautiful. Mm ... Lovely lips.' Renee fought back her repulsion. His eyes moved from the page back to Renee. 'But no, I've never seen her before.'

'Have you seen anything unusual around Goorungah lately? Any people hanging around that you don't recognise?'

'Bit of a crowd you've got down there today. Haven't seen many of them before.'

'I'm not talking about the protesters, Mr Gawlor.'

He shook his head slowly, as though he was bored with the questioning and glanced back towards the television. 'Am I under suspicion or something? Can we hurry this up a bit? I don't know the girl. I haven't seen anything unusual. I've been a good boy just like my lawyers keep telling me I should be.'

The mention of his lawyers, dropped casually into the conversation.

'This is just routine, Mr Gawlor. We're asking everyone around town.' It was only a slight stretch of the truth. 'Do you remember where you were on Tuesday morning?'

'Hm ... let me see.' He held his chin and looked past them. 'I was knitting a scarf for my grandmother.' Smart arse. 'I remember because I woke up early, fretting that I'd run out of pastel pink, and that is her favourite colour, you see.'

'Can anyone attest to that? Tiffany?' That was hopeless, of course she'd cover for Worm, but it was worth seeing the reaction.

'Tiffany wasn't here. She was in the city,' Worm answered for her.

Renee looked over at Tiffany, who nodded. 'It's true, I was with Mum in the city.'

'Can I get your mother's details?' Tiffany gave her a name and number and Renee jotted it down as something to follow up when she got back to the station. 'Was anyone else here ... while you were knitting?'

'Chika was here.' The dog leaped to its feet upon hearing its name, saliva dragging across Worm's pants.

'Anyone else? A person, maybe?'

'Naww. Chika, you're not enough.' He leaned down and played with the dog's ears.

'What is it you do for a living, Mr Gawlor?'

'J,' he said randomly.

'Excuse me?'

'The only letter that doesn't appear on the periodic table.' He motioned back towards the game show on television. 'Weren't you paying attention to Eddie?'

'Again, Mr Gawlor. What do you do for work?'

'Wholesale supply.'

'Right.' Renee returned his stare. The confidence of him. 'And I understand Archibald Ford is a regular customer of yours?'

He glared back and it was the first time she noticed a hint of defensiveness.

'How long did you say you were out here for, Detective Renee Taylor? Hold on a second, if I'm not wrong, you're Nurse Valerie's daughter, aren't you? Fancy that. Such a lovely small town we have here, where everyone knows each other.'

'We should leave you get back to your show, Mr Gawlor.' Roger, who had been standing by silently, suddenly spoke, turning to face Renee. She could feel his anxiety. 'Renee? Thank you for your time this evening, Mr Gawlor.'

'Any time.' He grinned as they turned to leave. She could see that he was enjoying Roger's stress. 'Give my regards to Mumsy!'

Renee remembered they weren't just looking into this recent death any more. She turned back. 'What about Caroline Forrest and Bessie Shields? They disappeared from this town about thirty-five years ago. Did you know about them?' She knew he wouldn't say anything but years of being a cop in the city had taught her the value of catching someone by surprise. Guilty people go quiet. The wrongly accused profess their innocence. In most cases, anyway.

'They were lovely girls who I had the pleasure of meeting on a few occasions.'

'When?'

'I don't remember.'

'Where?'

'Downtown somewhere, I think.'

'Some people say you and Bessie were spending time together.' She didn't want to mention Mrs Shields by name and put her in harm's way.

'Some people say a lot of things.'

'Do you know anything about her disappearance?'

'She was here one day, gone the next. I think she probably went off looking for adventure. She was bored in the town, wanted the city.'

'What about Caroline?'

'No idea what happened to her.'

All good liars know it's best to stay as close to the truth as possible. He knew Bessie, clearly, but what could she prove now, so many years later? She had bugger all on him. Anyone who lived in town back then would have known them. He smiled at her as if reading her thoughts.

Renee reminded Tiffany to call if she needed anything and they left, Renee relieved to be out of that house and away from Worm's breath and his slobbering mutt. 'The audacity of him. Wholesale supply! Can you believe it? He didn't even try to cover himself.'

'Shh … he can probably hear you,' Roger said as he wound up the passenger-side window.

'I don't care, he's a drug dealer.' Renee wound her window down.

'He might be dealing drugs, but we have no firm evidence of anything, Renee. Just keep your voice down.'

She rolled her eyes as she started the engine and pulled away. She let the silence hang as she drove. There were kids walking along dressed in sports gear kicking balls and carrying rackets heading to the indoor sports centre. 'Did you have a chance to look around?'

'A little.'

'He had two mobile phones.'

'So what?'

'Only dodgy people have two mobile phones.'

'My wife has two mobile phones.'

Renee looked across at him as she turned the corner. 'Maybe your wife's dodgy.'

'Renee, cut it out. There's no need to be nasty.' Roger turned his head away and looked out of his window.

'Why does she have two mobile phones?'

He paused. He was wondering whether he could trust her. 'Her boss gave her one for work and she has one for me and the kids. She says it helps her separate work from home.' There was a softness to his voice when he talked about his wife. 'Me and the kids got her the latest model for her birthday last month.' He smiled. 'She loves it.'

'Sorry, Roger.'

He glanced across at her, surprised. 'What for?'

'I was a bit of bitch.'

'You've got a lot on your plate.'

'It's no excuse.' She wanted to know about Trish, her work and how they'd met, but didn't feel the moment was right to ask questions. 'I'd love to meet her.'

'My wife?' His eyes sparkled.

'Yeah. Maybe when all this blows over and things calm down a bit.'

He nodded, smiling. 'That'd be nice. You'll like her.'

They turned into the station where a crowd of people had already gathered out the back in the parking lot. 4.55 pm. They didn't have a room big enough inside for the press conference so Stacey had cleared a section of the bitumen lot and set out a few rows of chairs. Renee spotted Mulligan on the back steps waiting behind a row of microphones. Her stomach dipped as she swung out of the car. 'Okay, we better get it over with.'

Melaleuca

The area was full of a motley collection of the local community and the media, including Lennon McGorrie. Jillian Crawley from Channel Five was front and centre in an entirely inappropriate fluorescent pink dress, directing the cameraman to a position near the lectern. Renee stepped up next to Mulligan, palms slightly sweaty as she gripped the edges of the lectern. Roger had taken up position at the back. He nodded at her and smiled. To the right, Nettie and Millicent stood together, and Clarence a bit further back.

Norm sat right at the front, fixing her with a beady eye, and Mrs Ford sat next to him, back straight, palms together. A stack of placards stood propped against the wall as the protesters rested on chairs. Renee cleared her throat nervously.

Mulligan leaned in. 'Better get on with it, Taylor.'

'Thank you everyone for coming.' Her voice came out shaky and barely audible. *Renee, pull yourself together.* She pushed her shoulders back.

'Welcome everyone. At approximately 6.45 on Tuesday morning, the body of a young woman was found dead near Fletchers Drive down by the Goorungah Creek. She had been murdered. She appears to be in her twenties, with dark brown hair and tan skin, approximately 1.70 metres tall, and she was wearing denim shorts and a purple top. A photofit image of her has been created.'

Stacey, standing behind her to the right, wheeled around a board with the image pinned to it.

'We are asking anyone who might know her to come forward and identify her. If anyone saw anything either early Tuesday morning or Monday night, or has any suspicion of any wrongdoing, we are asking them to come forward too.' Stacey replaced the artist's impression with an enlarged colour printout of the necklace found on the woman's body.

'The deceased was also wearing a pendant featuring a rare yellow sapphire. This appears to be the same necklace as belonged to Caroline Forrest. Caroline Forrest and Bessie Shields disappeared on 20 August 1966 from this town.'

There was an audible gasp from the crowd as Stacey unveiled the photographs of the two girls. The media pressed forward their questions, crowding each other out.

'Do you have any suspects?' This question came from multiple journalists, but Jillian Crawley was the loudest and closest.

'Not yet, but we have some promising leads that we're looking into.' Renee didn't want to encourage futile optimism, but she needed to give the town some reassurance that there was movement on the case.

'And what about motive?' Jillian jumped in again while she had the stage. 'Anything on why someone would commit such a heinous crime in a quiet country town like Goorungah?'

'We don't know the motive yet, Miss Crawley,' Renee replied succinctly and scanned the crowd for the next question, keen to move on and take attention away from Jillian. Such inflammatory questioning would only serve to build anxiety in the community.

'Was the woman Aboriginal?' She recognised his voice before she saw it was Lennon standing at the back away from the other journalists, next to Clarence. He stomped out his cigarette and stepped forward when she made eye contact. 'You said she had tanned skin but what does this mean? I think the community would like to know.'

'Mr McGorrie, racial identity is not something we can confirm with a DNA analysis, but given her physical appearance we are working on the assumption that she was Aboriginal.'

Millicent reached across and held Nettie's hand. Renee pressed on. A few more questions were raised, but they essentially covered the same ground and Renee was not able to give any further insight. She looked across at Mulligan, who nodded for her to wrap up. 'If anyone has any information about the young woman whose body we found on Tuesday or the disappearance of Bessie Shields and Caroline Forrest, please come forward.'

But her voice was drowned out by the clamour. At the back of the crowd, she saw Worm slip away into the shadows of the trees. He caught her eye and gave her a lazy salute as he left.

It was 7.30 by the time Renee got home. Goodness, Mum was going to be starving. She liked to leave the car at the station and walk home but given how late it was, she decided to drive the short distance home.

'Mum?' Renee sang out into a house that felt strangely empty. 'I'm sorry, Mum. I'm late again. Today was hectic …' She threw her bag on the table and went to get a beer out of the fridge, but there was still no answer. 'Mum?' A loud groan came from the bathroom. 'Mum!' She rushed down the hallway, heart thumping in her chest, to find her mother lying naked on the tiles.

'My goodness, Mum.' She reached for a towel to cover her body and kneeled on the floor. 'What happened?'

'I slipped. I was having a shower. I'm so bloody clumsy.' She whimpered and reached for the edge of the bathtub, trying to pull herself up, but grimaced and held her lower back.

'Wait, don't move. You may have broken something.' Renee helped her mother lie back down. 'I'll call an ambulance.'

'No.' Val reached for Renee's hand. 'I don't want an ambulance. Just let me lie here for a bit and then help me into bed. I'll be fine in the morning.'

Renee leaned down, keeping hold of her hand, 'Mum, you're hurt. I can see you're in pain. Please let me call an ambulance. Where does it hurt?'

Her mother pointed at her hip.

'You'll need to get that X-rayed. What if you've fractured something?' Renee wriggled out of her mother's clutches and left to find her phone. 'Don't move, Mum.' She felt an overwhelming fury towards her mother and the entire hopeless situation. She had worked so hard over the years to never be at the mercy of others. To be in control. Independent. Yet, here she was, with her mother lying naked on the floor, pitifully in need of the help of others. She got up to get her mobile and make the call.

'Emergency services, what is your emergency?'

'Yes, I need an ambulance – my mother has slipped and hurt herself.' She gave the address and returned to the bathroom floor.

'They'll be here soon.' Her mother was curled up with her face in her elbow. 'Mum?'

She sat down on the tiles and reached for her mother's face. She pulled away but Renee had already seen the tears. Her anger evaporated as quickly as it had arrived.

'Come here, Mum.' She fixed the towel around her mother's body, wiped the hair from her forehead and let her head rest on her thigh. Renee patted her back and her mother's sobbing deepened. Big whole-body heaves. 'There, there.' She patted her back. 'It's going to be okay, Mum.'

'I'm sorry, Renee,' she said, wiping away snot and tears with her skinny, twisted hand.

'Shhh ...' Renee patted and cooed until the sobbing softened. 'They'll be here soon. Everything's going to be okay.'

Her mother whimpered and hugged her leg. Renee imagined how much she would hate the prospect of returning to the hospital as a patient. She'd be cared for and washed down by her former colleagues. For a proud woman like Val, that would be excruciating.

'Come on, Mum, let me try to put some undies on you at least, hey?' Her mother's body started to wobble. Renee leaned over. 'Mum, are you laughing or crying?'

Her mother erupted into laughter.

'You're ashamed of your old mama's fanny!'

Renee started laughing too.

'I'm not ashamed, Mum. I just thought you'd want some undies on.'

'That's the least of my worries.' Her mother was struggling to get the words out between her fits of laughter. 'But go on then, grab those red lacy ones.'

'Mum!' Renee went into the bedroom to search her mother's top drawer. She was bent over giggling now too. Delirium had taken hold. She found a pair of sensible cottontails and a nightie and returned to the bathroom.

'These ones?' She moved the undies in a sexy motion against her hips, as her mother watched and laughed, naked on the floor, with just a towel covering her. They heard the ambulance pull up out the front, no siren tonight, and then the front gate opening and closing.

'Quick! Slide them on. So they don't see my hairy old fanny.' She slid the undies up her legs.

'Mum! Here, arms up.' She wiggled a nightie over her mother's head and pulled it down as much as possible to cover her waist.

'Hello?' A man's voice called from the front door, following by loud knocking.

'He sounds sexy too,' her mother said, winking at her.

'Yes, come in!' Renee called. 'It's open. We're in here.'

Renee helped her mother explain what had happened to the paramedics and then watched as they carefully moved Valerie onto a stretcher. She reached out to hold her hand as they passed through the lounge room and loaded her mother into the ambulance.

'Is she going to be okay, Dr Mac?' Renee asked the doctor when he came out of her mother's hospital room. Renee had ridden in the back of the ambulance with Val as she'd protested against any medical intervention that didn't involve painkillers.

'She's sedated now. She needs sleep.' He was a short pudgy man with round glasses and pink skin.

'Do you think I overreacted? She really didn't want to come here.'

'You did the right thing. If she's fractured her hip, we'll need to keep her in for some time.'

'When will you know for sure?'

'We'll run scans as soon as we can. From my initial assessment, I don't she's broken anything, but we need to play it safe. How did it happen?' the doctor asked. He gave her *the look*. Oh, the guilt.

She'd been meaning to get someone in to put a railing along the side of the bath for months.

'She slipped in the bathroom.' She would beat herself up enough when she got home without the added disapproval from this man. 'I know, we should have a better hand railing. It's my fault.'

'That's not what I was thinking.' He motioned for her to walk with him and she followed him down the hallway towards the entrance. 'I know Val's been on the list for a carer for some time now. You've moved back to look after her?' Renee nodded. 'That must be tough.'

'That's life.' She shrugged her shoulders.

'Being a full-time carer for someone with arthritis as progressed as your mother's can't be easy, Renee. Are you managing to take care of yourself? Let us take care of your mother for a while. I want you to go home and get a good night's sleep. When you wake up in the morning, you can come visit her. Okay?' She smiled. He had kind eyes. He turned to the nurse on reception. 'Can you get Lonnie back up here?'

Then he turned back to Renee. 'You rode in the ambulance, right? When you came here?'

Renee nodded. She hadn't even considered how she was going to get home.

'Lonnie will be here in a minute. He's the medic who you came here with. He'll give you a ride home.'

'Thanks, Dr Mac.'

Later that night, once she arrived back home, she did a quick check of the eggs and adjusted the lamp, which had shifted slightly when the paramedics had pulled the stretcher across the mat, and then got into bed.

As she stared at the stars glowing on the ceiling she thought about her apartment in the city and wondered what it would be like to be there again. The beautiful anonymity of bustling city life. When she couldn't sleep in the city, she'd often go for late-night walks through the park and along the river. No one knew her there, but if she went for a night-time walk here everyone would be talking about it the next day. 'I think the local detective's gone cuckoo – I saw her out walking the streets at one am.'

The faces from the press conference drifted in front of her. Worm's salute, Jillian Crawley's violently pink dress, the grief-stricken expressions of Millicent and Nettie. Lennon McGorrie's patronising question. Roger's reassuring smile. They merged into one and floated away. And then she slept.

Chapter 17

1965

Caroline loved the feel of the cold, damp earth in her hands as she pulled out weeds from the courtyard garden. It was mid-afternoon on Wednesday, her second week working at Hereford Downs. She had completed her morning jobs, then she'd prepared the lunch for the men and eaten the leftovers, and now she was enjoying tending to the garden knowing that Mrs Cunningham had made a trip into town and wouldn't be looking over her shoulder any time soon.

The night before, Bessie had thrown rocks at her shack again, trying to get her to come out, but she ignored it this time. She hadn't talked to her friend since they spent the night at the shed with Worm and Gappy, and she was actively avoiding her now. If Bessie wanted to ruin her life getting mixed up with those two, then that was her choice. She loosened a mound of dirt in her hands and let it crumble down into the garden. A worm remained slithering around in her hand, and she placed it carefully down beneath the parsley so its delicate skin wouldn't get burned by the sun. Footsteps came from behind.

'Caroline?' It was Chester. 'Come, I want to show you something.' He held out his hands to pull her up, and she shrugged and accepted.

'Show me what?' she asked.

'Just come.' She looked up towards the house. Chester read her mind. 'Don't worry, Mum won't be home for ages.'

She followed him down a garden path and out a small metal gate that screeched on its hinges. She had never gone beyond the house fence before. 'Where are you taking me?' She glanced back again to see if Mrs Cunningham was home yet.

'It's a surprise.' They weaved further along a narrow dirt path overgrown with shrubs and ivy until they came upon another gate. Chester opened it and led her through to an orchard full of trees overflowing with citrus fruits. 'Here, let's fill this for you.' Chester passed her a bag and reached up to pull off a mandarin. She opened the bag and he placed the mandarin in it.

'You sure your mum won't mind?' Caroline asked.

'Course not. Look how many we have! There's plenty to go around. Take some extra for the other families on the camp.'

Chester filled the bag with mandarins and moved on to the lemon tree until the bag was bulging.

'That's plenty, Chester.'

'Let me just get some of these grapefruits for you.' The grapefruits were higher up and there was a ladder placed by the trunk. 'I ran into Worm at the saleyards this morning,' Chester said, looking up into the tree branches.

'Oh yeah ...' She couldn't see his face. Why was he telling her this?

'Said that he had a good time with you and Bessie the other night.'

Caroline felt her pulse stop and then start again. Milli couldn't find out about that. 'I wouldn't describe it as a "good time".' She should've known that Worm would be the type to shoot his mouth off.

'Yeah, I thought it was a bit strange. Didn't pick you for one to hang out with Worm.' He came down the ladder and handed her two grapefruits, which she put in her bag. 'Is everything okay?'

'I went because Bessie wanted to. Thought someone should look out for her.' She saw something that looked like relief pass across Chester's face. He looked up to the branches once more. 'Why do you care anyway?'

A moment passed as he seemed to struggle to find words. Caroline was intrigued. Was he interested in her?

'I just wouldn't want you to get in any kind of trouble.'

'You think I can't handle myself?' She wanted to add that she didn't need his protection when she already had Milli, Pa Quincey and everyone else on the camp, but stopped short.

'It's just that I've heard some stories about them.'

'Down at the pub?'

'Yeah. I've seen them get into a few punch-ups down there.' He wasn't telling her anything that she didn't already know. Milli said Worm often got drunk and into fights at the pub. 'It's just that …'

'Chester.' She said it sternly.

'What?'

'I can look after myself.' She smiled when she said this, encouraging him to see the strength in her.

'I know you can. I just want to make sure that you know those guys are no good. And if you ever get stuck, you can call me.' He looked sincere, genuinely concerned for her safety, as he held out the bag.

'I'll be careful,' she promised, taking the bag and starting back up the hill. 'Now come on – we better get back up to the homestead or I'll have your mother to worry about and, quite frankly, she scares me more than Worm.' She turned back to him suddenly, worried that her tongue had loosened too much, checking to see if she'd offended Chester, but he was smiling.

'She scares me too.'

After her initial reluctance, working at Hereford Downs became surprisingly pleasant. Chester continued to pick her up each morning, and then she tended to her chores, prepared the lunch, snuck in some leftovers, and returned to the camp with Chester, chatting along the way about everything from annoying siblings to their mutual suspicion of religious indoctrination. Caroline told him all about her life on the camp, and he shared his ideas for how he would improve Hereford Downs and innovate the agricultural methods.

Caroline continued avoiding Bessie, which was easier than expected because Bessie seemed to be taking the same approach to Caroline, and she didn't see Worm or his sidekick Gappy again. The days passed in pleasant monotony for a few weeks but then the evening she'd been dreading arrived. Dinner for the Armstrongs.

They were early, of course. Caroline spied them out of the kitchen window while she was cutting the chicken. She didn't even have it in the oven yet, and here they were, one hour early.

'Caroline?' Mrs Cunningham appeared in the doorway, dripping in pearls, with big bouffy hair, a satin blue dress that Caroline had ironed and laid out for her earlier, and reeking of musk perfume.

'Yes, ma'am.' She turned to face her boss, apron covered in chicken fat and sweating profusely from running around the hot kitchen for the last few hours.

'The guests are here.' Mrs Cunningham gave her a look that filled her with panic. How anyone can get so worked up about a meal would forever baffle Caroline. 'Drinks?' she prompted, as though Caroline was an idiot.

'I'll be right in, ma'am.' Caroline smiled stiffly and watched her boss turn away in a huff. She looked around the kitchen. There was still so much to be done. She tried not to panic. She could hear the Armstrongs being welcomed into the parlour by Mr Cunningham as she poured four glasses of champagne and put them on a silver tray. Chester was joining them too, but he must've been held up in the yards somewhere, and Simon had gone down to the city to meet with some of the university staff. She took off her dirty apron before she entered the parlour, trying not to shake, and approached Mrs Armstrong with the tray of drinks.

'Ahh ... Here she is! You stole my girl!' Mrs Armstrong laughed at Mrs Cunningham.

'Now, you know that's not true!' Mrs Cunningham said, amused by Mrs Armstrong's backhanded compliment. All of this was said without a greeting to Caroline. 'I heard you were getting along just fine without any help.' Mrs Cunningham didn't say anything about Mrs Armstrong receiving assistance from her daughter around the house, because it would be too much of an offence to take a stab at Lola's dismissal from school.

'She was wonderful around the house.' Mrs Armstrong continued talking about Caroline as though she wasn't there, as Caroline offered Mrs Cunningham and then the two men glasses of champagne. She was relieved to get out again, and as she left she could hear them making a toast to Mrs Cunningham's birthday.

Back in the kitchen, she opened the oven to check on the chicken and turn the vegetables, then started on the appetisers.

'How's it going? You need a hand?'

Caroline turned to see Chester still wearing his farm gear. He was removing his hat and jacket.

'Chester, your mother's going to kill you when she sees you still in your work gear.' She continued preparing the appetisers.

'You really won't let me help you?' He came closer and she could smell the dirt on him. He smiled softly and it calmed her slightly. 'I know it's important to you to get this right, but really, they're just stuffy old people,' he said, and it made Caroline laugh.

'I'm okay, Chester. Please go and get ready before your mother comes back.' He left and she took the plate of appetisers in to the guests. The party moved into the dining room and she could hear their delight when Chester entered. Maybe this would actually turn out okay. She breathed a sigh of relief as she stood in the kitchen listening to the party chatting merrily, then assessed the plates all lined up, ready to go in. She took the main course through.

'Oh, smells delicious,' Mr Armstong said as she placed a plate down in front of him and continued around the table. Chester smiled at her as she set his plate down.

She returned to the kitchen to pick up more wine and was refilling glasses and half listening to their conversation when one story caught her attention. A man called Vincent Lingiari from the Northern Territory had walked off the land. He was demanding equal pay for Aboriginal workers.

'They're demanding equal pay?' Mr Armstrong demanded as he cut into his food. 'What kind of tomfoolery is that?'

Caroline topped up Mrs Armstrong's glass of wine, trying not to make eye contact with anyone although she could feel Chester's eyes on her.

'The blacks are getting too confident. If we don't draw a line now and say "no", they will just keep pushing and pushing,' Mrs Armstrong said.

Caroline took a step back to check on the table. Everyone's glasses were full. She turned to leave hurriedly, keen to avoid being in the room for the rest of this conversation, but Mrs Cunningham reached out and grabbed her arm.

'Another plate of bread. Please make sure it's warmed before serving.'

Caroline left as Mrs Cunningham rejoined the conversation. 'I absolutely agree. It's for the good of the nation. We must present as one, and to do that we need to assimilate the blacks – well, those who *can* be assimilated – as a matter of urgency. It's already gone on too long.'

Caroline reached the kitchen and held on to the end of the table to stabilise herself, drawing air into her lungs. She hadn't realised she was holding her breath. The conversation had affected her in ways she couldn't articulate. She felt more than angry and more than scared. Invisible. Like her feelings existed, but her body didn't. She was irrelevant to these people.

'Are you okay?' It was Chester. He had followed her in.

'What are you doing in here? You're going to get me into trouble, Chester. I'm fine.'

'I can see you're not. I'm so sorry, Caroline. They're bloody vultures, those Armstrongs, and my mother's not much better.' He poured a glass of water, pulled the chair out from the table for her to sit and handed the water to her. He sat down too. 'Have some.' She took it reluctantly and told him again to go back into the dining room before his mother found them, but he refused. 'I don't want to. I'd rather stay with you.'

She could smell his faint cologne and for the first time she noticed the strength of his upper body and his rigid jawline. He looked handsome in his crisp white shirt.

'Do you like it here on the farm?' she asked, feeling her body again. She was still there.

He smiled and leaned back in his chair, seeming relieved that she'd stopped asking him to go away. 'I do like Goorungah. And I like being with my brothers. How about you? Do you like it here?'

'It's crazy sometimes. Kids and dogs everywhere, and Milli's always nagging me, but the camp is my home.'

'If you could go anywhere in the world, where would you go?'

'I don't know. I've never been asked that question before. I would like to see the ocean.' She looked across at him and tried to imagine what it would be like to be by the water with him. A peaceful feeling came across her. 'How about you? Where would you like to go?'

'I want to go to Sydney.'

'Why Sydney?'

He grinned shyly. 'I like designing things … and building. I would like to see the Harbour Bridge, and the Opera House before they finish building it.'

They felt a presence behind them and turned.

'The bread?' Mrs Cunningham was staring straight at Chester.

Melaleuca

Caroline got to her feet. 'Sorry, Mrs Cunningham. I'll bring it in right away.'

'Let me help.' Chester leaped to his feet, but Mrs Cunningham stepped in his way.

'Chester, your father would like you back in the dining room immediately.'

Chester gave Caroline a knowing grin out of his mother's view, and then went back in. The conversation was increasingly boisterous. Mrs Cunningham gave Caroline a hard stare, shook her head in dismay and turned to follow her son.

Caroline put the bread in the oven. When it was hot, she cut it into slices and, with dread, re-entered the room to find that everyone had finished their meals and moved back to the parlour. There was no need for the bread any more. No doubt she'd hear about that later from Mrs Cunningham.

She cleared the plates from the dining room, piling them high in the kitchen sink and, on the request of Mrs Cunningham, hurried back to the parlour to refill the men's glasses. They were drinking whiskey now and Mr Armstrong was standing over the old record player taking song requests. It was going to be a long night. She knew how much the Armstrongs could drink and that they loved to stay up late and carry on into the early hours.

'Caroline, what would you like to hear? Some Patsy Cline maybe?' Mr Armstrong asked. He was breaking protocol by talking to her so openly and for a brief moment the room shifted its gaze to her.

'Thank you. Whatever you like, Mr Armstrong.' He grinned back at her and she eagerly left the room. She turned on the tap to fill the sink with hot water and scratched left-over food from the plates into the bin. The music got louder in the room next door.

'Mmmm ... That warm bread smells wonderful.' It was Mr Armstrong. She turned as he came up behind her. 'Can I have a little?' Suddenly she felt his hands on her waist and she could feel his breath on her neck.

'Mr Armstrong.' Caroline moved quickly away from his reach and found the plate of sliced bread on the end of the bench. 'Ahh, here it is. I'll bring some in right away.'

He came towards her again, placing his hands on her hips, and she froze, wondering whether to slap him away, or tell him to stop, or move away again. She could smell whiskey as he leaned in against her body, and in her mind all she could see was the look of disgust on Mrs Cunningham's face. She couldn't move. She had failed the dinner party. All she had to do was help Mrs Cunningham celebrate and then she'd keep giving her leftover sausages to take home to Milli at the end of the day so Pa could eat a decent meal and give his leftovers to Star dog. Mr Armstrong's lips sucked on her earlobe and his belly pushed up against her. All she had to do was disappear. It was easy. She wasn't even there. She didn't exist. Invisible.

'What the fuck are you doing?' Chester boomed, his voice bringing her back into her body, and Mr Armstrong stumbled back, doing up his front zip. The two men eyed each other. 'Your wife wants you back in the parlour, Mr Armstrong.'

Mr Armstrong started laughing and Chester moved forward, grabbing him by the shirt collar. 'I should throw you out the fucking door, you mongrel.' Mr Armstrong stopped laughing, and Chester pulled his face in closer. 'If I ever catch you anywhere near her again I'll belt the living daylight out of you.' When Mr Armstrong didn't reply, Chester shook him. 'You hear me?'

'Okay, okay.'

Chester pushed him out of the kitchen then turned to Caroline. 'Are you okay? I'm so sorry. Let me take you home.' He put his hand on her shoulder but she shrugged it away.

'I'm okay. Seriously. Please. I need this job.'

'You used to work for them. Has he ever tried anything like that before?'

Caroline looked down. She felt ashamed, but didn't know why – what had she done wrong? Nothing. So why did she feel guilty?

'He used to look at me all the time. Once he tried to keep me from leaving the room but I managed to dodge him.'

Chester suddenly became strangely calm, his face set – it frightened Caroline.

'Chester, if you interfere or do anything, I will lose this job and I need it. He'll stay away from me now.'

Eventually Chester relented but insisted she stay in the kitchen, and he brought in the dirty dishes, then helped her scrub and clean. When Mrs Cunningham came in to check on her, Chester pulled his mother to the side where Caroline couldn't hear, and eventually she heard the Armstrongs leave.

Chapter 18

A few days after the evening with the Armstrongs, Chester was late. He had been on time ever since the first day, but today he wasn't. She waited by the fireplace with Pa Quincey, which she didn't mind at all because he was in a good mood and had stories to tell. When Chester did eventually arrive he didn't greet her with his usual smile, and as they drove away from the camp along the dirt road he tapped and hummed despite the radio being off. After a few more minutes of this strange behaviour, she couldn't take it any more.

'You alright, Chester?' He slowed the truck down to a stop and looked across at her. 'Chester, what are you doing?'

'Caroline.' There was something about the way he said her name that sent shivers through her. Had she done something to upset him? Why was he being so serious?

'There's a dance on Saturday,' he continued.

Caroline smiled. Is that what he was getting all worked up about?

'A dance?' She'd heard about these dances, but they weren't for people on the camp. They were for the rich white farm kids. Not even Worm or Gappy would be welcome at one of those flash dances.

Melaleuca

'I was wondering if you'd come with me.'

She took a deep breath. Surely Chester knew better than this. What was he playing at? 'Chester,' she said, hoping that she wouldn't need to launch into an explanation about how the town's hierarchy operated. 'You know why I can't come with you to the dance. People aren't going to like that and you know it.'

'I don't care what *people* like. I want you to be my date.' His expression was pained and she had the urge to hold his hand, but she didn't want to encourage his advances. The truth was cold and cruel.

'Look, Chester. I like you, I really do, but this just is not the kinda town where a fulla like you can take a girl like me out to a dance.'

'Hold on. Did you just say you liked me?' He sat straight, with eager eyes. It was not the effect she had hoped for. She wanted to deter him, not encourage him.

Finally she met his gaze and smiled. 'Of course I like you.'

'So, that's all that matters.'

'What do you mean, "that's all that matters"?' She rolled her eyes at him but couldn't help smiling.

'I would love it if we went to the dance together, but, honestly, I just want to spend more time with you. At the dance, in this beautiful big rig,' he gestured around the inside of the vehicle, 'at the camp, if you let me. I'd love to meet more of your friends, and get to know Milli and Pa Quincey some more.'

'You're crazy, Chester.' She laughed.

'Crazy for you, Caroline.'

She stopped laughing, and this time he caught the moment perfectly – he leaned in and kissed her, and she kissed him back.

She wanted the moment to last but could hear a car coming along the road behind them. A group of young larrikins slowed down and peered inside as they drove past. 'Woo-wooo. Get a room, you two!' they called out.

'What are you looking at?' Caroline called back, momentarily surging with confidence from the euphoria of the kiss. She didn't recognise them – probably farm boys from further west. Caroline turned back to face Chester, who shrugged, seeming just as surprised at her outspokenness. This time she took the initiative and leaned in to kiss him. When their lips parted, she whispered, 'I want to go to the dance with you.'

Caroline waited outside their shack trying not to let Star jump on her and dirty her dress with his paws. He sensed the excitement in the air and ran zoomies around Caroline. Milli had found her a yellow silk dress in the church's charity bin – probably a dress that once belonged to the wife of a wealthy pastoralist, but it didn't matter because it was her favourite colour and it was beautiful. It was two sizes too big, but she had brought it in using Mrs Cunningham's needle and thread. It glistened in the sunlight as she waited for Chester, shifting from foot to foot to calm her nerves.

For the past few evenings Milli had been teaching her how to dance the waltz around the backyard. Apparently, she'd learned by watching some of the patrons at the pub after they'd had a few drinks and cleared the chairs to the side. Caroline didn't want to let her sister know that maybe the Goorungah pub was not the best place for picking up dance moves, but she didn't want to sound like an uppity snob and let her sister swing her around the backyard.

Milli had been angry when she first found out about Chester's invitation. They'd been out the back tending to the oils after

Melaleuca

Sunday church one morning and Milli had asked Caroline who was making her cheeks all rosy. She probably could have guessed who it was because Caroline had been returning from Hereford Downs in a good mood for the past few weeks, but she asked anyway, and Caroline confirmed that it was indeed Chester Cunningham. She reluctantly told her about the dance, and Milli scowled and ranted until she finally calmed down and admitted that she was relieved it wasn't Worm or Gappy, but she still had her concerns.

'Oh, girl, now why'd you have to go fall for that boy? You know this is gonna end in heartbreak?' Milli had cried.

'I tried to tell him "no", Milli, but he don't care what people think.' Caroline had immediately regretted telling her.

'That dance is for the white kids, Callie. You ever see any Murris go to them dances?' Milli had lectured her like a little girl as Caroline picked the petal sticks from the blossoms she'd picked from the garden. She eventually softened, got up from tending to her oils and came to stand next to Caroline, placing her hand beneath her chin to lift her gaze to meet hers. 'You know it's just cos I love ya. I don't wanna see you get hurt.' Caroline had stared back sadly, and Milli had taken her in an embrace, pulling Caroline's skinny body against her soft curves.

Now as Caroline stood out the front of her shack on the day of the dance, she patted her hair again on the sides making sure there were no fly-away strands. After Milli had accepted she was going to the dance, she'd helped Caroline style her hair that afternoon and even let her borrow some of her spray. She felt reasonably satisfied that it would hold in place. Pa sat beside her, chipping away at his emu egg, carving landscapes and animals into its hard blue-green shell.

'He's late. He promised me he wouldn't be late.' She didn't expect Pa to respond. The old man was not one to get caught up in the romances of the young ones around the camp, even if she was his granddaughter. But his chuckling surprised her. 'What you giggling about, Pa? It's not funny!'

'He's not late, girl, you just nervous – time's going slower for you today.' He was right, she realised. She wanted to ask him about Nana Tamar, but years of silence on that subject cautioned her against raising it now. She sensed that just speaking her name would open a torrent of grief; his love for her was too much for words. Let her memory rest peacefully in his heart.

She had told Bessie about Chester's invitation that morning. She should have known better than to expect her friend to be happy for her. 'You womba, girl,' Bessie had said as they stood filling their buckets by the communal tap.

'You don't know anything, Bessie.'

'I know that he's a rich white boy and you're a poor black girl.' She'd spat it out fiercely.

'Yeah? So what?'

'Have you even thought about who's gonna be at that dance tonight?' Bessie gently shoved her to the side and put her empty bucket beneath the tap. 'Whitefullas, that's who. And they all gonna be laughing at you, cos you reckon you can date a white man.'

'Stop it, Bessie.' Caroline stood with her hands on her hips. She didn't want to hear this from her friend. Bessie was supposed to be on her side but after that evening with Worm and Gappy, Caroline had realised that Bessie cared more about having a good time than looking out for her.

Finally she spotted the ute coming up the dusty path. He got out, looking handsome with his freshly shaved face, pressed white shirt and grey slacks.

'I got this for you.' In his hand was a flower corsage of white melaleuca blossoms, green eucalypt leaves and yellow roses. He must have cut the flowers himself from the garden. They were tied with a white ribbon. He helped her pin the corsage at her waistband and stepped back to judge the effect. 'You look stunning in that colour.'

'Yellow's my favourite.' She touched the corsage gently and prayed that the evening would go smoothly. Chester seemed calm, which was a good sign.

'Chester Cunningham.' It was Milli marching over from the shed. Caroline had begged her earlier not to hound Chester and ruin the moment.

'Sorry,' she whispered and Chester took her hand and squeezed it reassuringly.

'It's okay.'

'So.' Milli stopped, hands on hips, and looked Chester up and down. 'This is the man who's makin my sister daydream more than usual?' Milli had met Chester before around town but they hadn't been introduced properly. 'So much for just giving my sister a lift to work, huh?' Caroline wanted to disappear. 'Now you're taking her to a dance?'

'Milli!' Caroline said under her breath and scowled.

'Nah, it's alright. I'm just bossin him.' Milli smiled, clearly enjoying the role of protective sister. 'But you have my sister home before midnight or there'll be big trouble, you hear?'

'I will,' Chester promised. 'I'll take good care of her.'

'Come on. Let's go.' Caroline pulled him towards the car, and then turned back to her sister. 'It's just a dance, Milli. Relax!'

As they drove out of the camp, she spotted Bessie standing to one side watching them leave. Neither girl waved.

They drove towards the town hall, where a sea of white faces was huddled around the outside, the women all dressed up for the occasion in their colourful dresses, the men with their stiff ironed shirts and polished shoes. Chester held her hand and gently guided her through the crowd. 'It's going to be okay,' he whispered.

As they approached the entrance, Caroline put her hand through his arm and let him lead the way into the hall. She had been inside plenty of times before because the church often used it as a function centre when it was raining. It was an old building with tall ceilings and scuffed wooden floors. Tonight, though, the dance organisers had prettied up the place for the occasion, adding tall vases filled with roses – red and white – and they had lined the entrance with long red carpets. People stood around outside, sipping their glasses of punch, eyeing off any newcomers. Although it was a small town and most people were already well acquainted, an unusual air of formality prevented them from rushing towards one another and laughing and chatting like they normally would.

The music had already started when they entered and there were at least six couples swaying on the dance floor. Chester spotted two of his friends standing to one side and motioned Caroline over to where they stood with their dates, although she needed no introduction to one of them – Lola Armstrong.

'Caroline, this is Hector and Patty Fitzgerald. They live on the big property further west.'

She knew the house he was referring to. It was a grand white homestead with manicured lawns and a white picket fence around the perimeter.

She greeted the boys and, as though reading her mind, Chester explained, 'The boys went to boarding school down in the city, that's probably why you don't recognise these two handsome faces.' He went to pinch Patty playfully on the cheek.

'Get outta here, ya ratbag,' Patty said, pulling away and putting his hand out to shake Caroline's. 'Nice to meet you, Caroline.'

Hector similarly introduced himself, and despite the vast difference in their appearances – Hector was pale and skinny, while Patty was strongly built with dark features – they had similar gestures and voices.

'This is Lola,' Patty said, turning to his date.

Lola smirked at Caroline. 'Hi, Caroline. Fancy meeting you here.'

'Hi, Lola.' Caroline explained to Patty that they were already acquainted because she used to work on the Armstrong property. She caught a look from Chester at the mention of the Armstrongs, so she shook her head slightly then smiled to assure him she was fine.

'And this is Janelle,' Hector said, introducing his date, a stunning brunette in a long flowing orange gown.

Both women looked at her with pity and judgement. Neither extended their hand to Caroline.

'Nice to meet you,' Caroline lied. The men chatted among themselves about agricultural mechanics and tractor sales. Away from their gazes, the two women changed. Lola's eyes narrowed and Janelle's mouth twisted in disdain.

'Your dress is pretty,' Lola commented. Caroline could feel her eyes go up and down and then she winked at Janelle with a knowing grin.

'I like your corsage too,' Lola said, then laughed into her hands.

'Thanks.' Caroline reached down and touched the eucalypt leaves. It was comforting in the face of these two women. Whatever they had going on with their men, it was nothing compared to the feelings she shared with Chester. What they had was something genuine and sweet.

'Did you make it yourself?' Lola continued. Caroline ignored her and looked around the hall again to see if she recognised any of the faces. Maybe there would be someone else there she could go and talk to and get away from Lola and Janelle, but her eyes fixed on the exit. 'Did you make it yourself?' Lola repeated louder, leaning in.

'Chester gave it to me.' The exit was not far away. Maybe this was a mistake. She looked over at Chester but he was lost in conversation with the men. He had promised her that he would look after her.

'You know, you can tell how much a fella likes you by the gift he gets you. Patty bought me back a set of emerald earrings from the city last month. I'm not wearing them tonight because they don't go with my dress. *And* they're too expensive to wear to a local dance.' Janelle gave exaggerated approval by nodding earnestly while Lola explained. 'I'm saving them to wear when I go down to the city. Patty said he'll take me to a dance down there soon.'

'I'm sure they're real pretty,' Caroline said, and wondered if she would ever see anything pretty in Lola ever again.

'Maybe Chester will get you something nice *one* day.'

Much to Caroline's relief, a man appeared on stage and the crowd fell silent as excitement quivered around the room. He was about sixty years old with a big belly that made his tuxedo stretch around his waist.

'Good evening, folks of Goorungah!' he bellowed. 'I am honoured to be your master of ceremonies on this wonderful Saturday evening!' As he introduced the band, the crowd cheered and clapped. The men all started heading towards the back, and the girls to one side of the room. Caroline was ready for this part, and she smiled confidently at Chester. Milli had explained that this would happen at the start of the night, and then the master of ceremonies would invite the men to lead their partners to the floor. Milli had worked with the team doing the catering for a few of the dances over the years and seemed proud she could impart this knowledge to her younger sister.

Lola and Janelle stood a few feet to her left and she was relieved to have some distance from them. She looked across the room and thought proudly that Chester was easily the most handsome among the men. He caught her eye and smiled back. The taunting of the girls was in the past now. She would simply avoid them for the rest of the evening, now she knew Lola hadn't changed from that nasty girl who had watched her clean porridge off the floor, and Janelle was similarly nasty, and focus on having a good time with her date. She'd show everyone! Who cared what people thought anyway? Chester was right. Even Bessie could get lost with her stupid warnings about this evening. She'd probably be getting drunk with Worm and who knows what else. Caroline was going to make a life for herself. She was strong, and beautiful, and Chester liked her, and nothing else mattered.

'Now, gentlemen,' the master of ceremonies announced and the crowd hushed in anticipation. 'I invite you to please take the hand of your partner and lead her to the dance floor.' She winked at Chester as he walked towards her and held out his hands.

'Can I have this dance, beautiful lady?'

She beamed, and felt her heart beat with the light and warmth of a joy she'd never known before. She took his hands and he guided her into the middle of the room. The band launched into an upbeat country song and all the couples around them dived right in to a lively jig. Chester guided her through the moves, swinging her around with strength and ease, and Caroline let her body relax and move in time with the music, thinking that she'd never had so much fun in all her life.

After a few more songs, the master of ceremonies came back on stage and called supper. A mad dash to the back of the room followed, where there was a large table neatly laid out with plates of sandwiches and freshly brewed tea. Hector and Patty came to sit with her and Chester, but Janelle and Lola mingled with some other ladies. Caroline could see them across the room and wondered whether she should make more of an effort to go and join them, but she was so comfortable sitting next to the men and listening to them go on about cows and fences and rain and wheat crops. It was not her cup of tea, but there was something soothing about the monotony and predictability of their conversation. They weren't talking about other people, like Lola and Janelle would be.

She could see Lola and Janelle pointing at people around the room, sneering and giggling.

The music began again with less formality and excitement than before as the initial ice had been broken and all the partners had

Melaleuca

been established. Chester beckoned Caroline to the dance floor once more and they swayed to the gentle country ballad.

'Are you having a good time?' he asked as Caroline leaned against him and moved with his rhythm.

'When's the next one?' she asked in response, moving in close to him so her head was just beneath his chin, feeling the warmth of his chest. Out of the corner of her eye, she caught Lola at the side of the room staring directly at her. It took her a moment to realise that Janelle was by her side, and they were both sharing the same expression. Satisfied evil glee. Why weren't they dancing with Hector and Patty?

Caroline lifted her head and quickly glanced around the room. The dance floor was empty. How long had she and Chester been the only couple dancing? She let go of Chester's hand and turned in a circle around the room to see that the entire crowd was watching from the sideline. Her heart started to beat wildly.

Chester was looking around the room in astonishment, as though trying to make sense of what was happening. She stepped back away from him. Lola and Janelle started to laugh and some of the others followed. She spotted Patty and Hector with their heads lowered as though in shame, avoiding eye contact. So that's what Lola and Janelle had been up to in the break. They'd been organising this. For her to be embarrassed and alone on the dance floor.

'Do something, Chester.' She wanted to grab his face and plead for him to fix it. He had said he would look after her. She wanted to sink into the floor and never be seen again by these people. She wanted to scream at them and tell them they were awful human beings.

'I'm so sorry, Caroline.' That's all he could say. The music had stopped and the master of ceremonies stood helplessly on the stage.

'We're not dancing with an Abo,' one of the girls yelled. Caroline didn't recognise her face, but made a mental note of the tight auburn curls and round freckled cheeks.

'Yeah, this is no place for you lot. Go home!' one of the men sang out, another face without a name, but his cruel eyes would forever be etched in her mind, and cheers followed from around the crowd.

Chester took her shaking hands. 'I don't care what they think. Please stay with me.'

She was frozen in place.

'Hector! Patty!' he yelled at his friends, but they shrugged uselessly as Janelle and Lola stepped in front of them, guarding them. Caroline pulled her hands away from him and ran towards the exit. 'Caroline, come back! Don't go!'

She bolted out the door, leaving the laughter and jeering behind her, welcoming the freezing air and windy night. She ran faster, trying to get as far away from the hall as possible, adrenaline propelling her forward. She ripped off her shoes and continued barefoot with them in her hands, pulling at the flowers Milli had neatly woven through her hair, feeling naive and stupid.

Chester caught up with her a few blocks down from the hall. It was late and the street was empty. Most houses were dark, their occupants having retired for the evening. The sound of the music starting back up and cheers of rejoicing could be heard from the hall. She stopped, exhausted, as he caught up to her.

'Please, Caroline. I'm so sorry. Don't leave. We can go someplace else. I don't even care what those people think.'

'They're your people, Chester. Whether you like it or not, you are white and I am black, and this town of ours is never gonna let us forget that.' She shoved him in the chest and he took her in his arms and tried to hold her, but she pushed him away.

'Please, Caroline. I'll do whatever you want me to. You want me to go back and shut that place down right now? I will. I'll do it.'

'You're asking me now?' she yelled back at him. 'Why didn't you do it back there? You could have got on stage and taken the microphone from the master of ceremonies. You could have gone up to Hector and Patty and given them a piece of your mind. But no. You chose not to. You chose to stay quiet. And now it's too late. The damage is done.'

'I'm sorry,' he said and fell silent. They stood opposite each other on the dark empty street. There was nothing left. The night was cold and Caroline's heart was hurting. She pulled off the corsage. Maybe Lola was right. If he really liked her, he would've given her something that wasn't homemade.

'I'm sorry too, Chester. I may be young and people think I'm a dreamer, but I'm not stupid. I can see a path to heartache and tears when it's in front of me, and this here with me and you, it isn't gonna happen in this town.'

'At least let me drive you home,' he pleaded, reaching for her as she started walking away.

'Just leave me be, Chester.' She left him standing there and headed back towards the camp, to Milli, who would scold her for being foolish but hold her until her heart mended. And Pa, who would tell her a simple story by the campfire that would seem like nothing at first, but then the meaning would blossom later and meander through her life. The camp might laugh and tease her and tell her she was silly, but then they would welcome her back into their world, the same harsh world that she knew was destined to be hers too. Maybe Bessie was right. May as well just have some fun and live for the moment.

She realised she was still holding the corsage and with a sudden burst of fury she wrenched it apart, scattering the flowers on the ground, the yellow rose petals and white melaleuca blooms bright against the darkness.

Chapter 19

Saturday 12 February 2000

Her phone was ringing. Renee sat up, adrenaline spiking as images from the night before flashed across her mind. Her mother lying naked on the bathroom tiles. The flashing lights of the ambulance. The all-white of the empty hospital corridors. She jumped out of bed and pulled open the curtains. It was still dark outside so she fumbled around for the switch, finally lighting up her bedroom.

She had been so tired last night, returning late from the hospital, that she had dropped everything on the floor and fallen straight into bed. Now as her phone continued ringing, she scrummaged around her clothes, convinced something bad had happened, probably to her mother – maybe she'd taken a turn for the worse, or maybe there'd been another murder, maybe Lisa Moore was right to fear further killings, and she would be to blame. Her fatigued mind raced through increasingly paranoid possibilities for her phone to be ringing so early in the morning until, finally, she located it in her jacket pocket.

'Detective Taylor speaking.' She coughed to clear her husky throat and sat at the end of the bed to steady herself. 'How can I help? Who is this?'

'Good morning, Detective. This is Adriana calling from the state intel hotline in Brisbane.' Not her mother. A slight relief came over her. 'We have a call for you.'

'From who? What did they say?'

'Actually, he's on the line now.'

She glanced across at the time. Five am. Who called police hotlines at this hour? 'I tried to take a report, but he insisted on talking to the detective leading the case.'

'What's his name? Is he serious?' Renee scratched around on the floor, found a notepad and went to sit at the kitchen table.

'Like I said, Detective, he wouldn't tell me anything.'

'Okay, put him through.'

Renee could hear clicking as the call was transferred. She waited, hoping the call wouldn't disconnect, until finally the gruff voice of an elderly man came through the line. 'Hello? Can you hear me?' His voice was a little hoarse and she guessed he was probably around her mother's age, maybe a bit older.

'Yes, this is Detective Taylor. You've called through to the tip-off hotline. What's your name, sir?'

'My name's Graham Bell.' He said it very clearly and seriously with a slight British accent – English-born but living in Australia a long time, Renee guessed. Renee knew that the hotline received a lot of hoax calls, but this man didn't sound like he was fooling around.

'Thank you, Mr Bell, can you tell me what you know about the woman found in Goorungah?' Renee tried to write in her notepad, but the ink in her pen had run out, so she ran for the one in the mug on the kitchen table but it was no longer there.

'I don't know anything about that woman. That's not why I'm calling.' There was a hint of frustration in his voice.

Melaleuca

'Then you're calling about Bessie Shields and Caroline Forrest?'

'Yes. I'm calling about those Aboriginal girls who went missing back in the sixties. I saw it in your press conference on the news last night.' She had missed the news because she'd been busy helping her mother after the bathroom fall, but she assumed they'd showed the same photograph of the girls. 'They were asking anyone to call in with information. Is this the right telephone line?'

'Yes, please go on, sir.' Renee scratched around behind the cushions on the couch trying to locate a pen. She was sure she'd seen her mother do a crossword here a few days ago.

'I never heard about it back when I was driving those roads. I was a trucker when I first arrived in Australia, you see? I did the long stretches from Brisbane city all the way out to Quilpie in the west. Eleven-hour stretch of road, so you see some things. And sometimes you just think you see some things. It gets lonely and the imagination can run wild.'

'Sir, sorry – what does this have to do with the missing girls?' Renee shook her head trying to wake herself up.

'Well, nothing, directly. I'm just providing you with some context, Detective. I'm saying that the stretches of road are vast, and people see strange things on those outback tracks. But I did see that girl.'

'Which girl?'

'Keep up, Detective. The girl they showed on the news last night. Well, they showed two girls, but it was that Caroline that I saw.'

'You saw Caroline Forrest?' Her pen was finally working. 'Did you say you saw Caroline Forrest, sir?'

'Yes, I remember seeing her, and I know it was on the twentieth of August because I had to get to Cunnamulla that evening with a load, reload up, and then turn back in time to get home to my family for my daughter's birthday on the twenty-first.' That was the day Nettie Shields and Millicent Forrest had reported last seeing the girls.

'What exactly do you remember, sir?'

'This girl – Caroline – she was bolting along on a bike. I could see her in the distance as my truck was approaching. Her feet were smashing down on the pedals, and when my truck got closer she didn't move off the road, so intent was she in getting to her destination that maybe she didn't hear or see my truck. The gush of wind from passing sent her off her bike and she toppled over into the grass.' Renee closed her eyes and tried to imagine the scenario playing out. 'So, I slammed on my brakes and stopped the truck as soon as I could, a few hundred yards along, then ran back to check on her. She was okay, a bit scratched on her knees and palms where she'd broken her fall, but she was fine. I tried to help her up but she waved me off.'

'Did she say anything? Where she was going or if she was in trouble?'

'No. I asked if she needed a hand getting to wherever she was going, but she said she was fine and didn't need any help.'

'How did she seem?'

'Scared, but more than anything I would say she seemed very focussed. Like she was on a mission.'

'And then what happened?' Renee tried not to be distracted by the cockroach crawling across the kitchen floor then underneath the fridge.

'Well, she picked up her bike and kept going. You know, I never would've remembered it, if it hadn't been for the news report last night. I never even knew those two girls went missing.'

'Did you see where she went?'

'I saw her turn off the main road out of Goorungah and up towards the industrial estate.'

'And what did you do then?'

'Well, like I said, I had a load to deliver further west so I got on my way. I mean, she was fine, just a bit scratched up from the fall, bleeding a little from the knees, but she was able to ride again, no problem.'

Renee took down the man's number, gave him hers and told him to call her back directly if he thought of anything else.

It was still early, around six am. Too early to call Mulligan. So she decided to go for a look around the industrial estate herself. Maybe being in the area would help her get into Caroline's mind and better imagine what the man had just relayed to her.

She veered right from the main road heading towards the city and then right again into the abandoned industrial estate, the direction Graham Bell had said he'd seen Caroline Forrest turn in, and past a deserted house that probably once belonged to someone who serviced the area.

She'd been to the area a few times as a kid, but she'd never examined it from the perspective of an investigator. Despite the perfectly clear sky, the place still felt cold and dark. Long shadows were cast by the huge wheat silos, old empty fuel tanks, truck weighbridges and cotton sheds, all made from galvanised steel and concrete. Even the ground felt cool.

She walked towards the old cotton shed, pushed the timber plank doors open, which screeched loudly as they swung on their old rusty hinges, and went inside. When she was a child, this shed had been filled with giant mounds of soft cotton seeds that provided an exquisite place to run around and jump in, the closest thing to bouncing on clouds. It was empty now, just a few bits of scrap metal laying around in cobwebs on a cold hard dirt floor and pigeons cooing high above out of sight.

Renee wondered if Caroline had ridden her bike up to the shed. Had she gotten off and looked around inside? Did she meet someone here? Maybe Bessie and Worm were waiting for her and they'd all agreed to run away together? Maybe they chose this location because the shed was large enough to hide a vehicle in? A getaway car, perhaps.

She went back outside to look around. Two concrete silos towered above and she remembered how the neighbourhood kids would dare each other to climb them. They weren't friends as such, just a bunch of ratbag kids whose parents had to work during the holidays and couldn't take them away to the beach. They were pulled by the yearning for mischief and the company of other kids to pass the long summer days with, with their social groupings in constant flux depending on preferences for games and locations. 'Go on, bet you can't climb to the very top! Scaredy cat, aren't ya?' She shook her head at the memory of how they would tease each other into what was, in no uncertain terms, quite a dangerous feat. Never one to shy away from a dare, Renee would stare down the taunting onlookers and take the challenge. She'd climbed the old concrete tower on numerous occasions and every time her breath was taken back by the view at the top. Vast paddocks of wheat stretched as far as the eye could see.

That same urge for the thrill of height came over her and she started walking towards the base of the silos. Ever since she could remember the silos hadn't been in operation. Probably easier for the owners of the industrial estate just to leave them there, rather than arrange for their destruction and deal with the hassle of removing all the concrete and steel.

As she approached, numerous signs still warned trespassers of prosecution, which had only ever served to make their childhood dares all the more exciting. The first part was always the trickiest. This required the person to haul their body up over a section of about two metres of ladder that was locked off with a gate of metal panelling. Whoever had the appropriate legal access simply used their key to open the gate and continue up. As kids they would stand on each other's shoulders and monkey their lithe little bodies up. Overcoming this barrier was much more difficult today but she made it and continued up the ladder, steadying herself against the refreshing gusts of wind.

There were thirteen flights of stairs with a small flat landing separating each one. She stopped on the fourth landing to catch her breath, remembering the exhilaration that drove her as a teenager to ascend the ladder, to be on top of the world. As a fifteen-year-old, she would come here alone and look out past the country town that encompassed her daily existence, away from her fears for her mother and her worsening arthritis, and the nasty school kids who teased her for being a geek because she couldn't afford to buy books so had to spend hours at the library. The shackles of her youth would disappear as she looked out beyond the rolling hills and wheat fields towards someplace else.

Maybe it was this eagerness to look into the distance that had kept her from taking in the details of the industrial estate immediately below as a teenager. Now with the eyes of a police investigator she scanned the immediate surrounds. There was a small dwelling hidden away in bushy undergrowth down behind the cotton shed and out of sight from the main road. It was wooden, no more than four by four metres, with a corrugated iron roof, and tucked away right at the back of the industrial estate.

She descended the ladder and walked back to the front of the cotton shed. There was a narrow path to the left that she hadn't noticed previously. She followed the path along, pushing away branches and the occasional spider web until she came upon the cabin she'd spotted from above. From the front, she could see that it was made of rough timber logs with a tin roof.

She lowered her head and stepped through the doorway onto timber floor panels that creaked with her weight. They were broken in parts and she had to be careful where she stepped. It was a single room, with a dirty old sofa in the middle that may have been beautiful colours once but was now an ugly beige covered in stains and dirt. Cigarette butts, broken glass and empty beer cans littered the floor. A faded magazine with torn-out pages showing a busty naked woman was crumpled up beneath a coffee table next to the sofa. Fold-out chairs were stacked in one corner of the room and Renee imagined that a group of people might have come and gathered here.

She opened a drawer to the coffee table and found cigarette papers, matches, more pornos, a scattering of loose tobacco and a plastic Coke bottle with a short piece of water hose sticking out. A homemade bong. She opened the drawer beneath it, and jerked back: a thick black funnel-web spider sat cosied up in the corner. It was time to get out of there. But then she noticed something else in the drawer. Sunglass frames. Blue and oversized. She'd heard that description recently. Nettie Shields. She had said Worm gave Bessie gifts, including a pair of oversized blue sunglasses. Had Bessie been here? Had she been here with Worm? Did Caroline come too? Renee pulled on her gloves and, carefully dodging the spider, reached in, picked up the glasses and placed them in a plastic bag for further inspection at the office. It was hard to believe they could survive thirty-five years, but then again it looked like the place had been abandoned for that long.

Chapter 20

As Renee drove down Main Street towards the centre of town, there were hordes of cars and people crowded around near the swimming pool. Unfamiliar faces walked past, towels over shoulder, zinc smeared across their faces. Kids in bathers and parents milling around, gossiping. It must have been Goorungah's turn to host the regional swimming competition.

She had tried to call Mulligan but he wasn't answering, and as she approached the station she realised why he may have been held up. The protesters were back and their numbers had grown significantly. She estimated the crowd to be about one hundred, plus a few who'd wandered down from the swim meet for a stickybeak. The press conference, far from alleviating the protesters' concerns, seemed to have increased them.

She slowed the vehicle to see if there was anyone she knew. If Nettie was out there, she could ask her to come in and look at the sunglasses she'd just found, but she couldn't spot her. Lennon was there. She sped up before they could make eye contact.

Stacey was at her desk even though it was a Saturday and her rostered day off. 'What are you doing here?' Renee asked, looking around the office. Roger was also at his desk on the phone.

'Sarge called me in to help manage the phone lines. We're getting calls from all over the country now following the press conference so Mulligan wanted all hands on deck today.' Stacey rolled her eyes, clearly unimpressed with the situation. Her kids were probably down at the swimming carnival while she was stuck here. 'How's your mum? I heard she had a fall.'

'Goodness, what time is it?' Renee felt a surge of guilt. She'd been so preoccupied following up on the hotline tip-off she'd completely forgotten about her mother.

'Taylor, where the bloody hell have you been?'

Renee turned around. Mulligan was standing in the doorway to his office, sweat dripping from his head.

'I'm sorry, Sarge, I tried to call you bu—'

'In my office now. We've got Chief Superintendent Dupont threatening to come from headquarters this morning to check up on us, and I'm trying to convince him we're fine.' Renee followed him into his office and took a seat in front of him. 'Tell me how your meeting went last night with our local Citizen of the Year.'

'Worm?'

'Yes, the charming Mr William Gawlor. What did he have to say for himself? You went and saw him yesterday afternoon, right?' Mulligan's phone started to ring and he glanced down, pressed a button, and Renee heard it go through to Stacey's line. Without any other internal noise she could hear the protesters yelling from outside. 'It's been relentless here this morning.' They were chanting and Renee and Mulligan both paused to listen.

'WHAT DO WE WANT? JUSTICE!'

'Bloody hell, I wish they'd just keep it down.' He shook his head, looked down, closed his eyes and took a deep breath in. 'Worm.

William Gawlor. Tell me how you went with him yesterday.'

Renee proceeded to update Mulligan on the little they'd learned. 'He's obviously dealing drugs. Mobile phones all over the place. It's likely that he's taking the stuff as well. Looked like he hadn't had a decent night's sleep in a decade. But of course he didn't offer up anything specific.'

'Did you look around his place? What'd you see?'

Renee tried to think back to the afternoon before. 'The young woman, Tiffany. A spoiled mutt. Mobiles. A few car magazines. He said we'd have to get a warrant to search if we wanted anything more.'

Mulligan sat back, 'I'm not surprised. He knows how the system works. He won't be saying anything without a warrant.'

'So why haven't you been able to pin him for any drug charges? Can't we get a search warrant?'

'I've tried. But you know it's not that easy, Taylor. The head honchos always want to take their time and get to the source. A few of them have tried to come out undercover. But Worm's no silly bugger. He might look like a rough old thug, but he's got all his oars in the water.'

'Yes, but I don't think we should give up on that line of enquiry just yet.'

'Hmm ... go on.'

'There's a young woman there. Tiffany. I don't think she's safe.'

'Why do you say that?'

'She's skinny as a rake. She's years younger than Worm. He bullies her.'

'It's not illegal to be thin and with an older man, Taylor.'

'Yes, but it is illegal to sell drugs, and Worm is clearly getting her to do drug runs for him. Archibald Ford told me as much.'

Why was Mulligan so intent on defending Worm? Was he that concerned about Worm's legal team? Whatever, she needed to show Mulligan what she'd discovered that morning. She reached into her backpack and pulled out the plastic bag containing the sunglasses.

'What's this?' Mulligan cleared his throat and leaned forward.

'Sunglasses. I found them in a shed on the industrial estate this morning. I think they belonged to Bessie Shields. But let me start from the beginning.' Renee held up her hands as though pleading for Mulligan to be patient and listen, and he nodded. She explained the tip-off she'd received early that morning, describing how Graham Bell had seen Caroline Forrest riding towards the industrial estate in a frenzied race to get somewhere, and how she'd fallen off her bike.

'How'd he know it was her?'

'He recognised her from the photo Channel Five has been including in their regular evening updates.'

Mulligan scoffed. 'Really? Bit of a long bow, isn't it?'

'That's what I thought, but he mentioned this incident occurred on 20 August 1966.' Before Mulligan could put words to his expression of sheer scepticism, Renee added that Graham Bell remembered because he needed to get back to his family for his daughter's birthday.

'How's your mother?'

Renee blinked. *What?* 'Mum's fine. I think we need to get forensics out to the shed where I found these sunglasses.'

'I heard she had a fall last night.'

'Sarge, I thought you said that Dupont may be coming out. Don't you think it would be good to have something to show him? This represents progress.'

He sighed. 'Taylor. I need real progress. Not paranoid reports to the hotline from some bored old man with nothing else to do. And the sunglasses prove nothing other than what we already know. Bessie Shields liked to spend time with the local boys. How do you even know that they belonged to Bessie Shields?'

'Because her mother told me the other day!' She could feel her heartbeat starting to race. How could she convince him to take action? Any action.

'Huh!' He leaned forward with his head in his hands. 'That proves noth—'

'We need to go back there and keep searching.' Renee said, breathing deeply to find her cool. 'We need to get the forensics team out. They can do a thorough sweep of the area.'

'Taylor. We have a crowd of protesters out the front of the station. The chief superintendent could show up here any minute now. We're not spending our time running around like chickens with our heads cut off.'

Renee didn't know what to say. This could be important given the connection between the past missing women case and the current victim. She understood that there was politics, but surely this was too significant a lead to ignore.

'Renee?' It was Stacey at the door. 'You have someone here who wants to see you. Joshua Cunningham is in the waiting room.'

'Thanks, Stacey.' She started walking towards the front reception area, hearing the protesters shout from outside and feeling her stomach churn, as she tried to slow her mind. What the hell was Joshua Cunningham doing here?

Chapter 21

'Sorry to show up like this.' He shrugged apologetically. His hair hadn't been combed and the bags under his eyes made him look ten years older than when she'd seen him at his mother's funeral a few days earlier. 'I just really need to talk to you.'

'It's okay.' Renee opened the partition. 'Why don't you come through? We can talk in here in private.' He followed her down a corridor to the small interview room they reserved for interaction with the public. It was a stark room with no windows that did nothing to elicit calm. 'Have a seat.' His eyes were red, like he hadn't slept, and she thought for a second that maybe she could smell booze on his breath.

'I did try to call,' Josh explained as he took the seat offered to him. 'I left a message. Did you get it?'

'Just now. Sorry. I would've called you back, but it's been a bit hectic.'

His eyes softened and she had a fleeting urge to give more details – the fox had killed the chickens, her mother had taken a bad fall and she was sick and tired of her boss not supporting her – but he had come here, to the station, to see her in a professional capacity. 'Josh, why are you here?'

'I'm here about that woman you found.'

'You knew her?' Renee's mind raced. Was this a confession? How did Joshua Cunningham know the dead woman? She tried not to show her surprise.

'I know this is going to sound crazy, but you need to hear me out.'

She strained to keep a neutral face and speak calmly. 'Go ahead, I'm listening.'

'Do you know Millicent Forrest?' Josh looked around the room, as though checking for cameras.

'Yes, that's Caroline's sister. What about her?'

He took a deep breath. 'I saw on the news that the same necklace Caroline Forrest was wearing was found on that woman by the creek.'

'We don't know if it's actually the same necklace, but it certainly looks the same.' He went quiet. 'What do you know, Josh? You can tell me.'

'Dad gives Millicent Forrest money. He has for years, I've seen it. He used to try to hide it, pretending he was paying her for some tea tree oil she makes, but he was lying.'

Renee hadn't managed to go out to see Chester yet and she still had questions about the morning of his wife's death. If he wasn't by her bedside, then where was he? What was more important?

'Okay.' Renee was connecting the dots in her mind. Chester Cunningham was paying Millicent Forrest. 'How much money? And why are you suspicious about this?'

'It was a lot. I used to check his wallet when he came home, and there was always a few hundred bucks missing. When I was younger, I remember thinking that maybe she was a prostitute and I kept my mouth shut to not embarrass Mum. What could I do if Dad was seeing a prostitute? He's not going to listen to me.'

'But now you have another theory for the payments?'

'Look, I put it out of my mind for a long time. I didn't want to think about it, but then I saw the news, and that you'd reopened the case about these two missing women.'

'Caroline Forrest and Bessie Shields?'

'Yes. I never heard of them.' He held his hands up. 'Nothing. I didn't even know that two women went missing from Goorungah. I mean, did you know, Renee? No one ever talked about it, right?'

'Nope,' she agreed. He was silent, and she could see he was carefully constructing something in his mind. 'What are you thinking, Josh?'

'I suddenly realised Caroline is Millicent's sister. What if Millicent saw something?' He bit his lip.

'Millicent Forrest saw something? Like what?'

'Like, maybe an accident.'

'An accident?'

'Yes, like maybe Dad was responsible somehow for those two girls going missing?'

'Your dad?'

'Maybe he was drunk or something and ran them off the road?' He spoke more rapidly now, as though he knew what he was saying had mind-blowing implications but he had a compulsion to get it out. 'I'm not saying that he killed them, but maybe he caused their deaths somehow, like by accident?'

Renee thought Chester seemed like a reasonable man and had heard he was well thought of in the community, but sometimes it was the quiet typical family man who was capable of the most heinous crimes.

'Or I don't know, maybe it was intentional. When we were kids, my father would leave us for days on end, without telling us where he was going. He'd worry Mum sick, and then get angry with her when she asked where he went. So maybe the old bastard is a sicko and did something to them.'

Renee remembered how Josh had commented on his father's inattentiveness, but she hadn't realised it was this bad. Perhaps the death of Josh's mum was allowing him to give voice to long-buried enmities.

Still, it was a hypothesis worth testing.

'And Millicent saw it?' Renee asked.

'Exactly.' Josh was clearly relieved that Renee was listening. 'Millicent saw it, and Dad bribed her for silence. I reckon she figured rather than coming to the cops, she worked out a deal with Chester. Pay me, and I'll keep my mouth shut.'

'Okay, so you're saying that there were some payments going on between Chester and Millicent, and you think Chester was lying about it being for essential oils or something? But what does any of this have to do with the woman found earlier in the week?'

'Dad wasn't by Mum's side when she passed on Tuesday morning. That was the same time that young woman was murdered, wasn't it?'

'Yes.'

'And at the funeral, Dad had scratches on his neck.' Renee couldn't remember seeing any scratches at the funeral but then she hadn't been looking for them. 'Mum passed within a few hours of that girl being killed. And Dad was nowhere to be found. The hospital staff were trying to call him all night. And then he shows up with scratches on his neck. And there's a body found.'

'Josh, your father probably slept through the morning and missed the phone calls.' Renee wasn't sure she believed that, but there was no evidence of any kind at this point. Best she did not encourage Josh too much.

'Maybe. But he's hiding something. He's always been hiding something.'

Renee could see Josh's frustration. He'd been alone with his own thoughts for too long. She knew the feeling. He was desperate to tell someone, despite the repercussions of being correct. His father could be a murderer but sometimes having an answer was better than a life of wondering. Ignorance was not always bliss.

'You think I'm crazy, don't you?'

'I don't think you're crazy, but, seriously, have you talked to anyone else about this? What does your wife think?'

'Nothing. I haven't mentioned it to her.' Josh looked down. 'I went and saw Millicent Forrest before I came here.'

'You what? Josh. This is a murder investigation. That was ill-advised.'

'I know. I'm sorry.' He met her eyes with a level look. 'I couldn't help myself.'

'What'd she say?'

'Nothing. Once I told her my name, and tried to explain why I was there, she shut the door in my face. Seriously, Renee, what do you think? Do you think Dad has anything to do with this?'

'I don't know. But I will need to follow this up as well as report what you've just told me to my boss. Is there anything else you need to tell me or is that it?'

'That's it.'

'Okay. You should probably hit the road and get home to your family. I'll call you if we find out anything.'

'Umm ... Renee?'

Why did he look so sheepish?

'I think I've missed the bus back to Brisbane.'

She looked at the time. It was already noon. The eight am bus had left hours ago.

'You didn't drive?'

'No, the family went back last night and they needed the car.'

'Okay, so stay at the motel and get the next one in the morning ...'

'Could I stay at yours?' Please, no. His eyes were pleading. 'I don't have enough money for a room.'

'Seriously? What the hell is going on with you? Actually, don't tell me. It's fine. You can stay at mine.' She was too tired to argue, and there was something beaten about him.

'I'm so sorry, Renee. I'll make it up to you.'

'It's fine. You can sleep on the couch.' She escorted him back out to the front reception, told him the location of the spare key and that she'd see him in a few hours.

Roger and Stacey were at their desks when she re-entered the office. The phone lines seemed to have quietened down, but she could still hear protesters chanting out the front.

'Why's Joshua Cunningham here?' Stacey asked, leaning forward, quivering. Her enthusiasm for weekend work had suddenly returned with the possibility of town gossip.

'Do you know if Dupont is coming out?' Renee asked, ignoring her question.

'Not sure. Sarge hasn't been out of his office since you arrived.'

She looked at Roger. 'Anything useful?'

He looked up from a small pile of scribbled notes. 'Not really. A couple of things that need checking out first. There is one ...'

Melaleuca

Renee put her hand up. 'Tell me later once you've checked them out.'

She figured Mulligan's current preoccupation with the phones would give her a good opportunity to slip out to ask Chester a few questions. Just in case Sarge decided that was a bad idea, too.

Renee drove north and turned up the driveway to Hereford Downs. She had never been on the property even when she and Josh were dating. It was an impressive place with rose bushes lining the driveway all the way up to an enormous homestead.

Chester was sitting out on the front verandah when she pulled up, almost as though he was awaiting the arrival of someone. She wondered if he knew that his son was lurking about town accusing him of heinous crimes. Probably not.

'Afternoon, Mr Cunningham,' she called out as she walked towards the front steps, wondering if he'd recognise her. 'My name's Renee Taylor. I'm—'

'I know who you are. You dated my boy. I saw you at the funeral with your mum. How's she going?' So he remembered who she was, but she guessed he had no idea she was there on police business. Maybe he assumed she'd come around to pass on her condolences.

'She's fine thanks, Mr Cunningham. And I'm sorry about Mrs Cunningham.' He didn't get up, but he motioned for her to take the seat next to him. She didn't take it.

'Mr Cunningham. You may not be aware, but I'm working at the Goorungah Police Station now. I'm a detective there.' Josh hadn't lied. There were scratches on his father's neck and they looked recent.

'Oh yes, old Norm did mention something about that last time I popped down to get the paper. Come home to look after your mum, hey? You're a good daughter. Better than my ratty good-for-nothing kids.'

She winced. Josh had mentioned when they dated that his father could be nasty and was neglectful, but she'd always thought he was exaggerating. He'd raised it again today. At least Josh lived in a huge house and had plenty of money. Not that it mattered if there was no love.

'Mr Cunningham, I'd actually like to ask you a few questions about the woman we found down by the creek earlier in the week.'

'Terrible tragedy, that one. Do you know who she was yet?'

'No. We don't know. I was wondering if maybe you had ever seen her.' She pulled out the artist's impression from her backpack and placed it in front of him, studying the movement of the deep wrinkles across his face.

'You think I had something to do with it, do you?' He looked up at her. 'I saw the news. I'm not an idiot. I knew you'd be around here.'

Renee pulled out the photograph of the necklace.

'This is either the same necklace that Caroline had, or it's a replica.' Chester's head lifted at the mention of Caroline. 'Did you give the necklace to Caroline, Chester?'

'Yes, I did. It was her favourite colour, yellow.' His face softened with the memory. 'What I don't understand is what it is doing on this young woman.'

'What was your relationship with Caroline?'

'She was the love of my life.'

Renee paused. This did not accord with what Millicent had

said. But perhaps she didn't know? Had Caroline kept an affair secret from her sister?

'Do you know what happened to Bessie and Caroline, Mr Cunningham?'

'If I knew that, I probably wouldn't be such a grumpy old bastard with shit-for-kids that don't respect me and a wife who never really loved me. My life would have taken a very different turn. Not knowing what happened to Caroline has pained me every day of my life.'

'But it's true that you were in a relationship with Caroline and you gave her the necklace?'

'Yes.' He looked sad and defeated, no energy to argue.

'And the woman we found by the creek?'

'I don't know her.'

'How'd you get those scratches on your neck?'

He felt around beneath his jawline as though he'd forgotten they were there. Then his head snapped up. 'Shaving!' He said it with immense indignation, understanding the weight of Renee's implication.

'And your whereabouts on Tuesday morning?'

'Tuesday morning? That was the morning Sally passed. I was here.'

'Why weren't you by Sally's side? The hospital staff had called you and said she was close to passing. Wouldn't you want to be nearby?'

He huffed in frustration and bit his lip. 'I was hungover.'

'You didn't hear the phone ringing?'

'I'd taken it off the hook. I wanted to drink in peace. I drank the whole fucking bottle. Is that illegal?'

'No, Mr Cunningham.'

'You know, instead of coming up here questioning me, you know where you should be?' He didn't wait for her response. 'Down at that mongrel Worm's place. He's got so many young women around this town hooked on drugs, it's a fucking miracle he's still a free man. Why don't you get down there and question him?'

'We're investigating all angles, sir.'

'Good. Do a better job of it.' He stared her down until the sound of her phone ringing in her pocket broke the silence.

It was Mulligan. She thanked Mr Cunningham and went back to her car. The sun was low on the horizon and Mulligan was not in the best of moods.

'Where the bloody hell are you?'

She wanted to say investigating a murder, rather than sitting around on her arse taking phone calls, afraid of the big boss, but she bit her tongue. 'I'm just leaving Chester Cunningham's property now.'

'What? What are you doing out there?'

She explained that Joshua Cunningham had come into the station earlier and revealed some details about his father that made her suspicious.

'Like what?'

'Well, apart from Chester not being by his wife's bedside when she passed, and that coinciding with the time of death of our Jane Doe, Josh said that he saw scratches on his father's neck. And, indeed, I just confirmed that he does have scratches on his neck, which he said were from shaving, but there's more.' She paused, making sure she had his attention.

'Go on. I'm listening.'

Renee explained how Josh suspected his father was bribing Millicent Forrest.

'Why was he bribing her?'

'Well, according to Josh, Chester may have been responsible for the death of Bessie and Caroline, and he thinks Milli might have witnessed it. It's hush money.'

'Joshua Cunningham suspects his old man of murder?'

'Yeah, I know. He said it fit in with his experiences of his dad – apparently Chester often disappeared when they were younger.'

'Okay, so what'd Chester have to say?'

Renee was surprised that Mulligan wasn't more annoyed with her for going to see Mr Cunningham before updating him and seeking his permission.

'Well, he denied it all, of course. He did admit to giving Caroline the necklace, but that was it. Reckons he doesn't know what happened to Caroline and Bessie, and doesn't know the girl.'

'Hmm … did you believe him?'

Renee shrugged. 'I don't know. I would have said he was telling the truth but liars can be very convincing.'

'What does he think happened?'

'Same as everyone else.'

'Which is?'

'Worm. So I'm going to see him first thing in the morning.' There was complete silence. 'Sarge?'

'But we don't have anything new on him. Nothing concrete, anyway, just more suspicions.'

'We need to bring Worm in for questioning.'

'Not yet. Find me some evidence.'

'He knew both girls and he likes to control young women. He deals drugs. He is a criminal.'

'Concrete evidence.'

'You're scared of him?' Renee asked. She was getting tired of his cowardice.

'No, I'm not scared of him.'

'Then let's go over there right now. Everyone in this town thinks he's guilty of something. He has that young woman Tiffany hooked on something. She's afraid of him.'

'You're not going until I say so, Taylor.'

'Okay. Fine.' Renee couldn't stop herself. She hung up on him.

The sun was setting over Goorungah as she drove into town. It had been a clear sunny day but now when she looked out to the west rolling deep purple thunder clouds were moving in, bringing the smell of rain.

Josh was sitting on her front porch sipping a beer when she pulled into the driveway. She had just questioned his father about a murder case. He could be a witness. What was she thinking, letting him stay? Even as she understood the stupidity of it, she knew she wouldn't turn him out. She and Josh had unfinished business. Might as well see if she could lay a few ghosts to rest. And if she found out more about Chester Cunningham as a result, so much the better. She walked up the porch steps and Josh smiled at her.

'Want one?' He pulled a beer loose from a six pack and offered it up to her.

'Maybe later. Here, let me put those in the fridge.' She leaned down and picked up the remaining beers. 'I see you've had a trip to the bottle-o.'

'I got you some fish and chips as well, but they might need reheating. They're on the bench.'

'Well, you are quite the house guest.' She forced a smile back and walked inside. She placed her bag on the table, then reached for her phone and dialled the hospital.

The nurse on duty said that her mother was still resting and that they'd call back as soon as she woke up. Relieved to hear that Val was okay, Renee went into the stillness of the bathroom, got out of her sweaty clothes and turned on the shower. The water felt good. She let it flow over her face and hair and tried to forget everything that was going on outside of the bathroom. Joshua Cunningham wasn't really drinking beer on her front porch. Her mother wasn't really crippled by arthritis and lying in a hospital bed. A woman hadn't been murdered down by the creek. The authorities really did care about the two Aboriginal girls who'd gone missing. There was no king-pin drug dealer giving methamphetamine to the young people around town. The steam turned reality into a pleasant mirage.

She turned off the shower after having gone well over her self-imposed one-minute limit. She didn't care tonight. She put on a singlet and jean shorts and went back into the kitchen. At least he'd thought to get beer and food. He hadn't completely lost the plot.

'Have you eaten yet?' she called from inside. She emptied the fish and chips onto a plate and placed it in the microwave. He was still sitting on the porch. She could smell the cigarette smoke and wondered when he'd taken up smoking.

'Not hungry,' he called back. She waited for the microwave to beep and went to sit with him on the porch.

'I thought you said you came home to look after your mum. Where is she?' He put his cigarette out in an empty beer bottle.

'She's in hospital. Had a fall last night.' The chips tasted good.

'I'm sorry, Renee.'

'It's okay.' She shrugged. 'She's happy there. They're giving her morphine or something. Gives us both a little holiday from each other.'

'Val's still Val, huh?'

'Worse, if anything! Won't eat a decent meal. Still telling me to grow my hair.' Renee held back the more intimate details, the feelings of helplessness and frustration at seeing her mother's gradual decline. 'It just scares me how much she needs me.'

Josh smiled softly and she winced, remembering he'd just lost his own mother. He didn't need to hear her whinging about Val's frailty.

'You remembered I liked chicken salt and vinegar.'

She ate greedily now, trying to recall the last time she'd actually sat down and eaten. Maybe that doctor had a point about looking after herself.

'Josh?'

'Yeah?'

'We are taking your comments seriously.'

'What does that mean?'

'We spoke to your father this afternoon. I thought you should at least know that we're following up.'

He took a long drag on his cigarette and looked into the distance with bitterness. 'Good. What'd he have to say for himself?'

'I can't discuss details with you now, Josh. But I just wanted to reassure you that we're taking you seriously. You seemed a bit worked up at the station. Is everything okay at home?'

He scoffed. 'At home?'

'It's okay, we don't need to talk about it if you don't want to.'

'Hmm … I don't want to burden you.'

She was about to say it wouldn't be a burden but stopped herself.

It would be. She was giving him a bed for the night. That would do for now. She finished her meal. She could hear people shouting from the pub next door. A few teenagers walked by, talking loudly and laughing at one another.

'I should get to bed. And you must be exhausted too,' she said.

Josh's phone started to ring. He silenced it.

'Who's that?'

'Dad. It's the fourth time he's called. Did you tell him I was still in town?'

'No. Does he normally call you so frequently?'

'Never. I know this must be weird for you, Renee. I'm sorry.'

She watched him turn off his phone. 'Come on, I'll make up the couch for you.'

'What's that?' Josh pointed to the corner where the eggs lay under the lamp.

'A fox killed Mum's chickens, so I rescued their eggs. Maybe they'll hatch and keep the family line going.'

He looked puzzled for a moment and then laughed. 'You've always had a heart of gold, Renee.' He reached out and touched her hand. She let him take it. 'I'm sorry.'

'What for?'

'Leaving you.'

Her heart stopped and once again she was sitting on the bean bags in the library feeling all the euphoria of teen love.

'Why did you leave me, Josh?' She let her hands fall away. She couldn't let herself be hurt again.

'I don't know. I needed to work on myself.'

'Tell me the truth. You didn't think I was good enough for you.'

'No! Is that really what you think?'

'I just thought we had something.'

'I thought you deserved more than me. You're smarter and more courageous. You had a brilliant life in front of you and I needed to sort myself out. I sometimes wonder what would have happened if we had stayed together …' He stepped in and tried to take her hand again but instinctively she stepped back.

'It would never have worked out,' she said. And to Renee's surprise, she realised she meant it. Josh was not quite the man she thought he was. He had been an adolescent crush when neither of them really knew who they were. That was all. A weight lifted off her.

'I'm sorry,' Josh said.

She smiled but moved away, putting some distance between them. 'You know, Josh, it was a long time ago and it really doesn't matter now.' She meant it.

She grabbed one of the sheets and spread it across the couch, refusing to make eye contact but feeling more kindly towards him now that she felt less for him. 'Just forget about it.'

Renee left the room swiftly, fell onto her bed and lay on her back with her arm across her eyes blocking out the light. The people at the pub next door were getting rowdier and she considered shouting over the fence, but that usually served against the desired effect, even if she was the local cop. She thought she might have trouble sleeping but instead fell almost immediately into a deep, exhausted slumber.

'Renee!' She sat up in bed. It was pitch black. There was movement in the house, and smoke. 'Renee!'

She hurled herself out of bed and flicked on the light. Smoke was everywhere. She could barely see through the haze. 'Josh?' It was thicker in the hallway, and as she made her way down it she coughed and spluttered. She could smell petrol. A loud crashing bang came from the lounge room. 'Josh!' No answer. She crouched down and felt her way to the lounge room. 'Josh? Where are you?' The curtains were in flames. The entire kitchen was ablaze. She was choking and suffocating from the smoke. She tripped over his body sprawled out in the middle of the lounge room. 'Oh my goodness, Josh? Talk to me.' There was the sound of footsteps in the kitchen. Someone else was in the house. She heard them run out the back and bump into something. The rubbish bin maybe.

She felt for Josh's body and finally located him, but he remained motionless on the floor. His head was smothered in thick warm liquid. Blood. 'Help!' she screamed and coughed. 'Josh, stay with me.'

She pulled his body along the floor, needing to get him outside in the fresh air, as flames spread from the curtains to the couch. She got hold of both arms and pulled his body with all her might. 'Help!' The heat burned her skin and she could no longer open her eyes. Her body said bolt but she couldn't leave Josh behind. She pulled harder and dragged him out the front door, collapsing on the porch, heaving breathlessly. Beyond the roaring blaze of the flames she could hear the faint sound of sirens. Then she passed out.

Chapter 22

Sharp repetitive beeping sounds pulled at her consciousness. She rubbed her forehead. Her vision was hazy and the room around her was a blur of white and grey. It smelled of disinfectant. She felt groggy. Painkillers? But she still felt pain. The skin along her right thigh throbbed. She tried to move it and the throbbing became a shooting pain along her entire right side. She lifted the sheet and looked down to see that her right leg was bandaged.

A warm hand reached across her forehead. 'Mum?'

'I'm here, darling.' Her mother came closer so Renee could see her face.

'What happened, Mum? Where am I?' Outside the window, she could see rain teeming down.

'You were in a fire. You're okay now.' Renee looked around, grimacing – the movement hurt her neck. 'We're in the Goorungah hospital,' her mother informed her.

'You're awake?' Mulligan came into the room with two cups of coffee and put one on the table next to Val.

'What time is it?'

'It's ten o'clock on Sunday morning. Not that you should be worrying about the time. You need to rest after what you've been through.' Her mother ran her hand across Renee's forehead as the night's events flooded her mind. She had been to see Chester. Josh had stayed over. They drank beer and ate fish and chips. He'd given her the 'it wasn't you, it was me' spiel and she'd gone to bed feeling relieved and a little lonely, but above all deeply tired. Then the fire had started.

'Where's Josh?' She tried to move her body into a seated position, but the pain was excruciating.

'It's okay. Calm down – Dr Mac said you need to rest,' Val said, putting her hand on Renee's shoulder. 'Josh is okay. He's in the city hospital – they flew him in the chopper down to metro emergency. His injuries were a little more severe than yours.' Val stopped herself and looked across at Mulligan as she said this, and Renee knew she was keeping details secret.

'What does "a little more severe" mean?'

Val looked strained and Mulligan jumped in. 'Josh has been placed in an induced coma. It's just to help with any swelling around the brain. They'll bring him out of it soon, and I'm sure he'll be fine.'

She lay back down. 'How did it start? It was deliberate, wasn't it?' Renee racked her brain trying to think who would want to do this. Was she getting too close to someone? She wouldn't put it past Worm to light a house on fire with people inside. Or maybe it was Chester … Was he capable of this? He *was* the last person she'd spoken to. Maybe he got terrified about the truth surfacing.

'We're not sure yet.'

She remembered smelling petrol. 'I know someone lit it. I'm sure I heard someone else in the house running away. There was petrol. Who do you think did it, Mulligan?'

'I don't know, but we'll find them.' He nodded at her. 'I interviewed an eye witness to the murder investigation this morning.'

'What?' She sat up and a sharp pain went through her right leg. 'Who?'

'Do you remember those Aboriginal kids you saw down by the creek?'

How could she forget? The three delinquents swinging off the rope into the water that she'd come across the day after the murder.

'The leader of the pack. Calvin.' She remembered the stocky young bloke who was probably all of fourteen years old and already sporting a few home-done tattoos along his knuckles. 'Well, he reckons he saw Chester drive down that road the morning the murder took place.'

'Are you serious? I knew those little bastards were keeping something from me. Did he come into the station?'

'No, I came across them walking the streets this morning. I was driving around, seeing if I could find who may have been responsible for setting your house alight.' Mulligan's phone started to ring in his pocket. He moved to the corner of the room to take the call.

'Do you need anything love? Are you thirsty?' her mother asked. 'Do you want me to ask the nurse to get you anything?'

'No, Mum, I'm okay. How are you?'

'I'm good, darling. Don't worry about me.'

'Hold on a second, have you been discharged yet?'

Her mother shook her head. 'Nope. Who would've guessed? Both Taylor women in the Goorungah hospital. Talk about bloody hopeless.'

'Who was that?' Renee asked as Mulligan came back over, scratching his head.

'Stacey. She said Chester Cunningham is at the station.'

'Chester?' She glanced at her mother. 'Really? Has he come in to confess?'

'I have no idea, but I'll let you know.' He reached for his umbrella.

'No way, you're not going without me! I'm coming.'

Renee got out of bed, grimacing from the stabbing pain in her ankle. She must have rolled on it again last night. She tried to ignore the agony that radiated from her thigh.

'Renee!' her mother scolded. 'Please lie down and rest.'

'I'm fine! Look at me.' Her entire body throbbed with pain, but she managed to stand. 'Where are my clothes?'

She was able to change and leave before any medical staff returned.

When they arrived at the station, Stacey met them at the back door, wide-eyed and fast talking. 'Oh, my goodness, Renee! I didn't think they would let you out so soon. Can you believe it though? He's here! Chester Cunningham is here.' Renee followed Mulligan down the corridor and through the main office as Stacey chattered anxiously. 'Do you think he's here to confess? I can't believe it. Poor Sally.'

Roger was on the phone but immediately ended the conversation. 'Renee. Are you okay?'

'I'm fine, Roger.' He looked genuinely concerned and Renee was touched.

'Where is he?' Mulligan asked.

'In the interrogation room,' Stacey said.

Renee could tell from her bright eyes she was scared, but also enjoying the drama. No doubt having a respected community member show up at the police station after a fire was thrilling for her – all the gossip she would have to share with Lisa later over a glass of chardonnay while watching the kids play in the backyard. Chester Cunningham fronting up at the station with a confession was sufficient material to fuel town gossip for years.

Mulligan looked hard at Stacey. 'Where?'

They didn't really have an 'interrogation room'.

'The small interview room,' Stacey clarified.

Mulligan paused. 'What's that noise?' They could hear chanting from the street. 'You've got to be kidding me! Are those protesters at it again?'

Renee walked over to the blinds and pulled one slat down to peer out. She'd seen a few of them on the way in, but the group had grown in the few moments since her arrival. The same woman was standing with the microphone shouting, 'What do we want?' and the crowd responded with, 'Justice.'

She spotted Lennon over to one side and wondered if they knew there was a suspect in the station. Is that why they had chosen to gather on a Sunday morning? Or had they heard about the fire at Renee's house?

'You stay out here, Madden,' Mulligan barked. 'And, Taylor, grab a tape recorder.'

Chester was waiting in the same room that Renee had talked to his son in the day before. But unlike Josh, there was an element of calm about Chester, as though he was resolute in his decision to be there and had little doubt about what he was about to say.

'Mr Cunningham,' Mulligan began, taking a seat opposite Chester. Renee took the one next to him. 'Interesting that you have decided to grace us with your presence rather than the bedside of your son. You are aware he is in intensive care in the city? In an induced coma?' Renee took a deep breath, imagining Josh unconscious in a hospital bed, and hoped his wife or sister or someone was by his side.

'I'm well aware of that. The best way I can help my son is to be here right now and tell you what actually happened.' Renee also took a seat. 'In 1966.'

Mulligan leaned in. 'We're listening.'

'Shortly after you stopped by the farm yesterday, Renee, I had a call from Millicent Forrest.' Renee could see that he was struggling to find a place to begin his story. 'Millicent informed me that Joshua had been around to her place earlier yesterday with some strange questions about our relationship.'

The tape recorder buzzed softly. Renee glanced down to make sure it was working properly. She started making notes just in case. Out of the corner of her eye she could see Mulligan watching and waiting for Chester to proceed.

'What did Millicent tell you, sir?' Renee asked, getting increasingly frustrated by Mulligan's passivity.

He sighed and shook his head. 'She told me that Joshua wanted to know why I was paying her. According to Millicent, Joshua alluded to some sort of conspiracy he'd worked up in his mind – bribery of some sort relating to me being responsible for the disappearance of Caroline and her friend Bessie, and that Millicent had borne witness to the event.' Renee watched a range of emotions play across Chester's face. Incredulity and anger settled into sadness.

'Do you know what may have given Joshua that impression, Mr Cunningham?' She already knew after her conversation with Josh the day before, but she wanted to hear it from Chester's perspective.

Angie Faye Martin

'Hmm ...' He closed his eyes for a long time, as though preparing his thoughts, and when he opened them again Renee realised the extent to which they were bloodshot. 'I imagine it is because I was indeed giving Millicent money. But it wasn't for the reason Joshua suspected.'

'Then why?'

'Because Millicent raised my son.'

Chapter 23

1965

It was late spring, a few months after the night of the dance, and Caroline continued working on Hereford Downs, much to most people's surprise. She had hoped Mrs Cunningham would let her go after the humiliating public rejection at the dance but her employer's desire for a clean house trumped every other concern. So to avoid difficult conversations around the brutal prejudice Caroline had been subjected to, Mrs Cunningham had decided that what had transpired at the dance was all Caroline's fault for not trying harder to 'fit in'. Clearly Caroline had got the steps wrong during the dances, worn the wrong outfit and hadn't made more of an effort to have polite conversations with the ladies during the breaks. Apparently this was enough to justify the entire dance turning against her.

She heard that Mrs Armstrong had reported back to Mrs Cunningham that Caroline had actively avoided her daughter Lola during the break and didn't come to talk to her or Janelle, which was true, but only because they would have been outraged, then vicious, if she had approached them. But anything would do to appease the two women's consciences and this seemed to make them feel better. It was all too much for Caroline to argue with and she let the snide comments go unchecked as she went about her daily duties around the house. She was tired with a fatigue that couldn't be remedied by sleep.

When Mrs Cunningham told her she had to stay away from Chester from now on, Caroline agreed – she had already decided to do that anyway – and Mrs Cunningham arranged for Simon to collect her from the camp instead. That plan went along smoothly until Simon's application to study law was accepted. Caroline found herself hoping that Mrs Cunningham would let her move on. She even put forward Bessie's name as an alternative, thinking that maybe a short stint on a property would be good for her friend, but Mrs Cunningham refused to take on anyone without experience, and so Caroline was stuck again in the suffocating confines of the ute with Chester.

They would sit alongside each other on these trips exchanging superficial conversation, never making eye contact. Neither of them spoke of what had happened. Caroline would occasionally feel him looking at her, but resolutely refused to turn her head. The small wage Caroline brought in from working at the farm, supplemented by an occasional bag of sausages from Mrs Cunningham, was enough for her, Milli and Pa to not go hungry, and so that was sufficient motivation for Caroline to keep forcing her body to move through the motions of getting up each day and working. Clean, cook, garden, eat, sleep, repeat.

But over time, Caroline felt herself sliding away. She would sit and stare at her food of an evening, not wanting to make Pa Quincey and Milli worry but with no will to pick up the fork. She would even try to put the food in her mouth and swallow, but she just couldn't do it. All her energy went into maintaining the most essential of routine tasks like brushing her hair and cleaning her teeth, and even those tasks were not completed each day. Caroline was exhausted by everything. The herbs lost their fragrance and sunsets no longer made her gaze around in wonder at the beauty of the world. Mrs Ford's singing at the end of the Sunday church service didn't stir her and Pa's stories became dull and meaningless.

Caroline had experienced plenty of hardship, but late one afternoon, as she filled a bucket at the communal taps in a tired daze after work, she realised that for the first time in her life she had no desire to see the coming day. She didn't want to work on Hereford Downs, nor put up with the nagging demands and judging looks of Mrs Cunningham, nor feed her big gutsy family of men. She didn't want to go to church and listen to Pastor Ford preach about generosity and watch Mrs Ford fuss over baby Archie while Aunty Nettie struggled to feed her baby. And she didn't want to sleep in a cold shack next to her overbearing big sister, nor feel the painful burden of caring for Pa as he got more and more frail with each passing day, moaning in his sleep about ailments he'd never admit to when awake.

'Are you avoiding me?' Bessie said, making her jump. Bessie had been over a few times in the last few weeks to try to get her out of her shack, but she always said she was too tired and needed to rest for work. It was partly true, she was too tired, but she was also ashamed of herself for going to the dance and not listening to Bessie's warning in the first place.

'No. Why would you say that?' Caroline tried to act indignant, but her friend was right.

'Ummm ... because you never want to hang out with me any more.'

'I told you. I'm busy.' Caroline turned off the tap. She didn't want to argue with Bessie. She was wearing new sunglasses on her head. Oversized and fluorescent blue, and Bessie wore them like a crown. 'Where'd you get those from?'

'Worm.'

'Oh my goodness, you're not still hanging out with those two losers.' She picked up her bucket and started walking back towards her shack.

'Don't be like that, Callie,' Bessie said, stepping out in front of Caroline. 'You're too young to act this old and boring.'

Caroline put the bucket down. 'What's that supposed to mean?'

'It means exactly what I just said. You're carryin on like an old woman with a broken heart. Who cares about Chester Cunningham? He's just some stuck-up farmer. Why don't you come out with me sometime? I've been makin bungoo doing some jobs for Worm. You could do it too.'

'Do what?'

'I can't tell you. You have to come and check it out for yourself.'

'Stop being like that, Bessie. Just tell me.'

'Okay, fine. I'm selling a bit of yarndi for him. That's all. He's training me up and soon I'll go down to the city with him and Gappy.'

If there was a chance of getting away from Mrs Cunningham and Chester, and not having to swallow her pride every morning, then maybe it was worth checking out. Selling yarndi was illegal, but wasn't that bad? And lately Bessie had money. She wanted to have some money so she didn't need to work at the Cunninghams and be this sad pale ghost of a woman.

'Alright then. When?'

Later that evening, she told Milli she was going to the pictures with Bessie, and on the way there Worm and Gappy picked them up. The moment she stepped into the car and saw Worm's sneering face and Gappy's empty grin she knew she had made a huge mistake.

They went back to the hut behind the silos and sat around in the same arrangement they'd sat in a few weeks earlier with Worm on the couch next to Bessie and Caroline and Gappy on stools across from them. Worm pulled out a joint and offered it around, and this time Caroline felt so anxious she took it, wanting to escape the feeling. For a moment it lightened everything and she felt peaceful for the first time in a long time.

'Here.' Bessie passed a bottle of something that made Caroline lurch back when she took a sniff.

'What is it?'

'Whiskey,' Worm answered for her.

The dope made Caroline suddenly brave. 'So, what's the deal, Worm? Are you going to drug me again, like you did last time?' Bessie almost spat out the mouthful of booze she'd just poured into her mouth. 'What? You think I don't realise what happened?'

Bessie and Gappy looked away, but Worm met her stare straight on.

'Did you like what I gave you?' he asked, unfazed by the direct line of her questioning. 'I can give you some more if you like.'

'Liked it?' Caroline thought for a moment. What was there to like? It was oblivion. 'I was unconscious.'

Out of the corner of her eye she could see Gappy and Bessie eyeing each other nervously.

'Bessie told me she has been working for you.'

'Oh, did she now?' Worm cocked his head to one side and gazed at her. 'I heard about your little adventure at the town dance. Can't say I didn't try to warn you about those snobby farmers though?' He leaned back on the couch with his hands behind his head and pushed his groin forward. 'Are you up for the work now?'

'Sure. I can sell weed for you.'

Worm looked across at Bessie and started chuckling. 'Is that what your friend told you? Bessie Boo ...' Bessie pretended not to hear and walked over to the record player, 'have you been telling fibs to Miss Soup Kitchen?'

Caroline felt her heart start to race, the weed giving her a strange sense of disorientation as the air suddenly felt very thick. 'Bessie?' Caroline called over to her friend. 'What's he talking about?'

She thought she heard something outside and turned, but Gappy put his hand on her back. 'Relax.' The record started to play a slow, mournful melody and Bessie swayed to the music, her back to everyone.

'What's going on?' She went to get up, but this time Gappy held her down by the shoulder. 'Gappy, let go of me.' Bessie kept dancing, moving drunkenly to the music, and Worm stood up and looked past Caroline to the door. Caroline turned to see what he was looking at and two men stepped inside.

One of them was wearing riding boots and jeans while the other wore a shirt and tie. He was much older, sixty perhaps. They looked out of place in every way and Caroline started to panic.

'Greetings, gentleman,' Worm announced, reaching out to greet them with a handshake. The men took his hand to be polite but remained silent. 'You're just in time! It's Caroline's first run today, and we've just finished having our briefing, haven't we, Caroline?'

Melaleuca

He winked at her as she stood paralysed.

'Is this them?' asked the older one. He appeared as though he'd finished up an office job moments earlier. Caroline's heart thundered. He smiled at her and she fought the urge to vomit. Worm took a bunch of notes from the men and gave them to Gappy.

'Bessie!' she hissed across at her friend, who was now looking to the ceiling, swinging herself to the music, arms hanging floppy at her sides. Terror filled her every cell. Gappy counted the cash and put it in his pocket. 'Bessie!'

'You wanted to make easy money, didn't you, Callie?' Bessie slurred, eyes vacant.

'Not like this. We have to get out of here.' She scanned the room for something to use as a weapon.

'What did you think I was selling?'

Caroline grabbed her friend's arm and yanked her towards the door. 'We need to go, Bessie.'

Worm stepped in front of her and leaned in close. 'Listen here, you little bitch. Bessie is a grown woman. She can make her own decisions. Isn't that what you've been telling her for the past few weeks? It was alright to turn a blind eye then, so why do you care now?'

Caroline yanked her arm back. 'This isn't right, Worm. You can't do this.'

'If you don't want to be here, then leave. Let your friend do the work. She can handle both of them. I've seen her do it before.'

Caroline shuddered at the thought and glanced over at Bessie, who was guzzling liquor directly from the bottle.

'She's only doing it because you give her so much booze and drugs, Worm. If she was sober, she'd come to her senses.' The

305

weeks of frustration and melancholy were boiling up into rage. Caroline pushed Worm hard on his chest. He stumbled then regained composure and stepped back, shocked.

'Oh, really? That's how you want to play?' Worm said, eyeing Caroline menacingly.

She didn't feel scared any more. She was too tired and angry to feel anything resembling fear. 'Fuck you, Worm. You're not having my friend.' She spat it out, just as a loud cackling came from behind her. Bessie was in fits of laughter on the couch. For a second, Caroline assumed her friend was laughing from the shock of seeing her stand up to Worm, but then she followed the direction of Bessie's gaze to the entrance of the cabin. The two men had silently left.

'You've scared them off.' Worm pounded his fist against the wall. 'I told them you two were cool. Fuck!' He pounded the wall again. 'You fuckin freaked them out, Caroline!' He pushed her hard against the wall. When she got back up and stared him down, he raised his fist. She wasn't going to be intimidated by this man. He slammed his fist straight into her face, knocking her head back. The pain sent her into a dizzy spiral and for a second she thought she would fall to the floor, but she held herself up against the wall and got back on her feet. Worm stood in front of her, shaking his head. She spat the mouthful of blood that had formed directly into his eye.

Bessie and Gappy stared, mouths wide open.

Caroline went to Bessie and pulled her by the arm. 'Come on, Bessie. We're leaving.' Her friend got to her feet in a stupor and followed. 'Gappy, take us home.'

'Don't you fucking dare, Gappy,' Worm muttered, wiping the blood from his face. 'Make them walk. And bring me Meredith.'

Chapter 24

She left Bessie at the turn-off to her shack, having walked the two miles without saying a word to her. She was still affected by booze and weed and whatever else Worm had given her and went from laughing deliriously to sobbing and apologising. Caroline returned to a dark, silent cabin and tried to slip in unnoticed.

'Is that you, Callie?' Milli sat up in bed, reaching around for the kerosene lamp.

'Shh ... Go back to sleep.' The room lit up as her sister turned the knob on the lamp.

'Oh my goodness!' She held her arms out in shock and disbelief on seeing Caroline's swollen, bloodied face. 'What's happened to you? Who did this?'

'It's nothin. I'm okay,' Callie said, lying down on the bed and pulling the blankets over her body.

'Caroline Forrest, you tell me right now who did this,' Milli demanded, leaning across to see the full extent of the injury. It stung when she touched her cheek. 'Stay there. I'm going to get something to clean it.'

Caroline plopped herself down, hoping that Pa wouldn't wake, but sure enough his head poked around the corner.

'What's happening?' he asked, and when Caroline stayed quiet he came into the room. 'Princess?'

'It's nothing, Pa. Please go to bed.' But when he saw her face, he slumped down into the bed next to his granddaughter and held his arm around her.

'What's goin on, my princess? What's happenin here?' He started to sob with such an air of defeat and helplessness that Caroline felt her heart throb with pain.

'Please Pa, don't cry. Go back to bed.'

'Who did this to you?'

Milli came back. She sat in front of Caroline with a warm cloth and started to pat her face. No one spoke, and Caroline sat and let them nurse her. She could smell the melaleuca in the warm water and allowed it to ease her mind and the tears that made their way down her cheek too.

'I'm so sorry.' The words came from every part of her. She loved Pa and Milli more than anything, and to know she'd caused them this level of devastation was too much. 'It won't happen again.'

'Shh … We'll talk in the morning,' Milli said, continuing to wipe her face and neck. 'Just tell me now, where is Bessie? Is she safe?'

Caroline assured her sister that Bessie was safe at home, and the two sisters crawled into bed next to each other. Pa pulled out his mattress and laid his thin frame down in the doorway to their room, guarding them from whatever monsters were on the other side.

A few days had passed while Caroline made excuses not to go out of her shack, not wanting sympathy from the adults or stares from the children. She'd sent Milli out to tell Chester she was sick when he came to collect her on the first day after the incident, but now three days later the bruising had subsided somewhat.

She pulled the sheet aside from where she lay in bed and peered through the opening to take in the scene. Kids were playing a game of rounders in the dirt, Aunty Nettie was hanging clothes up on the line and Uncle Kevin was sitting on a log by the fire having a smoke and yarning with Pa.

She remembered how Bessie had come over the day before when Milli and Pa Quincey were out. Caroline figured she had waited for them to leave so she wouldn't have to explain her role in the incident. She had tapped at the side of the shack and Caroline thought about telling her to go away but then rolled over in bed and told her to come in and lie next to her. For a long time they just looked at the ceiling together in silence before Bessie finally said she was sorry.

'Do you really mean it?' Caroline had asked, rolling over to face her friend. 'Will you do it again?' Bessie stayed on her back looking at the rafters and wouldn't answer Caroline. 'Why do you do it? We can get you a job on one of the stations?'

Bessie leaned over and Caroline could see there were tears flowing down her friend's cheeks. 'Callie, you've been sayin for months that you're going to get me a job on the station. Mum's been tryin too. And Clarence.'

'You just have to be patient, Bessie. Something will come up.' She reached out and wiped the tears away.

'Nobody wants me, Callie. I'm not like you. You're neat and nice and know what to say. I'm just a big blabbermouth. Who would want me around? You see the look that Mrs Ford gives me at church. Those white women think I got the devil in me or something.'

Caroline had indeed noticed the looks that Bessie got in church and whenever they went down the shops. There was something reckless and wild about Bessie that Caroline loved, but the local ladies around the town did not. Where Caroline saw an adventurous, playful spirit, they saw a threat.

'We'll look after you on the camp, Bessie. We'll protect you here. You don't need to go out with those men.' Caroline said it to make her friend feel better, but she felt scared too – after all, she had been willing to sell drugs to get away from Hereford Downs. Who was she to tell Bessie how to make money?

'I don't wanna be a weight on people, Callie. Mum's already hungry and tired all the time lookin after the rest of the kids, and who knows what's wrong with Dad? He gets madder everyday, wakin up yellin in his sleep about whatever happened all those years ago. And Clarence. He's old enough to find a woman and make his own family. I gotta look after myself, Callie.' Her friend let out a guttural sob. Caroline put her arm around her and told her that everything would be okay, even though she didn't really believe it herself. Bessie slowly drifted off to sleep and remained next to Caroline for the night.

As she was looking out the window, reflecting on her conversation with Bessie, the yellow ute came up the drive and she heaved herself up to get ready for another day of work at the Cunninghams. She collected her bag, went out and got in the ute. She looked down at the floor, not wanting Chester to see her eye.

'Are you okay?'

'Just drive, Chester.' She continued looking down as he started the engine and drove back out the driveway.

'Callie, what's wrong?' She looked up and allowed him to see her face, figuring he would see it at some stage that day. She couldn't hide forever. He grimaced, slowed the vehicle and pulled over to the side of the road. 'Who did this to you?'

'It was an accident.' She looked ahead, wanting him to just keep going, regretting she hadn't given it another day for the bruising to dissipate. 'It's nothing, Chester, please just keep driving.'

'I'm not going anywhere until you tell me who did this.' He leaned back in the driver's seat so he could see her full body. 'Did they hurt you somewhere else? Tell me, Callie.' His eyes scanned her neck, legs, arms and face.

'I'm not going to tell you, Chester. You'll just make it worse.'

'So it wasn't an accident?' he persisted and she sighed. 'It was Worm, wasn't it?' She almost laughed at how quickly he was able to guess. 'I knSew it.' He held the steering wheel and looked at the road, the veins pulsing through his wrists and along his quivering forearms.

'Chester. It's okay. We're going to be late, Chester. Come on. Just drive.' She had no time for this.

'Are you serious right now? I'm not going anywhere until you tell me exactly what happened.'

'Chester, you're *not* my man. We're not together. It's not your responsibility to fix any of this.'

It was true. He couldn't argue with her. 'Can you at least tell me what happened? As a friend? Can I at least be that to you, Caroline?'

Caroline knew he wasn't going to budge. Maybe it would be nice to tell someone everything? 'Bessie told me she was making good money working for Worm.' His eyes widened. 'Yes, I know. Stupid. But I haven't exactly been feeling myself lately.'

'Selling drugs?' Chester asked.

'Well, that's what I thought. Just weed. It's natural ...' She started to explain and shrugged when his face didn't change.

'You were going to deal marijuana?' He looked at her incredulously.

'Chester, do you want to know what happened or not?'

'Sorry. It's just … very unlike you.'

'Yeah, well. Like I said. I haven't been feeling myself lately. Since … I just want to make enough money to get away from here.'

He nodded. He also didn't want to talk about the dance again either. 'I'm sorry. Please, go on.'

Caroline looked out the window, across the paddocks just starting to sprout rows of new seedlings, letting her mind go back to that evening. She told him what happened.

'Who were the two men?'

'I don't know. I'd never seen them before.' Caroline went on to describe their appearance – the younger one who looked like a farmer and the older man who looked like he worked in an office. Chester didn't recognise them from the description either.

'I am going to kill Worm.'

'No, you can't,' Caroline said tiredly.

'Caroline, we can go to the police about this. We can tell Sergeant Mulligan.'

Caroline laughed. 'Sergeant Mulligan? What am I going to tell him? I went to sell drugs for these blokes but they wanted to pimp me instead and I'm sorry, I'll deal weed, but I'm not going to be a prostitute – that's where it crosses the line for me? Umm, no, I don't think so.'

Chester fell silent. 'What about Bessie?'

'She's fine. She came over yesterday. She didn't get hurt like I did. But I think she's been doing it for a while.'

'Sleeping with men for money?'

Caroline nodded. 'I tried to get her to promise me she wouldn't do it any more, but I'm not sure …'

At work that day she managed to avoid Mrs Cunningham for the most part until lunch, when she spotted the black eye while Caroline stirred the stew.

'Oh, that looks nasty.' There was no sympathy in her voice. It wasn't her fault Worm punched her in the face, but Mrs Cunningham would think it was. It was the same with the dance. How could anything possibly be something other than Caroline's fault? If it was Caroline's fault it would mean people like Mrs Cunningham would need to take a good hard look at themselves. Caroline didn't answer and Mrs Cunningham didn't push her, so lunch was prepared in silence as Mrs Cunningham came and went as normal, offering an instruction here and there. Caroline had never been more relieved to leave the property than she was that afternoon.

The following day, she waited outside her shack for Chester to arrive. The swelling in her eye had subsided and she was beginning to feel better. Pa Quincy and Milli were being very supportive, and her conversation with Chester the previous afternoon had made her feel a little better. Chester had said he thought she was brave for standing up for herself and her friend, and his compliment gave her a new sense of pride.

She watched the little kids across the other side of the campfire playing with some new puppies, expecting Aunty Nettie to come out rousing on them to keep their uniforms clean and get to school. The signs of late spring were all around. Wildflowers blossomed, the earth was warming up, and baby animals ventured further from their mothers. Pa was sitting by the fire with Star, boiling his billy for a cup of tea and she could hear Milli inside scratching around getting ready for work. If Chester was going to be late, she figured she may as well join Pa for a cuppa so she went inside to grab a mug.

'Haven't you gone yet?' Milli called as she folded up blankets inside Pa's room.

'He hasn't come yet.' The shack had been a mess when she'd walked out ten minutes earlier – now the dirt floor had been swept clean of crumbs and the bowls and plates were neatly arranged on a freshly laundered tablecloth.

'Well, what are you doing in here? You be ready when he comes.' Milli still nagged but more gently these days.

Caroline grabbed her mug and left to sit on a blanket in the dirt with Pa. He reached for the freshly brewed tea and poured some for her. She brought it close and let the steam warm her face. After a while, she took a sip as Milli emerged from the shack and walked past on her way to work, stopping briefly to wrap a blanket around Pa's shoulders. The kids had left for school and the camp was quiet now.

'Pa, how'd you know Nana Tamar was the one for you?' The old man smiled softly and continued gazing into the flames. Caroline only had fleeting memories of her grandmother from when she was a young child. She was a kind and gentle soul. Caroline would lie between her grandparents at night, fighting off sleep, listening to their soft chatter in traditional language.

'We were promised to each other. That's what the old people would tell us. We didn't argue with the old people.' He chuckled quietly. 'Not like you, cheeky girl.'

It sounded so easy to Caroline. She wished someone would simply tell her what to do. 'How'd they know, Pa? How'd they get it right for you and Nana Tamar?'

'I don't know, Princess, but I was one lucky fulla. Your grandmother was the most beautiful woman in all the country.'

'Can you tell me what she was like?' Caroline asked, even though she'd heard all the stories before.

'When Tamar looked at me, even before we were promised to one another, I'd feel like a king. She made me feel proud and strong.' He sat up straighter as he remembered his beautiful wife. 'And when we were married, she did her hair all up nice in flowers and feathers and everyone around the camp told me that my bride was the prettiest, smartest, kindest woman they knew.' He laughed a little as he said this, and Caroline could see he was back in that place, an excited young groom with the whole world ahead of him.

'Why you laughing, Pa?'

'They probably tell every groom his bride is the prettiest, I s'pose, now that I'm thinking back, but, gee, I believed it at the time. My Tamar. She was beautiful.'

'I believe you, Pa.' She smiled across at him. 'Look at me – I must've got my good looks from somewhere.' He shared her grin and reached out and touched her cheek.

'You remind me of her, little princess. Cheeky and dreamy.'

'And beautiful?' Caroline grinned back.

'Yes, and beautiful.'

He put down his tea and reached across to take Caroline's hand in his. His fingers were thin and frail, and she worried about him still having to do manual work at the abattoir. The smile left his face. 'But I know it's not easy now for you young ones.'

'That's not true, Pa. You don't need to worry about us.' She didn't want to see the sadness in his eyes.

'You're old enough now to accept the truth, Princess. Most of the old ways are gone. I wish I could tell you which way to go. But when you're not sure what to do, just know that the spirit is still here.' He took Caroline's hand and placed it on the ground, closing his eyes. 'It's still here.' She inhaled deeply, closed her eyes and welcomed the overriding calm, letting Pa hold his hand over hers as her fingers touched the sand. 'This is yours, my princess. This earth. Listen. Can you hear it?' Birds chatted and fluted, children sang; there was the distant sound of water falling from the tap. 'Are you listening?' The sound of the breeze passing softly against the leaves, a distant truck, an animal moving in the bushes, probably a lizard or a snake. 'This is your Country. You belong to it and it belongs to you.

'Can you see?' She opened her eyes. 'Look up.' They looked to the sky together. 'That's your sky. This is your Country, and it still beats with the rhythm of our blood. Our blood, that pumps through here.' He tapped at her chest. 'If you want to know which way to go, you gotta listen to this *ere*. Be strong. Be brave. The true way is in here.' He tapped at his own chest. 'Just gotta listen carefully.'

She heard the familiar sound of Chester's ute coming up the driveway. 'I have to go, Pa.' She pulled up Pa's blanket, which had again fallen around his side, and squeezed him in a gentle embrace before walking towards Chester.

'Sorry I'm late.' He looked different today and it was more than his freshly shaven face. His eyes sparkled.

'What kept you? I hope your mum doesn't get too cranky with me.' He started the engine and drove back down the track. They had become used to chatting about insignificant issues to pass the time on the morning ride, but this morning silence hung heavy. 'Are you okay, Chester?' Maybe she'd said too much the day before. Maybe he didn't want to be near someone who had associated with Worm. He pulled the ute off to the side, veering down towards the creek out of sight from the main road, and parked in the shade of some bushy eucalypts. 'What are you doing, Chester?' she asked, puzzled by the detour.

He turned off the engine, then glanced down at his hands and took a deep breath before looking into her eyes. 'I can't do this any more.'

'Do what?' He was going to tell her that she was dirty. She spent time with deviates like Worm. The shame made her want to retch. And just when she was starting to feel comfortable around him again.

'Pretending. Pretending that there is nothing going on here.' Hold on a second. This was not the direction she was expecting him to go in.

'I don't know what you're talking about, Chester.'

'Tell me you don't feel anything, Caroline.' She looked away from him and brought her hand to her heart. The truth was easier to feel than before. She just had to pause and listen for it. She looked down at her hands and back towards Chester. But before she could respond, he said, 'Don't say anything.' He got out of the vehicle and came around to open her door. 'Come with me.' She followed him to the opening of a walking path, feeling the same rush of excitement she felt that day following him towards the citrus orchard.

The forest was still damp from the morning dew and the birds sang from branches up high. She could hear the trickling of water as they approached the creek. They came upon a cluster of rock boulders and Chester jumped down first, then turned and reached out his hand to guide her down through the crevasse. They continued along a narrow path until it opened into a lush meadow bordered by melaleuca trees. She was definitely going to be late now, but she didn't care any more.

Chester stepped back and allowed her to take in the scene. A patchwork quilt was laid out on the soft green grass, a few cushions cast here and there. The quilt was surrounded by a ring of sweetly scented dark pink eucalypt blossoms. They had been neatly picked and placed around the edge. She turned to face Chester, who was still standing behind her.

'Caroline, I want to be with you. We don't have to tell anyone. It can be our secret. We can stop here each afternoon when I drive you home. No one has to know.' He came closer and reached for her hands. 'I'll save money from selling cattle at the sale yards then we can move to the city.' He paused, letting her hands fall away from him. 'Say something, Caroline. If you don't want me, just say it. I can't go on like this.'

She picked up his hands again in hers and kissed him softly on the lips. His arm reached around her waist as he pressed his lips more firmly against hers. She could feel his body tense and shiver as it pressed up against hers. She stepped back, grinning, touching her lip with her finger. 'So this is why you were late this morning?'

Chester shrugged, smiling back. 'Do you like it?'

'It'll work for now. But we need to get a move on, if we're going to keep this secret like you say.' She pulled him back towards the path. 'Come on, your mother is going to have a fit, we're so late!'

Spring had turned to summer and each day she waited eagerly for Chester to come and collect her from the camp. They would chat and share some fleeting kisses on the journey towards Hereford Downs. Then she would go about her daily work around the house, trying to catch glimpses of him from the windows. Sometimes she would see him just before lunch out near the washing line, and if Mrs Cunningham was safely out of sight they would kiss in among the linen sheets.

During lunch, he would compliment her cooking just enough to get a smile out of her. Sometimes she wondered if Mrs Cunningham suspected their romance had reignited, but she was fairly certain Mr Cunningham was oblivious, given he was always off in his own world of cattle prices and wheat sales. Caroline had never felt so happy in all her life.

Milli and Caroline filled their buckets from the communal tap. Washing clothes was an arduous but necessary job and the sisters had perfected a streamlined routine over the years. Milli would wash the clothes in the first bucket and wring out the excess water, then pass the piece of clothing to Caroline, who would rinse it in the second bucket of water, then hang it up on the makeshift clothesline strung between two trees.

'I was talkin to Aunty Nettie last night,' Milli said, breaking the silence but maintaining the same rhythm of scrubbing and dunking, then scrubbing and wringing.

'Oh yeah,' Caroline murmured. 'How's Aunty going? Still pretendin she's not in love with that stockman?'

Milli tried to stifle her grin. 'Don't talk about Aunty like that, Caroline.' But she couldn't help breaking into laughter, knowing full well Aunty Nettie was sweet on a dashing stockman who came into town from time to time. Her moods were obviously correlated with the droving seasons that dictated his coming and going, and who could blame her? She had to put up with quiet old Uncle Kevin, who could go three months without saying a word. 'You know, that's how rumours start, and Uncle's likely to come and thump anyone talking about his missus like that.'

'Married love, eh? Would you ever get married, Milli?'

Milli looked at her. 'Why you askin me that?'

Caroline fell silent. She had not told her sister of their plans – to save money, to leave for the city where judgement might be less harsh. She was hoping to pick the right moment. Besides, she had a secret she was not yet ready to share with anyone, and her sister knew her too well. Caroline knew that if she started to talk to Milli about Chester, she would tell her the one thing she hadn't told him. She was pregnant. Very early days, but nevertheless.

Milli continued to squeeze the water out of the clothes. 'Come on now, girl, be serious for once,' she said. 'Aunty Nettie reckons her shack is full to the brim with gundanoos – you know how they took in some of Paula's kids after she turned to the drink, and now with the little ones all growin up so quick, well, there just isn't any room.'

'Yeah, those little kids are gettin too cheeky, should be in school now,' Caroline said, feeling her arms getting tired as she stretched up to peg the dresses on the line.

'Well, Aunty wondered if we'd take Charlene,' Milli went on. 'Reckon she needs a bit of privacy now she's almost a woman, and with our little shack only having to fit you, me and Pa, well, I thought it'd be the right thing to do to say yes.'

Suddenly Caroline realised that Milli knew, somehow, and that she was trying to draw an admission out of her, giving her time to find the right moment to reveal her pregnancy rather than ask directly. The appreciation Caroline felt for her sister's tenderness was spoiled by a rush of guilt. Caroline wasn't planning on raising the baby in the shack so there was no reason for concern about space. Soon she would be gone.

'Let's tell Aunty that her girl Charlene can come over whenever she's ready,' Caroline said, thinking that maybe it would be nice for Milli to have some female company once she left with Chester and the baby.

'Okay, I'll tell Aunty Nettie tonight when I see her,' Milli said and Caroline noticed how deflated she looked.

She'd been holding off telling her sister about the baby but seeing Milli's face now told her it was time to open up and let her in. She pegged the skirt on the line and reached down to take her sister's hand. Milli dropped the piece of clothing she was working on in the bucket and looked up, letting Caroline guide her palm towards her bulging abdomen. Their eyes met and emotions welled between them as they realised the miracle and heartache that this little one would bring. Caroline let her sister's hand fall and bent down to pick up the last piece of clothing that Milli had let drop in the bucket and began wringing it out.

'Well, that's done for another day, sis,' Caroline said, hanging the last piece of clothing while her sister sat quietly watching. 'Come on, Milli, you stoke the fire and I'll get the water.' She patted her sister on the shoulder and lead the way back to the shack, not used to being the one taking charge.

'Wait,' Milli said, reaching for her hand. 'It's Chester's?'
'Yes.' Caroline smiled.

They lay together on the picnic rug spread out on the grass under the shade of the paperbarks, enjoying the warmth of the waning sunlight filtering through the tall trees, listening to the trickle of the stream that flowed nearby.

Caroline got up. She undressed to her underwear and slowly walked into the water, which was stained a golden light brown from the melaleuca leaves.

'Come in,' she said, moving into the deeper part of the pool, glancing back to entice him with her smile. 'The melaleuca is strongest in this part, good for healing.'

Chester took off his shirt and trousers, and made his way into the water. 'And why do I need healing?' he asked, moving closer to her.

'Everyone needs healing. Just being in this world breaks you down.' She twirled the tips of her fingers, making ripples across the surface. 'Sometimes even the smallest things can cause the biggest scars.'

'I need to get away from here, Caroline. All my parents talk about is the crops and money and the farm. And with Simon gone, it's becoming unbearable. Sometimes their expectations make me feel like I'm going to explode.'

'Milli does the same to me.' She waded deeper into the water and he followed, submerging himself from the neck down.

'But you always seem so calm.'

'That's just when I'm around you. You make me feel safe.' She felt his hands reach around her waist, pulling her in. She wrapped her legs around him and pressed her lips to his and they kissed as the sunlight flickered through the trees and the robins and finches danced from branch to branch.

As far as she was aware, only Milli knew of their love affair, and this secrecy served to provide them with a warm cocoon in which they could hide against the world. But they both knew it couldn't last forever.

'Chester?' she said softly into his ear when they were laying back on the blanket, checking he hadn't drifted off to sleep after their lovemaking.

'Mmm …?' he murmured, sleepily reaching out and pulling her in closer to his chest. 'It's not time yet, is it? Let's stay a little longer.'

'Chester, we're going to have a baby.' She looked up into his face.

'Really?' Chester's eyes widened as he propped himself up on his elbows. 'How do you know?'

Caroline laughed softly. 'I've missed my monthly, three times.' She paused, considering his expression. 'You're happy?'

'Are you serious?' His hand gently rested on her lower abdomen. 'This is the most wonderful news ever! What's wrong?' He noticed the look in Caroline's eyes and stopped, suddenly realising the enormity of the situation. 'It'll be okay. Don't worry. I'm going to take care of you. Of us.'

She was still and quiet. 'What am I going to do, Chester?'

'What are *we* going to do?' he corrected her. 'Caroline, you're not alone.'

'I know, but it's not you I'm worried about. It's this town.' She sat up and regarded him seriously. 'The way they looked at me with such disgust on the night of the dance, don't you remember?' He said nothing, but reached to hold her hand. 'We can't bring a child up in this town.'

They both fell silent, knowing it was the truth, but not knowing the solution.

'Let's go someplace else, Caroline,' he said. 'Some place far away from this shithole and its arrogance. We always planned to get out of here together one day. This just means we have to bring our plans forward a little. We can start a new life someplace else, maybe by the coast or in the city, somewhere big enough for us to disappear.'

Caroline felt a burst of optimism. 'I heard that people mix more in the city – one of the girls from the yumba has a cousin living in the city dating a German man, or maybe he's Austrian, but a whitefulla all the same.' Imagine a life somewhere they could raise their child as a family without fear of judgement and abuse. 'Oh, but what about money, Chester? You'd be leaving behind everything. I don't have anything as it is, but you stand to inherit Hereford Downs. How can you leave all that?'

She thought about the vast stretches of land and wealth that would one day be his. That money would eventually be handed down to the child growing inside her. Maybe it would be better for them to continue meeting in secret. But what would they tell their child? The little boy or girl would never know where they really came from. It wasn't a difficult decision, really.

'Caroline, if this town won't accept us then I don't want to live in it. The farm means nothing without you. Let my brothers have it. Besides, I'm good with my hands and I know how to fix things. I could get a job as an apprentice carpenter.' He looked at her pleadingly. 'I'm not saying it would be easy at the start, but we could make it work. Let's just get out of here. Come on, let's go next week.'

'Next week? No! What will I do without Milli?' Caroline began to panic.

'I'll be with you, I'd be by your side the whole time,' he said soothingly.

'No, you'd have to work, and I'd be by myself in a town where I knew no one. I need Milli to help with the birth, Chester, please. I'll come with you, we'll make a new life, but please let me have the baby here. I'm scared to do it without my sister.'

'Okay, we'll wait until you've had the baby here,' Chester said.

'Thank you, and for now we best be getting going or the whole camp is going to know we're still together,' she said, getting up.

'So what? Let them know, let them all know – why do we need to keep this a secret?' he asked, shaking out the picnic rug.

'We've been over this, Chester – I don't want people to know. We need to keep this a secret, for just a bit longer,' she pleaded with him as they returned to the car. 'Until we come up with a solid plan.'

'Well, they're going to know soon enough anyway, if you're already three months along, unless you wanna tell everyone it's an immaculate conception and then they might start to really wonder ...' He tried to lighten things up, but she wasn't in the mood for joking. 'Oh, come on, it's going to be okay,' he said, taking her by the waist and leaning in to kiss her on the lips.

'Let them think the baby is someone's who's just passed through,' she said. 'It'll be easier that way, less questions. We don't have to say one way or the other. Just let people think what they want. Just trust me on this one, Chester. We should keep a low profile.'

The sun had set and a cool breeze hung in the air as they drove back towards the camp in silence, both apprehensive of what lay ahead. Chester seemed far from convinced, but Caroline felt certain it was better to keep it secret.

Chapter 25

Autumn had arrived and it was becoming more uncomfortable to move around in her clothes in the stifling heat. Despite her baggy dresses, her six-months-pregnant stomach was now very visible. She had told Mrs Cunningham when it had become difficult to hide the pregnancy any longer that the father was a man back at the camp who did not want to marry her. Mrs Cunningham's lip had curled in disdain, rapidly followed by outrage at the loss of her help. 'You have no idea how hard it is finding someone reliable.' Some of her anger had been soothed by Caroline promising to work up until the birth, then return after the baby. Caroline had not felt even a pang of guilt at the lies. Mrs Cunningham's contempt for her condition had seen to that.

She had finished the floors and clothes and was in Chester and Simon's room dusting. The room didn't really need dusting – she just liked to be near Chester's things. She arranged his drawings into neat piles on his desk. The one on top was a sketch of a bookshelf.

Mrs Cunningham was in the parlour working on a tapestry, as was her morning routine. The men were all outside in the yard and the house felt still and peaceful. A light breeze flowed from the half-open doorway onto the veranda and she sat for a moment on Chester's bed, leafing through his pile of sketches. There were barns and chicken coops and go-karts, all impeccably drawn with exact measurements alongside. When she came across a sketch of a baby's cot she lay down on his bed to soak in the details, thinking what a wonderful father Chester was going to make. The base was on rockers and each side panel had a small teddy bear shape carved out. She closed her eyes and imagined her baby in the cot, and rocking him or her back and forth wondering what colour she would paint the wood. Maybe a light yellow ... her favourite colour, the same as Chester's ute.

'What are you doing?' Mrs Cunningham was standing over her. Caroline scrambled to her feet, grabbing the papers before Mrs Cunningham could see what she had been looking at.

'What is that? Give it to me.' Mrs Cunningham snatched the drawing of the cot from her hands. She stared at it for a long time as Caroline stood paralysed, expecting an explosion of wrath, but without saying a word Mrs Cunningham collected the rest of the papers, placed them back on Chester's desk and left the room.

She hovered over the fireplace the following morning, waiting for the familiar rumble of bubbles from the billy. Pa had sent her out to fetch him some tea, too tired to rise out of bed. She spotted Bessie approaching from the distance. She hadn't really spoken to Bessie since her pregnancy had become visible and the gossip had spread around the camp. She hadn't been deliberately avoiding her – Bessie had been away from the camp a lot – but she was relieved all the same. Things had not been the same between them since that night at the Worm Hole. Bessie had stayed away from Worm for a week or two, but then started going over there again, doing whatever she was doing.

But Caroline knew she would have to have the conversation some time – now was as good a time as any.

'Bessie!' she called out to her friend and waved.

Bessie put the bucket beneath the tap, turned on the water then looked up at her friend coldly. 'Hi.'

'What's going on with you?' Caroline asked carefully.

'That's a bit rich coming from you! When were you going to talk to me about being pregnant?'

'I didn't know what to say.'

'Don't give me that shit, Caroline. You're all high and mighty with me, telling me not to sleep around, and here you are, knocked up with a kid.'

'I was going to talk to you, Bessie. I was just waiting for the right time.'

'Bullshit. Whose is it anyway?'

'I don't know,' Caroline lied. She was no longer sure she could trust Bessie, and it would make for trouble if word got out.

'Are you seriously not going to tell me?' Her friend leaned in close with her big sparkly eyes and Caroline couldn't help sharing.

'It's Chester's.' Caroline couldn't make eye contact.

'Chester Cunningham's?' Bessie hissed. 'I thought you two broke up. Holy Jesus, if Mrs Cunningham finds out …? The whole camp thinks it's just some fulla. So what are you going to do?'

'Not sure yet,' Caroline said.

'Does Milli know?'

'Yeah, she knows. But you can't tell anyone, Bessie. You promise?'

'Yes, I promise. But, seriously, what are you gonna do when it comes along?'

Melaleuca

'We might leave together.'

'What?! You can't.' Bessie looked genuinely horrified.

'I can. It's not safe for us here, Bessie.'

'But you said you'd take care of me. You said you'd get me a job on one of the properties. You told me I just had to be patient. Caroline Forrest, you can *not* leave me here. Take me with you. I can help with the baby.'

Caroline looked at her. 'I thought you were too busy workin for Worm. What about him?'

A look of fear crossed Bessie's face. 'I don't wanna live like that any more, Callie. It's gettin bad – he scares me.'

If she got Bessie away from Worm she would be better off, but what if Worm came after them? Could Chester's work support three adults and a child? She had to think of the baby.

She would need to talk to Chester. She smiled at Bessie and put a hand on her arm. 'I'll think about it.'

Milli was sitting out the front of the shack with a needle and thread, mending a work uniform.

Caroline found Pa's mug and poured him his tea. He sat up in his bed and she propped the pillow behind his back. He had been sick but they weren't sure of the cause.

Nothing changed for Milli and Pa, but everything was changing for her. She needed a break from the shack so she reached up to the top shelf where they hid some coins, put two shillings in her pocket and walked back outside.

'I'm goin to the shops. Gonna get some flour. Want anything?' Caroline asked Milli.

'Get some milk for Pa. He's getting too thin.'

Goorungah was bustling on a Saturday morning as people from the farms came into town to stock up on supplies. It was right on lunch time as she passed Alfie's cafe, packed to the rafters with patrons eating burgers and fish and chips. She'd never eaten in there. It was too expensive. She continued past the pub where she could hear the radio blaring with the races and men in heated conversation about jockeys and the condition of horses.

She walked into the grocery store and, spotting Mrs Cunningham, ducked her head and went to the back of the shop before she could be seen. After what had happened the previous day, Caroline could not think of anyone she would less like to run into. Maybe Worm.

She found the flour and waited for Mrs Cunningham to purchase her items before moving back to the front of the store. She recognised the hair of the woman in the line in front of her. It was Lola Armstrong. Lola from the dance. For a second, Caroline wanted to rip open the bag of flour and throw it in her face. She breathed and moved her hand down to her belly, remembering her unborn baby.

'Hi, Caroline.' Lola smiled falsely.

Caroline said nothing and watched as Lola placed her items on the counter, silently pleading for the cashier to hurry up and process the transaction.

'Not long to go now,' Lola said, glancing down at Caroline's protruding belly. Caroline continued ignoring her and berated herself for making the trip to the shops at such a busy time of day. 'Whose is it?'

'No one you would know,' Caroline said, placing the flour and milk down on the counter as Lola finished paying the cashier and picked up her bag of groceries.

'I heard it was Chester's,' Lola said it loudly so everyone could hear and then turned abruptly and walked away. If there was any mercy in this world, it would be the last time Caroline would ever lay her eyes on that girl. She watched her strut away out the door, then paid the cashier and took her items.

On the way out, Caroline spotted Lola again, sitting on the bench next to the girl from the dance – the one with the red hair and big rosy cheeks who had called out at her. The girl was eating a bag of potato chips and offering some to Lola. They spotted her walking. It was too late for Caroline to cross the street so she put her head down and walked as quickly as possible, hoping they would just let her pass. She was almost there when she felt a hard obstacle knock her left foot, sending her body slamming down onto the concrete. She instinctively curled in, landing on her left side, minimising the impact on her baby.

'Oh my goodness, are you okay?' Lola said in mock sincerity, bending down to help Caroline up. Caroline pushed her hand away and picked herself up and dusted off her hands and knees. Her knees and palms were scratched and bloodied. She looked Lola straight in the eye.

'Whatever happens to me in this lifetime, I promise to never become heartless and cold like you, Lola Armstrong.'

'What are you talking about? No need to be so serious now. Calm down.' Lola held her hand to her chest in deep indignation.

'You tripped me. I'm carrying a baby and you tripped me. What kind of person does that? Actually, don't answer that. I don't want to know. I hope I never see you again in my life.'

Chester's yellow ute arrived to pick her up for work. Everyone was used to seeing it but she wondered if people would stop and look harder this morning. She collected her bag and went out to get in the ute. She looked down at the floor.

'Are you okay?' he asked. She continued to look down so he started the engine and drove back out the driveway. 'Callie, what's wrong? Did something happen?'

Caroline told him about the incident at the store. 'Your mother was there. I thought she'd left but she must have overheard.'

Chester slowed the vehicle and pulled over to the side of the road. He turned to look at her. 'So what if she did? She has no proof and she won't want to believe it anyway. We'll get out of here soon, Callie. I promise. Why do you want to wait? I don't want to scare you, but you know as well as I do that the government will take our baby if he or she comes out pale. And that's likely given I'm the father. Why don't we just pack up now and go?'

Caroline knew it was a danger. Out here it was easy for them to come by the yumba and take the little kids when no one was watching. But she needed her sister. At least until the baby was born. What if something happened during the birth? What if the baby came out sick or she couldn't feed it? At least if they were in Goorungah she would have Milli close by.

'I need Milli, Chester.'

'I know. It's okay.' Chester reached into his pocket and pulled out a tiny drawstring bag. 'I got you this.'

'What is it?' Caroline let the contents fall on her lap. A shining crystal pendant hung on a thin gold chain. 'It's beautiful.'

'It's yellow sapphire. Your favourite colour.'

'I love it.'

Chester cupped her face in his hands. 'And I love you.'

Chapter 26

It was an unusually warm winter's day and Caroline had just finished clearing the table from the men's lunch. Mrs Cunningham was sitting at the table eating a sandwich. She had become icy, aloof and overly critical of Caroline's work since seeing the drawing of the cot and hearing what Lola had said in the grocery store. But she had not raised the topic again and Caroline had not had the courage to. She thought it was peculiar. This woman's grandchild was growing inside her and she seemed to not care at all. Caroline was both relieved and perplexed by her behaviour.

Caroline had told Bessie how carping Mrs Cunningham had become and it had made her friend protective. At church the day before, Mrs Cunningham had come over with her perennial frown to tell them the soup was too cold and Bessie had inserted herself between them and – astonishingly – apologised to Mrs Cunningham and taken it upon herself to reheat the soup. Caroline smiled, thinking how her friend had changed. She looked forward to the moment they could all get out of Goorungah together.

As she stood by the sink washing the last of the plates, she felt a pain in her lower abdomen and warm fluid running down her legs. Aunty Nettie had said this would happen but the baby wasn't due for another month. She looked at Mrs Cunningham, who had just finished the last bite of her sandwich and become immersed in a magazine.

'I think the baby's coming,' Caroline whispered at first, and then repeated it louder.

'Oh good Lord, your water has broken.' Mrs Cunningham rushed to the hallway closet and came back with a towel. 'Watch out, hold this – you're getting mess everywhere. Now, stay here while I fetch Chester to get the ute. We'll need to get you to the hospital.'

Caroline stood paralysed in the kitchen. Of all places to go into labour, it had to be in the kitchen of Hereford Downs. She heard Mrs Cunningham calling out to Chester. He would be in the stables at this time of day, thankfully not down in the paddocks far out of earshot.

The back door opened and slammed. 'Caroline?'

An overwhelming contraction seized her body and she jerked forward, holding her middle, and sank to the floor. *Not here, baby. Please don't come in this old witch's place.*

'Chester!' She didn't care about hiding her feelings for him any more. Mrs Cunningham already knew anyway even if she didn't have the courage to admit it. 'It's coming! The baby's here early!' He rushed over and she threw her arms around his shoulders, gently getting her to her feet. 'It hurts.'

'Take deep breaths. We're going to get you to the hospital right now.' He guided her out the back door with his arm around her to hold her up and Mrs Cunningham followed them out. 'Mum, are you coming?' Chester called back to his mother. Caroline looked at him, surprised. They had both lost themselves in the moment and were openly showing their feelings for each other. Caroline

Melaleuca

wanted to tell him that his mother didn't care. That she's ashamed of her. But she couldn't put her thoughts into words. The sudden realisation he was becoming a father seemed to have left Chester yearning for maternal support and Caroline felt her heart breaking for him as she watched the scene unfold.

Mrs Cunningham took a step back and watched on coldly.

'Mum?'

She turned and went inside without saying another word as they reached the ute and another contraction took over her body. Chester yanked open the door and Caroline slid in along the bench seat. He rushed round to the driver's side and started the engine.

'Hurry! Chester!' she begged, resting her head on his thigh and holding her stomach as she felt the ute moving down the driveway. Another wave of pain washed over her. She thought of what Aunty Nettie had told her. 'It's all about the breathing. You gotta focus on breathing in ...' she could see Aunty Nettie doing the movements as they had chatted out the front of her shack one night, '... and then out like this ...' Caroline held the image in her mind as the ute roared along the country road towards the Goorungah hospital where this little one would make its grand entrance. Think good thoughts. Don't think of Mrs Cunningham. Think of Aunty Nettie. Breathe like Aunty Nettie showed you.

'We're nearly there, Caroline.' She could feel the ute take a hard corner and she could see the pine trees out the window from where she lay. They were the pine trees that bordered the hospital. Nearly there.

Chester helped her out of the car and to walk up the ramp to the entrance of the hospital as a nurse hurried out with a wheelchair.

'It's early. Our baby is early,' Chester called out.

Caroline collapsed into the wheelchair and heard the nurse tell Chester to wait in the waiting room of the hospital. He wouldn't listen and tried to follow them down the corridor, but the nurse closed the glass behind her. Caroline felt the wheelchair move her away from Chester. She looked up to the nurse. 'Can't he come with me?' The nurse ignored her and kept pushing her away. She looked over her shoulder and saw him on the other side of the door, and screamed out, 'Tell Milli!'

'It's a little boy,' the doctor announced, as Caroline let her head fall back on the pillow and he placed the tiny body on her chest. 'A nice healthy boy.'

She felt him squirm on her belly as she lay exhausted from the effort. She lifted her head to look down at his pink wriggling body, tiny nose, tiny fingers, tiny everything. She nuzzled into him with her nose and giggled with relief. 'You're perfect.' The nurse came over and said she'd need to take him now to give him a bath. Caroline had reluctantly let her take him when she heard her sister's voice down the hallway demanding to know the whereabouts of her sister. She started to laugh from an intense combination of post-birth-induced delirium, the relief of having seen her healthy baby boy, and the audacity of her sister to charge into a hospital shouting out demands. She lay there propped up with pillows, listening to Milli's rapid footsteps getting closer, and all she felt was warmth and gratitude.

'Callie?' Milli burst into the room.

'Excuse me, ma'am,' the nurse called out from where she stood bathing the baby. 'No visitors allowed down here.'

'Ma'am, with all due respect, that is my sister.' Milli shot back in her 'proper' voice. The nurse shook her head and shrugged in resignation, and turned her attention back to washing the baby. Milli took this as permission and hurried over to her sister's side.

'I'm here.' Milli's voice was soft now and Caroline felt her hand wipe hair from her sweat-drenched forehead. 'Sorry I'm late, but you didn't gimme much notice. You okay?'

'I guess. Where's Chester?'

'He's at the camp waiting for an update.'

The nurse brought the baby over, freshly bathed and wrapped in muslin, placed him on Caroline's chest and left the room.

'What are you gonna call him?' Milli asked, taking a seat next to Caroline and leaning her cheek against her shoulder so she could take in the baby.

'Francis. What you reckon? You like it?'

'I love it.' Milli had reached to touch his little cheeks when Caroline heard footsteps coming along the corridor.

The doctor re-entered with his clipboard and pen. 'Well done, Caroline. He's a very healthy boy.' He stood at the end of the bed and Caroline took in his appearance for the first time. He had unusually thick bushy eyebrows and a narrow face. 'He is quite pale-skinned for an Aborigine. Can you tell me – who is the father?'

Caroline looked at Milli before answering, 'We don't know.'

'The father's a white man, isn't he?' Neither woman responded. 'It was that young gentleman who brought you here, wasn't it? Chester Cunningham?' The doctor paused as he studied Caroline, the baby and then Milli, who had taken a protective stand next to Caroline. Baby Francis wriggled on her chest and she held him a little more firmly. 'How old are you, Caroline?'

'I'm eighteen.'

'That's quite young to be raising a child on your own. I understand you're not married?' He put the clipboard down on the bed and stood across from Milli.

'No.' Caroline knew better than to add any details. She could have said she lived with her sister and grandfather and the baby would be surrounded by love, but that would only fuel this man's disapproval.

'I heard you live on the camp.' Caroline felt Milli's hand reassuringly on her shoulder and wondered why her sister was staying so quiet. It made her nervous. 'I understand there's been an outbreak of measles there recently. We had a few of the young ones come in.' Caroline hadn't heard of any measles cases but she didn't want to appear to be calling the doctor a liar so she said nothing. 'And I heard that sometimes there's a bit of fighting out there, bit too much booze ...' Caroline thought of Worm and Gappy luring Bessie away and getting her drunk and wanted to tell the doctor it all came from in town. 'It's not a good place for a little baby, is it.' The doctor put his hand on the baby's head, and Caroline fought the urge to slap it away.

'I can look after my baby, Doctor, if that's what you're worried about.'

'Oh, I'm sure you can. I have no doubt about your maternal abilities. It's other people I'm worried about. You know there's no shame in letting someone in a bit better position raise your little one. You want to give the baby every opportunity to have a good start in life, don't you?'

Fighting back tears, Caroline looked up at Milli, wondering why the hell her sister wasn't saying anything, but when she saw her sister's face there was nothing but terror etched across it. 'Doctor,' Milli said, her voice quivering with fear. 'My sister will give this baby everything it needs in life.'

'Of course.' He smiled thinly, picked up his clipboard and headed towards the door, but before he left he turned back. 'But I will need to arrange for a welfare check in the coming days.'

Caroline woke early to the daylight outside the hospital window. The baby was in the cot next to her bed, finally asleep. He'd slept in the nursery overnight, but the nurse had dropped him off crying for a feed in the early hours. Caroline had fed him, and placed him in his cot, then nodded back to sleep herself. She was down in the small dark room at the back of the hospital; the one reserved for Aboriginal women, where they'd shifted her from the birthing suite the day before. She had been there a few times to bring Aunty Nettie supplies after she'd given birth. It had felt so full of life when Aunty Nettie was there with a new baby and some of the other kids meeting their new sibling, but this morning it felt cold and lonely.

The door opened. Caroline expected a nurse to come in but it was Milli sneaking through, holding an index finger up to her lips. 'Shh ...' Caroline watched as Milli shut the door as slowly as possible behind her so as not to create a sound, and tiptoed over to where Caroline lay. 'We need to get you outta here.'

'What are you talkin about?' Caroline tried to sit up but felt a stabbing pain through her abdomen from where she'd stretched her muscles the day before giving birth. 'The doctor hasn't said I can go yet.'

Milli walked over to the cot and picked up the sleeping baby Francis, who immediately started to protest. She brought him to Caroline. 'We don't have time, Caroline. I've been talkin to Chester and he said his mother is plannin to come down this morning to speak to the doctor. He overheard her telling Mr Cunningham last night. Apparently she'll say anything to get baby Francis into foster care and away from her son. She wants the baby gone. She's going to say that you're unreliable and unfit to be a mother. We need to get you out of here right now. Do you hear?' Milli held baby Francis in one arm and tried to help Caroline out of bed with the other. She packed the towels and baby clothes her sister had brought into a bag, and added some hospital-supplied nappies and bottles. Caroline followed Milli as she walked towards the door and peered down the corridor. 'Come on, it's clear.' She held on to her sister's hand as they walked briskly down the corridor and out the front door of the hospital.

'Where's Chester?' Caroline said, trying to keep up with Milli as she charged on ahead out of the hospital grounds and onto the road. She had presumed he'd be waiting in the ute.

'He's at home. You two can't raise suspicions or Mrs Cunningham is likely to call the cops. We gotta plan. Come on, keep up.'

Caroline raced after her. The baby was crying now and she desperately wanted to stop and comfort him, but Milli kept walking, so she raced on, soothing him as much as she could.

'Chester's packin up his ute this morning. He's gettin as many supplies in there as possible, to hold you two over for a month or two until he's able to get a job. He's tryin to do it on the sly so his parents don't cotton on, so it's takin him a while to get sorted.'

'He's comin to get me?' They crossed the footbridge over the creek and took the alleyway behind Main Street to pass the town as discreetly as possible.

'Yes, he'll be waitin for you under the trees just before the turn-off to the camp right on eleven o'clock. And you're to go and meet him as soon as you've packed while it's quiet around the camp so no one sees you leaving. This has to be kept secret, Callie.'

They were past the main part of town now and Milli was clearly running on adrenaline. 'Milli, please. I need to stop. The baby needs to stop.' She could go no further. Heaving to catch her breath, she halted to check on Francis. Milli looked over her shoulder, then she stopped and came back to Caroline.

'I'm sorry, Callie. I'm sorry to scare you like this.' Milli pulled her over into the branches of a low tree, out of sight of passers-by. 'Sit here for a moment.' Caroline let Milli place baby Francis in her arms as she lowered herself onto a soft patch of green grass. The earth felt good beneath her and baby Francis's cries lulled. Milli finally took a breath, and Caroline reached out her hand to hold Milli's, and noticed it was trembling.

'Thank you, Milli.'

When they reached the yumba, the camp was slowly coming to life. Uncle Kevin was feeding his dogs and a few kids were poking sticks into the fireplace. Caroline followed Milli into their shack where Pa was waiting at the kitchen table. Caroline kneeled down next to Pa to help him hold the baby and then laid little Francis down on his lap so Pa could take him in. He smiled gently. 'Well done, Princess.'

She put her arms around both of them. Neither of them spoke for some time, until finally Caroline broke the silence. 'I promise I'll visit as soon as I can, Pa.'

'I know, Princess. Chester's a good man. He'll take care of you. And I want you take care of him too.' Caroline promised she would. She couldn't hold back tears. 'It's not goodbye. I'll see you again soon,' Pa said and wiped the tears away.

Milli came back out from the bedroom where she'd been packing clothes for their trip.

'I don't wanna go, Milli,' Caroline sobbed. 'Can't I just stay a few days?' But she knew she had to leave.

'Come on now. Don't do that.' Milli dropped the bag and came over to where Caroline sat. 'We'll see each other again soon. I need you to be strong. You have to do it for your son. You're a mum now.'

'I know. But it's too hard without you. I don't even know how to feed him.' She would have said anything to try to convince Milli to let her stay, but that was the first thing that came to mind.

'Yes, you do, Callie. You've helped Aunty Nettie and the other women around here plenty of times with their newborns. You know how it's done.' It was true. But still she didn't want to go. 'I need to go to work now.' Milli got up and dusted her skirt. 'We have to keep things as normal as possible so no one gets suspicious.'

'Please, Milli.' Caroline reached out to grab her hand and try to pull her back down, but her sister stood up straight and flicked it away.

'We need to be strong. You need to get away before anyone realises you've gone. We'll see each other again when things calm down a bit. I'll come and visit you when you get set up.' Caroline watched as her sister reached into her pockets. 'And take this,' Milli said, handing over a small bundle of notes. 'It's not much, but it'll cover petrol and you can buy some food.'

Caroline looked down at the notes that she knew were her sister's life savings. She didn't want to take it, but the overwhelming realisation that she was now responsible for another human life was dawning on her. It was a terrifying thought but the fear was surpassed by another stronger feeling. She looked down at his little squirming body and tiny nose as he lay contently in Pa's lap – it was sheer blissful love. She folded the notes into her bag and let Milli embrace her. Caroline's heart ached as she thought how much she would miss her sister and the hours they spent preparing meals for their little family. Then she watched as Milli kissed baby Francis's face, soaking in his scent and feeling his precious new skin with her cheeks, blessing him with all the love and promises of an aunty, knowing it could be years before they met again. Then she walked out the door. Caroline watched out the window as Milli walked away, wanting to take in every last moment as Pa called out, letting her know he was off to boil his billy for his morning cuppa.

'Hush now, baby boy,' she soothed Francis.

'Babies won't eat if they're not calm,' Aunty Nettie had warned her. 'You gotta start looking after yourself more, Caroline, now that you're gonna be a big mama. Put some fat on those skinny bones of yours, so you can grow a nice little chubby baby.' She sat down to feed Francis, looking down at his soft cheeks. This baby was Chester all over, light skin and blue eyes. The government officials would be watching this one like hawks. He gurgled and looked up into her eyes, satisfied with his feed, and she held him in close.

She thought about the aunties and their advice as she looked over all the bits and pieces Milli had packed for the long trip ahead. It was mainly things that Milli had gathered from church and around the camp. It was only then that she remembered the promises she'd made to Bessie to think about taking her with her. They weren't supposed to be going so soon. They were meant to have a few weeks to prepare for the departure. She felt panicked at the thought of Bessie feeling betrayed once again and got up to go and see Aunty Nettie.

Chapter 27

Sunday 13 February 2000

'So let me get this right – you're saying that Millicent raised your son? The son you had with Caroline?' Renee asked, looking across at Mulligan to see if he was keeping up. He had his head down and seemed to be looking at something on the floor.

'Yes. Caroline had a baby boy the day before she went missing. Francis was mine.'

'But Milli said you weren't even together, that she didn't know who gave Caroline the necklace.'

Chester smiled. 'She wasn't going to have Francis exposed until he was ready. She knew I would never harm Caroline. She wasn't keeping my secrets, she was keeping theirs.'

'Wait, did you know about this, Sarge?' Why didn't she know about this? Why wasn't it recorded on the files?

Mulligan shifted uncomfortably in his seat. 'People knew about it but it just added weight to the idea she and Bessie skipped town. It didn't change anything. Nobody knew it was Mr Cunningham's child. Far as anyone knew they went on a couple of dates and it was over. There were any number of men around camp could have been the father.'

Renee stared at him incredulously. There was not a single thing

Melaleuca

in the file about the baby. Why had he not mentioned it?

'We tried to keep it a secret,' Chester said. 'Caroline and I were afraid the baby would be taken from us at birth if the authorities knew I was the father. They did that in those days.'

Chester's face was drained of colour – the memories were taxing on him. Renee wondered how Josh would take this news. He had a brother. Francis.

Renee regrouped. 'So you were giving money to Millicent to raise the baby?'

'Yes. That's correct. I told Sally and anyone who asked that I was investing it in a small business and there would be a return on it many years from now. It gave me an excuse to go check on Francis and Milli too. That was our cover. I never thought Joshua paid it any attention. But I guess …' He looked away sadly, unable to finish his sentence.

'Please continue, Mr Cunningham.'

'I underestimated the extent to which a boy needs his father.'

'How so?'

'I covered Francis's needs with my regular payments to Millicent, and I provided Joshua and Roxy with everything they could have wanted in terms of money – university education, house deposits, help with the grandchildren. But I wasn't really there for them. Not in the way they needed me.'

'How do you mean?'

'I never asked them how they were going. Particularly Joshua. If I looked at him closely, I thought of Francis. I guess in some way, not consciously, I was trying to be fair – if I couldn't really be there for Francis, then I wouldn't really be there for Joshua either. I thought when I met Sally that maybe I could move on, but I just couldn't.

I went back to thinking about Caroline and Francis and the life we could have shared together. I've spent my entire life wondering what if. And look what I've done. Joshua has gone mad – traipsing around town, asking questions, trying to figure things out.'

'So that's why you're here now? You feel guilty for putting Josh in harm's way?' Renee clarified.

'Yes. Of course. I should have come clean years ago. I've ruined our relationship. I've endangered my son's mental health by not being upfront. If I had told him that I had lost both Caroline and his brother, and that the grief nearly killed me and made me mean then maybe he wouldn't have been driven mad with anger and suspicion. He wouldn't drink so much and act so impulsively. Now he might never wake up. And I will have to live with that.'

Renee looked at Mulligan, who looked impassively back at her.

'So, where is Francis now?' Renee asked.

'The money I gave Millicent was generous. It was enough to send him to the best private schools down in the city. He did well academically and now he lives in one of the wealthy suburbs with his wife and children.'

'Does he know about you?'

'No.'

'Does he know about Caroline?'

'Yes, to the extent that he knows that his mother went missing after his birth and he was raised by his auntie. But Millicent lived with him in the city from shortly after the birth. She only came back to Goorungah ten years ago. Even now she visits him there. He's never even been to Goorungah. Seemed best for everyone.'

'And what about Caroline? What happened to her?' Mulligan jumped in.

Melaleuca

'I honestly don't know. I wish I did.'

'So when was the last time you saw Caroline?' Renee asked.

'The day before she went missing – when I dropped her off at the hospital in labour. Milli and I had arranged for us to meet under the trees before the turn-off to the camp. But she wasn't there. After speaking to Milli later on that day, I suspect Caroline went to find Bessie because she'd been missing for a few days. But I don't know. I don't know where she went.'

'And if we asked Millicent about this, would she give us the same story?' Mulligan asked.

'I guess there's only one way you can find out,' Chester replied matter-of-factly, and Renee knew he was telling the truth.

'So you agreed to look after Francis financially?' Renee asked.

'Yes.' Renee thought Mr Cunningham had aged years since his wife's funeral just a few days ago.

'And you think Josh went mad with suspicion because you were what?' Renee asked.

'Not there for him ... I guess.'

'Emotionally unavailable?'

'I wasn't there for Francis and I loved him. I spent all my time wanting to be with my firstborn and feeling guilty, and I didn't see what was right in front of me ...'

'Sally, and Josh and Roxy.'

'I know now. I've learned my lesson. The hard way, no less.' He looked up, eyes welling with tears. 'Are you a mother, Renee?'

Renee was taken aback by the personal nature of the question. If he hadn't asked with such tender sincerity she would have ignored him.

'I'm not, Mr Cunningham. I don't have children.'

'They pick up on the silences just as much as they pick up on the laughing and shouting and the arguments and the joking. They hear and see everything. Such an incredible responsibility we have as parents, to raise and shape and nurture these little humans. And despite our best efforts, we often just ... fuck it all up.'

'I'm sure it's not as bad as you think, Mr Cunningham. You can still make amends. Explain all this to Josh. He'll understand.' Chester pressed his fingers to his forehead, and Renee pushed a glass of water in front of him. 'Have some water.' Chester drank the entire glass down, took a deep breath and readied himself.

'Mr Cunningham, where were you the morning of your wife's death?' Mulligan asked.

'I was at my home.' The tension in the room returned. Mulligan was holding Chester's gaze with scepticism. 'I'm not proud of it,' he went on, 'but that's the truth. I went home and drank myself into a stupor.'

'You know we have an eyewitness placing you very close to the scene of the crime?' Mulligan pressed on. Renee remembered – the cheeky kid who she'd caught swimming at the creek on her second day on the job.

'Must've been somebody else. It wasn't me.'

'Why did you keep calling Josh?' Renee asked, recalling that the night before when Josh stayed over he had received relentless phone calls from his father.

'I was worried about him. He was going around town asking questions about the disappearance of Caroline and Bessie. It was only a matter of time before Worm and his nasty crew caught wind of his snooping, and then who knows what they'd do to stop him being a nuisance. Lord knows, they're capable of anything, those low-life bastards.'

'So tell us more about Worm,' Renee said.

'He's a germ. They've been peddling drugs in this town for years. Everyone knows that – it's not much of a secret. But they're also known for abusing women.' She watched as Chester eyed off Mulligan. 'It was widely known that Worm and his cousin hung around with Bessie. Caroline told me that they gave Bessie drugs and pimped her out. They'd been known to harass young women around town. But no one would speak up because they were afraid they'd get a visit from them.'

'Why didn't you report it?' Mulligan asked.

'Who said I didn't?' Mr Cunningham stared fiercely at Mulligan now. 'I came and told your father, but a fat lot of good that did.'

'What are you talking about?' Renee asked, cutting through the tension in the room.

'Why don't you ask your boss?' Chester said, not taking his eyes off Mulligan. 'Ask the sergeant here about his father. People came forward, a few of the women. Meredith Walker did – she's still over there, last flat on Wilsons Lane, have a chat with her – but Mulligan Senior never did anything. He was useless. Either he was scared of Worm and his crew or he was in on it.'

Mulligan put his hands palm down on the table. 'Enough speculation, Mr Cunningham. I appreciate your concern about my father's negligence but he's not here to defend himself, so shall we return to the facts and evidence. Speaking of which, do you consent to a DNA sample?'

'Sure. I've got nothing to hide.'

There was a knock at the door. 'What is it?' Mulligan barked. Stacey poked her head through the opening, teeth clenched.

'Sorry! Dupont's on the line. He wants to make sure Renee's okay after last night.'

'Fine,' Mulligan muttered. 'We're finished here anyway.'

Renee was relieved to escape the stuffy room. The call with Dupont was brief and to the point. It was clear he was using his concern as a facade to get more information about how Goorungah Station was handling the press and public opinion, but she conveyed a message of calm control, knowing that would be what Mulligan wanted. She didn't mention anything about Chester – she needed to debrief with Mulligan first – so she ended the call, promising more regular updates on her health.

When she returned to Chester his shoulders were slumped and his face forlorn. She stopped herself from feeling pity for him – this man was not off the hook, despite his confession.

Renee took his DNA sample and then joined Mulligan where he sat waiting in his office.

'What'd the boss want?' Mulligan asked as she sat down opposite him.

'The usual. I assured him we're across everything. I didn't mention Chester yet. Too early.'

'Good.' Mulligan nodded.

'So what do you make of all this?' Renee asked. Mulligan looked out the window deep in thought, watching the rain as it teemed down on the bitumen. She could see the blood pumping across a vein in his forehead.

'I think he's lying.'

'Hmm ...' Renee thought for a moment. 'He seemed fairly

genuine to me. I mean, why would he lie about any of that?'

'I just don't know if it all adds up,' Mulligan said. 'I still think he's involved somehow.'

'Really?' Renee asked. 'How?' Mulligan got up and walked to the window and peered out the slats. The rain was unrelenting. 'Mulligan, we need to talk to Worm again. We need to talk to him about Bessie and Caroline as well as our current victim.'

'We don't have any evidence, Taylor.' There was a knock. It was Roger. 'Come in.'

'The fire department called. They confirmed what we already suspected. The fire last night was deliberately lit.'

'Thanks, Madden,' she heard Mulligan say.

Someone had tried to hurt her. Kill her even. And maybe her mother too – not that many people had known she was in the hospital. Or could it have been Josh they wanted?

'Taylor?'

'Yes, Sarge?'

'Are you okay?' Mulligan asked, concern showing across his face. 'Why don't you get some rest?'

It was generous of Mulligan to offer but she didn't want to show she was intimidated. 'I'm fine. Really I am.' She wasn't though. Her head pounded and her lungs still hurt from breathing in smoke and a slow-burn anger was growing in her gut. They could have hurt her mother. 'I'll be back in a minute.' The office was suffocating – she needed to move to think. She went into the kitchenette and filled a glass of water.

'Renee, I could have done that for you.' Stacey took the glass out of her hands before she could reject the offer. She hadn't even heard her walk up from behind. 'Can I get you anything else? You look a bit pale, hon. You want a Panadol or something?'

Renee was relieved that at least Stacey knew her well enough by now not to tell her to stop working. 'I'm good, Stacey.'

'I'm so sorry about the fire. I heard the kitchen was damaged. I'll arrange someone today to go over there and fix it, okay.'

Renee didn't have the energy to argue with her and simply nodded her agreement.

'Do you want to stay at our place tonight? I'm sure Keith won't mind. I can't imagine you'd want to go back and stay in that same house tonight.'

'I'm okay, Stacey. Thank you.' It was nice of her to offer, but, honestly, Stacey was the last person she would want to stay with. Besides, Renee was intent on standing her ground. She took the glass of water, put it down without drinking any, thanked her again, and returned to Mulligan's office where he still stood by the window looking out.

'I want to talk to Meredith Walker. Chester said Meredith Walker was the only one to ever come forward to the authorities. She might give us something we can use against Worm.' He remained silent, thoughtful. 'Mulligan. We're wasting time.' She knew she was niggling at him, but why was he being so passive? 'I'm going to talk to Meredith.'

'I've seen her out there.'

She followed his gaze out to the protesters. 'Then I'm going out to find her.'

'Taylor,' Mulligan called out to her as she left. She felt his eyes on her as she marched out of the front reception, through the rain, down the concrete stairs, past the dripping wet flag, all the while ignoring the stabbing pain in her ankle.

Melaleuca

The crowd was screaming despite the rain pelting down. She searched for Meredith, but it was a sea of unfamiliar faces. She squinted, trying to focus her vision. A man was standing in front of her. He was holding her by the shoulders. It was Lennon.

'Renee? Are you okay?' Why did everyone keep asking her that? She felt herself sway and, again, Lennon asked if she was okay. She felt herself slipping. The ground pulled her down.

Someone had put a towel beneath her head. Faces hovered above her. They slowly came into focus. Roger held an umbrella to cover her.

'Here. Drink this.' Stacey put a glass of water in front of her and she sipped it. Mulligan came into view. The protesters around her had dispersed, giving them space. The remaining few stole glances in her direction.

'Roger, Stacey, take her home,' Mulligan said. 'Taylor, you *need* to rest.'

Roger and Stacey helped her to the car at the back parking lot and drove her the short stretch home. It took almost as long as walking, but in the car at least she had privacy while crossing Main Street. No doubt everyone had already heard that the new cop, the one whose house got burned down, just fainted. Roger and Stacey supported her to the porch.

'I'm fine, really. You can go now.' But they insisted on opening the door and leading her to the couch.

The house smelled of smoke. The firefighters had been able to save most things but they would need a new kitchen. 'I'm okay. Really.'

After they left, she remembered the eggs. She limped to the corner to check on them. They were shattered from the flames. If nothing else, she had wanted the eggs to last. She really wanted to see the chickens hatch. She kneeled down, ran her fingers over the cracked shells and felt herself start to shake.

Chapter 28

The next morning Renee felt groggy with sleep, the whole house reeked and there was no way of cooking breakfast. She had no wish to stay there a minute longer. Fuck it. She grabbed her keys, got in her car and drove through the pouring rain to the last flat in Wilsons Lane where Chester had said Meredith Walker lived.

Renee guessed Meredith Walker was probably in her mid-fifties – thin, skin so white it was almost translucent, with long wavy blonde hair. She wore a floaty black dress with tassels and a silver necklace with a crescent moon.

'Renee Taylor,' Meredith stated, opening the door wide, slightly swaying. 'Get in here out of that rain.'

'You know who I am?' Renee asked, shaking her umbrella out and stepping inside. It was warmly lit inside and a little hazy – the air hung with a mixture of cigarette smoke and sandalwood incense.

'Of course I know who you are dear. You're Val's girl. She's a solid sheila, that Val. Come through, love.' Renee followed Meredith into the kitchen, remembering that her mother had said she was friends with the woman. 'What brings you here?' She was swaying again and Renee could smell alcohol on her breath. There was an ashtray piled with cigarette butts on the coffee table and Stevie Nicks sang in the background. 'How is she? I see her at the pokies from time to time. Poor love. That arthritis has really got her, hey?'

'She's okay. She had a fall the other day, so she's in hospital now.'

'Oh no – I should pop up and see her.'

'She'd like that.'

'So what are you doing back in Goorungah? I thought your mum said you'd moved down to the big smoke.'

'I did. I'm just back for a few weeks to help out with Mum.'

'You're a good daughter. Wish my daughter would come back and visit me more often. Moved down south with some no-hope loser.' She looked up to a photo on the wall showing a young woman at a hen's night, sipping cocktails out of pink penis straws. 'Now if I recall correctly, your mum said you joined the police force. Why on earth would you do that?' She laughed, but then stopped herself. 'Sorry, hon. We need good people like you in there.'

Renee ignored the comment and continued. 'I've actually been transferred here.'

'Right. Have a seat.' She nodded to the thin round kitchen table, the type they sell to cashed-up city dwellers in vintage shops who spend entire weekends deciding on the colour scheme for their matching Smeg kettle and toaster. Here in Goorungah, in this kitchen, it just looked tired and sad.

Renee took a seat. Meredith grabbed her ashtray off the coffee table in the lounge room, placed it on the kitchen table and took a cigarette from her pack on top of the fridge.

'Smoke?'

'No, thanks.'

'Drink?'

'Just water.' Meredith poured a generous glass of vodka and added a dash of lemonade for herself and then got Renee a glass of water.

'That's a nasty scratch you have there.' Renee had forgotten about the bump on her forehead. She'd hit it when she landed on the porch during the fire. Meredith must not have been out otherwise she'd know about the fire, but now was not the time to go into it.

'What can I say? Goorungah's keeping me busy.'

Renee felt self-conscious as Meredith's big eyes seemed to sum her up. 'Your mum does that too.'

'What?'

'Purses her lips.' No one had ever commented on the similarities between her and her mother. She was surprised that she felt complimented. 'Val purses her lips when she's frustrated. You never noticed?' Renee shook her head. 'Well, go on then. You obviously didn't come around to get on the booze with me.'

'Have you seen the news? About the young woman who was found dead by the creek?'

'I did.' She took a deep draw of her cigarette. 'Terrible ... Have you found him?'

'Not yet. Mrs Walker?'

'Call me Meredith, love.'

'Meredith, I've been hearing reports of a bloke called William Gawlor – Worm?'

Recognition flooded her face. She picked up her glass and swirled the liquid, staring hard at its centrifuge and then tapped the bottom on the table.

'Worm.' She said the name like it was falling to the ground, like someone might say Hitler or Satan. No further explanation needed.

'You know him?'

'Everyone knows him.' She took a mouthful. 'Do you think he's got something to do with this?'

'I'm not sure,' Renee said truthfully.

'I wouldn't put it past him.'

'Chester Cunningham came down to the station yesterday.'

'Good old Chet! He was a lovely young man, but, gee, he turned into a grumpy old sod.'

'He said that I should talk to you about Worm.'

'Oh, did he? I wonder how he knows. This town talks too bloody much.'

'Mr Cunningham said that Worm assaulted you.'

'Worm assaulted a lot of young women. That was common knowledge.'

'Can you tell me about it?'

Meredith hesitated for a moment then poured another vodka. 'All the young ones would get pissed at parties and carry on. He and his cousin from the city would lurk around outside in their flash hotted-up car. What was his name now?' She pinched her forehead trying to remember. 'Something to do with his teeth ... Gappy! That's it. Skinny little pissant, but he was strong.' She took a sip of vodka. 'He had an older brother who would sometimes come too. Trav. They'd wait until the party was over and we'd be stumbling around trying to make our way home in the dark. Then they'd chuck us in the car and take us to their hangout.'

'Behind the silos?'

Meredith nodded. 'That's the one. They called it the Worm Hole. What a ridiculous bloody name. You been there?'

'I have.'

'Well, that's where he beat me up. I was the only one to ever go to the cops. That's probably how Chet found out. I was the only one to ever speak up, but I didn't get very far. I knew straight away no one was going to take me seriously. I was just a drunk tart "asking for it".'

'I'm sorry that happened to you, Meredith. It must have been horrifying to have that happen in your hometown. Can I ask, Meredith, why did he beat you up?'

'Because I wouldn't go along with it. They ran a prostitution ring from there. Once they'd get the girls hooked on whatever drugs they had in excess at the time, they'd line up men from nearby towns. The girls would get a cut. But I put my foot down. Drunk though I was, I sobered up pretty quick when I saw what was happening. I didn't want to be paid to have sex with strange men and I refused. That pissed him off.'

'I know it's painful, Meredith, but can you tell me what happened?'

'We were in the hut behind the cotton sheds. Gappy had already passed out on the sofa. Worm and I were drinking and things were getting heavy. I had slept with him previously, I ain't no angel. But this night there was a knock and then a man I'd never seen before enters. I just remember looking at Worm and him saying nothing. I knew straight away what was happening and I tried to wriggle free.'

'What was Worm doing?'

'He was holding me down and telling me that I should have known. That I should have expected it.'

'And the man?'

'He must've got freaked out because I wasn't willing. The look on Worm's face when he noticed that he'd left. I'll never forget it.

Pure rage. He held me down and told me he was going to kill me, and kept saying some stuff about "good girls" and "bad girls".'

'Can you remember what exactly?'

'He was slurring and full of rage. It was something like "good girls get presents, and get looked after" and ...'

'And bad girls?'

Meredith took a gulp of vodka and looked to the ceiling, searching her memory. 'He said something like "bad girls get taken down" or "bad girls go under".'

'And you reported it?'

'I did. I reported it to Mulligan Senior and another cop. Neither took me seriously though. Just told me to stay away from him. Told me I was asking for it with what I was wearing and how much I had to drink.' Meredith fell silent and filled her glass again. 'Sure I can't offer you anything, love?'

'I'm good.'

Meredith tapped her glass on the table again. There was more to come. Renee could sense the battle within. She knew from experience that silence was the best encouragement.

'The afternoon I lodged my statement down at the police station I was with Mum, and when we got home I told her I wanted to be by myself for a while and brush down my horse. So I walked down to the stables – Mr Schilling let my horse agist on his property – I went into the stables, got my riding gear, and my horse was just lying there, all frothy at the mouth. She'd been poisoned.'

Meredith got up and shook her body, as though trying to shake off the awful memories. 'Goodness, Renee. I haven't thought about this stuff for years.'

'I'm sorry, Meredith.'

'It's okay, love.'

'Do you think Worm poisoned your horse?' Meredith nodded. 'Do you think he abducted Bessie Shields and Caroline Forrest?'

'I don't know. Probably. I know Caroline and Bessie had been to their hangout before because one night when I got there – this is before the bastard beat me up – Worm was real pissed off. He reckoned that Caroline Forrest had just ruined his night.'

'Did he say why?'

'It was something about ruining a deal. He'd set something up, and Bessie was "a good girl" but Caroline was a "bad girl", and she'd lost him a heap of money.'

'Worm told you all of this?'

'He was drunk and angry, but we ended up just playing cards and smoking some weed, and then I went home.'

Caroline and Bessie had been in the hut where Worm hung out. Renee already suspected this because she'd found the sunglasses there.

Renee remembered the files: the blank files. They had done nothing. Renee knew that she should have Worm's hut searched and a forensics team out there. There might still be evidence there that could link Worm to Bessie and Caroline's disappearance. But she found she was hesitating to call Mulligan. It was, after all, his father who had ignored Meredith's assault, who had not followed up on Caroline and Bessie. She took a breath and told herself to calm down. Just because his father had been negligent didn't mean Mulligan was. A bit slow on the draw, maybe. A bit reluctant to fight the lawyers. But he had given her the lead on this – why would he do that if he didn't want her to investigate fully?

She called him. 'Sarge. We need to get forensics out to the industrial estate now.'

'Slow down. Where are you? I thought I told you yesterday to go home and rest. We've had some developments this morning.'

'What developments?'

'Where are you?'

'I'm just leaving Meredith Walker's house.' She waved to Meredith, mouthing a *thank you*. 'I'm on my way to the station now.'

'Good. That's where I am. Get here now.'

Renee parked out the back and hurried into the station through the rain. No protesters today. The rain was keeping everyone else off the streets. Dark thunderclouds filled the sky. It was eerily quiet for a Monday.

She discarded her wet coat on her chair. The office was silent. Stacey and Roger weren't there. Must be at lunch. On her way to Mulligan's office, she picked up a report from the lab that was sitting on her desk. That was fast! Surely the results of Chester's DNA test. Would they find a match with the DNA under the victim's fingernails? She thought not. Her every instinct said he was telling the truth. She pulled the report from the envelope as she sat down across from Mulligan at his desk.

'What developments? What's going on?' Renee asked, desperate to read the report in her hand.

Mulligan faced her, shuffling through papers. 'We have a DNA match,' he announced, pulling out one slip of paper and holding it up. 'The DNA found under the girl's fingernails matches that of Chester Cunningham.'

Melaleuca

Renee was shocked and reached out to hold the seat. 'Where is he now?'

'You don't need to do anything. You need to relax and get yourself better after the fire. I've sent Madden and a few officers from headquarters have joined him to make the arrest. They'll take him straight down to the city lock-up. With all the protesters here, it'll be mayhem keeping him at the Goorungah watchhouse.'

She looked down at the floor, taking in the news. Irrefutable proof that Chester had killed the woman. Maybe he also killed Bessie and Caroline, and everything he'd told them earlier today was a lie. Renee's head pounded with confusion.

'Can I see the report you read?' She wasn't sure why she was asking. She needed to see it in writing.

'Here.' Mulligan handed over the single-page report. She scanned its contents. Sure enough Chester's DNA matched that taken from the woman's fingernails. She felt exhausted all of a sudden.

'But who was she, Mulligan? Who was the woman?'

'We may never know. You should go home and get some rest.'

She agreed. She looked down at the report Mulligan had just given her. Chester Cunningham's DNA results. She looked at Mulligan, confused. Did he have a copy? But how could he? She turned her attention back to the report she had with her, the one that had been waiting for her on her desk when she arrived, and scanned the results. Mulligan's report could not be a copy, because these results said that there was no shadow of a doubt. Chester's DNA was not a match.

'But, Sarge, how can this be right?'

Mulligan stared at her. 'What?'

'This is the report on Chester's sample and it's no match. So how do you have one that is?'

Mulligan stared at her, a vein pulsing in his neck. 'Chester's sample? What do you mean? I sent the sample myself.'

Renee stared at him. 'But, Sarge, so did I. There must have been a mix-up. I know I labelled it right. I'll call the lab.' Renee picked up Mulligan's landline, held it loosely against her ear and began to dial Petrovic. It was so quiet in Mulligan's office she was sure he would be able to hear Petrovic's phone ringing too. Once, twice.

Renee looked up and met Mulligan's cold, blazing eyes and froze in place, like prey before a predator. Suddenly, Renee knew what had happened. Every nerve ending screamed 'Shut up! Get out!' But he leapt at her with alarming speed and struck the phone clear from her hand. It smashed against the wall.

'You stupid bitch,' he snarled and pushed her face against the wall, ripping her hand up behind her back.

'Mulligan!' she cried, trying to twist to look at him. He reached for her other wrist and yanked it behind, gripping it firmly so she couldn't move, and clipped on some handcuffs. 'What are you doing? Get off me! Mulligan! Get off me,' she screamed, terrified. Gone was the kindly yet stern boss who had seen it all. Mulligan's eyes were blazing, nothing behind them but rage, and he was uncommonly strong. There was no one around. The office was empty. She felt something cold and metallic against her forehead. The scent of gunmetal sent a shiver through her body. Renee went still.

'Shut up.' He pressed the cold muzzle hard against her temple. 'Move,' he growled. She stood motionless, paralysed with fear. Her eyes darted around the office for a weapon. 'Move!' A jolt of pain reverberated through her skull as the heavy piece knocked her temple.

'Why are you doing this?' Renee asked, as he pushed her out of the office and down the corridor towards the back parking lot. He was stronger than she expected. Had he been working with Worm? Why was he framing Chester?

They reached the back door. He shoved her outside and across the parking lot. She tripped in a puddle of mud as he opened the boot of his car. 'Get in.'

She stood staring at him, eyes wide. 'Please, Mulligan. We can talk. Whatever you've done, I'm sure it's not that bad.'

He smacked her across the face with the gun and the world went blank for a moment. 'Get in, Renee,' he growled, shoving her and sending her hip hard into the metal frame of the car. She howled in pain. He seized on her momentary distraction and pushed her harder into the empty hollow of the boot. She fought against him, kicking at him, then tried to crawl back out, but her hands were cuffed. He pushed her in deeper and slammed the boot shut.

She was surrounded by darkness. The sound of the rain beating down on the car drowned out all other sounds, until she heard the front door open and close and then the ignition. The car started moving. She imagined it leaving the parking lot. She tried to feel the direction of the turns and memorise them so she would be able to return if he took her someplace, or tell someone where she was if she managed to reach a phone. What on earth was he going to do to her? This was bad. Very, very bad. She eased the panic brewing by focusing on the turns.

She scratched around to see if she could find the latch to one of the back seats. Nothing. After about ten minutes the car slowed and stopped. Her heart was pounding and everything hurt but she readied herself for an opportunity to escape. If he was stopping, the boot might open soon. She heard the front door open and close, and then what sounded like a gate squeaking on its hinges. She heard him get back in the car. The tyres rolled over stones now, rather than smooth bitumen. They were on a driveway. It bumped a few times in potholes then came to a stop.

The driver's door opened and closed again. She waited, then heard footsteps going away from the car, into the distance, until once again there was nothing but rain. She waited. The adrenaline subsided slightly, enough for her to feel the pain in her forehead. She reached to check her head and felt warm thick liquid. She heard footsteps returning to the car. She breathed deeply, calming herself.

The boot opened and Mulligan stood before her. He pointed the gun towards her. 'I really don't want to have to use this, Taylor. But I will.' He pulled her out. She stumbled into him and instinctively jerked away, not wanting any part of his body to touch hers, standing upright, hands cuffed behind her back.

'Mulligan, how about we just sit down and talk? I'm sure we can both figure it out, whatever it is.'

'Okay, let's do that. A talk would be nice. See that shed over there?' He motioned with his eyes, which were cold and calm. 'We're going to get out of the rain and go and have a little talk in there.'

Renee looked around. There was a main house – a modest old Queenslander on short stilts. She figured it was Mulligan's home. She'd driven past along this old back road many times but had never really noticed it before. There was nothing unique about it to make a passerby look closely. Behind the house, further up a gently sloping hill, there was a garage made of concrete slabs with a tin roof, large enough that it could probably fit three or four vehicles. Renee looked back at Mulligan. There was a cold emptiness to his expression with a hint of tired disappointment, as though he were the victim in all of this, just doing what he had to.

She walked in front and he followed a few feet behind, holding the gun loosely pointed in her direction. The earth was muddy and her clothes and hair were dripping wet. Blood made its way into her eyes and blurred her vision. She estimated they had driven about two hundred metres from the main road. The grass at the side of the driveway was high but she could still run through it. If he fired, she could duck into the grass. It was a long shot but the alternative lay ahead – a cold concrete garage. She kept pace with him as best she could so as not to indicate her resolve and waited for the moment to bolt. A lone crow flew overhead. It squawked. Mulligan stopped to look up and she took the chance to bolt.

She was quick off her mark. 'Taylor!' A shot fired behind her as she ducked into the grass. He missed. She got about fifty metres away from him, her heart pounding inside her chest as she clambered through the brushes, hands cuffed behind her back. She could hear him coming. He would catch her soon if she didn't make another move, so she got up again and ran. Another shot. She couldn't slow down now, she needed to get away. The third shot came, pounding through her left shoulder, jolting her through the air. Unable to break her fall, her body hit the ground, and she rolled in shock and agony.

'I should just finish you off right now.' He stood above her, shaking his head in disapproval. Renee stayed silent, agonising pain shooting through her shoulder. 'But I feel like we have unfinished business. We were going to have a chat, weren't we? And I want you to meet someone.'

Mulligan pulled Renee to her feet and made her walk back to the path. They continued until they arrived at the shed. There was a padlock and a combination lock. He dug inside his pants and pulled out the key, then swivelled the numbers around the lock faster than she could see.

'Can never be too careful,' he said, more to himself than to Renee. He loosened the lock and pulled the door open. 'After you.'

Renee froze and he shoved her hard from behind, which sent her stumbling inside. She turned to try to escape again, but Mulligan stepped in after her, slamming the door shut behind him, pushing Renee further into the garage. Blood was streaming out of her left shoulder where the bullet had entered and she was feeling faint.

'Rodney?' It was a woman's voice.

Renee turned away from the door. A figure, long and thin, approached her. Renee wasn't sure if she was delusional from the blood loss or if there really was a woman in a long black dress coming towards her.

'Honey, we have company,' Mulligan sang out from where he was bent down next to the entrance to take off his muddy boots. 'Come on now, Taylor, I know you've had a big day, but it's time to relax. You're going to be at home here.'

Renee stared around the room, frozen. She looked down – a straw mat bordered with sunflowers said *Welcome*.

Chapter 29

1966

Caroline tried to act as natural as possible as she approached Bessie's shack where Aunty Nettie was out the front, hanging washing on the line. She dropped everything as soon as she saw Caroline coming up with the baby.

'Caroline Forrest! Have they let you out already?' Caroline grimaced at the prospect of lying to Aunty Nettie. 'I heard you only gave birth yesterday. You must be a healthy one – made me stay in that dark little room at the back for five days after I had Clarence. Here, give me a look at him,' she cooed and pulled the blanket gently back to peer in and see the delicate features.

'He's gorgeous, Callie. What'd you call him?'

'Francis. He just had a good feed.' Caroline was proud that he'd already taken to her breast and Aunty Nettie smiled and nodded. 'Is Bessie inside?'

'That girl,' Aunty Nettie mumbled, shook her head, and returned to the bucket of clothes. 'Hasn't been home in two days. Would you believe it? Couldn't even be here to help her best friend give birth.' Caroline's heart raced thinking of where Bessie may be. She felt overwhelming guilt for not asking about her sooner. She hadn't even thought of Bessie when she was giving birth, she only wanted Milli there with her.

'What do you mean, Aunty Nettie? Where is she?'

'Lord knows!' Aunty Nettie said as she wrung the water out of the sheets. 'I don't know what I'm going to do with the girl, Callie.'

'Did she tell you where she was going?' Bessie would be with Worm, Caroline was sure of it.

'Of course not.'

She checked the time. It was nine o'clock. She had two hours before she needed to meet Chester at the waterhole. If she waited, then she could get Chester to drive over to the Worm Hole and together they could get Bessie and bring her back to the camp. They'd be able to tell her their plan had been moved forward and they had to leave today, but they'd send money as soon as they were settled and she could come and join them. But if she waited and something happened to Bessie in the meantime, or if she was already in trouble, then Caroline would never forgive herself. Maybe she was over there passed out alone with no one looking out for her?

'I'm sure she'll be okay, Aunty Nettie,' Caroline lied and scanned the surrounds for Clarence's bike. She spotted it underneath an awning close to Aunty Nettie's shack. Caroline could get the bike, race over there now, help her friend home, and then meet Chester. But what would she do with Baby Francis?

Pa was sitting in the shack with his cup of tea when she returned. 'Pa?'

'Yes, Princess?' She laid baby Francis down next to her grandfather, as slowly as possible, not to alarm him.

'I need you to watch him for a bit, would you, Pa? I just need to duck out. I'll be back in half an hour.'

'Where you going?' Pa looked up, eyes tired and scared.

'I need to check on Bessie. I'll be back soon.'

'Leave her be, Princess. You've got a son now, you need to put your child first. Forget about that girl.' It was true. She had a son, but how could she leave her friend alone if there was something wrong, especially knowing what Worm was capable of – the manipulation, luring her with drugs. If she was fast, she could get Bessie home safe and be back in time to get her baby and leave with Chester.

'She's my friend, Pa. I'll be back soon. Just look after Francis. Please.'

She snuck past Aunty Nettie, who was hanging laundry over the line, grabbed Clarence's bike and pushed it out onto the driveway before jumping on and racing down the dirt road. It was terribly painful, especially on the bumps, but she persevered, thinking of her friend and the danger she may be in. She hit the bitumen and kept going, out of town towards the industrial estate. The silos loomed in the near distance and she prayed that Bessie would be okay when she got there.

Just as she veered right off the main highway towards the industrial estate, a truck came whirling past and the wind gust made her swerve. She tried to brake but it was too late and she fell off her bike onto the side of the road. The truck slowed down and the driver ran back to check on her.

'You okay, young lady?' the truck driver called out as he approached. He offered his hand, she accepted, and he pulled her up onto her feet. She brushed the gravel from her knees. Blood oozed from her grazed skin.

'I'm fine. Thank you.' She staggered back over to the bike.

'Are you sure?' Caroline heard him say in an English accent but she didn't bother replying. She needed to get to Bessie.

She left the bike at the front of the cotton shed and raced down the side path to the shack. When she arrived, Gappy was holding a rifle pointed at a glass bottle on the fence. Shooting practice. Bessie was nowhere to be seen. 'Where is she?'

'Oh, look who we have here,' Worm said. He was sitting on a torn-up couch that had been moved outside onto the grass facing away from her, towards Gappy. She walked around to get a better view of him and realised there was another man sitting next to him. She didn't recognise him at first, but then he reminded her of someone. The sergeant. It was the sergeant's son.

'What are you doing here?' she blurted out, surprised to find him there. He must've been only fifteen or sixteen, far too young to be hanging out with Worm and Gappy, but then who was she to talk.

'Now, now, Miss Soup Kitchen, that's no way to greet our new friend,' Worm continued smugly. 'This is Rodney. Rodney Mulligan. Better known as the sergeant's boy. We like to keep our friends close and our enemies closer, if you know what I mean.' Worm put his arm around Rodney Mulligan and laughed. The boy smiled awkwardly, but looked confused, as though he was pretty sure Worm was taking the piss but was too intimidated to call it out.

The gun went off and the glass shattered. 'Good shot, Gappy. Can't say much for your teeth, but you got a good set of peepers on you. Now give Junior here a go before his dad returns.' A loud moan came from inside the shed. Caroline burst inside to find Bessie stretched out on the couch, holding her stomach and sweating profusely.

'Callie, you're here?' Bessie's eyes were glazed and red. 'I thought you forgot about me.' Caroline felt her friend's forehead. She was burning up. Caroline grabbed an empty cup off the floor and raced outside to the tap against the shed to fill it up with water.

'Had second thoughts, have you, Soup Kitchen?' Worm called out from the couch. She ignored him and started back inside with the water, but he got up and came towards her. He had the rifle. 'We have plenty of work going. New clients coming in all the time. Sarge will be here soon.' He winked and Caroline tried to push past, but he stepped in front of her.

'Get out of my road, Worm.' Caroline locked eyes with him, but he wouldn't move. 'I'm taking her home. Now move.' She heard Bessie cry out from inside and charged past Worm, pushing him to the side.

Worm reached out and pushed her back.

'Get away from me, Worm.'

He pushed her harder and this time she slipped back and fell hard on the floorboards. Agonising pain in her head. Everything went blurry around her. Then the agony faded, along with the colours of the bush, the smell of the eucalypt and the taste of blood.

Chapter 30

Monday 14 February 2000

He undid the handcuffs, pulled out a seat at a table and beckoned her over. 'Come, sit.' Renee followed in a trancelike state, holding her wrists from where the cuffs had torn at her flesh, and collapsed into it, then turned back to look at the woman. She was in her fifties, around the same age as Meredith Walker perhaps.

'Grab some warm water, dear,' Mulligan said to the woman, who immediately went to the small sink and filled a bowl. 'Taylor has a little shoulder injury. Now, Taylor, pass me your car keys.' He must have planned to get rid of the car at the station. Her car would still be there because he had driven to this place in his car.

She did as he asked, figuring she was not in any position to refuse, and watched as the woman came to sit next to her with the bowl of water. She seemed nervous and scared but she was composed in her movements. Renee didn't say a word as the woman gently dabbed a damp cloth against the bullet wound.

'That's the spirit!' Mulligan said. 'I knew you two would get along.' And then it dawned on her. An Aboriginal woman in her fifties. Caroline had straight hair. This woman had curly hair. Just like in the photos. She searched Mulligan's face and he smiled back in response to her questioning eyes.

'Bessie?' The woman stayed silent and continued dabbing her arm. Renee looked back at Mulligan, who nodded and shrugged innocently. She glanced back up at the woman wiping her shoulder and for a split second there was a flash of horror in her eyes, but then the glazed nothingness returned.

'What the fu—'

Mulligan held his hands up to stop her. 'I know you must have a lot of questions, Taylor. But it is very late. Tomorrow will be a big day for me. I'll have to explain another disappearance. And this time that of a police officer, so no doubt HQ will be sending people out. So I would appreciate it if you saved your questions for later.'

Mulligan stood up, gave Bessie a kiss on the cheek, which Bessie neither grimaced at nor leaned in to, and walked to the door. 'I will see you both, bright and fresh, tomorrow.'

Renee lay on a single mattress, trying to focus her mind away from the pain that radiated from the wound. Mulligan had left, locks clicking from the outside. Then she had frantically run around the room checking the perimeter, searching for slats or openings. She had known then it was a futile quest – everything was tightly sealed off – but she had to try. Eventually Bessie came over to where she had stood in the middle of the room, staring up at the skylight in the centre of the ceiling, and coaxed her gently to the single mattress she lay on now. Renee remembered taking some medicine that Bessie had held out for her, realising they were completely at the mercy of a psychopath. How else could one describe him? What normal person locks a woman up in a room for nearly thirty-five years? Renee passed out quickly from whatever Bessie gave her.

When she came to it was early morning and sunlight shone through the small glass opening in the ceiling. She looked around to assess her surroundings and potential escape routes. There was a lounge room set up to one side, complete with a brown velveteen couch. A kitchenette was to the other side with a small four-piece dining room set that reminded her of her own cramped kitchen in her city apartment. There was a toaster, kettle, mini-bar fridge and electric stove. An oil painting of horses following a trail through snowy mountains rested on one wall and three pot plants hung from the ceiling. To the back of the garage, a small bathroom had been sectioned off with bamboo partitioning.

Her new 'roommate' sat on the couch watching an evangelical service. The television was broadcasting an African-American preacher bellowing, 'Is Jesus Christ your saviour?' He stood on a stage cloaked in a purple satin gown in a massive church arena with a crowd of thousands. 'Did Jesus Christ die for your sins?' Renee noticed Bessie nod in response, her eyes unfocussed. Bessie wasn't even here in this shed in Goorungah. She was in the audience of a Baptist church in Atlanta, Georgia, surrounded by fellow believers.

Renee looked again towards the skylight where clouds migrated across the square, sending shadows dancing along the walls. She guessed it was early morning. Mulligan had not returned and she thought of him going into the station. When would they discover she was missing? It was Tuesday morning, so Stacey and Roger would be expecting her at work. Surely it wouldn't take them long to become concerned, given that the last time they'd seen her was Sunday, when they'd escorted her home feeling sick. How would Mulligan react when Roger and Stacey become worried and insisted on going to check on her at home? Would he lie and pretend she'd already called in sick, buy some time? Would he try to pin her disappearance on Chester too? And her mother. It hurt to think of how her mother would worry about her sudden disappearance. She pushed those thoughts aside and moved to get out of the bed, which sent a sudden stab of pain shooting through her arm.

'Taylor? Is that your name, dear? Come and sit here with me. This preacher is a good one. You might like him.' She seemed more confident than she had the night before, and Renee obeyed her command. Something about her physical frailty but strong voice reminded her of Val.

Renee took a seat next to her as the woman lowered the television volume. 'My name's Renee. I'm a policewoman.' Renee wanted to ask this woman so many questions but how could she, and where would she start? If indeed this was Bessie Shields, she had possibly been held captive in this shed for more than thirty years. Her face was like a shadow of the girl in the missing persons photographs. Deep rings under her tired, wide eyes, light wrinkles on her forehead.

'Why'd he bring you here?' Bessie asked.

'I don't know.' It was true. Renee didn't know. Why *did* he bring her here?

Bessie nodded as though she shared her experience. 'He brought me here because he said he couldn't trust me not to tell.'

'Tell?' Renee asked.

'Tell people what I saw. And he's right. If I had the chance, I'd tell the world. But why are *you* here? Did you see something too? What did you see?' The woman searched Renee's eyes, peering in close. Renee could hear her breathing. The lady's eyes were familiar.

They were like her mother's, Nettie. The same eyes that had told her to trust her instincts. That people were afraid of something in this town. But there was more. They were like her older brother's too – Clarence? And then it dawned on her ... Bessie's eyes were the same as the woman by the creek. Renee saw it now.

Bessie started suddenly. She had also found the answer to her question. It was in Renee's eyes. Her daughter was gone. 'Dawn's gone, isn't she?' Bessie started to sob uncontrollably. 'My daughter. My baby.' The woman collapsed on herself as the grief ripped through her body. Renee patted her back softly as she pieced together this revelation. The woman they had found by the creek was this woman's daughter. She must have escaped from this hell and ran away. Then Mulligan had caught her and murdered her so as to keep his dreadful secret. Renee almost doubled over in revulsion as she realised that Dawn was probably Mulligan's daughter.

'I'm going to get you out of here, Bessie. I'm going to get you back to your family.' The cop in Renee felt obliged to assure protection and safety, but the words even felt hollow to her.

Hours later, Renee heard locks clicking and Mulligan entered. She quickly slid the toothbrush that she had been sharpening into a knife beneath her thigh.

'Back to having two girls!' he announced cheerfully, placing a tray down on the table and adjusting his gun in its holster. Bessie sat next to her on the couch, staring at the television, looking even smaller than when Renee had first arrived. The news of her daughter's death had taken something out of her.

Renee glanced across at Mulligan as he went to a drawer and got out some plastic cutlery. 'I've had one hell of a day, let me tell you. You're quite the popular policewoman, Taylor. Got the whole town worried.' She could smell meat wafting from the tray he'd placed on the table. 'Don't worry though, I think people are naturally going down the same track they went with our Bessie and Caroline. A little runaway.' He kept talking as he laid plates and cutlery on the table. 'All got a bit too much and you left town. It was kind of helpful that you passed out in front of the crowd, because I didn't have to exaggerate all that much. It really was all getting a bit too much for you. People are even starting to wonder if you lit that fire yourself.'

She could feel the rage growing inside her, and wished the makeshift shiv was sharper. But it wasn't ready yet.

'Right, well.' He stood back, looking at the table to assess his preparation, and then turned his attention to Renee and Bessie. 'You two are quiet.' He came and stood in front of them. He was neatly shaven, smelling typically of sunscreen and dressed in his police uniform. Renee could see the shiv going through his stomach, or maybe his carotid artery. But it wasn't ready yet.

'Oh, now, you've been crying? Bessie, what's wrong?' Mulligan came closer. The woman didn't move. She let him bend down on his knee, take out a handkerchief and wipe the tears from her cheek. All this time in the shed with him, she had grown entirely passive. Renee wondered what she had endured at the hands of Mulligan before arriving to this state of defeat. 'There, there, darling. I take it you've heard about Dawn? I'm sorry.' Renee noticed the slightest grimace in the woman's body. She was trying to control her anger. 'We told her over and over again, Bessie, that she had a good life here with us, but she just wouldn't stop trying to leave.'

'What the fuck, Mulligan?' Renee studied the gun in his holster and wondered if she could get to it before him. 'Why?' He ignored her and continued patting Bessie.

'Come to the table. I don't want to have this discussion in front of Bessie.' He pulled a seat out at the table and Renee took it. He sat next to her and adjusted the covering on the bowls. 'I can see you have questions.'

'Did you kill her? Did you kill the girl by the creek, Mulligan? You know you're not going to get away with any of this. Someone will figure it out. Roger and Stacey will know by the way you're acting.'

'Taylor, calm down and lower your voice. You've already upset Bessie this morning. We have all the time in the world to go over this. I need you to understand the position I am in. The position I was in.' He looked across at Bessie, stroking his chin.

'Go on then. Explain.' Renee could feel her heart racing. She wanted to hurt him so badly but controlled her breathing and remained silent.

'It was 20 August 1966. Dad and I went out to Crystal Ponds for a swim and Worm and Gappy were there. After a while, Dad got bored and said he wanted to go home for a rest but I was having too much fun with the lads, so he said I could stay with them and he'd come get me later. I was having so much fun splashing around with the boys …'

'You were friends with Worm? I knew it! You lying bastard.'

'Well, interestingly, that day at Crystal Ponds was actually the first time I'd hung out with them. They were older than me and I was still a teenager.

'I remember Dad speaking to Worm and arranging to come get me later. I couldn't remember ever seeing them together before that day, but they seemed familiar with each other. He said he didn't mind, because he had planned to meet up with Worm later anyway. So the day went on and Worm and the boys were drinking and carrying on, trying to impress the girls by throwing themselves off the highest ledges, and then we ran out of beer. So we all piled into Worm's car and drove back to his hangout, the Worm Hole, behind the cotton sheds. And that's the first time I met Bessie.' Mulligan looked across and smiled at Bessie, who was sitting on the couch, focussed on the television. Renee suppressed an urge to vomit.

'Bessie was already at the hangout?' She couldn't bring herself to say Worm Hole – what a stupid fucking name.

'Yes, she was in a bit of a state already, had drank herself into quite a stupor.' He shook his head disapprovingly. 'I was concerned and tried to get her something to eat, but Worm and the boys told me to forget about her, and eventually I did get carried away with having fun again, drinking, shooting bottles, playing music on the old record player. Until Caroline turned up.'

'Caroline came to the hut?'

'Yes, dear Caroline came bursting through the pathway, knees all scratched and bleeding, demanding to know where Bessie was. We were all standing around outside, and Bessie was inside, just having a nap. She was fine. I don't know why Caroline thought it was her responsibility to come and "rescue" her. If she had just gone away, none of this would have happened.'

'None of this …?' Renee couldn't believe her ears. Mulligan displayed not a hint of guilt or remorse.

'Look, Taylor, Dad and I actually did good that day. Bessie would be dead if it wasn't for my father.' Renee stared at him, speechless. 'Caroline came out to fill a cup with water for Bessie, and then as she tried to go back inside Worm stood in front of her. Instead of just minding her own business and leaving, she insisted on going back in. So Worm shoved her and she fell. Wasn't even Worm's fault. It was an accident.

'We all looked on in shocked silence. Even Dad. He had just arrived to pick me up. And then we heard Bessie. She'd managed to get herself up to come and check on Caroline. She bent over her friend screaming. Poor Bessie. It was a shock for her. And then she got afraid. Obviously didn't realise that Dad and I are good guys. She started to bolt. Worm ran after her and brought her back. I remember Dad and Worm arguing about what to do with her. Worm wanted to kill her because she was a witness to Caroline's death. Dad said he could arrest Worm for murder, but Worm said he'd tell everyone why he was there. And he said he was there to collect his son, but Worm cackled and said he wasn't an idiot. He had secretly taken photos of Dad with many of the women who had been in the shed. Dad was just lonely, because he was missing Mum, but he told me later those photos could never be shown to anyone. I never saw them, but I believed him. So he pleaded with Worm not to kill her, and Worm said he wouldn't if he kept her quiet. So Dad brought her back here.'

'Thirty-five years ago.' Renee said it slowly to see if the sheer magnitude of time weighed on Mulligan. It didn't.

'Yes – like I said, Dad was a good man. He may have gotten a bit lonely after Mum's death, but he wasn't a murderer. He did the right thing. He brought Bessie home and took good care of her until he passed, and then I took over providing the care.'

'Care?' Renee spat out the question.

'Oh, don't judge me, Taylor. Look around. She's had everything she ever needed. Food, medicine, entertainment and, well, until a few days ago, she had plenty of company ...'

'Mulligan, were you Dawn's father?'

'Goodness, no!' He laughed as though it were a joke. 'Dawn was my sister. The old man was Dawn's father.'

'Did you kill her?' Mulligan looked down at his hands. 'Mulligan, did you kill Dawn?'

'There was no other choice. I built a life here for Bessie and me, and she kept threatening it.'

'You really think that poor woman over there is happy, Mulligan?'

'Of course she is. She loves me.' His self-satisfaction was disturbing.

'This is sick, Mulligan. You're sick.'

'The world is sick, Taylor.' He got up from the table and went over to where Bessie was lying down. 'Come on, love, I brought us some scrambled eggs and bacon. You must be starving.' Mulligan pulled her up from the couch and brought her to the table where she sat slouched over. Renee and Bessie stared vacantly at the food Mulligan had heaped onto each of the three plates.

'You're not going to get away with this, Mulligan.'

'Bessie, eat up, darling,' Mulligan said, ignoring Renee.

'Too many stones have been turned. You can't keep this covered up forever.'

Mulligan chewed his bacon. Bessie looked at her meal, taking slow, small bites. The church congregation had broken into song. 'This little light of mine, I'm gonna let it shine.'

'And then guess what?' Renee insisted. 'Guess what's going to happen then, Mulligan?'

Mulligan slammed his fists on the table. 'Quiet!' He got to his feet, pulled the gun from its holster and walked towards Renee. He aimed it at her head.

'Taylor, I'm doing you a favour, letting you stay. I could've just knocked you off. It would've been easier. It's still an option.'

Renee looked directly into his eyes and he smiled, lowered the gun and walked to the door.

'Wait.'

Mulligan turned back.

'You bribed that witness, didn't you? The kid who said he saw Chester.'

Mulligan clenched his jaw.

'What kind of a police officer bribes a witness — a vulnerable youth, no less? The corrupt kind.' She waited for him to pounce on her as the anger raged behind his eyes. But he just smiled faintly, turned and left. The locks clicked once more. Renee turned back to face the room and Bessie.

'So Mulligan has kept you here ever since that day?' Renee asked, pacing back and forth in the kitchen. Bessie calmly went about cleaning up the breakfast plates. The gospel music had finished and she'd switched the television off.

'Yes. Now come on. You need to have a shower. We need to disinfect your wound with salty water. You can change into one of these dresses.' She watched Bessie scrummage around in some dresser drawers and pull out a thin orange cotton dress. It was too small for Bessie. She guessed it was Dawn's.

Renee followed Bessie to the other side of the room. Her body was lead. She stood silently as Bessie fussed around, laying out items for her to use — a spare toothbrush, a wash cloth, some soap — all the while mumbling instructions about the importance of keeping on top of personal hygiene. There was a flush toilet, shower, wall cabinet and chair. No sink. Bessie placed the towel on the chair and turned on the shower, moving her fingers underneath the running water to feel the temperature. 'There. Don't be too long. Hot water tank will last about a minute.'

Renee undressed, placed her clothes on the chair and moved under the shower. She enjoyed thirty seconds of warmth before the water turned cold. Mulligan must have lit the fire. It had to have been him. Unless it was Worm ... How could Mulligan do this? Keep a woman confined for more than thirty years. How did he get away with it? She scrubbed at her skin. How did she not see it? No one had seen it? Or was it worse than that? Did everyone know and simply not tell her?

'That's enough now!' Bessie yelled. She turned off the taps, dried her body and slipped on the dress. There was no mirror. Probably a good thing. She didn't want to look at her face. Her reflection would intensify the reality of this horror to an unbearable magnitude.

'How often does Mulligan come out here?' Bessie was sitting on the couch now with a bowl of boiling water. Renee sat on the rug next to her.

'It varies. When he's in a good mood, he comes for breakfast and dinner every day. When he's in a bad mood, he won't come for a week. I think he's in a bad mood now.' Bessie dabbed a cloth into the water and gently wiped the wound. Renee grimaced in pain – the bullet had torn straight through.

'How much food do we have?'

'Plenty. If he was going to starve me, he would've done it years ago.' Renee had checked the cupboards. There were tins of beans and tuna, rice, pasta. There was a two-plate electric stove, toaster, kettle and bar fridge containing milk, lettuce, tomato, margarine and a few condiments. Someone would come within a day or so, surely. They would not need a big supply. As long as they had water.

'Does Worm know that you're here?' Bessie continued to tend to her wound.

'Yes, he knows. I've heard Rod and him on the phone together. That's why Rod can't arrest him for dealing all those drugs. If Rod arrests Worm, then Worm will tell the authorities that I'm here.'

Renee had insisted that she and Roger talk to Worm and Mulligan had done everything he could to stop her bothering him again. The fire would have solved his problems if she had died. Was it Mulligan who lit the fire, then? It seemed likely. Worm wouldn't need to bother. Worm would reveal his secret if she got too close.

'Why was Dawn wearing Caroline's necklace?' Renee asked.

'I took it from Caroline's body. I wanted something to remember her by. And when I had Dawn, I gave it to her.'

Chapter 31

Renee heard keys wriggling in the door again. She was propped up against the couch on the floor again. Bessie sat on the sofa, quietly absorbed in the televised preaching. It was before sunrise on the fifth morning she had been there. Mulligan had already delivered their breakfast but he'd forgotten they were out of pepper and had returned to the main house to get some. How much longer could she cope with this? The gospel music. Mulligan's smug self-righteousness. Bessie, her body here, but her mind and spirit wandering elsewhere. This small strange suffocating world. This distorted reality. Surely someone would come for her? Where was Roger? Had Josh woken up? What if he had seen Mulligan light the fire? Did anyone believe that Chester was telling the truth? Maybe Lennon McGorrie would figure it all out? Over the past few days she had beaten herself up for not seeing the blatantly obvious. Of course it had been Mulligan, with his resistance for external interference in the case, his protection of Worm, his undermining of her theories, his increasing frustration with her and the alacrity with which he leaped onto Josh's theory about Chester Cunningham's culpability.

A loud thudding noise came from the door. Usually she heard the lock jiggle a little when Mulligan returned, but this was different. She got up, putting her ear up to the door. Again she heard a thud against the door. It wasn't Mulligan.

'Help!' she yelled at the top of her lungs.

A voice came from the other side of the door. 'Renee?'

'Who's there?' The door handle wobbled as someone jerked wildly from the other side.

'I can't open it!' the person yelled in frustration, banging loudly against its steel facade.

'Meredith? Is that you?'

'I'm here, Renee! I'm going to get you out of there.'

'Where's Mulligan?'

'I've dealt with him. Don't worry about him.'

'Have you got the keys?'

'Yes, but there's a combination lock on this thing!' The door rattled loudly as Meredith banged it from the other side.

'Okay, calm down. I need you to go inside Mulligan's house and call the station. Get some backup out here.'

'Shit.'

'What?'

'I can't, I'm too scared.'

'But why Meredith? You dealt with Mulligan.'

'I ... I ...' Meredith's voice faltered from the other side.

'Talk to me, Meredith?'

There was a long pause. 'I opened my boot to get a torch and he ran at me. His face was all contorted. He looked like a monster. I didn't think, I smashed him with the torch on his head and he went down. He wasn't breathing. I left his body over there.'

'So that's okay, Meredith. I know it must have been frightening. It was self defence!' Renee tried to calm herself and Meredith. She needed to stay focussed. Bessie was standing right behind her, like a shadow. She needed to stay strong and calm for Bessie.

'I know. I left his body over there.'

Renee bit back her impatience. 'You said, Meredith. Please, go inside and call for back-up.'

'I left it over there. But it's not there any more. He's not there any more, and he's got a gun.'

Renee remembered the time she had talked a suicidal man down from a ledge in the city. He had been up there for three hours, drunk and desperate, crying that his life was over because he had lost his job and his wife and kids had left him. There was a moment when she thought she had lost him. The man leaned out from the ten-storey building, holding on to the window with one hand. Instead of panicking, her pulse slowed, her breathing steadied and she saw the world with the most brilliant clarity. She had locked eyes with the man and felt only compassion and warmth. 'It's your decision, but I'm here and I'm not going anywhere,' she'd said, and her calmness promised safety. She knew he understood. He crawled off the ledge and came inside.

Renee had somehow forgotten that she was at her very best when it really mattered.

Mulligan was out there. With a gun. Meredith was losing it. Bessie stared at her, eyes frantic. Renee breathed. Her pulse slowed. Her mind cleared. She saw Mulligan in the station the day she'd asked for the old case notes. 'In the filing cabinet,' he'd said. She'd watched him walk from his desk to the steel cabinet in the corner of his office. It only had two drawers and he'd needed to kneel down to open it. He'd fiddled around with the combination on the top drawer. He'd glanced up at her and she'd politely moved her eyes towards the window, even though the blinds had been drawn and there was nothing to see outside. She remembered how Mulligan spoke to himself as he moved the numbers. He'd said his father was born on the same day as Queen Elizabeth. He was strangely proud of such a coincidence, and he'd said it when he opened the lock as though it held significance.

'Meredith! When's the queen's birthday?'

'What are you talking about?'

'The queen's birthday! When was Queen Elizabeth born?'

'12 June, I think.'

'Okay, try 1–2–0–6.' Renee listened for the clicks.

'No, didn't work.'

'Fuck,' Renee said.

'That's just the public holiday. Queen Elizabeth was born on 21 April,' Bessie said quietly. She had gone back to sit on the couch.

'Meredith. Try 2–1–0–4.'

Renee imagined her fingers rolling the numbers into place.

'No! That's not it!'

'Bessie, do you know what year?'

'1926.'

'Meredith, try 1–9–2–6!'

Click. 'You got it!' Renee heaved open the steel door.

'Are you okay?' Meredith asked, checking her over. 'Did he hurt you?'

'I'm okay.'

'Who's that?' Meredith looked across at Bessie. Terror came across her eyes as she realised the identity of the woman. 'It's not.' In complete shock, Meredith looked to Renee for answers.

'Not now, Meredith. We need to move. Bessie?' Renee called. 'Come on now, we need to go.'

They walked out the door. Renee saw the sun rising over the hills. It had occurred to her in confinement that she may never see a sunrise again. She heard a click from behind her and froze.

He was still alive. And he had a handgun.

The three of them faced freedom with the menace right behind, but before she could get a handle on the situation, Meredith flung herself around to confront Mulligan. Renee tried to stop her but Meredith had lunged towards Mulligan, attempting to push his gun away. As she did, a bullet left the cartridge. Deafeningly loud, it pierced through the air, hitting Meredith in the neck and sending a shockwave through her entire body. Meredith fell to the ground and the gun flew out of Mulligan's hands and landed on the ground off to the side.

Renee lurched towards the gun. She grasped the grip and rolled on to her back. As Mulligan threw himself upon her she pointed the gun at him and fired at his chest. His body heaved and then slumped into hers. She wriggled out from underneath him as a pool of blood formed a puddle around his body. Mulligan took his last breath, and his body dropped motionless to the ground.

There was a moment of stillness. The sun peeped over the horizon. Mulligan was gone. Renee looked over to where Bessie huddled over Meredith and raced to her side.

'Meredith, where did he get you?'

'It's fine. It only grazed my neck.' Blood oozed out. Renee needed to get help.

'How did you know I was here?'

'When I found out you'd gone missing, I was worried. I remembered as you were leaving my place you got a call from Mulligan.'

Renee strained her memory. It felt so long ago.

'When you left my place, you were speaking to Mulligan and going to the station. Then I saw Mulligan on the news saying he hadn't talked to you since he saw you at the station when you collapsed. So when you went missing I decided to have a look around. I drove around for a bit and ended up at the industrial estate. Mulligan and Worm were there – they had cleaning equipment. I think they'd gone out to get rid of evidence. They didn't see me. I parked some distance away, but I could see them talking and they seemed to be on such good terms that I knew both of them were in on it.'

'Why didn't you call Roger?'

'I don't know Roger that well. I don't know any of the police. I didn't trust anyone at the station – they let me down before. I wanted to see for myself.'

'Wait here. I'll call an ambulance.'

Renee raced inside Mulligan's house. She found the phone on a bench in the kitchen and dialled triple 0. As she requested an ambulance to the property, she looked out the window to where Meredith sat in the mud holding her neck, Bessie by her side. Meredith would be okay. The ambulance would be there soon. She breathed a sigh of relief as she looked around the kitchen. It was immaculate. Everything perfectly in its place. How could a psychopath go hidden in plain sight for so many years? Then she thought of his co-conspirator. Worm. As soon as he heard whispers of what had happened here this morning, he would know he was in trouble. She needed to get to him before he skipped town, but first she needed to call Roger for backup.

Melaleuca

She felt each turn like a map etched into her subconscious. These were the roads she'd walked as a kid, the roads on which she'd learned to ride a bike. It was the street she'd sauntered down when she skipped school as a teenager. It was her town. And there was no room in it for bastards like Worm. She drove to the house next to the sports centre and parked outside.

She'd left Meredith and Bessie as soon as the ambulance arrived. She'd taken Meredith's car and Mulligan's gun.

She pulled into the driveway as Roger screeched his car to a stop immediately behind her. They nodded at each other as they approached the door. She imagined Worm inside and wondered whether he would be on high alert, or whether his arrogance would prevent him from stressing about police.

Roger pounded his fists on the door. 'William Gawlor, come out with your hands above your head.' The dogs rushed and barked at the front door, but even over their barking, Renee heard the back door open and shut and the faint sound of footsteps running from the back door.

The side gate was locked so she hurled herself over the wood-panelled fence, landing heavily on her side. As she looked up, she could see Worm leaping over the back fence into the football oval. She got up and raced towards him, flinging her body over that fence too and this time landing painfully on her shoulder. She couldn't think about the pain now and forced herself back on her feet. Worm raced across the oval, towards the trees on the far side. She followed, running as fast as she could, bare feet on the green grass, and then entered the nearby scrub.

It was quiet. She looked around. She could smell his cheap cologne on the air. He wasn't far. Normally the birds would be greeting the sunlight at this time but the scrub was still. She tightened her grip on Mulligan's gun. 'I know you're in here, Worm. You can't get away with this any longer. I know what you did.'

She scanned a grey panorama of melaleuca bark – papery-soft layers. How do you ever really know someone? People are cloaked – some with such thick bark, it's obvious to everyone including themselves that they're hiding something, but others dress in so many thin papery layers they don't even know themselves they're hiding from the world.

'I know you killed Caroline, Worm.' A twig snapped to her left and she tightened her grip on the gun.

'I know about you and Mulligan Senior, and the photos of him you threatened to share. And I know how you've blackmailed Mulligan all these years, by threatening to tell the world he has Bessie trapped.' She paused and listened. 'He's dead, by the way.' Soil crushed to her right this time, and she turned to point the gun in that direction. He was close. 'You can't blackmail him any more. You're on your own, Worm. What do you think about that?'

A hand grasped her from behind and she was yanked back. He held her mouth and pulled her towards the ground, but she elbowed him hard in the groin and he lost his grip on her body. She leaped back out of his reach and turned to point her gun towards him.

'You really think you can beat me?' She settled into her stance and eyed him calmly. 'Get on your knees and put your hands behind your head.'

'You got nothing on me, bitch.' He grudgingly got to his knees and glared back at her.

'Hands behind your head!' Renee walked closer. 'What's underneath the floorboards in the hut behind the cotton sheds? Did you really think you were going to get away with this? So many people in town despise you, Worm. You're going away for a very long time. I'm arresting you for the murder of Caroline Forrest.'

She could hear footsteps coming through the scrub. 'Madden, I'm over here.'

'Are you okay, Taylor?' Roger asked her, as he assessed the situation.

'I'm good. Cuff him.'

Chapter 32

Roger and Renee arrived at the police station with Worm cuffed in the back seat. Stacey met them at the door, wide-eyed and uncharacteristically speechless. Roger escorted Worm to the holding cell and Renee took the opportunity to take a seat at her desk while Stacey put a cup of coffee in front of her and a blanket around her shoulders.

'I just got off the phone to the hospital,' Stacey informed her as Roger re-emerged, 'Meredith and Bessie are there and they're doing fine.'

'Thanks, Roger. Thanks, Stacey.' Renee gulped her coffee, finding the warm fluid and anticipation of a caffeine hit soothing. 'What about headquarters? Has anyone checked in with them?'

'Yes, Dupont is on his way out now. He'll be here any minute.'

'I don't understand anything,' Roger admitted. 'But it's okay, I will. You must be exhausted.'

She was, but adrenaline was still pounding through her veins. 'Worm killed Caroline in 1966 when she tried to rescue Bessie from his prostitution ring. Bessie witnessed the crime and Worm wanted to kill her too, but Mulligan's father pleaded with him to let her go.'

'But Mulligan's father was a cop – why did he have to beg Worm? Why didn't he just arrest him?'

'Worm had collateral on Mulligan Senior in the form of some kind of sordid photographs of him with women at the hut, so Mulligan Senior had no leverage. Worm agreed not to kill Bessie if Mulligan Senior kept her silent, so he locked her in the shed.'

'And Mulligan knew?' Roger asked, dumbstruck.

'He was there on the day Caroline was murdered and, yes, he carried on keeping Bessie captive when his father passed.'

Roger and Stacey stared at each other in shock, and Renee paused to let them come to terms with the information. Their boss was a psychopath and a woman had been held captive for more than thirty years in their hometown.

'So, where's Mulligan?'

'He's dead. I shot him.' She took a sip of her coffee. Was it bad that she felt good? He was gone.

'There's more. The murdered woman at the creek was Bessie's daughter, Dawn. Mulligan Senior was the father. She had escaped and was threatening everything Mulligan held dear. He murdered her.'

Roger's jaw dropped. 'His own sister?'

'Yes, his own sister.'

Chief Superintendent Dupont arrived from headquarters and Renee gave him a run-down on everything that had happened. Forensics were sent to the hut, where they found human remains beneath the floorboards. Someone had recently been there and pulled the boards up. Renee supposed Mulligan and Worm had tried to get rid of the body – Meredith Walker had said she'd seen them out there.

But they'd been sloppy and there was still plenty of DNA samples in the form of hair. Mulligan's boots in the laundry matched the prints found at the creek crime scene. Chester was released from prison and Renee was informed that he immediately went to be by Josh's bedside as he continued to recover from the fire.

Later that day, Renee lay in her bedroom feeling a sense of calm that had escaped her for months. Stacey and Roger had accompanied her home and spent the afternoon fussing around the house, helping Val tidy up and do odd jobs. Val was still healing herself but had stubbornly insisted on coming home the minute she found out what happened. True to her word, Stacey had organised for the kitchen to be fixed and the smell of vegetables cooking in the oven drifted through the rooms. They had insisted she lay down and rest and, for once, she didn't protest. She drifted in and out of a restful sleep, thinking how nice it felt to hear the voices of colleagues and her mum nearby, until she heard a knock at the door.

'Renee? Are you awake?' It was her mum.

'Mmm …'

'Honey, you've got a visitor. I'll tell him another time, hey?'

'Who is it?'

'Some journalist. McGorrie?'

Lennon was here to see her. Why? She was intrigued. 'No, it's okay, Mum. I'll come out.'

He stood at the door, holding sunflowers. 'I got you these. I wasn't sure. Sorry if it's inappropriate. They are from everyone – they are all pretty proud of you.'

'They're beautiful.' She took them and gestured for him to sit next to her on the deck.

'You did it. You not only found out who murdered that young woman, you solved the mystery of two missing Aboriginal women that spans three decades.'

'No thanks to you, Lennon. The media pressure was not a big help.'

Lennon met her glare levelly. 'I'm sorry you felt pressured, Renee. We kept the pressure up because we knew that finally someone was listening. Someone cared about these women when no one had cared before.'

'It's quite a story,' Renee said, relenting and turning to face him. 'Are you looking forward to writing it?'

'I would rather not have to write any more stories about missing or murdered Aboriginal women, Renee.'

She smiled sadly. 'And I would rather I didn't have to tell their relatives, Lennon. But if I can catch the men who do it, then that's something.'

Later that evening, Renee sat in the lounge room watching the evening news with her mother. She was certain that they had enough to convict Worm for murder and conspiracy. Chief Superintendent Dupont had agreed. They had her testimony and that of Bessie as a witness.

'What happened to the eggs?' Val asked from her armchair.

'Didn't make it through the fire.'

'Sorry, love. I know you were excited about seeing those chickens hatch.'

Renee shrugged. Compared to all those around her who had lost so much, she felt silly for being so upset. The news started up and Jillian Crawley appeared on the screen. She was reporting from the front of the station. 'In what has been a dramatic turn of events, an unsolved cold case has led to the discovery of the murderer of the woman whose body was found almost two weeks ago here in the small town of Goorungah. The accused is Sergeant Rodney Mulligan.'

'Who would've guessed it, hey?' Her mother shook her head in disbelief. 'I never liked him much, but this.'

'Sergeant Mulligan died at his property outside of Goorungah in the early hours of this morning, from a gunshot wound fired by an officer in self-defence when it was discovered that he was keeping Bessie Shields, a missing girl last seen in 1966, captive against her will. He had kept her in confinement for more than thirty years. Bessie's child, Dawn Shields, had never been outside until she broke free on the day she was also murdered. It is unclear whether Rodney Mulligan was the father of Dawn Shields. It was the body of Dawn Shields that was found by the creek two weeks ago. Bessie Shields is being cared for in hospital but overall is in a stable condition.'

Renee went to the sink to get water.

'Where are you going?' her mother called. 'You're on!'

Renee only half-listened from the sink. She looked out the window and hoped that the residents of Goorungah would feel safer tonight.

Jillian Crawley thrust the microphone into Renee's face. 'Constable Taylor, is it true that you were held captive by Sergeant Rodney Mulligan?'

'What I can tell you is that Sergeant Rodney Mulligan is now deceased and an investigation is pending as to his involvement in the murder of Dawn Shields and the confinement of Bessie

Shields. I can also report that William Gawlor was arrested today on suspicion of the murder of Caroline Forrest in 1966 and he is being detained here in the Goorungah Watch House.'

'And may the bastard rot in hell,' her mother announced, slapping down on her thighs in triumph. 'What a daughter I have raised! Why are you so quiet?'

'I'm just thinking.'

'You should be proud of yourself, Renee.'

Renee sat back down. She hoped Roger and Stacey were okay with their families tonight. And she looked forward to hearing how Bessie had reunited with her family. She hoped Josh had made it home to his family and that he could start to patch things up with his father. She thought about Lennon McGorrie and what he'd said to her on the deck earlier that evening. He and the protesters were proud of her. That made her feel good.

Chapter 33

A week later, Renee thought it was time to pay Bessie Shields a visit. Bessie had settled back into her mother's place and Renee had received reports from the social worker that she was doing well. She had tried to see Bessie when she went to the hospital to visit Meredith, but social workers were only allowing immediate family through to her room. She had spent so long confined to a small space the hospital staff were cautious of exposing Bessie to foreign germs before improving her general health and immunity, and they also didn't want to overwhelm her with meeting people.

Renee tapped lightly on the front door and heard rustling inside.

'Constable Taylor, is that you?' Nettie peered through the screen. 'We thought you'd never come around.' The old lady smiled and opened the door. 'Get in here. Don't be a stranger.' She entered and the house felt different to when she had been there previously. There was noise and warmth. 'I've got biscuits in the oven. You're just in time. Make yourself at home.' Nettie left to go to the kitchen. Bessie sat in one of the comfortable old lounge chairs. She was watching tennis with a teenage girl who Renee guessed was Audrey. There was a fireplace in the corner of the room and Renee remembered when she'd last visited the house Clarence had been chopping wood.

Bessie looked up and held out her hand to greet Renee, but stayed quiet and returned her attention to the tennis. Audrey sat next to Bessie, painting the fingernails of her other hand.

'Nice colour,' Renee said, taking a seat in the adjacent armchair.

'Thanks. Aunty Bessie said her favourite colour is violet. Hey, Aunty?' Renee watched for a moment as Audrey painted the rest of Bessie's nails.

'You're that cop from television?' Audrey asked.

'Sure am.'

'My Uncle Clarence said he thought you was a stickybeak but now he reckons you're real deadly.'

'That's nice to know. How's your uncle going?'

'Still womba as hell. He's out the back, listening to his shitty country music. Do you follow tennis?'

'Not really.'

'Me neither. But Aunty Bessie can't get enough of it. She reckons she's gonna hit the courts with me this arvo and teach me how to play. Hey, Aunty?'

Bessie met Audrey's gaze and smiled. 'You're a cheeky one, aren't ya?'

Nettie came back in carrying a plate of steaming biscuits. 'Now what can I get you to drink?' She placed the biscuits on the coffee table in front of them. 'And Audrey, you better not be giving your aunty any grief.' The teenager grinned defiantly back at her grandmother.

'Just black coffee, thanks, Mrs Shields. No sugar,' Renee said as she watched Audrey with amusement.

'Well, you're easy. Bessie, cuppa tea?'

'Yeah, Mum.' She seemed tired but well.

'I'll get it for Aunty Bessie,' Audrey said, jumping to her feet. 'You want milk and sugar too, hey, Aunt?'

'Yes, darling.'

Renee sat back and watched the television until Bessie broke the silence.

'You got Worm?'

Renee nodded.

'Good. I'm too tired to be angry, but I can rest better now knowing those two got what they deserved.'

'We'll need you to testify in court, Bessie. Do you think you can tell them what you told me?'

She nodded slowly. 'Of course I can.'

'Thank you, Bessie.'

'I'm not the one who should be getting thanked. You're a strong woman, Renee. But I hate to tell you, you got a lot more work in front of you. Lord knows, our people need tough ones like you.'

Audrey came back out holding a cup of tea. 'Here you go, Aunty Bessie. And this is for you, Renee – Nana said to give you this.' Audrey handed Renee a flyer:

11 am Saturday 13 May 2000

Crystal Ponds Reservoir

MEMORIAL

In honour of Caroline Forrest and Dawn Shields

Yours truly,

Nettie Shields, Bessie Shields and Millicent Forrest

The day of the memorial dawned dry and overcast. Three months had passed since Bessie had been freed from captivity. Finally the residents of Goorungah could rest knowing that justice had been served and the culprits had been caught. The families had chosen a small clearing near Crystal Ponds to honour Caroline and Dawn. It was late autumn and the air was cold.

Renee got out of her car and went around to the other side to help her mother out. She'd tried to convince her to stay home in the warmth, but Val wouldn't have a bar of it. Renee looked around as they started walking down to the location of the ceremony. The car park was packed.

She spotted the Cunninghams over to one side. They had all decided to attend – Josh, his wife Lucinda, Chester and Roxy. She left her mother with an old friend and walked through the grass over to Josh.

'Josh?'

He turned around and smiled. 'Renee, come here.' He looked good and sounded different. 'You remember my wife, Lucinda?'

'I do.' She looked different too. Her face didn't hold as much tension. 'How are you, Lucinda?'

'Well, thanks.' She smiled. It felt genuine.

She went on to greet Roxy and Chester and returned to her mother, then assessed the surrounds. A light mist hung in the air, blurring the landscape of forest greens and browns. A small wooden stage stood at the lower end of the clearing, weathered from years of exposure to the elements.

She saw Stacey and Roger, each with their families. Carissa Bremmer from primary school was there. She made a mental note to catch up with her sometime. Stacey's older sister, Lisa, the one who had teased her at high school for wearing second-hand clothes, was standing over to one side. She made a mental note to avoid her at all costs. Norm, the man who had warned her of the brown snake, was sitting on a bench with the two other old men from the post office.

She saw Mrs Ford and remembered the day it had all started. Archie had also come along. Calvin and his entourage of tough guys looked uncharacteristically quiet and innocent sitting next to their families, snuggling into their mums and aunties. The protester with the loudest voice who had stolen the microphone from McGorrie was sitting at the edge with a group of people Renee vaguely recognised from the protests. Then she spotted Lennon sitting in among them. He looked up and smiled at her; she couldn't help but smile back.

The families of Caroline and Bessie sat closest to the stage. She spotted Millicent Forrest. Nettie held her granddaughter Audrey on one side and her daughter Bessie on the other. Renee took her mum's hand and squeezed it gently.

The women struck their wooden clap sticks in perfect synchrony to the cadence of the land, creating a beat for the rest to follow, and the dull thundering of the didgeridoo filled the valley as the men took it in turns to enter the circle. Renee watched as their ochre-painted bodies mimicked that of eagles soaring high on the winds: arms spread wide, feet pounding the ground. She recognised Clarence dancing. Clarence: honouring his niece, Dawn. One of the men dancing looked familiar. She stared at him hard and had a sudden shock of recognition. He looked like Chester. He looked like Caroline. This was, surely, Francis, honouring his mother. The day was appropriately overcast and even the birds and tree frogs paused their song as though to pay their respects.

The crowd fell silent as an elderly woman made her way on to the small stage. Renee recognised her as one of the protesters.

Her body was frail and she walked with a limp but her voice was strong.

'Our girls were taken, but their spirits never left us.'

Renee lowered her head and thought of the photograph of Bessie and Caroline. Bright eyes and big smiles, reflecting all the excitement and anticipation of teenage girls about to set off on adventures through life.

The old woman continued, 'Their pain was our pain. We weren't there on those awful days when the devil came their way, but we felt the pain and we been feeling it for all these years. Our women cried, and our men tried to drink away their rage.' The lady paused and tapped her walking stick against the wooden stage as the crowd silently looked on. Renee looked around. The family were crying – tears of grief mixed with relief. A flock of birds broke the silence, wild squawking echoing throughout the valley. 'We all know who did this!' And she thumped her cane more aggressively against the wooden stage. 'But this world looks down on Lore. Oh, we all know that too well. So we were patient and we watched, and today we saw white man's law finally catch up.' Renee watched as the women tapped their clap sticks.

'Caroline and Dawn – may your spirits fly high!'

Epilogue

She ran down the slope, her favourite part of her morning run. A week had passed since the memorial. So much had happened since she'd returned to Goorungah on her outback secondment three months ago. Mulligan was dead. Worm was behind bars. Bessie was reunited with her mother and family. Caroline and Dawn had been laid to rest. So why did she still feel like she couldn't relax? She slowed her pace to a walk and checked her fitness tracker. Fifty minutes. Better than when she'd first arrived. Her fitness was improving despite everything that she had experienced. It was still early and her mother would probably be asleep so she opened the front door as gently as possible.

'Morning, darling,' her mother called from the kitchen as she sat on the front porch to untie her shoelaces. 'Here you go.' Val awkwardly carried out her water bottle under her arm and sat on the chair on the porch.

'Thanks, Mum.'

'What a glorious morning.' Although it was cold, there was not a cloud in the sky nor a hint of breeze. Rays of sunlight glistened off the remaining dew on the grass.

'Mum?' Renee removed her socks and looked up.

'Ooh, I know that tone. It's too early in the morning for that tone.'

'Why did you never want to introduce me to my father?'

'I honestly thought you would be better off not knowing. I thought you could just leave it in the past and get on with your life.'

'Well, I think I need to meet him.'

'Okay.' She seemed unperturbed. It wasn't the reaction Renee had been expecting.

'How do I find him?' Her mother laughed. 'Why are you laughing, Mum? It's not bloody funny.'

'Sorry, darling. It's just that you're asking me where someone lives when you're one of the most esteemed policewomen in Australia right now.'

'It's kinda funny, I s'pose,' she admitted grudgingly.

'Well, you know his name, don't you?'

'Floyd Chapman.'

'He grew up in Tooladdi. So you could start by asking around there, I s'pose.'

'Do you ever think of him?'

'I used to. All the time. Not so much these days.' Her mother walked down to the water tap and kicked over the pot plant saucer, releasing the murky water; the same pot plant saucer Renee had emptied after Norm warned her about the snakes. She watched as her mother turned on the tap with her knee and filled up the saucer with fresh water for the birds. It had rained so much in the last couple of weeks there was no threat of snakes any more. There would be enough water down in the creek beds to stop them from venturing into town.

'My boss in the city called me yesterday,' Renee said as her mother returned to sit on the step next to her. 'He asked me if I wanted to stay out here. Become the sergeant. Now that the position's vacant and all ...' She watched for her mother's reaction. There was a flicker of excitement and Renee could tell her mother wanted her to stay. 'Mind if I hang around for a bit longer?'

'S'pose I can put up with you.'

'Good, because I already accepted the offer. But with a condition – I told them I'd accept if I could start in the position when I get back from out west. After I meet Floyd Chapman.'

'I think that's a very sensible idea, Renee.'

Renee brought out a plate of honey on toast and a pot of tea to share. They sat on the porch and watched the morning go by.

'I thought maybe we could go into the farmer's markets today. It's Sunday,' Renee said, watching to see if her mother would pick up on her hint.

'You wanna buy more chickens don't you?'

Renee nodded and smiled. 'Why not?'

Renee watched the green turn to brown as she drove out to Tooladdi on dusk. The day before, she and her mother had wandered around the markets and picked out five newly hatched chickens. They'd shared a beer on the back deck and listened to the chicks' soft happy clucking as they made themselves at home. Social services had organised a carer to start that day, which was perfect timing for Renee's outback adventure.

The sun was setting over the horizon and she pulled into a service station for a coffee. She sat next to the window where she could see the passing traffic. Three cattle trucks passed and one caravan. She sipped at her coffee and checked her phone. There was an email from Lennon McGorrie. It read:

Melaleuca

Dear Renee

I have an opportunity I would like to present to you. I have run it past the chief editor and she likes the idea. Would you be interested in contributing to a new column in the National Indigenous Post? *Past surveys indicate our readership wants to hear more about improvements in the justice system, and I thought what better way to gain insight than for our readers to hear directly from you – a Murri policewoman with real experience? We could call it 'Taylor's Watch' maybe, brought to you by Detective Renee Taylor. What do you think?*

Lennon

She clicked reply, and typed:

Dear Lennon,

I like it. But you'll have to change the by-line from 'Constable' to 'Sergeant, Goorungah Station.'

Chat when I get back.

Renee

She watched the truckies pull into the fuel bowsers then canned her cup and walked outside. As she crossed the bitumen, the tail of a brown snake caught her eye as it slithered off into the mulga scrubs, and she knew she was on the right path.

The highway was straight and narrow across undulating hills. The soil was red and covered in low shrubbery. The occasional kangaroo and emu appeared in the bushes. Another hundred kilometres to Tooladdi. She had no idea where Floyd Chapman lived or how she was going to find him, but if Tooladdi was half the size of Goorungah it wouldn't take long to find him.

Angie Faye Martin

Signs reading *Slow Down* signalled the entrance to the outback town. She passed the pub and the swimming pool and stopped out the front of the local cafe. The man behind the counter told her that the Chapmans lived in the big house down by the creek, at the end of the road. Renee followed his directions and stopped outside a tall timber house on stilts. Two little kids played in the driveway on toy cars. A woman sat on the front porch. She looked familiar. Her eyes welled with tears.

'I knew you'd come find us one day. Floyd!' she called out. 'Come! Look who's here.'

'My name's Renee.'

'That's a beautiful name for my niece.'

'You're my aunty?'

'Whether you like it or not, bub.' She smiled warmly and reached out her arms.

Author note

When people ask why I chose to write this novel, the answer is never straightforward. Perhaps the simplest explanation is that I needed a creative outlet to explore the complexities I was negotiating when I began writing. At the time, everything felt confusing – juggling a career in the public service, my identity as an Aboriginal person, the dynamics of Australian politics, and questions of community, belonging, ethics, courage and authenticity. It was a period of deep reflection on what it means to be true to oneself and how to navigate the tension between right and wrong. I found a sense of peace whenever I immersed myself in this story. Though entirely fictional, it was rooted in many of the concepts and values I was grappling with in my own life.

This book means the world to me, not only because it offers a chance to tell a story I hope readers will find engaging and suspenseful, but also because it provides a window into the lived reality of many Aboriginal people. The novel touches on issues like land theft, the loss of language and culture, and the unequal value placed on Aboriginal lives by society, especially within the justice system. It's a story that speaks to both personal and collective resilience in the face of these ongoing challenges.

Although I am a Kooma/Kamilaroi woman, I have not referred specifically to my nations in this book because while I have tried to make the content as authentic as possible it is, after all, fictional. Some words that are spoken broadly across many Aboriginal communities are used, such as gunji (cop), muntha (bread) and womba (crazy).

The yumba was a camp on the outskirts of small towns in south-western Queensland such as Charleville, Cunnamulla and Quilpie. It is an Aboriginal word meaning 'camp' from multiple languages in the area, including my own language, Kooma. My father, Garry 'Sonny' Martin, and his siblings were raised on the Charleville yumba and he has written about his experiences growing up on the fringes for *Meanjin*, *The Saltbush Review* and *IndigenousX*. Prior to the 1967 Referendum, Aboriginal and Torres Strait Islander people had limited rights compared to non-Indigenous Australians. Each state was slightly different, but generally speaking during the early- to mid-1900s Aboriginal and Torres Strait Islander people who had survived the Frontier Wars were being displaced from their traditional lands and moved onto government reserves or missions – many religious but not necessarily. The people who remained on the yumbas or fringe camps managed to avoid forced removal by filling a gap in the labour market, often as stockmen or domestics on cattle properties. I pay my deepest respects to all people who lived on the camps and stood so strong in the face of poverty and hardships. It is my only hope that I have used my education and privilege to give the injustices you faced voice, and I hope I have done this in a way that makes people feel heard.

I am also proudly descended from hardworking farmers of Anglo-Saxon, German and Welsh origin who settled in these regions.

Many of these families, including my own, built a community and looked after the integrity of the land in the ways they knew best. While I explore many blatant acts of prejudice and bigotry in my novel, I also hope to shine a light on the generosity and kindness of non-Indigenous Australians living in these regions.

Acknowledgements

I owe my deepest gratitude to my husband, Pedro, whose unwavering belief in me, and endless words of encouragement and support, have been the bedrock of this journey.

To my sister (and stylist!), Lou-Ellen, whose thoughtful feedback and steadying presence have been invaluable when I've ventured off into the wild world of creative chaos.

To Mum, whose high expectations always pushed me to reach for the stars, knowing I'm capable of more than I give myself credit for.

To Dad, whose stories of the old days have given me a sense of identity and connected me to a legacy of strength and resilience.

I am profoundly grateful to Jo Mackay, whose editorial genius shaped my raw ideas into the polished story you see today.

A special thank you to Amy Matthews for taking me on as a mentee when I was such a novice, guiding me through the fundamentals of creative writing.

I am also forever grateful to those who offered feedback and advice on drafts along the way: Prindi, Belynda, Trina, Ross, Samia, Laurie, Kitty, Laura, Jen, Casey, Mel, Janet and Aunty Carole. Your support means more than words can say.

To the great team at HQ, whose belief in this book and in me gave me the confidence to pour my heart into every page. Annabel,

Johanna, Anne, Karen-Maree and her wonderful sales team, Chloe and Stuart – thank you for everything.

A special thank you to FNAWN for its leadership, community and collective wisdom, and to Flinders University and Writers SA for creating the HQ First Nations Commercial Fiction Fellowship – an opportunity that helped me make this book a reality.

I'm also grateful to Darren Holt for the stunning cover which perfectly captures the spirit of *Melaleuca* and to Alex Hotchin for the beautiful map of Goorungah.

And finally, I offer my deepest respects to the First Nations women who have suffered violence. Their strength and resilience were an inspiration for this work, and their stories are a reminder of the need for justice and change.

Book Group Discussion Questions

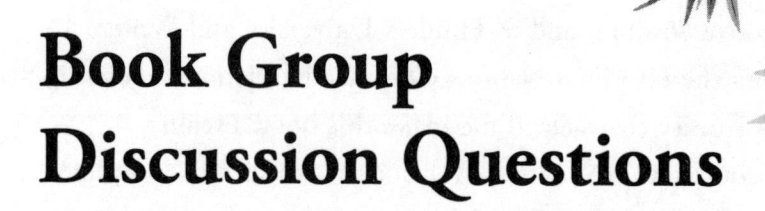

- What were some of your favourite scenes from the book? Why did they stand out to you?

- What was the most challenging or difficult part of the book for you to read or understand?

- *Melaleuca* alternates between Renee's perspective in 2000 and Caroline's in 1965. How did this dual timeline structure influence your reading experience?

- How did the characters of Renee and Caroline grow throughout the story? How do you think their feelings towards other characters evolved?

- Were there any unexpected twists that caught you by surprise?

- Did any of the characters feel suspicious to you from the start? How did your feelings towards them evolve over the course of the book?

- The bark and oils of the melaleuca tree are important symbols in the story, along with brown snakes, chicken eggs and the name 'Renee'. Did you identify any other recurring images or metaphors? How did they enhance the overall meaning or emotional impact?

- *Melaleuca* is set in Goorungah, a fictional town in regional Queensland, where oppressive summer heat gives way to the biting cold of winter. How did the setting and atmosphere of the book affect the mood and tone of the story?

- Was there a line or passage from the book that stood out to you? Why did it resonate with you?

- How relevant are the themes or messages of the book to society today?

talk about it

Let's talk about books.

Join the conversation:

@harlequinaustralia

@hqanz

@harlequinaus

harpercollins.com.au/hq

If you love reading and want to know about our authors and titles, then let's talk about it.